**Piper Milton** is a moth⟨...⟩ ⟨...⟩nd
lives on the south coast. ⟨...⟩ ⟨...⟩vel.

# Clementine and Claudia

Piper Milton

*Sylvia
With love from
Piper*

SILVERTAIL BOOKS • *London*

First published in Great Britain by Silvertail Books in 2016
www.silvertailbooks.com
Copyright © Piper Milton

1

The right of Piper Milton to be identified as the author
of this work has been asserted in accordance
with the Copyright, Design and Patents Act 1988
A catalogue record of this book is available from the British Library

ISBN 978-1-909269-04-0

To Peter

*'Take away love, and our earth is a tomb.'*
Robert Browning

# Prologue

Smoke from the engine stacks bled into the night sky as the late afternoon train sped south-west out of Waterloo station, bound for Weymouth. En route it would stop at many stations including Winchester, Southampton and Poole. Soldiers in khaki greatcoats, unable to find a seat, collected in the corridor outside the first-class compartments. A pungent mix of body odour, dried mud and cigarette fumes hung in the air. Silent in thought, some stood staring into the dark at the frozen landscape beyond the windows, whilst others, perched on knapsacks, swapped stories and jokes. A hip flask was passed back and forth between a weather-beaten sergeant and a Royal Naval rating. Pausing between swigs, the NCO would steal a glance at the activity within the compartments, thirsty for the normality of England, for life's trivia; the elderly gentleman reading *The Evening News*; the lady with an ostrich feather in her hat and pince-nez clothes-pegged on her nose who was struggling to follow a knitting pattern; a mother soothing her baby.

Through the glass partition separating the first class passengers from the soldiers, a small boy sat on his mother's lap clutching *The Child's ABC of the War*, and stared in awe at the heroic figures, wishing he was twelve years older so he too could fight the Kaiser. His excitement was such that his parent pulled the blind down over the window and told him to sit still. Frustrated, he turned his gaze to the subaltern sitting opposite who was chatting to a young woman with a red cross on her coat. The soldier's uniform was too clean, his boots too shiny, no trench mud to satisfy little Henry. Even the arm sling proved a disappointment. Not a bayonet or bullet wound; he had merely tripped down some steps and cracked his elbow. Henry's attention stole back to the corridor, and, wriggling free of his mother's arms, he climbed from her lap. Pressing his face against the glass panel of the door he saw a zigzag of lightning from a distant storm. *Exploding shells! Into action!* The corridor was a trench, the pile of duffel bags were sandbags. A Tommy stretched his arms. *Take care — keep low! The sniper will get you!*

The train powered on, the screech of its wheels on the tracks like the demonic flight of German shells, the unearthly sound of the fireman's whistle like the approach of doom.

# 1

'Duck!' shouted the little boy, causing the nurse to start. It amused her that an infant could make her jump so, when she was able to sleep perfectly through heavy artillery. Henry's mother smiled apologetically and pulled him away from the door and Clementine watched him once again settle on her lap and reopen *The Child's ABC of War*. Frowning, she thought how immoral it was for publishers and toy manufacturers to use the war to boost their profits by targeting the young. When she had been a girl, *A* had been for antelope, not attack, and *B* for baby, not bayonet. She looked at the mother, a seemingly respectable middle-class woman and wondered if it was naïvety or stupidity that caused her to provide her offspring with such unsuitable reading material.

To Clementine's right sat a second lieutenant with whom she had been conversing. His fingers fidgeted nervously with his Sam Browne belt, suggesting he was not as old as the thirty-plus years he looked. In truth he was barely twenty-two, a veteran of war but ill- experienced with the weaker sex. Somehow he had survived nineteen months in Flanders, nineteen months that had stolen his youth and destroyed his dreams. Even his memories had not escaped. Balmy days up at Oxford, where he had read History before living it, contained too many faces he would never see again.

From out of his wallet he produced a photograph of his wife, the young girl he had hastily married in the early days of the war. To this stranger beside him he confessed that he barely knew his bride, and that the brevity of time — a total of five days they had spent together as man and wife — had not been conducive in developing the relationship. What worried him most was that even those five days did not count any more; the man he had been no longer existed. Both he and his wife had changed and between them they had produced life — a daughter called Hope, who in less than an hour he would meet for the first time.

Throughout the rest of the train there was much speculation as to the reason several of the carriages were missing that evening. General opinion was that they had been requisitioned to move fresh troops to the ports. Nowadays the war failed to arouse the passions of 1914, for what sort of person could get excited at the thought of more young men going off to defend their mothers, wives and sisters knowing the odds of them returning in one piece, if at all? And especially now there was more awareness of the kind of horrors they faced. Now well into its third year and responsible for hundreds of thousands of the nation's youth already lying slaughtered in the rat-infested soil of Northern France. The war dragged on, relentless; the thought of even more troops being sent out only added to the passengers' sense of despair.

There wasn't a civilian on board old enough to remember August 1914 who could not also recall those fresh-faced youths who had rushed to enlist in Kitchener's New Army, as patriotic fervour had swept the land. Then their only fear had been that they were going to miss out, because everyone said it would be a short campaign with victory before Christmas. However, as Christmas came and went with no sign of peace, and news of the barbaric conditions under which the soldiers lived and died filtered back, the queues had dwindled and eventually, with a rapidly depleting Army, the government had been forced to introduce conscription.

The soldiers on board this train could be called the lucky ones, for the majority were on their way home; some to enjoy a few days leave with their loved ones before returning to their battle positions across the Channel, whilst others, broken in mind or body and no longer capable of serving King and Country, were returning for good. For most it would be the first time in over a year they had seen their families, and the atmosphere amongst them was so intense one could almost smell the anxiety.

The train drew into a dimly-lit station and the second lieutenant, along with young Henry and his mother, rose to depart. The only new passenger to enter the carriage was a major in the Cavalry. He was tall and his boots looked as new as his bespoke uniform. He placed himself in the seat opposite the nurse, and as the train got under way his gaze settled on the young woman. She was reading Rupert Brooke's 'War Sonnets'. He recognised that she was a member of the Voluntary Aid Detachment. As his eyes moved up to her wide-brimmed hat, she turned her head to glance out of the window. He saw, to his surprise, that her honey-coloured hair was short and straight, a good couple of inches above her collar. He rather suspected it could be the reason the elderly woman in the corner, who was busily clicking away with her knitting needles to produce regulation socks for the troops, kept staring at her so disapprovingly. Short hair was still associated with women's emancipation, and probably she had heard stories of fast, short-haired girls dancing the nights away with soldiers on leave.

He studied the VAD's face. She had good fine features — not beautiful but, he thought, strikingly attractive — and he felt quite sure that those pale-blue eyes had never seen the interior of a West End nightclub. Suddenly, as if aware that she was being scrutinised, she glanced up and their eyes met. He smiled and, shyly, she smiled back. He thought he had never seen such gentleness in a face before, and he knew she was totally unaware of her loveliness.

Clementine turned away and stared out of the window into the night sky, thinking of the family she was longing to see. Such was the pressure of work in the hospital in France that she had been unable to take leave for almost twelve months. Then yesterday she had received a letter from her younger sister Claudia informing her of her imminent marriage. It had been an impulsive decision to come home, so no one would be expecting her.

She had been nursing since 1915, a few months after war broke out. After taking a series of first-aid and nursing classes and obtaining the necessary certificates, she had worked in a local hospital gaining experience before signing up as a VAD. When she had announced to her parents that she was being sent to France, she had received mixed reactions. Her father, a retired brigadier, proudly patted her on the back and told her she was a true Ellacombe, whereas her mother wept and tried to persuade her to engage in a safer form of war work, like Claudia, who served teas in Service canteens to soldiers on leave. Claudia herself was of the opinion that Clementine had to be perfectly mad to want to spend the best years of her life emptying bedpans; she didn't particularly like her own job, but discovering the freedom it gave her, so totally unknown to girls such as themselves before the war, she stuck at it.

Taking her sister's letter from her pocket, Clementine read it once more, a small frown appearing at Claudia's description of the man she was to marry the day after tomorrow. *'He's an Hon. — The Honourable Alexander Rufus Henry FitzPatrick. His brother was Patrick, the Earl of Moundsmere — who died at Mons. Unfortunately he had a son otherwise Alexander would have been next in line. I suppose it's still a possibility, for the child is very young. Imagine me a Countess — absolutely ripping, don't you think!'*

There was little else about him except that he was thirty years of age and had 'divine looks'. Claudia then went into great detail about her wedding dress — how she had managed to acquire the silk and then persuade a London designer to make it for her all in the space of three weeks. She mentioned nothing about her fiancé's personality, whether she had met his family, or even how she came to know him. At best Claudia was not much of a correspondent, but she did write occasionally and neither she nor their mother, who wrote frequently, had ever mentioned him before. Remembering some of the types her sister favoured, Clementine felt a trifle uneasy, but she was aware that Claudia firmly believed money was the path to happiness so she gave a wry smile, for The Honourable Alexander FitzPatrick was bound to be rich!

Clementine's thoughts turned to Coppins, the family home where they had lived since their parents had returned from India ten years before. The house had belonged to Brigadier Ellacombe's great-aunt, with whom Claudia and Clementine would stay in the holidays after being sent home to attend school. Brigadier Ellacombe inherited the house and twenty acres of farmland when she died suddenly of pneumonia at eighty-two. It was a lovely house, Georgian in style but with parts said to be older. By most standards it could not be described as large, and certainly The Honourable Alexander FitzPatrick would be used to much bigger and grander properties, but to Clementine it was home and she had loved it from her first visit, when she was eight years of age.

Clementine tried to imagine the activity and excitement that would be taking place at Coppins for, much to her sister's annoyance, the wedding breakfast was to be held there. It was years since they had had any kind of celebration and it would be wonderful to see the house lit up and glistening like it had before the war. The last time she had been home in February 1916, half the place had been shut up to conserve labour and fuel, and there had been a rather depressing air about it. Coppins was a house that needed to be lived in — but with coal shortages and staff down to a husband-and-wife team, it was little wonder it felt unloved. However, the wedding would change that, albeit for a short while.

In her letter Claudia described to Clementine how she had failed to persuade their father to let her hold the event in London. She had used every pretext she could think of; that it would be more convenient for wedding guests, that it would be so much easier with regard to catering, 'Papa, do consider poor Mrs Best. How on earth will she manage to provide sufficient food for fifty guests? You surely haven't forgotten we are in times of rationing. And what about staff? Who's going to serve everything? You know perfectly well there's no help to be had. All the single men have enlisted and the girls are at the munitions factory. And don't forget the house — it will take forever, getting it presentable.'

'Nonsense! We are at war! And it is up to the likes of us on the Home Front to set an example.' Brigadier Ellacombe saw through her immediately. 'Your grand friends will just have to take us as we are — simple country folk coping in times of hardship. If it doesn't suit you, then I suggest you put your marriage off until the conflict is over.'

Clementine smiled as she imagined the scene. All her sister's persuasive charm wasted on the stubborn, no-nonsense manner of their father, who abhorred pretence under any circumstance.

A deep snore from the old gentleman beside her, who had fallen asleep behind his newspaper, made her start and the knitter leaned forward and gave him a cruel poke with one of her needles. He woke abruptly and for a moment appeared confused until his thoughts cleared. Clementine hoped he didn't think she was responsible for his rude awakening, but catching her eye he smiled.

'I've been up to Harley Street to see what can be done with my rheumatism,' he told her.

'Oh! And did they help?'

'If they did I'd eat my hat,' interjected the knitter.

He chose to ignore the woman, giving Clementine a bemused look.

'A waste of money,' he said in a softer voice. 'A warm climate is what you need, they said. A warm climate indeed! "Where do you suggest?" I asked. "The French Riviera?"' Clementine giggled and somehow it encouraged him to start regaling her with a graphic account of his recent illness. She felt she should interrupt him before he went into more detail, suspecting he thought she might have a magic cure for his ailments.

'I'm not a properly trained nurse,' Clementine said. 'I've only a very basic medical knowledge.'

'That's quite right,' the knitter said self-importantly. 'She only does menial tasks.'

Clementine caught the cavalry officer's eye and noted the glint of amusement. She was relieved when, seconds later, someone called out that they were approaching Southampton. Immediately both the woman and the old gentleman began gathering their things together, and before many more seconds had passed the brakes were squealing and the train was drawing into the station.

There was a flurry of activity throughout the carriages. Everyone seemed to get up at once. Coats were fastened, luggage lifted down from the racks above the seats. The soldiers in the corridor rose from their backpacks and busied themselves, dusting cigarette ash from their coats, straightening their caps. As they stood waiting to disembark, Clementine studied some of their faces, wondering whether this was home for them, or whether they were about to board ships to take them back across the English Channel.

Peering out of the window she caught sight of a handful of women and children lining the platform. They stood in the shadows contorted with cold and anxiety as they strained to see the faces of the soldiers waiting to burst from the doors the moment the train stopped. The cavalry officer also rose, but only to assist the old gentleman, who had difficulty with his luggage. Clementine was surprised how tall he was, well over six feet and with a strong physique that made lightweight of the tin box as he lifted it onto his shoulder. He had the sort of looks that many girls would swoon over, thick wavy hair and quite the darkest brown eyes she had ever seen. And had it not been for the fact she had just witnessed his kindly act, she would probably have guessed him to be conceited and arrogant.

Once the rush had passed, Clementine did her bit to help the old fellow, helping him to his feet and down the steps on to the platform. The major managed to find a porter before the train started off again, handing him some coins with instructions to get the man and his luggage into a taxi.

'Would you mind if I open the window slightly?' Clementine said finding herself alone with the officer.

'Not at all,' he said, preoccupied with staunching the flow of blood from a gash on his hand. Clementine sprang to her feet her brow wrinkling. The bleeding seemed profuse.

'Do let me see — how did you do it?' she asked, removing the already soaking handkerchief. She made him sit down and dabbed at it. 'It's deep enough for a stitch.'

'And I suppose you just happen to have a needle and thread with you,' he said with an uncertain smile. Clementine grinned as she pressed her thumb against the palm, which immediately arrested the flow of blood. With her other hand she took out from her pocket a small first aid box that contained lint and bandages. She placed a pad over the wound and bent the officer's fingers over it. 'Grasp it firmly if you can,' she said, whilst unrolling a bandage.

'How fortunate to be travelling in the same carriage,' he said 'Do all nurses travel so well prepared?'

'I just happened to have it with me, luckily for you. How did you do it?'

'That old chap's tin box — it had a jagged edge which I failed to notice.'

She folded the bandage down the centre, narrowing it, and then proceeded to wrap it over the knuckles of his clenched fist, tying it round and round. As she worked, the officer couldn't help noticing her hands; in shape they were fine and sensitive, the kind one might expect a musician or artist to have, but they were so rough and inflamed, especially around the joints, they looked more like a kitchen maid's.

Clementine became aware of his gaze, and feeling ill at ease under his scrutiny longed to replace her gloves.

'How did you get that?' he asked, touching a nasty-looking scar on one of her fingers.

'It was septic and had to be lanced.'

He noted her embarrassment and remained silent.

Eventually she tied the ends of the bandage firmly into a reef knot. 'You are going to be a bit handicapped until the pressure can be released on your palm.'

'How long do you think that will be? I've arranged for my car to be dropped at Dorchester. As it is, I don't think I shall be capable of driving.'

'It's the only way to staunch the blood, unless of course you prefer to hold your arm in the air.'

'I didn't mean to sound ungrateful. I'm not entirely sure what I should have done without you. At least it seems I shall survive the journey.'

'Fingers crossed.'

'If only I could.'

She chuckled as she put her gloves back on. 'I leave at Wool. If you can hold on until Wareham, I'll change the dressing, and if it's possible to release the pressure without the bleeding restarting, you may still be able to drive your car, but no promises.'

'It would be most welcome if I could. I'm already behind schedule as it is. Another delay would be best avoided. Do you work in London?' he asked, knowing that practically every hospital in the capital was bulging with casualties of war. When she told him that she had just returned from France he was visibly surprised, and learning that she had been there for two years, he stared at her in wonderment. He knew the conditions those nurses had to endure, and she only looked a slip of a girl, small-boned and rather thin.

'I'm really quite tough,' she said, as if reading his thoughts. It caused him to smile and she smiled too, her eyes lighting up with subtle radiance, and he thought she was undeniably lovely. He wondered why she had chosen such a way of life; to live in poor conditions away from family and friends when she could have stayed at home in comfort hardly aware there was a war. It was a bitterly cold winter and, he knew even colder in Northern France.

'Do you sleep under canvas?' he asked aware that many did.

'Not any more. They erected huts for us shortly before Christmas.'

'They spoil you!'

'Well, I must admit they are quite luxurious after the old bell-tents. We even have proper beds.'

'And roaring fires, running hot water and thick rugs, I'd wager.'

'Oh, if only,' she laughed. 'The first thing I shall do as soon as I get home is wallow in a deep scented bath. The water will be almost too hot to bear and I shall stay there for hours and hours.'

It suddenly struck her that her mother would not consider her conversation with this stranger to be at all proper. In fact, she would be horrified, but then Clementine wondered what her mother would say, should she ever discover that hardly a day passed when her young daughter did not bathe some poor soldier straight from the trenches.

The major stared at her with a wistful expression. 'You're too beautiful to be hiding away in such a filthy job when you could be breaking all the chaps' hearts at home.'

What had induced him to utter such a crass remark he couldn't think. He only knew he regretted it the moment he said it. 'I'm sorry,' he told her immediately. 'I do hope I haven't offended you.'

'Please don't apologise,' Clementine mumbled.

An uneasy silence followed while she felt awkward and wondered if perhaps she took her work and life too seriously. He, on the other hand, was annoyed with himself; he should have realised she was not the sort of girl to take such a remark as a compliment. She was obviously dedicated to the life she had chosen and was as much a patriot as any soldier.

'How long is your leave?' he asked, attempting to clear the air.

'About ten days. I have to catch the boat train on the eighth of February.'

'So you'll be returning to France?'

'They need all the nurses they can get.'

His eyes lingered on her face. He was not surprised. Again he acknowledged how different she was to any girl he had ever met.

'And what about you? I can see you've been wounded,' she said eyeing the small braided stripe on his left sleeve. 'When did that happen?'

'Last summer. I got hit by shrapnel and was sent home. The last few months, I've been helping out at the War Office. But I certainly wasn't as lucky as your patients,' he added with a smile. 'Where they sent me I swear there wasn't a nurse under forty.'

Clementine grinned. 'They obviously felt your rank deserved the more experienced Sisters. Where were you fighting?'

'At Thiepval.'

Memories of last summer invaded her thoughts and it was Clementine's turn to stare with quiet awe. Back then, a day never passed when she hadn't been rushed off her feet as convoy after convoy of wounded arrived from the Somme battlefields. The hospital had been overrun with casualties, and many had been shipped straight back to England without receiving any medical aid, for there had been neither staff nor facilities to cope with the numbers. Everyone had worked round the clock; eighteen and twenty-hour shifts being normal, whilst in the background, like the devil's heartbeat, the heavy guns had hammered away. The Somme Campaign had claimed over six hundred thousand victims in little over four months, and this man bore scars of it beneath his immaculately tailored uniform.

'Will you remain at the War Office?' she asked, wondering if his fighting days were over.

He shook his head. 'I'm expecting orders to return any day.'

Her stomach sank. She didn't want him to go back, she wanted him to stay in the safe confines of the War Office where his handsome face and strong body would remain whole and his treacle-coloured eyes would continue to see. He must not become like the rest; the poor wretched creatures that she was accustomed to seeing with missing limbs, missing minds, or missing faces. This war was a destroyer of beauty; one only had to look at the ravaged land of Northern France that more closely resembled a mud desert than the charming countryside it had once been.

'Are you an admirer of Rupert Brooke?' he asked as she picked up the volume of war sonnets from beside her.

'A friend lent them to me for the journey. They are very moving and I can understand why they are so popular but…' She paused as if in reflection. 'Most of the men I've seen who die don't even die with dignity, let alone romanticism.'

He stared at her small unsmiling face and was saddened. It had always rather irritated him to hear young women blindly eulogise the dead poet, whose works he felt were illustrative of the fact that Brooke had never experienced battle, let alone trench-life with its headless corpses, blood-bloated rats and stench of decomposed bodies. This nurse understood, as she had first-hand experience. Part of him wished she didn't.

The train sped on, stopping more frequently as it passed through the New Forest. A few passengers boarded, but as their carriage was near the front of the train, the couple were left undisturbed. War dominated their conversation. He was a major in the Hussars and as a reservist had been sent out to France at the outset. He had seen little action with his horse, for this war had limited use for the animal apart from transport and communication, and he had ended up alongside the Infantry in the trenches. 'The only successful charges my regiment have made in this war have been on foot.'

Their backgrounds made it impossible for them to remain strangers. He had once spent a short leave in Le Touquet, the smart seaside resort where Clementine and a friend sometimes walked on their rare free afternoons, and could remember passing all the hospital tents just a few miles away.

'Le Touquet is the only place where you can get a cup of unchlorinated tea,' she said, 'and it's wonderful just to be able to stroll amongst the sand dunes and let the wind blow the smells of the hospital away.'

He nodded. In general he found it difficult to talk of his experiences to those who had not served in the war. It was something he had in common with most soldiers. Things they had seen were too brutal to bring up in genteel conversation, and as a result memories tended to fester and relationships strain. Sometimes it was a relief when leave was up to get back to those who understood; those filthy frightened men alongside whom one lived in the trenches. But, it was different with this young nurse who helped with the wounded fresh from the Front Line, and for whom the war held no glory; he felt at ease with her.

It was the same for Clementine. When he remarked on the shortness of her hair, she had no compunction about confessing that liberation had indeed been her motive for taking the scissors and chopping it off — liberation from lice, which despite all her efforts, she had repeatedly caught from new casualties. She was able to tell him because she knew he would understand, and together they joked about the little creatures that had no respect for class or culture, yet it struck her as ironic that she would have to think of a more palatable reason to give her mother.

It seemed no time at all before the train was pulling into Wareham. Clementine felt a thrill of excitement as she realised how close to home she was, for it was from here on warm summer afternoons before the war that her parents had sometimes hired a boat to take them up the river to Poole Harbour. Choosing one of the several small islands in the picturesque bay, they would picnic on the sandy shores. Clementine and Claudia would have swimming races and dig for cockles with their little brother Timothy, if the tide was low. And whilst their father made use of his binoculars watching for rare birds, their mother would relax on a deckchair in the shade with a novel.

Clementine began removing her gloves. 'I'll quickly see to your bandage and if we can release the pressure you can have your fingers back,' she joked.

'That would be nice.' He watched her start to unravel the dressing, conscious of time racing ahead, never to return. She would vanish like many of the men he had seen fall on the battlefields. He would never see her again. If only time would stop and give them sanctuary. He experienced a feeling close to the desperation he had felt when his mother had arrived to take him out for lunch after his first half-term at boarding school, when he had been seven. The bliss of seeing her, only to lose her a few hours later, had been almost too much for him to bear.

The wound had stopped bleeding and Clementine placed a thick wad of lint in the palm. 'I believe you might be able to drive your car after all, if you're careful,' she said with a smile catching his eye.

In an instant, as if they had travelled through a tunnel, everything seemed to go black, momentarily perhaps, but emerging into the light there was a clarity that had not been there before. Suddenly she was conscious of the intensity of his gaze. The darkness of his eyes seemed to have a force, which threatened to unbalance her, and for a long moment she felt vulnerable. It was as if the train had run off its rails and was racing into the unknown. A nervous sound came from her throat, and summoning her common sense she continued with her task.

17

'Would you hold the lint a moment with your other hand whilst I sort the bandage out?' she said, feeling like an inexperienced probationer under inspection.

'You're trembling,' he murmured. Clementine's face glowed crimson as he let go of the lint and took her hand in his. She watched as he, with immense gentleness, stroked the calluses on her fingers. Clementine couldn't move. In the background the train was rushing ahead. Cocooned in this railway compartment she could see what was coming. But strong as she had thought she was, she hadn't the strength to resist when he drew her into his arms.

# 2

Claudia tried to study her reflection in the looking glass above her dressing-table, but the mirror needed re-silvering and it was like looking at oneself through a spider's web.

'It's like everything else in this house, old and worn,' she muttered as she opened one of the drawers and felt towards the back where she had concealed a packet of *Black Cat* cigarettes. Lighting up, she inhaled deeply, savouring the instant calm. In just two days it would be all over and then she could relax, no more worrying about something going wrong. She and Alexander would be married and life would change for the better. 'The Honourable Mrs Alexander FitzPatrick' she drawled, feeling a thrill at hearing it spoken aloud.

She thought of the first time she had seen him, unbelievably only two months ago. What had started out as an unpromising evening selling raffle tickets for the Red Cross quickly took an upward leap when she had first set eyes on him standing across the crowded room. Despite another girl pointing him out as one of the few eligible bachelors still alive and in one piece, he was one of those people you couldn't fail to notice. Wealth attracted Claudia; she could sense it as others can sense danger. It drew her like a fly to a sun-lit wall, and upon discovering that she knew his friend, she worked her way across the room. Once she had been introduced it had been fairly easy to charm him, make him laugh — for she knew that having fun was generally top of most soldiers priorities; wanting only to forget and have a good time.

Claudia resented the war. One moment she had been basking in her first adult summer, enjoying all the attention her beauty attracted, the next she was in limbo. If only she had known how abruptly it was all going to end, she might not have behaved so impeccably. She had loved being eighteen, been deliriously happy and thought that life could only improve. But those long hot, lazy days had drawn to a close before she was ready and had never returned.

What had made that summer especially good was that she had attracted the attention of Duncan Farraday, the eldest son of a local gentry farming family. Duncan was a few years older than Claudia and considered one of the best catches around. It was a real plus that she liked him too. They had met at one of the tennis parties the vicar was fond of giving during the summer, and thereafter she and Clementine had been drawn into his circle, receiving numerous invitations to picnics and social events held by his family. Quite soon she became aware that with a little more encouragement, he would propose. But at the time she had been in no hurry to settle down. Life had suddenly taken a turn for the better. She was having a wonderful time and getting to know people she would never have met in the normal way, namely Duncan's friends who would either sail into Swanage Bay in their expensive yachts or motor down to enjoy a night or two of the Farradays' hospitality.

Claudia had loved the giddy feeling she got from all the attention and thought to keep Duncan on a string whilst waiting to see who else might stray into the web she was weaving. The Farradays were very proud of their friendship with the van Raaltes of Brownsea Island, who lived in the castle at the harbour entrance. It was widely known that they sometimes entertained royalty — a fact not lost on Claudia.

However, whatever dreams she had were dashed on 4 August 1914, the day war broke out. Along with thousands of other young men, Duncan Farraday enlisted, went to France and promptly got himself killed.

As Claudia stared blindly ahead taking a final inhale of her cigarette she thought of Duncan and wondered what might have happened if there had been no war. Would they have married? Would they have been happy? She had read somewhere that usually in a relationship, unless one is extremely fortunate, one party loves more than the other. Well, in their case Duncan had most definitely been the adorer, and she had to confess it suited her that way; she preferred the comfort of knowing herself to be in control. Yet here she was, about to marry a man who had never divulged what his feelings were towards her. With Alexander she had been the pursuer, armed with tricks and games to chivvy things along. It had been a challenge and though she had won and got the prize, she didn't feel quite as she had imagined she would. Her joy had fissures — moments of vulnerability which would surface in rare flashes of quiet and which always she chose to ignore.

Hearing footsteps approaching she jumped up and threw the cigarette out of the window. She was just closing the curtains when her mother appeared.

'Claudia my dear, are you ready? It's time we left, Papa's worried about the roads freezing.' Claire Ellacombe was in her late fifties, a pale thin woman whose lined skin made her look older, a consequence of having spent the best part of her life in India. It happened that as a child, her ayah had failed to protect her delicate complexion from the cruel sun. Thankfully her daughters' ayah had been more vigilant, taking great pride in her two blonde charges, especially Claudia, the fairest. The Indian nursemaid had loved telling the little girl that she had only ever seen the likes of her pale skin and hair in a book of Bible stories.

'You is angel from heaven,' she had been fond of saying, which with hindsight Mrs Ellacombe realised had probably contributed to Claudia growing up expecting to be the centre of attention.

She watched as her younger daughter, in a burst of gaiety, pirouetted, showing off the horrendously expensive dress that had been made in London. 'Well, Mummy, will I dazzle Alexander tonight?'

'I've no doubt of it, you look stunning, but please darling, Papa is down in the hall waiting and you know how impatient he is. So do hurry up.'

Brigadier Ellacombe stood in his tweed coat at the foot of the stairs tapping his walking stick. His rubicund complexion suggested he had already braved the cold taking a turn about the grounds, but in truth it was due to over-indulgence and too little exercise, something that had become more prevalent in the decade since his retirement from the Army. He was eleven years older than his wife, and the white side-whiskers he still favoured gave him the air of a figure from the past.

'We are going to be late,' he thundered as Claudia strolled down the stairs.

'Don't flap so Papa. We've plenty of time. Lady Moundsmere's invitation said seven o'clock,' she told him, cursing inwardly as she stuck a jewelled pin in her hat.

'The roads are treacherous at the moment,' he retorted, pulling on his gloves and walking to the door where a thickset man handed him his silk hat. 'Hold the fort, Best, but don't wait up. I expect we shall be late'

*

Miles away in Northern France where the incessant thunder of heavy artillery had become an accustomed part of life, an Army Medical Officer made his way along the ward of an Allied hospital tent. There were about forty beds and all were occupied with either sick or wounded. A Sister with a kindly face beckoned him over to a carrot-haired boy who lay baring his teeth as a nervous young VAD removed the dressing from his leg. Captain Charles Hamilton took one look at the suppurating, stinking wound and frowned.

'It requires drainage tubes and irrigating with hypochlorous acid every three hours, Sister.'

The soldier studied him nervously, his freckles barely noticeable. 'You won't take it off, will you sir? Please, I beg of you, I'd rather die.'

'No, you wouldn't,' Charles said firmly. Then: 'You may be assured I shall do my best.'

'Where's Blondie tonight, Doc?' enquired a cheeky-looking Cockney from whom he had extracted a piece of shrapnel embedded in the pelvis the day before. Charles smiled; the resilience of the British Tommy never failed to amaze him.

'If you mean Miss Ellacombe, she has gone home on leave.'

'She never said nuffin to us'

'Well, it was a sudden decision — a family matter.'

Sister Jenkins caught up with Charles as he was about to leave the tent. 'Sir, I thought you might like this,' she smiled handing him a photograph. 'It was taken on Christmas morning. Something to show the folks back home that we manage to celebrate too.'

He gave it a cursory glance before sticking it in his pocket. 'I dare say you've heard we're expecting a convoy this evening.'

She nodded. ' We are making preparations, sir.'

'Well, I'm just going back to my billet to snatch a couple of hours sleep before they arrive, but should you require me in the interim, make sure you send for me.'

The billet Charles shared with other medical staff was a building beside the railway station that had been requisitioned by the military. The track was in frequent use, moving troops back and forth to the Front, but he had become impervious to the noise of trains coming and going at all hours, and rarely was his sleep disturbed. In fact, he was usually so exhausted he prided himself he could sleep through anything.

His was a tiny room with a sloping ceiling with beams upon which he was always hitting his head. Sinking down onto the straw mattress, he blew the hair back from his forehead and was about to close his eyes when he remembered the photograph the nurse had given him. He took it from his pocket and held it near the gas lamp. Several of the patients and staff had gathered to sing carols beneath a large cardboard star, suspended from the apex of the tent. The padre could be seen giving Communion, whilst in the background, a bedbound youth was grinning at the camera. Charles was there too, accompanying a willowy VAD who was playing the flute, on a battered piano that someone had found. The occasion had really lifted the men's spirits, and those able to had sung along.

Charles smiled, remembering the joy he had experienced — a rare feeling for him these days. Despite having been reared in a country vicarage he didn't consider himself to be a religious man, but he would never forget that day, for in that humble make-do church he had sensed the presence of something magnificent. Many times in this war he had doubted God's existence, but suddenly and inexplicably, he felt sure they were not alone.

He decided to keep the photograph as a reminder to help him

in the days to come, when he knew his faith would again be tested. He was about to put the photograph down when he glanced again at the flautist. Neither of them natural musicians, they had both fumbled their way through the carols. The photographer had captured them both grinning, likely at one of their more momentous slips.

Almost eighteen hours ago, in the early morning when the ice had lain hard on the ground, Charles had watched Clementine climb into the seat beside the ambulance-driver at the start of her journey back home to attend her sister's wedding. She had waved and called out thanks as the vehicle rolled away, leading him to suspect that she knew it was he who had persuaded Matron to grant her leave at such short notice. He remembered how happy she had been, telling him: 'The family have no idea I'm coming — they are going to be amazed when I turn up on the doorstep.'

He turned down the lamp and lay back closing his eyes. 'Enjoy your leave, Miss Ellacombe, ' he murmered aloud. 'You certainly deserve it.'

*

Somewhere in the background a voice cried, 'Next stop Wool, coming up shortly.' It was like being woken from a deep slumber and for a moment Clementine was completely disorientated. With emotions running amok and threatening to overwhelm her she eventually broke free. How long she had been in the major's arms she had no idea, It seemed like minutes, yet commonsense told her it was more like seconds.

'I'm sorry,' he whispered as the train began to slow. 'I don't know what came over me — please forgive me.'

His words snuffed out the divine light of ecstasy leaving her with a mixture of shame and humiliation. She had let a stranger kiss her — a perfect stranger — and she had shown no resistance whatsoever. She sprang to her feet, and turning away, she reached for her bag in the rack above, wanting never to look at this man again.

Realising that his apology had had the opposite effect of what he had intended, he continued, desperate to try and relieve her obvious embarrassment.

'I know I shouldn't have done it but surely you're not going to leave me to bleed to death?' The unexpected witticism seemed to ease things and giving a half-smile she sat down and took hold of the bandage. Neither spoke as she worked, but the air was heavy with unspent words. She finished just as the train came to a halt. 'That will have to do,' she said matter of factly, stuffing everything back into her first-aid box, but as she started to rise he grabbed her hand and smiled sheepishly. He was acutely conscious of the seconds ticking away and desperate to resolve the situation as best he could. 'Please say you forgive me,' he pleaded. 'I feel I have taken advantage of you.'

Again the colour flooded her cheeks but somehow she managed a glimmer of a smile. 'Please, don't suffer on my account. Forget it ever happened.' And aware of tiny electric tremors from the touch of their hands she pulled back and began to put on her gloves.

'Forget it! How can I? I don't even know your name.'

Her whole being quivered with anticipation, but before she could speak she saw how his face seemed to close and finally understood the hopelessness of the situation. She was bereft, and feeling tears well in the back of her eyes she could only watch as he leaped up and reached for her bag. Even so she couldn't stop herself. 'I'm Clem.,' she heard herself say, but the words were buried beneath the loud shrill of the guard's whistle, saving her further humiliation.

The following seconds were taken up with frantic activity as he rushed to open the door and help her down onto the platform. For a brief moment they stared at one another, but too soon the train began to move and a thick cloud of steam descended. Suddenly he was gone.

She was still shaking when the porter, a gangly youth, appeared at her side and carried her luggage to the waiting room. When she handed him a few coins, he rewarded her with a toothy grin.

'Forgive me, I didn't recognise you,' she said. 'It's Danny Triggs. My, you've grown! You must be fifteen?'

'Last week miss.' Danny's older sister Ruby had been a housemaid at Coppins until marrying and moving to London, and he had sometimes come to help clean the brass and silver. He also owned a fine singing voice and Clementine remembered last seeing him perform a solo in the church choir at Christmas 1914. He had looked so angelic, and now here he was almost a foot taller with a face full of angry pimples.

'Is Ruby well? I hear she's had another baby. How is she managing to cope now that Frank has enlisted?'

His face clouded momentarily. He knew his ma worried about his sister, left with four little ones to bring up on the tiny allowance the Army gave her.

'Fine miss. She's working at a canning factory. Her skin started to go yeller when she done munitions, and she worried about getting ill.'

Clementine frowned. It was obvious the poor girl was struggling. 'Who looks after the children?'

'There's a nursery run by one of them Suffragettes.'

Clementine asked after the rest of the family, but before he could reply they were interrupted by the arrival of the station-master, Mr Green.

'Why if it's not Miss Ellacombe! Back for the wedding, of course! My, your sister's done well for herself. I hear the groom is related to Lady Moundsmere on that big estate near Dorchester.'

They spent a few moments exchanging pleasantries and then he asked whether she wished to use the telephone, as was the usual custom when one of the local families required a lift home.

'Lovely talking to you, Miss Ellacombe. There's a fire in the waiting room. Mrs Trott has come to do the cleaning and just made a brew — I'll make sure she brings you a cup. It'll keep the cold at bay whilst you're waiting.'

Best answered the phone. He could barely contain his delight when he heard her voice and said he would leave immediately, the moment he had harnessed the pony to the trap. Clementine was disappointed to learn that her parents were out for the evening, but was consoling herself with the thought of a leisurely bath and an early night when Mrs Trott appeared with a cup of steaming tea. 'Get that down inside yuh dearie. It be a bitter night and folk say gonna snow, but if yuh asks me, I reckon it be too cold for snow.' She paused a while, watching as Clementine sipped her tea, her interest aroused by the Red Cross uniform.

'Work in Lunnun? Me cozen's lad be there. He done got shot Christmas day just 'fore he be coming home fur leave. Near destroyed his mother, it did.'

Clementine sympathised, having known many cases of soldiers getting injured or killed just before taking leave. 'It's an enigma but some of the men I've nursed believe maybe the excitement of going home made them less cautious. Very tragic for their families who one minute are looking forward to a reunion and the next ...'

'Aye, be truth in that. I 'member when I be in service an happy cos next day be Sunday, me holiday, and I be seeing me sweetheart. Only be a few hours to go and then I goes an drops scalding water all o'er me bleedin foot.' She chuckled. 'Mine you, had its benefits, fur seeing me long face, my 'arry got into a tizz tinking I be getting weary of 'im. Well, if I'd known that be all I had to do to get 'im to propose , I'd done it long before.' After a pause that transported her back thirty years she looked again at the young nurse. 'Where say yuh work, my luv?'

When Clementine explained that she was based in Northern France, Mrs Trott stared at her with renewed interest. 'Yuh seen a sight or two, be sure.' Until the war she had always thought young ladies of Clementine's station such helpless creatures, and it filled her with satisfaction to think the youth of today were prepared to make such a valuable contribution to the war effort. 'Nought us knows wot we's capable of 'til put to the test, eh?' she said before scurrying off.

Clementine stared after her; the well-intentioned remark proving particularly meaningful, when not so many minutes before she had succumbed to the advances of a perfect stranger! The interlude since leaving the train had kept her mind busy, but now finding herself alone, the emotions she had fought to ignore rushed at her with such force that her head began to spin. For a moment she feared she was going to faint. Taking deep, calming breaths she looked about for someone or something to occupy her thoughts.

Never, in all her life had she done such a thing. Inevitably, opportunities had presented themselves at work, but she had always been careful to avoid getting into situations which might lead to familiarity. She tried to push it from her thoughts but the memory was all-consuming, and yet again she relived the most exquisite kiss she had ever known. However, the ecstasy was short-lived, guilt and shame soon taking its place. Perhaps worst of all was the niggling voice that asked, should history repeat itself, would she show more restraint?

Standing up, she began to pace up and down, desperate to get home and clear her head. Suddenly, as if in answer to her prayers, the door blew open bringing a gust of cold air and a short balding man with twinkling eyes.

'Best!' she exclaimed. 'How very good to see you.'

'My word, Miss Clementine, you're looking bonny,' he said squeezing her hand. 'How was your journey?'

'Tiring. I'll be glad to get home to a warm bed.'

'And so you shall, I left Mrs Best preparing your room and she said to tell you there will be a nice hot meal waiting for you when you get home.'

Home, she thought, savouring the word, and seeing Best pick up her case, she followed him out into the darkness where a pale-coloured pony attached to an old dog cart was snorting spectre-like vapours into the icy atmosphere.

'Oh, poor Oscar,' Clementine said as she stroked his velvety nuzzle. 'Did you have to leave your nice warm stable?'

'Had to bring you out of retirement, haven't we, old boy?' said Best as he handed Clementine a rug to wrap around her legs. 'Petrol's hard to come by since you've been away, and in London they say the cabbies are using the old hansom cabs again, just like the good old days.'

They drove from the station into the open countryside. It was a clear night and the sky glittered with stars. Clementine was struck by the contrast to the battle- scarred hinterlands of Northern France that she had travelled through earlier that day. But more than anything it was the silence that affected her, for she had become accustomed to the ceaseless booming of the big guns that some said you could hear in Dover. Here, sitting beside Best as Oscar trotted the three miles home along the familiar lanes, Clementine glanced up at the North Star, shining like a beacon, and felt the enveloping peace.

'Who would know there was a war on? I shouldn't think this countryside has changed much in centuries,' she said.

Best grunted. 'As I'm sure you know, looks are mighty deceiving, Miss Clementine. There's many a deep scar been caused here by this war, a lot of locals have had more than their share of tragedy.'

Clementine nodded. Her mother had kept her up to date with the local news in her letters. She cast her mind back to the day not long after war broke out, when she and Claudia had gone down to the station to wave goodbye to soldiers from Bovington Camp, and another occasion when they had helped send off a legion of volunteers — young happy faces brimming with excitement, who had rushed to enlist in case they missed out on the 'glorious victory'. How many of those boys, she wondered, were still alive?

The sudden cry of a fox pierced her thoughts and she heard Best cursing beneath his breath. 'Did you see them rabbits back yonder, I should have brought my gun — they were begging for the pot.'

'How is Mrs Best coping? The wedding must be a nightmare for her with everything in such short supply.' Best was the brigadier's old batman. He and his wife had joined the household staff on his master's retirement. However, since 1914 the domestics had dwindled to nothing; the gardener having enlisted and the two maids gone to work in the Cordite Factory at Holton Heath, leaving Mr and Mrs Best to run the house single-handed.

Best chuckled. 'Believe it or not Miss Clementine she's in her element, even though she's tearing around fretting that everything won't be ready in time. But you know Mrs Best she's always loved a challenge.'

'Have you met the bridegroom?'

'Briefly. He came to the house a few weeks ago.'

'And what did you think of him?'

'Oh, that's not my place to say, miss, but he seemed to be a decent sort, bit quiet like, but he went down well with Mrs Best when he told her her scones were the best he'd had.'

Clementine grinned. 'Ah, a flatterer!' A wise move, for which Mrs Best would reward him well in time to come.

'Oh well, I don't suppose I shall have long to wait before making my own judgement. The wedding's the day after tomorrow, I believe?'

'Aye that it is. It's all stations go, and with Master Timothy home tomorrow it will be just like it used to be.'

'So school have let him off,' said Clementine, excited that she would see her young brother again. 'I bet he's grown in the last year.'

'I'm sure you'll see a change. He's not a child any more.'

'What about my sister, do you see much of her?'

'It's only since the wedding's been arranged that she's come home more. Up 'till then she spent most of her time up in London.'

'Is that so? I don't suppose there's much down here to interest her.'

'That's true, things aren't what they used to be. No more entertaining like you knew, everything being scarce and all. Plus many of the big houses have been closed up or been turned into hospitals. It's not uncommon nowadays to find two or three families living under one roof, trying to make ends meet.'

Approaching a bend in the road he tightened the reins and a silence fell between them. A few yards on they came to a short rough track leading to two stone pillars marking the entrance to a drive. Clementine felt a thrill as all about her, the fields and the old oak tree she once fell from, breaking her ankle, came into sight. And then just seconds later, sitting on a small incline she spotted the house; late Georgian with long sash windows and light stuccoed walls.

At last! She was home!

# 3

Climbing from the car, Alexander Fitzpatrick glanced with affection at the tall twisting chimneys of the Elizabethan manor house, remembering how as boys he and his brother had once used them for target practice with their shotguns. Their grandfather Lord Moundsmere, who had found the raising of two young boys following the decease of his son and daughter-in-law a huge trial, had punished them harshly. Alexander recalled how the normally mild-tempered old gentleman had promptly confiscated the firearms for twelve months, telling the pair that the chimneys hadn't survived a civil war and four centuries for two hooligans to destroy them. At the time the brothers had been resentful, considering life unfair to deal them yet another blow. Alexander still cringed when he remembered their spell of rebelliousness and knew there must have been moments when their poor grandparents had been in utter despair.

As Alexander looked at the chimneys, each unique, stretching like graceful hands into the night sky, he thanked God that he and Patrick had been caught and those ancient clay pots had survived. He hadn't understood the importance of heritage and tradition then. He had taken much for granted. He didn't any more.

He made his way up the front steps to the heavy oak door where an elderly butler waited to welcome him and take his cap and swagger-stick.

'I missed the earlier train, Burrows — have they gone into dinner?' he asked, removing his Burberry.

'No sir Her Ladyship and guests are waiting in the Red Drawing Room.'

The Dowager Countess of Moundsmere's worn features did not betray the relief she felt at the appearance of her grandson; as the minutes had crept by she had begun to fear that she would have to entertain Alexander's fiancée and future in-laws alone, a prospect she did not relish at eighty-five years.

Alexander's tardiness was even more upsetting to Claudia as she began to fear he had changed his mind about marrying her. It was not in her nature to suffer in silence and she had struggled to conceal her anxiety, sitting like an ice sculpture unable to partake in polite conversation, hearing only the death knoll ticking of the clock. Such was her elation upon seeing him, she felt as if she had grown wings and was hovering off the ground. However, her contentment was short-lived for before the main course was served Brigadier Ellacombe was well into his stride discussing the war.

Since his retirement from the Army, he had been elected as a Member of Parliament, and the conversation was an interesting mix of opinions; even Lady Moundsmere was stirred into contributing the occasional pertinent remark. This war was unlike anything in his military experience and he was keen to talk to Alexander who had first-hand knowledge.

Claudia hated war talk and resented her father for introducing the subject, especially tonight of all nights. More than once she tried to catch his eye or lead the conversation in another direction and became increasingly irritated when her attempts failed.

Alexander was sensitive to Claudia's feelings, and though it would have been easy for him to collude with her, he instead encouraged the conversation to continue. He knew what form the discourse would take, and just the thought of their impending marriage was suddenly anathema to him. There was no way he felt able to discuss anything to do with it, and he was struck by the irony that it should be the war that offered refuge.

When her father started speaking of America's attitude towards the conflict, Claudia's patience finally ran out and in a voice like bitter chocolate she asked if there was a less depressing topic they might discuss.

'Like your wedding, I suppose,' Brigadier Ellacombe bristled, annoyed at being put out of his stride. Claudia blushed but reminded him that it was little over twenty-four hours away and that this was the last chance they would have to finalise the remaining details. He silenced her by stating quite emphatically that everything of any importance had already been decided upon and then continued with what he had been saying before. Mrs Ellacombe threw her daughter a sympathetic smile and confided in Lady Moundsmere that the wedding preparations had almost driven her husband crazy the last month.

'He can't wait for it all to be over. If and when our older daughter marries, I shall ensure my husband stays in London.'

The acrimony tended to sour the atmosphere, and soon afterwards Lady Moundsmere suggested the ladies retire to the drawing room for coffee, and allow the gentlemen to continue their conversation without further interruption.

Can I tempt you with a glass of port, sir? asked Alexander.

'Most certainly, there's nothing I enjoy more after a fine meal,' replied Brigadier Ellacombe. 'Haven't had roast venison for a while. Mrs Best makes a cracking pie, but I'd quite forgotten how delicious it is roasted.'

Alexander pushed the decanter towards him. It was the second time they had met and he was still undecided about him. The brigadier seemed typical of many of the old Colonial Army types he had met, plain speaking, down to earth but Alexander suspected he was more complicated than that. He had the feeling that an ambitious man lingered beneath the veneer of bonhomie and recalled Claudia telling him that apart from the house, what wealth the family had came from her mother's family. Claudia wouldn't thank him to tell her, but he could see similarities between father and daughter. The pair had crossed swords tonight because they had competed for centre stage. It would not surprise him at all if somehow he had not encouraged Claudia in her quest to marry well. The man must assuredly take some of the responsibility, having allowed his daughter considerable freedom in wartime London under the guise of war work. It had clearly been a gamble to set free a beautiful young woman in such chaotic times, but perhaps acknowledging that she shared his ambitious streak, it had not disturbed his sleep. However, that aside, Alexander was thankful for his company tonight. In fact, he wondered how he would have survived the meal without him.

Brigadier Ellacombe lit a huge cigar and leaned back in his chair feeling very full and relaxed. 'So tell me, Alexander, what plans do you have for when this war is over?'

'I expect Claudia has told you that I have a small estate in Wiltshire. The house is being used as a hospital for the duration and an agent manages the rest. He's old and will retire as soon as the war is over. Instead of replacing him I intend to take over the estate side myself and perhaps do a spot of horse-breeding. Having seen so many fine animals slaughtered since 1914, I know there will be a demand for good stock.'

The brigadier eyed him thoughtfully. 'Have you considered politics?'

Alexander smiled. 'I had a feeling you might ask me that. I

have, but not seriously. I don't think I am extrovert enough to succeed.'

Though having enjoyed a colourful Army career, the brigadier's greatest love had always been politics, and since his election a few years before, he had made a name for himself as an outspoken backbencher. He knew he was slowing up and would not be able to carry on for more than two or three years at the most. Timothy his son was only thirteen, and it was George Ellacombe's wish that he would one day follow his father into politics. How convenient, if in the meantime, Alexander was able to keep the seat warm until his boy could take over. So far, he liked what he saw of Alexander, and it certainly seemed he was to get a son-in-law to be proud of.

'Don't you worry about being extrovert. Claudia is extrovert enough for the both of you. Anyway, should you decide you'd like to give it a try some day, I will be delighted to steer you in the right direction.'

Claudia kept glancing towards the door, willing Alexander to appear, and irritated with her father for detaining him. It wasn't right that she be shut away with her mother and a Victorian-looking battle-axe, making polite conversation, whilst the men enjoyed themselves. Withdrawing would be a thing of the past once she began to entertain, she decided, as she turned back to Lady Moundsmere who was working on an elaborate piece of embroidery, which had surely taken years of toil. She dropped her gaze to her mother, who was behaving like a sycophant, showing great interest and asking all the questions only those unaccomplished with a needle would ask.

Mrs Ellacombe caught her daughter's eye, lamenting at her ungracious manner and wishing she would make an effort. She felt as if she was doing what should be Claudia's job. Couldn't she understand the benefits of keeping on the right side of Alexander's grandmother?

Claudia hid a yawn, knowing there was no way she would ever be induced to employ her energy in such a tedious occupation. Where were the men? Why were they taking so long? She managed to cheer herself up a bit by thinking about the house in Belgravia where she and Alexander were going to live, or rather she would, for she knew his orders to return abroad were imminent. Relaxing a little, she whiled away the minutes imagining how she would decorate the rooms. Modern would be the theme throughout, except for a few choice antiques. It would be fun, making changes, making her own decisions at last. She knew that by the time she had finished the results would be on a scale for all to admire.

'I had no idea you had another daughter, Mrs Ellacombe,' said the Dowager Countess. 'May I enquire if she will be at the wedding?'

'I think it most unlikely, Lady Moundsmere. I'm sure we should have heard by now if she were. It would seem Claudia's letter has either been lost or delayed.'

Claudia overheard and suffered a pang of guilt. She had meant to write sooner but there had always been so much to do, what with dress-fittings and everything.

'So she's nursing in France. You must be very proud of her?'

'Very much so, though I do worry, especially in light of the recent aerial attacks on the Allied hospitals. Only last week two nurses were killed in a bombing raid.'

'Your daughter's hospital?'

'Mercifully no, but next time.'

Lady Moundsmere decided it was time to change the subject. She turned to Claudia.

'Alexander tells me that you are involved with the YMCA. What exactly does your role entail?'

'I help serve teas at Lady Falkington's canteen,' the girl said thinking how oppressive the walls of this room were, with the dark panelling and tapestries. 'I also do hospital visiting, reading and writing letters, that sort of thing. It can be quite amusing. Some of the men are completely illiterate and ask me to write the most puerile things ...' She could hear voices approaching. At last!

She threw her soon-to-be husband a welcoming smile and made room for him beside her, but to her chagrin Brigadier Ellacombe squeezed his ample frame with its aura of cigar and alcohol fumes, into the space. Though disgruntled she took consolation in watching Alexander as he added to the logs burning in the huge stone fireplace. He was a good head taller than her father, and blessed with the sort of looks no one could fail to notice. Soon he would belong to her, not much longer now. No one could deny she had done well and she felt proud that she had possessed the courage to follow her dream. It gave her a thrill to think how they would draw attention. Wherever they went, people could not fail to think them a fine-looking couple. She would be somebody, her name would appear in society columns. Warmed from her thoughts, she rose from the sofa and went and stood beside him.

'I've just been thinking about the house. I can't wait to start decorating, but it's such a pity we can't move in sooner. Is there nothing you can do to speed things up?' she asked, giving her sweetest smile, and laying her hand on his sleeve with artful effect, displaying the pretty bracelet on her slim wrist. However, it wasn't the bracelet that Alexander noticed but the smooth alabaster skin and perfectly manicured nails which stroked the braid on his arm.

'It's hessonite and diamonds' she told him, 'a gift from my Godmother. She always promised it to me when I married.'

When he failed to comment she felt hurt as if he thought the jewels nothing but paste.

'I thought I told you,' he said breaking his silence, 'that the solicitor is awaiting a signature from the vendor and things cannot proceed until he receives it.'

'But if the signatory is serving in France it could be months!'

'It was your choice. You knew this at the beginning.'

Of all the properties they had viewed, none had matched up to this one. It was definitely the right place. 'It's just so frustrating having to wait.'

'Don't they say that the best things are worth waiting for?'

'Like you had to wait for me,' she teased. 'I do hope you realise that you've upset a good many of my admirers. Poor Johnny Dixon-Scott looked as if he was going to burst into tears when I told him I was getting married.' She didn't think it did any harm to remind him that she had quite a following.

'I was looking at those portraits of your ancestors in the hall after dinner,' she continued. 'Do you think we should get ours done? It would be such fun and we could host an unveiling ceremony. What do you say? I'd just adore Sargent to do them, he's got such style.'

'He's been in America since 1915, I'm surprised you didn't know. Besides, its not something I feel is appropriate at this time.'

Claudia knew he meant after the war and was about to say, 'All well and good if you survive, though a bit late if… ,' but had the good sense to stop herself.

Increasingly frustrated that the evening was not going at all as she had planned she began to fear that he might be getting cold feet. No matter how hard she tried this evening he seemed distant, and totally immune to any attempts she made at flirting. Perhaps it was the presence of his grandmother. Never could she imagine Lady Moundsmere as a young woman and was utterly convinced she must have been dull and boring. Then it struck her that by asking Alexander to show her the old bat's portrait they would get to spend a few minutes alone. However, her plan was thwarted before she even got the words out, when her father rose unsteadily to his feet and announced it was time to leave.

'You seem a little preoccupied this evening Alexander,' said Lady Moundsmere to her grandson when the guests had departed. He stood staring into the dying embers of the fire and turned to his grandmother, who sat very straight backed in her favourite armchair, the pale embroidery draped over her black bombazine frock.

'I apologise, I wasn't the best of company. The last few days have been rather hectic. I'm just tired. A good night's sleep will sort me out.' There was a long pause and in the mirror above the mantel he saw her reflection as she studied him over the top of her pince-nez.

'If you are having second thoughts,' she said eventually, 'it's not too late to call it off.'

Age had not affected his grandmother's mind; she was still as sharp as ever, and despite his misery he couldn't resist a smile, but she was a wily old girl and he knew he must be careful to allay her suspicions. 'I'm not having second thoughts, Grandmama.'

Despite his assurances she didn't entirely believe him. 'Claudia is a very beautiful young woman,' Lady Moundsmere replied. 'She must have many admirers.'

'I daresay,' he said, uneasy at her tone.

'I learned this evening that you have taken a house in Belgravia.'

'My place is too small so there was no alternative but to find somewhere else. However, there's a delay with the legal side and it looks like taking some weeks, so until it's completed Claudia will remain with her parents.'

Lady Moundsmere eyed him thoughtfully. 'Do you think in these times London is a suitable place for a beautiful young woman?'

'Possibly not, but she prefers to be in London so that she can continue with her voluntary work, and I think she is quite capable of …'

'Oh, I've no doubt of her capabilities.' It was said in such a way that one was unsure if it was meant as an insult or a compliment.

Alexander took a deep breath. 'Grandmama, I know that you don't particularly approve of Claudia, but you must realise that she is my choice, and I feel you should support me.'

He sounded convincing enough but her instinct warned her that something was wrong and a small worried frown creased her brow.

'Of course, my dear, but I must admit I was more than a little surprised when I met her. She just doesn't seem the sort of girl I envisaged you would marry. You haven't got her into trouble, have you?'

Alexander was taken aback by her unvarnished choice of words, and after a moments hesitation he gave a short laugh. 'What a thing to think, you know we are marrying because I am being posted overseas.'

'Yes, I realise that and am aware that many people are doing the same, but Alexander, do you not think it rather foolish to rush into marriage when you could go away and never come back. As there is no need for haste, why not wait until after the war? You could have a proper wedding then with friends and family. It would be far more satisfactory.'

He sighed, and there was a look in his eyes that she had never seen before.

'I know things are far from ideal, but in the circumstances it will have to do.' He turned away and started poking the embers, restless and uneasy.

She made one last attempt. 'What is troubling you, Alexander?'

He glanced over his shoulder. 'Nothing I need burden you with, Grandmama.' A silence fell between them and she decided not to press him further. 'What did you say you did to your hand?'

'I cut it on the train.'

'Who dressed it?'

A shadow crossed his face as he stared at the bandage. Strangely, Claudia had not even noticed. 'There was a nurse in the same compartment.'

'How fortunate.' His eyes were fixed on the ashes and she could not see his face. Rising to her feet, she rested a moment on her ebony stick. 'My boy, I want you to know that I have a vast store of common sense and wisdom, a legacy of my long life, and it would be a shame if you did not take advantage of it.' And with that she left the room.

# 4

When Clementine awoke the following morning the house was in darkness. Though still tired, she was too excited to remain in bed, so decided to wander about before disturbing her parents. Upon opening her wardrobe she found her clothes just as she had left them twelve months before, her nose twitching in revolt at the heavy scent of mothballs. She pulled out a warm dress and cardigan, thinking what a novelty it would be to wear something other than her uniform; like a snake with a new skin.

Glancing in the cheval mirror, she thought she had seen better-dressed refugees. The weight she had lost made the dress look like a hand-me-down and her shorn hair, with no headdress to conceal it, was noticeably uneven. She had a fair idea what Claudia, who fanatically measured the inches cut from her hair, would say, and knew a trip to the hairdressers would be insisted upon.

Creeping downstairs, trying to avoid the creaking steps, she was conscious of the ticking of the grandfather clock below dominating the silence. Waiting at the bottom was a black and white shaggy-haired Jack Russell whose tail wagged in delight when she bent to stroke him. He followed her as she roamed from room to room, familiarising herself with everything, and noticing changes which had clearly been made in preparation for the wedding. She ended up in the library, a large square room that had connecting doors to the drawing room. The walls were lined with Brigadier Ellacombe's military books and leather-bound classics, and two Gainsborough-style portraits of some distant ancestors who had been slave-owners in Jamaica. There was an air of tranquillity about it all that made her want to curl up on one of the squashy sofas in front of the hearth. Seeing stirrings of life amongst the ashes in the grate, Clementine threw on a small log before strolling over to the grand piano, where she played a few bars of a Bach Fugue. She was delighted to find it in tune and remembered Best saying that old Mr Brecon and his spinster sisters, who were always a popular quartet before the war, would be playing at the reception.

Struggling to release one of the long sash windows, she eventually managed to lift it enough to step out onto the terrace. The dog, seeing something move, tore off barking excitedly. Clementine waited, pulling her cardigan closer. An icy breeze slapped her face and taking a deep breath, she rediscovered a sweetness in the air that brought back memories of happier times. Leaning over the balustrade, she felt the cleansing power of the wind wash over her. Darkness was lifting, and then — instead of the lawn where they used to hold tennis parties — she found herself looking at a ploughed field. Even though it had been done in a good cause, a means of fighting the German Blockades, she couldn't help but give a sigh. Clearly nothing was safe. She shivered as a cold gust tore around the side of the house and was thankful when, panting with spent energy, Jack returned.

Tiny flames were licking the bark of the log, and kneeling on the hearthrug she took the bellows. Suddenly an explosion of embers shot out, one landing on her hand and making her jump. Immediately the memory of another spark stirred into being, transporting her back to the previous evening. Her heart sank with dismay. Why would the memory not go away and leave her in peace? It had disturbed her sleep, and caused her to rise early, knowing it would engulf her if she just lay there. She had shaken herself free, the excitement she felt at being home bringing a short respite, but now here it was back with renewed force. Was it trying to make her see something, make her learn from what had happened? Why wouldn't it leave her alone? After all, it was only a kiss!

Movement from the kitchen penetrated her thoughts, and getting to her feet she went downstairs.

Hilda Best, a grey-haired woman with florid cheeks, stood at the sink sorting through a pile of muddy vegetables that her husband had just brought in. She had a kindly face and smiled when she saw Clementine.

'Morning, Miss Clementine, did you sleep well?'

'Well, I didn't hear my parents when they returned,' she said, noticing the pot of tea on the farmhouse table.

'I'll fetch you a cup, dear,' said Mrs Best. 'Just let me wash my hands.'

'Remember what I said last night, Mrs Best. You're not to wait on me. I'm used to looking after myself now. You carry along with what you're doing. And don't forget, an extra pair of hands awaits your command. I am at your beck and call.'

Mrs Best gave her an uncertain smile.

'I mean it, I'm the best washer-up they've got at the hospital, and I'm not so bad at scrubbing floors either!'

Mrs Best shook her head and laughed. 'Well, well, who would have thought it?' From her expression Clementine guessed she was recalling the pre-war years when a maid would have carried early-morning tea and a biscuit up to Clementine's bedroom, then light the fire in her grate so she could dress in comfort. She was about to tell Mrs Best she was now more accustomed to waking up with a frozen hot-water bottle when she became aware of approaching footsteps and, recognising her mother's voice, darted behind the door.

'Mrs Best, who on earth has put those logs on in the library? It's far too early.'

'Sorry Mother, it was me,' grinned Clementine, stepping out from her hiding place. Mrs Ellacombe was stunned; it was almost a year since she had seen her older daughter.

'Clementine! Oh Clementine! Oh my dear! It's so wonderful to see you!' She shook her head in disbelief. Her prayers had been answered. Clementine, who adored her mother, hugged her tightly.

'I knew I shouldn't have relied on Claudia to tell you, and that I should have written myself,' the woman continued, wiping her tears, 'but your father said it was Claudia's privilege. I shouldn't have listened — I knew she would take an age. But what does it matter now? You're here, that's what's important!' She had never got used to Clementine working in France, and the strain of two years' constant worry about her safety had taken its toll. She was still an attractive woman who took care of her appearance, but Clementine was a little shocked to see she had aged noticeably in the last year.

'You should have let us know you were coming,' she ended up. 'I would have arranged a proper homecoming.'

Clementine laughed. 'Then thank goodness for Claudia. It seems to me you've already got enough to cope with,' she said, glancing at the line of pastry cases awaiting a filling on the sideboard, and the cake still to be iced. 'There was no time, anyway it was a decision taken on the spur of the moment. I happened to open Claudia's letter in front of our MO and I'm certain he persuaded Matron to allow me leave, though he would never admit it. As soon as I had her permission I managed to get a lift in an ambulance that was going to Calais. I had just half an hour to gather my things. I didn't even have time to change out of my uniform.'

'Well, the important thing is that you are home and this time for good, I hope.' But seeing the look on her daughter's face, her brow furrowed. 'Oh Clementine! Do you have to return? Surely you've done enough. Any one of the hospitals here would be only too pleased to have you. Let someone else take your place.'

'But, Mummy I have to go back — I promised. At this time of year half the nurses are convalescing themselves, and then when we are up to full strength in the spring the battles start, and there are always soldiers lying in agony waiting hours even for first aid.'

Conscious that she was in danger of letting Clementine's return to France mar her delight at having her home again, Mrs Ellacombe took a grip on herself. 'I'm so proud of you, so very, very proud,' she said emotionally, and she embraced her once again. 'Now come upstairs and surprise Papa.'

Outside Brigadier Ellacombe's door, Clementine's mother paused and gave her a knowing look. 'He's feeling a little indisposed this morning. He and Claudia's fiancé drank a whole bottle of port last night after dinner.'

Clementine laughed. 'That sounds like the sort of fellow I would expect Claudia to marry.'

Brigadier Ellacombe was still in his dressing room. 'What's all the commotion?' he grumbled as they entered his bedroom. 'Have we visitors?'

'Only one dear, and I've brought her up to see you.'

'You've done *what!*' he bellowed. 'Have you lost your senses, woman!'

'Don't worry, Papa, it's only me,' chuckled Clementine as her father emerged. She could see that the war had not had much effect on him. He was a little fatter and his complexion a little ruddier, but generally he was the same old papa.

'Clementine, my dear child, what a wonderful surprise!' he

said, hugging her fiercely. 'Why didn't you let us know you were coming?'

'We've been through that, dear,' said his wife. 'The fact is, she's here — and what with Timmy coming back today, we shall be a complete family again, albeit for a day. Isn't it wonderful?'

'It certainly is,' he said, suddenly clutching his head and groaning.

'Still feeling unwell dear?'

'Who was leading whom astray then, Papa — you or The Honourable Alexander FitzPatrick?' Clementine enquired.

'Well, he seemed rather apprehensive, I thought,' her father prevaricated, not disclosing the fact that he had drunk most of the port himself. 'But I suppose that's understandable when you think what the poor fellow's letting himself in for.'

*

Down the corridor Claudia lay in bed brooding over the previous evening. The dress she had worn with the panels of Brussels lace and blue sash, lay draped over the back of a chair where she had carelessly thrown it. Not once had Alexander commented on how lovely she looked. She felt she would never wear it again, for she would always associate it with the failure she considered the occasion to be. She was still angry with her father, whom she held responsible. How selfish he had been with his continued war talk. He had made her look an idiot at the dinner table; she would never forgive him for that. She lit a cigarette and felt an instant calm until she thought again of how distant Alexander had seemed. Perhaps it was just last- minute nerves. Well, let him have his nerves — just as long as they didn't prevent him from getting to the church tomorrow.

There was a knock at the door but before she had time to hide her cigarette, it opened.

'Caught you!'

'Clemmie! I don't believe it! Absolutely ripping!'

'Did you think I was going to miss your wedding?' her sister laughed rushing over to hug her sibling.

'Darling I'm stunned. And your hair — You've cut it, or should I say, hacked it. Just look at it! What on earth did Ma and Pa say? They must have had a fright.'

'About me coming home or my hair?'

'Your hair, silly.'

'Well, I think Mummy was so relieved to see me she didn't say much, and Papa hasn't yet noticed.'

'Rest assured he will when he recovers from his hangover and then just you wait. But seriously, it looks terrible; you'll have to get it rescued somehow. I can't have you looking like that at the wedding.'

'Enough about my hair. I want to hear about Alexander. Tell me all about him,' Clementine said sitting on the bed.

'Gorgeous, of course. Quite, quite gorgeous. I did tell you he's an Hon., didn't I?'

'I believe you did, but what is he like?'

Claudia chuckled. 'Where do I begin? He's perfect, of course. You know me, Clem, I don't accept second-best. He has it all — wealth, charm, looks. Such a catch! All the girls in London were after him.' She knew she sounded rather smug, but then it was only Clementine. 'They didn't stand a chance once *I* set eyes on him.'

She hopped out of bed, feeling much brighter. 'Oh, I'm so glad you're back. I just know you're going to like him.' She threw her cigarette out of the window and then with a theatrical gesture thrust her arm under her sister's nose to show off the solitaire diamond ring she wore on her engagement finger.

'What do you think? Isn't it spiffing?'

'It's beautiful, Claudia.'

'To think that just a few months ago I was beginning to despair whether I would ever get married, and now here I am unable to get over my good fortune. He's absolutely everything I've ever wanted.' Clementine gave her a discerning look. 'Well, he certainly has an impressive pedigree, but I would like to think that you love him too.'

'But of course, darling! I love everything about him.'

Clementine said nothing but she had misgivings, which despite Claudia's effervescence wouldn't go away. She listened as her sister rattled on, describing the house in Belgravia and all the plans she had.

'Just you wait, Clemmie. When the was is over I shall throw the most wonderful parties and you will come and stay with us, and I'll introduce you to lots of eligible young gentlemen.'

Clementine frowned. 'I doubt there will *be* lots of eligible young men when the war is over. Claudia, don't you ever read the newspapers?'

Claudia's face darkened. 'You know I don't,' she said crossly, 'and I certainly don't intend to start. I'm sick to death of war talk. Heavens, you should have heard Papa last night, ruining what should have been a perfectly lovely evening, and it's the same everywhere you go. Even the streets are full of shabbily dressed people trying to prove they're patriotic and *doing their bit*.'

She became conscious of her sister's disparaging look and burst out: 'I know you think I'm selfish but I don't care. I intend to enjoy what youth I have. It's hardly my fault that the government decided to rush over the Channel and help ghastly little Belgium.

What had they ever done for us? If I don't make the most of it now, I shall miss out, and who will care? At least you had a couple of years before the war when you were invited to parties and things. Don't forget I didn't come out until 1914, the year everything stopped dead.'

Clementine was ashamed of her sister's attitude and angry for the hundreds of young soldiers she had seen die, many even younger than Claudia. It was for the likes of her they had given their lives. What would they think if they could hear her, talking of what the world owed her and of the parties she'd missed!

'Well, how is it your Prince Charming isn't fighting in the war, or do aristocrats get special treatment?' she said.

Claudia smiled. 'Darling, he's a veteran. Did you honestly think Papa would let me marry a conshie, even with a background like Alexander's?' And with thoughts of wealth and position in her mind, she immediately went on to tell her sister about his family connections and how close she was to becoming the Countess of Moundsmere.

*

Alexander's best man, Piers Douglas, was of stocky build and stood five feet nine inches in his stocking feet. He could well remember the time when he had been taller than Alexander and used to tease him for his lack of height. Alexander had been the shortest boy in the year but then suddenly, when they had been about sixteen, almost overnight he had shot up and grown like a weed whilst Piers to his dismay, had never grown another fraction of an inch. It would have served him right had Alexander got his own back, but fortunately it wasn't in his friend's nature. However, Piers managed to adjust to the change and what he lacked in height he made up for with confidence and spirit. People were drawn to him and he had always been a popular figure with both sexes.

They had met at prep school when they were seven. Alexander's parents had decided to send their sons to different schools, and away from home and family for the first time he had been very unhappy. However, the boy with the thick sandy hair and smiling blue eyes at the desk next to his, who had already done a term, had shown compassion and taught him how to survive. They made an unlikely pair, one dark and serious, the other fair and fun-loving, but before long they were inseparable and Piers and Alexander had been friends ever since, despite going to different universities and joining different Armed Forces.

Piers had joined the Royal Navy at the outbreak of war in August 1914 and the following year had been awarded the Croix de Guerre for bravery at Gallipoli. He had been the only officer to survive on his ship, and after recovering from a bullet wound, successfully applied for a transfer to the Royal Naval Air Service, which allowed him to combine his two greatest loves, flying and sailing. Sent to Antwerp, he managed to survive six months before being shot down and shipped home with an injured foot. Now he was based in the New Forest near Beaulieu, training young pilots to fly.

Alexander was a little late meeting Piers at Dorchester station, and Piers was already outside when he drew up in the car.

'What an honour, the groom himself! Thought you'd be getting quietly drunk.'

Alexander shot him a look. 'Why do you say that?'

'Because I know *I* would. Are you not a lamb going to slaughter?'

'Well, for your information getting drunk doesn't work.'

Piers laughed, but something in Alexander's voice made him look more closely at him. The porter put Squadron Commander Douglas's luggage in the car and Alexander started the engine.

'So, my friend, you are actually going to tie the knot,' Piers said jocularly as they sped out into the countryside. 'I must say you're a dark horse, I had absolutely no idea you were serious about Claudia, though I can't say I blame you. She's a real stunner.'

Alexander said nothing. Piers knew this was out of character. They had been friends for twenty-three years and had been through a lot together. He thought of the plans they used to make about how they would celebrate when one of them married. Obviously the war had put paid to that. However, he had still expected to find his chum in fine form.

In the distance he spotted an old coaching inn, which the pair had frequented in the past, and said, 'I'm a little parched Alexander. What say you we make a start before luncheon?'

The two of them caused a stir with the landlord's daughter who helped behind the bar, and with whom Piers couldn't resist flirting.

'What's the matter with your friend, he looks a bit glum?' she asked as Alexander warmed his hands by the fire.

'He's a condemned man, I'm afraid,' Piers told her, 'getting married tomorrow.' They both laughed.

'So what is it, Alexander? Is the lovely Claudia giving you cause for concern?' Piers asked a couple of minutes later when he joined him by the fire with two glasses of whisky.' Do tell me I'm wrong.' Alexander's face grew darker. 'I wish I could.'

'Well, why the deuce are you marrying the girl if you're not sure?' Piers's features momentarily froze. 'Oh no! It can't be that you're doing the decent thing, can it?'

The expression on his friend's face answered his question.

Horrified, he shook his head. 'Alexander, you fool! I thought everything was a trifle hasty, but I would never have guessed that was the reason. Why didn't you tell me?'

'What good would it have done. Besides, I've felt so sick about it all that I just didn't feel like talking.'

'We've always managed to talk in the past.' Piers watched as his friend stared blindly into the fire. 'In fact, it might have done a lot of good. There are places, if you know where to go.'

'You mean abortion?'

'Well, it's too late now, of course — but yes. Not very pleasant, I grant you, but I would have thought preferable to a forced marriage. I take it you don't love her?'

There was a travesty of a smile on Alexander's face. 'What do you think?' He sighed deeply. 'I'm so confused I just don't know about anything any more. Over the past few weeks I've resigned myself to the fact that I have got to get married whether I like it or not. And after all, I'm thirty, I've enjoyed my freedom and it's all got to come to an end sometime. Let's face it, Piers, I've had a good innings, and if I have to marry, it might as well be Claudia.'

'Then what's the problem? Why the long face? Must be nerves.'

Alexander's eyes lingered on him a moment. 'I don't expect you to understand this, as I don't understand it myself. You'll probably think it ridiculous, but last night I met a girl on the train and she had the most incredible effect on me. For the time I was with her I was completely spellbound, and I can't seem to get her out of my mind. The point I'm trying to make is that Claudia has never had that effect on me, nor has anyone else, for that matter.'

'Are you saying that you've fallen in love with a stranger?'

'I don't know, Piers, but what other explanation can there be for feeling like I do? I never slept a wink last night agonising over it, angry that I should meet her at a time in my life when I am helpless to do anything about it.' Piers was the only person Alexander could trust to confide in, and he fully expected him to tell him in no uncertain terms to snap out of it, but instead there was a note of sympathy in his voice.

'I don't know what to say. I suppose I'm shocked because it just seems so out of character. As long as I can remember you've put barriers up when someone gets too close. I've always felt that you equated love with loss, and that it was fear of getting hurt that stopped you from giving and receiving love. It's understandable because, let's face it, you have suffered a lot of tragedy in your life, what with your parents and more recently, Patrick.'

'Are you saying my heart was frozen?'

'I suppose that's a suitable analogy, and having suffered frostbite in my toe, I can sympathise. I don't think I shall ever forget the excruciating pain when it thawed.' However, that aside, he felt it his duty to make Alexander see sense. 'It's a bit late if you're thinking of backing out. You'll be literally leaving the poor girl at the church steps.' He gave Alexander a long, hard look.

'Relax — you know I wouldn't do that. I am marrying for the baby.' He had been nine years old when his parents had died in a motoring accident in the South of France. Without his brother Patrick and the kindness of his grandparents he didn't know how he would have survived. Children need roots, family. He might be uncertain about Claudia, but he knew if he survived the war he would make a supreme effort to be the kind of parent he remembered, and if not, at least he would have given the child his name.

'I couldn't live with myself if I turned my back, Piers. I don't want my child having to grow up with the stigma of illegitimacy, so you may have no fears on that score. I shall be there.'

# 5

It had been decided that there should be plenty of warm sustaining dishes to satisfy the fifty or so wedding guests whose appetites were expected to be keen having survived an hour in a freezing church, and at five o'clock the following morning Clementine was in the kitchen helping Mrs Best with last-minute preparations. She stirred sauces, washed up, peeled vegetables and rolled pastry — did anything that she was asked.

All the vegetables were home-produced and a good many of them had gone into a huge saucepan, which Mrs Best was intending to make into soup. A neighbouring farming family who were good friends of the Ellacombes had provided sufficient meat, and it was generally accepted that there would be plenty for all.

A wonderful aroma wafted around the kitchen as Clementine removed some loaves from the oven and put them to cool on wire racks. Despite the early start she was enjoying herself and in a strange way knew she had the war to thank for that. There was no denying it had given her opportunities she would not have had. Leaving home had been an education and above all had taught her not to take people and things for granted. With that foremost in her mind she was able to see Mr and Mrs Best for the treasures they were.

As she filled pastry cases with mincemeat she watched Mrs Best pipe mashed potato onto some of the dishes and was about to ask if one day she would teach her how to cook when a tousled sandy-haired boy in a dressing-gown appeared, yawning widely.

Clementine's brother Timothy had arrived the previous afternoon with Brigadier Ellacombe, who had driven to Sherborne to collect him from school.

'Mmm, hot bread. I'm starving! '

'Don't touch,' said Clementine, lightly slapping his hand. 'Surely you can wait until breakfast Timmy. It's only half past six.'

'A growing chap needs plenty of fodder.'

'Timmy! You're not an animal and besides, you well know hot bread gives you indigestion.

His bottom lip drooped and he looked decidedly younger than his thirteen years.

'Oh let him have one of the buns you took out earlier dear. They must be nearly cool,' said Mrs Best, wiping her hands in her apron. 'We can't have the lad hungry, now can we?'

'Well you'll have to earn it,' smiled Clementine, realising that her young brother could prove very useful to Mr Best, who no doubt would welcome a helping hand. Rainwater had leaked onto the landing during the night and the poor man, on top of all his other tasks, had been compelled to climb up onto the roof and repair the damage. Behind schedule, he was beginning to panic, unlike his wife, who never seemed to get ruffled.

As Clementine had guessed, Best accepted Timmy's offer of assistance with alacrity and sent him off to get dressed in to some old clothes. On his return he was handed a bucket with instructions to clean out all the downstairs fires and lay them ready for lighting. 'And when you've done that, the drive needs raking.'

The sudden thought of breakfast and all the work it entailed made Clementine decide to persuade her parents and Claudia to breakfast in their bedrooms. Not only would it keep them out of the way for a little longer, but it would also enable some of the dishes to be placed in the dining room, freeing up the work space in the kitchen. When Clementine mentioned this to Mrs Best and suggested that she herself prepare the trays, she received a sceptical look. 'It would be a godsend if you could, Miss Clementine, but you know the Brigadier — he don't like no change.'

'Leave it to me' said Clementine, quietly confident that after two years nursing and sometimes having to deal with difficult patients, she would be able to handle her father.

Brigadier Ellacombe was not at all happy; he had been looking forward to his usual assortment of cooked dishes whilst leisurely reading the newspaper, and he saw it as an infringement of his rights — one more thing this wedding had disrupted. He felt obliged to concede, however he still made a fuss about the lumpy porridge and omelette that Clementine produced, pointing out that it wasn't her place to help in the kitchen. Mrs Ellacombe was a little more diplomatic and declined anything other than tea and toast, insisting she was too nervous to eat.

As much as she loved her parents, Clementine was aware they were rather oblivious to the effort required to keep a house the size of Coppins functioning comfortably, and that without the added burden of a wedding reception. She knew that part of the reason was because they had lived in India for so long with an abundance of staff who had indulged their every whim. She could well remember how the staff had spoiled both Claudia and herself, and knew that if they hadn't been sent back to England to attend school they would probably have grown into monsters. To this day she was still guilt-ridden whenever she thought of the sugar-coated bonbons that their ayah had regularly given them. The sisters had forever pestered her for the boiled sweets in a riot of pretty colours, but it was only after a chance remark made by Best years later that Clementine had learned they were bought from the market from her own meagre wages. Now Clementine could see how the adulation they had received from the local people had given them all a feeling of superiority.

This was the second time she had returned home since going to France, and she was becoming increasingly conscious that the absences had served to distance herself from her family. So many things would remind her that she had changed from the spoiled self-centred, middle-class girl she had been, and happy though she was to see her family, it wasn't long before she began to feel that she didn't quite fit in. Just last evening when dinner was a little slow in appearing, she had felt embarrassed to hear her parents talk about the 'good old days' when they had had twenty servants and one only had to 'click one's fingers'. Sometimes she wondered what the future held because it was becoming plain that things could never go back to how they were before 1914.

'You've been a real asset to me, Miss Clementine, you'll make some lucky man a fine wife,' Mrs Best said as the relief staff, hired for the day, began to arrive and Best lined them up to instruct them of their duties.

Minutes later, the door swung open and Mrs Ellacombe appeared.

'Are the bells not working? I've been ringing for ages — did no one hear? Where's Best? Has he stoked the boiler, like I asked? I don't want to be running out of hot water when we take our baths.'

'I'll go and fetch the breakfast trays,' said Clementine, excusing herself.

'We have staff now to deal with that. Your place is with Claudia. She needs your assistance, and I'll need you to help me too.'

It had been Claudia's intention to spend a leisurely morning relaxing and preparing for her role, but her plans went awry when she awoke with a headache, and a feeling that nothing was going to go right. Glancing outside and seeing the approach of dark clouds seemed the final straw. She couldn't believe God could be so cruel.

Clementine found her sister in complete disarray with clothes lying everywhere, the breakfast tray virtually untouched.

'What's going on? It looks as if a bomb has exploded in here.'

'I can't make up my mind what to pack.'

Clementine understood that Alexander's friend had offered the couple his home in Devon for their short honeymoon. 'You shouldn't need too much.' It wasn't as if there would be anyone else there, apart from a skeleton staff. 'A few outfits should suffice.' She held up a couple of dresses for selection, trying to be helpful, but what should have taken minutes seemed to take forever as Claudia kept changing her mind.

Just as Clementine placed the final outfit in the case, Timmy barged in followed by Jack, his tail wagging excitedly. 'Best sent me for the tray,' he said, bounding across the room.

'How many times have I told you to knock. And get that dog out — he stinks!' yelled Claudia.

'Look, you've hurt his feelings,' said Timmy as Jack piteously lowered his head. Clementine giggled.

'Then give him a bath,' retorted Claudia

'He can't have a bath this weather,' said Timmy, who was already spreading plum jam on some of Claudia's untouched toast.

'Oh yes he can, or else you must shut him in the stables. I'm not having his stench wafting around the place.'

After shooing her brother and the dog out, she went and stood by the window, staring out as the rain fell. She looked paler than normal, as if all colour had drained away. Her pallor served to accentuate the faint blue shadows beneath her eyes and around her mouth, and aware of time creeping away, Clementine wondered what she could do to buoy her up.

'I think it might clear,' she said, seeing a flash of sunlight peep out from behind a dirty-coloured cloud.

'Even if it does, it is still going to be muddy. My dress will be ruined.'

'That's probably why most people have summer weddings.'

'Really?' Claudia replied sarcastically, then rubbed her brow. 'Oh my head! Maybe I should take another aspirin. How long does it take for them to work? Oh God, I never envisaged feeling like this.'

Clementine watched as her sister swallowed another couple of pills, then pause as if something had grabbed her thoughts, her features fashioning an expression that Clementine couldn't decipher.

'Do you realise I could be a widow this time next week?' the girl said eventually.

'Oh heavens you *are* depressed! You mustn't be thinking things like that on your wedding day.'

'It's called facing facts. And let me tell you this,' Claudia went on, 'rumour has it that Primmie Driscoll has already ordered her widow's weeds — just in case!' Clementine looked incredulous. 'True,' continued Claudia, relaxing a bit. 'I think the family motto is '*Be Prepared.*' She chuckled, but her new mood was short-lived as she began to tense up again.

'I do hope Mrs Best doesn't let me down today; it would be so humiliating if someone picked up a smeary glass or a tarnished fork. I think I'd better go and check.'

'There's absolutely no need to do anything of the sort. I can assure you that everything is in hand. Please do not upset Mr and Mrs Best, Claudia, they are doing a wonderful job, and it wouldn't go amiss if you told them so. Everyone likes to be appreciated,' said Clementine. 'Just stop worrying about nothing and calm down. Why don't you go and have your bath whilst I tidy up here.

I'm sure you'll feel more relaxed. You're like an overstretched violin string waiting to snap.'

Claudia seemed strangely subdued on her return from the bathroom, disappointing Clementine's hopes that she might be in a better mood. Seeing her light yet another cigarette, she asked if everything was all right and watched as her sister stood by the open window inhaling deeply. There was no reply and the silence between them grew heavier.

'Claudia, for goodness sake, whatever is wrong?'

'My damned curse has started — that's what's wrong.'

Clementine stared at her not knowing what to say. 'Does it matter?' she asked.

'Of course it matters!' her sister exploded.

Clementine felt her face redden whilst the unblushing bride expressed her anger with more expletives.

'But surely Alexander will understand. These things happen. You're not to blame.'

'Oh yes, he'll understand. He'll understand perfectly!' Her face burned, agony etched into her eyes, but suddenly like a squeezed sponge her features crumpled and a tear fell. Privately Clementine wondered what sort of brute her sister was about to commit herself to.

'I'm sure you're doing him an injustice. After all, he can hardly blame you for an act of nature.'

'Oh God, you're so naïve!' Claudia snapped. 'Haven't you learned anything in France apart from emptying bedpans? No one would believe you're nearly two years older than me!'

Bewildered, Clementine watched as Claudia stubbed her cigarette out on the outside walls and lowered the window. 'Do I have to spell it out to you?' she said, turning to face her. 'He won't understand because he thinks that I am pregnant.'

Clementine felt herself shudder. 'Pregnant! Tell me, Claudia — were you pregnant?'

The ensuing silence confirmed her suspicions. She was horror-stricken. 'How could you — how could you do such a wicked thing?'

Claudia threw her eyes up. 'Why do you think, because it was the only way I could get him to marry me, of course! Oh, don't look at me like that. I'm hardly the first to have done it, and surely not the last. And if it hadn't been for my blessed menstrual cycle going haywire, he'd never have known.'

'He'd have found out sooner or later Claudia!'

'Never! The chances were that I'd become pregnant anyway over the next few days, and if not there was always a miscarriage to fall back on in his absence; he wouldn't have been any the wiser. Oh God, what am I to do?' She paced up and down the room, her face mirroring her suffering.

Clementine couldn't believe what she was hearing. 'I'm speechless! I wish you hadn't told me. Never in my wildest dreams would I have thought you capable of stooping so low.'

'Then it seems I can't expect any support from you. Fine sister you are!' Claudia said, turning her back and wishing she hadn't been so weak as to confide in her. She should have known the kind of response she'd get — for hadn't Clementine always been such a 'Goody Two Shoes', never putting a foot wrong. How stupid to think she might have become more worldly-wise after being away from home.

'Surely you weren't expecting my sympathy,' retorted Clementine. 'Do you know what I think? I think you are nothing but a scheming hussy and deserve all you get!'

Whenever they had fought before it had usually been Clementine who had given in; Claudia's temper was legendary in the family and Clementine found her tantrums hard to deal with. It was often easier to concede defeat but this time she had no intention of turning a blind eye to her sister's bad behaviour and Claudia understood this. She was more shaken than she showed by Clementine's reaction.

'What do you know? You've never even met Alexander. Why shouldn't he marry me after I gave myself to him? I might have been pregnant.'

'But you knew you weren't! It's utterly dishonest. It's a man's life we're talking about.'

As a silence fell between them Claudia marched across to the wardrobe and removed her wedding dress. She held it possessively as if she feared her sister might confiscate it. Clementine watched, and shaking her head with disgust, recalled how she had exclaimed at its beauty when she had first set eyes on it. Realising that Claudia was determined to go through with the ceremony, its pale elegance now left her cold. She was seeing a side of her sister she didn't like. Never would she have believed her to be so calculating, so ruthless. It was a far cry from the spoiled little girl who always liked to get her own way.

Earlier she had thought how the war had changed people — changed her — but perhaps what it really did was highlight one's true self; show people up for what they really were. Before 1914 it would have been impossible for a situation like this to arise because young ladies such as themselves had been chaperoned everywhere in order to protect their reputations. There was little or no opportunity for couples to be alone, and Clementine had sometimes wondered how a girl ever got herself a husband at all, for having one's mother or aunt always in attendance was not conducive to developing a romance. But war had altered this and the irony was, it was those very parents who had once cosseted their daughters who were now proudly boasting of them 'doing their bit'. Had they really no idea what was going on? Clementine had encountered girls in France who slept with soldiers, but though some could be described as fast, there were others, who like the troops, used the act as a means of escape from the horrors, and in all conscience she couldn't blame them. They asked for nothing but comfort, and what they took they gave. They were called immoral, but surely Claudia was the one without morals; what she had done put her beneath the women in the French bordels where the queues of soldiers often stretched onto the pavements. The whores might get paid, but at least their business was done with a certain integrity.

Noise from downstairs could be heard as the piano was being moved into the drawing room, reminding Clementine that in a few hours everyone would be assembled there to toast the happy couple.

'You can't possibly go through with it,' she said. 'Let me phone and tell him you're ill …'

'Don't you dare! I will go through with it!'

'Listen to me Claudia, at least my way you come out with some dignity. Tell Alexander you made a mistake. He will respect you, something he won't do if you decide to proceed. I'm sure that if you do that, he will still want to marry you, but for the right reason. Wouldn't you rather know that he was marrying you for love?'

Claudia gave a sarcastic laugh. 'If you think I'm going to risk making myself the laughing stock of society, you must be insane. Everyone expects a wedding today — and a wedding there will be!'

# 6

The rain stopped mid-morning, but it quickly began to freeze, making the journey to the church treacherous. Clementine travelled with her mother and brother in Brigadier Ellacombe's car, chauffeured by Bill Perkins, who lived in the village. He had worked at Coppins in various capacities since the age of fourteen, and despite having retired some years before, he agreed to drive the car, allowing Best to get things ready back at the house. A family friend would bring the bride and her father in Great-Aunt Jane's old landau.

Seeing how frail Perkins had become made Mrs Ellacombe fear for their safety. 'We're in no hurry! Just get us there in one piece,' she shrieked when they hit an icy patch and the car skidded. Her eyes met those of her son. 'Believe me you won't be grinning if we end up in a ditch.'

She turned to Clementine, who was looking out of the window with a plaintive expression. 'Did you ask Best to put hot-water bottles in the carriage? It's bound to be draughty.'

Clementine nodded, sure that the heavy black velvet cloak Claudia had had designed to wear over her wedding dress would not only provide sufficient warmth but also guarantee the dramatic entrance she so desired as she walked up the aisle.

'Don't you think Claudia looks beautiful? I'm sure I've never seen her more lovely.'

For her mother's sake Clementine struggled to summon some enthusiasm, but it was difficult. She couldn't stop thinking of the poor groom who had survived the trenches only to fall prey to her sister.

'I thought brides were meant to be happy,' said Timmy, still chafing because Claudia had insisted he wear a sailor suit. 'She doesn't look very happy to me.'

'Don't be silly, Timmy! The poor darling is clearly nervous — and small wonder. It's a big commitment she is making in these uncertain times.'

Clementine remained silent, not trusting herself not to blurt out the truth. However, she knew that even if she did, the chances of it altering anything were nil. No doubt their parents would be shocked and extremely angry, but their only concern would be that their single, sullied daughter get a ring on her finger as quickly as possible. She thought of the expression on Claudia's face when she had made a final attempt to make her understand just what she was doing.

'You say you love him, but what would your reaction be if he came home with his face blown away or his legs missing, perhaps both. Would you be able to meet his eyes and tell him you're glad that he survived, and that no matter what terrible things have been done to him, you'll always love him?'

Claudia had not answered, but Clementine could see that her determination remained undimmed.

'Darling, are you listening?' asked Mrs Ellacombe as an empty carriage moved away from the church. 'I said, is that the Fortescues?'

Clementine's long-distance sight wasn't as good as her mother's. 'I really don't know,' she said, shrugging her shoulders but Mrs Ellacombe's attention was already diverted by a speck of fluff on her new cashmere coat. Brushing it off, she asked Clementine to check that the feather in her hat hadn't drooped. Only when she was satisfied with her own appearance did she turn to her daughter. Despite the efforts of the hairdresser and the outfit they had hurriedly bought in Wareham yesterday, she couldn't resist a sigh. As Claudia had said earlier, Clementine looked like the poor relation.

'If only you had come home a little earlier, I could have got Mrs James to run up something, and Clemmie, do make sure you keep your hat on.'

Clementine gave her mother's hand a reassuring squeeze. 'Mummy do stop worrying, nobody will be looking at me.'

Nervous at upsetting Mrs Ellacombe again, Perkins parked the car as near as he could to the path leading up to the church entrance, so all she had to do was walk the short distance. As he climbed out and went to open the door, his mistress was trying to recognise the few cars parked on the roadside and the small group who were tiptoeing around the icy puddles, making their way towards the shelter of the building.

'Such ghastly weather,' she sighed again. 'I pray Claudia is warm enough.'

'I spy Alexander in the porch,' yelled Timmy. 'He's in khaki, Mother. I thought he'd be in dress uniform.'

'Oh well, I'm sure he looks very handsome whatever he is wearing. You should have seen Papa when we married. You wouldn't believe how splendid he looked. I remember walking up the aisle and my legs feeling so weak I thought I was going to faint.' Thirty years later, Claire Ellacombe's eyes still watered at the memory and she blinked rapidly, intent on keeping her composure.

Clementine knew she was going to find it difficult meeting Claudia's soon-to-be husband, having to summon the necessary excitement and happiness expected on such an occasion, when

70

she felt like an accessory to her sister's deception.

She forced her gaze towards the entrance where he stood, a tall figure with his back towards them, slightly stooped as he chatted to a boyish-looking officer of a different regiment or Service.

'That must be the best man,' said Mrs Ellacombe.

But Clementine barely heard a word. Alexander's face was hidden from view, but there was something strangely familiar about him.

'I think Claudia said he is a pilot,' continued Mrs Ellacombe as she gingerly stepped out onto the muddy gravel. As Clementine prepared to follow, Alexander chose that moment to look in their direction.

*

'Cor, you look icky,' said Timmy, who had been sent back to the car by his mother to see what had happened to his sister. He couldn't believe the change in her; in seconds all colour had drained from Clementine's face. She stared at him blankly, barely capable of coherent thought.

'I'll get Mother,' said Timmy anxiously.

'Don't! Timmy, wait. Don't … don't worry her. I came over dizzy. Just tell her that I'll join you when I've recovered.' He looked uncertain but her pleading smile reassured him and he hurried away, nearly slipping on a patch of ice. She watched as he relayed the news to their mother and saw her open the embroidered bag on her arm. Seconds later, Timmy returned with a small bottle of smelling salts.

'Ma said to take a good sniff and then join us inside.' Off he sped, returning to where Mrs Ellacombe waited in the porch chatting to Alexander and his friend.

What was she to do? She couldn't go in there! Oh no — Timmy was speaking to him, using his hands expressively, pointing to the car. Clementine froze.

'He's going to come!' she breathed seeing Alexander take a step in her direction, and fearing that her mother had asked him to accompany her from the car. He took another step. She could barely breathe. Only her legs which had gone numb, prevented her from opening the door and dashing off. She wasn't ready to face him, not like this, not here. She prayed for Divine intervention, uncertain whether she believed or not.

Though the following seconds seemed a blur, she thought she saw her mother shake her head. Thankfully, Alexander stopped and Mrs Ellacombe beckoned him. Without further ado he offered his arm, and in seconds the four of them had disappeared inside the church. Such was Clementine's relief she began to cry. However, for the rest of her days she would wonder what might have happened had Alexander come, and whether the prayer she had uttered had been answered or not.

She removed her hat and slumped against the seat, resting her face against the cold leather, allowing it to soothe the fever that was burning in her head. Dark clouds streaked the sky just as the landau drawn by two grey carriage horses sporting white plumes, appeared carrying the bride and Brigadier Ellacombe.

'Take me home, please, Perkins,' she said. 'Please take me home now.'

*

Inside the church, guests huddled together in the pews waiting for the bride. Only the choirboys' red vestments, and the splash of colour on the altar cloth seemed to take the chill from the air.

72

Alexander, sitting at the front, found the purity of the choristers' voices soothing, and involuntarily he remembered the evening he had first met Claudia.

It was at a charity function held by the Red Cross, organised to raise money for disabled soldiers and their families. He had promised to accompany his grandmother, but when she was unable to go due to a cold, she insisted he still attend. Discovering Piers up in London enjoying a few days' leave he dragged him along for support. As he had predicted, the function turned out to be rather dull — that is, until Piers recognised the two attractive young ladies who were serving teas. Before he knew, arrangements had been made for them all to meet later. His expectations had been quite different to his friend's; he had thought perhaps a trip to the opera, or ballet. He should have realised, seeing Piers smile, but he went along, little knowing what the meeting held in store for him. In a short time Claudia's looks and vivacity proved just the tonic he needed, and any objections he might have had vanished.

Over the following days the four of them did things and saw sights that he had not known existed. Piers was the perfect guide; he seemed to know every dance hall and late-night drinking establishment in London. It was such a marked contrast to the life Alexander was accustomed to. Even before the war he had not been one for the high life, preferring to remain in the country with his horses and books. Often Piers had tried to entice him to Town, telling him he was living more like a recluse than an eligible bachelor, but it had taken a spell in the trenches before he was prepared to admit that perhaps Piers had a point. If he was going to perish along with all the others, why not experience all on offer? Besides, he found the kind of escapism his books offered no longer sufficient to lighten his moods, and even riding affected him when pictures of the many beautiful creatures he had seen slaughtered in the name of freedom, pierced his consciousness..

'Live for today!' was his friend's motto, and for a while he did. For a few days he behaved uncharacteristically. Claudia was fun and carefree, and her extrovert behaviour caused much hilarity wherever they went. She enjoyed life, something Alexander hadn't done in a while. He was not of a promiscuous nature and in normal circumstances would have felt guilty sleeping with someone, especially of her background, whom he barely knew, but as she was so in command of the situation his conscience did not trouble him. Now he could not deny that he had acted like a bounder and a complete idiot, and had only himself to blame for the consequences.

Alexander felt Piers nudge him as 'The Arrival of the Queen of Sheba' began blaring from the organ. He glanced sideways and their eyes met. Piers half-smiled, but the smile was steely. 'Chin up, old man. It can't be worse than going over the top,' he winked.

Alexander smiled with resignation and rose to his feet.

*

Mr and Mrs Best were enjoying a well-earned glass of sherry with the temporary staff when Clementine slipped in through the side door. She was thankful not to be spotted for she was not up to explaining her presence. She paused a moment by the drawing-room door, watching sparkles of fire-light bounce off the crystal chandelier, illuminating the silver and polished surfaces. More tears began to fall, and taking care not to make a sound she crept up the stairs whilst Best asked them all to raise their glasses to the bride and groom.

The wedding ceremony seemed remarkably short to all gathered there, and before long they were back out in the churchyard, Claudia's black cape billowing in the bitter breeze. It was too cold to linger, and as soon as possible the wedding party departed for Coppins.

The procession created a stir with some of the war-weary local folk who braved the elements to watch them pass, all eager to snatch a glimpse of the beautiful bride. Claudia waved like royalty from the carriage window, remarking on their ruddy complexions.

On arrival at Coppins, the happy couple waited in the hall to greet the guests. Claudia looked enchanting in her ottoman silk gown, the train of which trailed around her tiny satin slippers. Her pale blonde hair was piled high with small curls accentuating her cheekbones and wide eyes. Beside her, Alexander made an imposing sight, making an effort to smile politely as he was introduced to a sea of unknown faces; his darkly handsome face contrasting sharply with his wife's ethereal beauty.

Claudia determined to make the most of the occasion; it was her day and she revelled in all the attention and took great delight in showing Alexander off. With most of the nation's unmarried men either dead or across the Channel, she couldn't help thinking that she had done awfully well for herself. Only a keen observer might have noticed the occasional shadow that crossed her face.

Having received the last of the guests, the bridal couple moved to the dining room where everyone was sipping sherry and already helping themselves to food. Piers was most complimentary about the assortment of dishes.

'I'm tempted to poach your parents' cook and whisk her back to Base,' he said to Claudia. 'My lads would give their eye-teeth to have some food like this. Mmm, quite, quite delicious!' Claudia's prime concern about having hot food had been that it seemed rather provincial, added to the fact that there weren't enough tables for guests to sit at, so she was especially pleased with Piers's kind remark and relieved that nobody seemed to mind too much having to rest their plates on their laps.

'How is your sister? Shame she missed the service,' Piers said casually, too interested in helping himself to another spoonful of crispy potatoes to notice her tight smile. Not ready to deal with Clementine yet, Claudia saw it as her cue to leave.

'Oh, she's fine,' she said, waving her hand dismissively. 'It was just a fainting fit, nothing serious. I believe my mother's trying to persuade her to come down. Do excuse me, Piers. I must go and introduce Lady Moundsmere to some of the guests.'

When she had gone, Piers turned to Alexander and, thinking of the younger Countess of Moundsmere, Alexander's late brother Patrick's widow, he said, 'I'm surprised Dulcie didn't come.' In fact looking about he could see that Alexander's side of the family was very poorly represented and wondered if this had been intentional.

'I did write to Dulcie, but she's still in mourning and didn't feel up to it. She sent her best wishes and a Georgian ironstone dinner service which I see on the display table.'

Piers nodded. 'I'm sure weddings can't be easy for her, especially yours. I must look her up when I'm next in Somerset. I always liked Dulcie even though she's something of a blue-stocking.' Alexander's brother had met her at Oxford, where she had been a student of English at St Hugh's College.

'My, what a wedding that was! Who would have thought we would live to see the day when fifty guests was considered a large party.'

Alexander allowed a splinter of nostalgia to prick his reserve as he thought of his brother's grand affair seven years earlier when he had married Dulcie at St Margaret's, Westminster. The church had been bursting with guests from all over.

'I wonder if we shall ever see the likes of those days again,' mused Piers.

'I'd be surprised,' said Alexander, taking his champagne and following him into the library.

Some guests were seated around a trestle table enjoying the repast. Piers found a chair by the fire and quickly began tucking into his meal. Alexander stood watching, delaying the moment when he would be obliged to go and talk to people.

'You should eat, it's really good,' Piers told him.

'I've little appetite at the moment.'

'You'll be lucky to get anything later. Believe me, it will all be gone in the next hour.' They listened to a rather ancient-looking string quartet in the adjoining drawing room. 'They're not bad, in fact, quite talented.'

'Well, the young ones seem to think so,' Alexander said, watching Timmy and his cousins merrily perform the Cakewalk.

'Look at the dog, he's joined in too,' laughed Piers, spotting the black and white terrier marching up and down beside them.

'I got my orders through this morning,' said Alexander suddenly.

'Typical! Couldn't they have found a more original wedding gift? So where are you off to?' Piers said, trying to make light of it, wanting Alexander to relax and enjoy himself.

'Not where I'd hoped. The Middle East is about the only place the Cavalry can do the job they've been trained for, but this time next week I shall be on my way back to France.'

'Rumour has it that they are under pressure to do something about the U-boats, and are planning a major offensive from Ypres towards the Belgian coast, targeting the U-boat harbours,' said Piers.

Alexander nodded. 'But why the deuce they want the Cavalry

is beyond me, for it has been proved time and again that we're too slow and vulnerable for this type of warfare. Armoured cars are far more effective. I wager that, if I'm still alive by spring, I'll be holed up in another stinking trench.'

Piers waved his finger. 'Remember my advice. Don't think of the future, think of the present.'

'Yes — and look where that got me.'

Piers chuckled.' Well, you have four days of unadulterated bliss awaiting you. Make the most of it. I'm sure your dear wife will more than oblige in that department'. As he got up to place his empty plate aside, he spotted Claudia and Mrs Ellacombe out in the hall with a young woman in a pink dress.

'I believe he's in the drawing room. Take Clementine in and introduce her to Alexander,' he heard Mrs Ellacombe say.

'I think we're about to meet Claudia's sister,' Piers said in a low voice to Alexander. 'By Jove, if I'd known the damsel was half as lovely, I'd have been down that path like a shot.'

Alexander smiled his first genuine smile of the day. 'You're incorrigib ...', the word faltered as his eyes became drawn to the young woman who was entering the room behind his wife. All his senses stirred as the space between them closed. Then he knew it was *her* — the girl on the train.

# 7

For a second, Alexander believed she was just a dream, that the girl who had engrossed his mind for the past two days, was simply an hallucination. But that thread of hope quickly vanished; everything about her was so vital, from the cropped honey-blonde hair and peachy complexion to the pale eyes, across which flashed a hint of alarm.

'Alexander, I'd like to introduce my sister Clementine — your new sister-in-law,' said Claudia, wearing an insincere smile as she turned to the young woman. She wanted nothing more than to get the moment over with. Inwardly she cursed her mother. Why couldn't she have left Clementine in her room instead of taking ancient Dr Gordon up to see to her. The silly old fool had diagnosed her problem as nothing but an attack of the collywobbles and insisted she come down and get some fresh air. But of course Claudia knew it wasn't nerves that had caused her to miss the wedding, and now she watched carefully as her sister and husband acknowledged each other.

'Don't look so shocked, Alexander. Surely I told you I had a sister,' laughed Claudia, whilst thinking Clementine's expression looked more suitable for a wake than a wedding. It was a fait accompli and she was married — and the sooner Clementine got used to it the better.

'I'm delighted to meet you at last,' Alexander said, proffering his hand, the very one that she had bandaged two nights ago. Knowing how deeply she had been affected when she had seen him outside the church, Clementine tried her best to smile pleasantly and make it easier for him. At least she'd had time to prepare; he was completely defenceless.

Claudia watched them shake hands. 'Sadly Clementine had to miss the ceremony because she felt faint,' she told him. 'Mummy's sure it's because the naughty thing skipped breakfast. Anyway, you're recovered now, aren't you, darling?'

'How do you do?' Clementine said, conscious of a nervous tic at the corner of his eye.

Disorientated, Alexander had the sensation that he and Clementine were cocooned in a bubble, separate from the vortex of disjointed faces and voices, until Clementine subtly made him aware that he was still holding her hand. It felt as if whole minutes had passed.

To Clementine his embarrassment was palpable, and to give him a moment to recover she turned to his friend from whose coat Claudia could not resist flicking a crumb.

Alexander cleared his throat. 'Forgive me. Please allow me to introduce Piers Douglas of the RNAS. He's my oldest friend — we've known each other since prep school.' She acknowledged the grateful look in his eyes. It was a much-needed breathing space for them both.

Piers was delighted to make Clementine's acquaintance. 'Where have you been hiding her, Claudia?'

'She's been nursing in France and only arrived home on Monday, much to everyone's surprise.' And Claudia hurried on to describe her sister's homecoming. Though both Clementine and Alexander made a conscious effort to look elsewhere, it proved impossible.

'How long are you back in England?' asked Piers.

'About a week,' said Clementine, and seizing the chance to divert the attention elsewhere, asked whether he was on leave too.

'Not really, I'm just enjoying a few days' break from training pilots.'

'How interesting,' she said politely, fixing her gaze on him as she struggled to think of something to say. She was so conscious of Alexander standing beside her, that her brain barely functioned. Fortunately Claudia stepped in.

'Just look at the young ones dancing. Dance with Clementine, Piers, teach her some new steps. In fact dance her off her feet. She could do with a bit of excitement.'

'What a ripping suggestion,' Piers said gallantly. 'How about it?'

'If you're brave enough to put up with my awkward feet, I'd love to,' Clementine said, anxious to escape. She took his arm and let him whisk her into the drawing room, very aware that if she was to survive the day it was imperative to keep her mind occupied, and the dashing young pilot, brimming with personality, struck her as someone capable of fulfilling that need. He was an incorrigible flirt, but right at this moment, he was just what she needed.

They danced until her feet ached and there were blessed moments when her thoughts were actually free of Alexander, though they were all too brief for he kept creeping into the conversation like smoke beneath a door.

'Perhaps you can explain why your existence was kept a secret from Alexander and me until today, Miss Ellacombe. Doesn't your sister like competition?'

'I'm certainly no competition for Claudia, Squadron Commander Douglas, and well you know it.'

'Absolute nonsense! You're quite divine. However, she's certainly no fool, keeping you quiet. I wouldn't mind betting that Alexander would have fallen for you instead, had you been around.'

Clementine froze. He was only joking, of course, but the reality of his words made her feel ill. He saw her go pale and remembering she had not been well, suggested they sit, but Clementine shook her head. She wanted to dance until she dropped.

In between dances she asked about his life in the Services.' It must be an exciting life you lead, Squadron Commander Douglas. Have you ever crashed a plane?'

Piers grinned. 'Charming!' Clementine laughed, and Piers led her off the floor to get something to quench their thirsts. 'To be perfectly honest I've crashed more times than I would care to remember,' he said as they rested on a window seat and sipped champagne. 'If it was peacetime, my Squadron Commander would have grounded me long ago. But good pilots are gold dust at this moment in time, and with the risk of sounding immodest, I'm rather a good pilot.'

'Then why is it you keep crashing?' she asked with an impertinent smile as the alcohol began to take effect.

'Because it's another world up there and you get almost drunk with excitement. I've always been a competitive sort, and once I got the hang of flying, I naturally wanted to prove I was the best and the most daring, and the inevitable result was that I bought it a few times.'

'It seems to me as if you are lucky to be alive, Squadron Commander Douglas. I hope that you have got it out of your system by now.'

'You mean you hope that I have grown up! Heavens yes, I've matured a lot since those early days and now I'm instructing new pilots and trying to stop them from doing the self same thing. They think me a right old stick in the mud — if only they knew!'

'How is it you're instructing? Wouldn't you rather be in active service?'

'I've seen seven months of active service and believe me, it seemed like a lifetime. I saw a lot of action and lost many friends. I'm not ashamed to admit that I was beginning to feel a trifle weary. The Hun really had the upper hand as far as machines were concerned, and their pilots were primed to the hilt to kill for the Fatherland. We were being sent out, novices straight from training school, and many were wiped out on their first sortie. It was not unusual for an old-timer like me, who had survived six months or so, to crack up mentally and have to be sent home in disgrace.' He paused in reflection and the look in his eyes reminded Clementine of a cornered fox she had once seen. It had affected her so much she had never hunted again.

'Are you telling me that this is what happened to you?' she asked quietly.

'Gracious, no! Though I do wonder how long I would have lasted. No, I just had a rather nasty accident and ended up in hospital for a few months. When I came out, the powers-that-be decided that I would be more useful training new pilots than getting myself killed in action.'

'Tell me about your accident.'

He shook his head. 'Another time, I want to hear more about you.'

'There's nothing much to tell. Before the war I helped Papa with his constituency work, writing letters, et cetera, and since then I've been nursing, and I suppose shall continue to do so until the war ends.'

Just then, a handsome, but ancient-looking woman with aquiline features, sitting in the library by the fire, acknowledged Piers with a smile and a little wave.

'I don't expect you've met Lady Moundsmere. Would you permit me to introduce you to her? Fear not, she's not as severe as she looks. It's all the black mourning that does it. I don't know whether you're aware of this, but after Alexander's parents died, he and his brother went to live with Lord and Lady Moundsmere. I was fortunate to sometimes be invited along during the hols. But I have to admit, even without the mourning she scared the life out of me. However, not for long. I soon realised what a top-hole character she is.'

As they approached, the lines on the matriarch's face softened. 'Ah Piers, the spring has gone on my pince-nez. Do you think you could mend it for me.' She handed him her eyeglasses and looked curiously at Clementine.

'So you came home after all,' she said after the introductions. 'Your mother was worried you wouldn't make it. She must be delighted, though I rather gather she's not so happy about you returning to France?'

Clementine grimaced. 'I think she accepts that I have to go back.'

'I'm sure she does. We all have our duty.' The old lady took the repaired glasses and clipped them on her beak-like nose.

'Thank you Piers. Now do you think I might trouble you to find Alexander. He is meant to be fetching me something to eat, but I expect he's been waylaid. Please remind him to avoid anything too rich.' She turned to Clementine. 'And in the meantime Miss Ellacombe can entertain me by telling me about her work in France.'

Piers found Alexander engaged in conversation with Brigadier Ellacombe and a bore who claimed to have been a friend of his late father. Rescuing him, Piers relayed Lady Moundsmere's message, and together they went to discover what was left of Mrs Best's banquet.

'By the way, Alexander, I've decided to take up your grandmother's invitation to stay on at Grangefield for a day or so, and wondered if your old motor-bike is still lying around somewhere.'

Alexander looked carefully at him, the spoon laden with carrots hovering in mid-air. 'It's in the stables, but do check it over — it's a while since it's been used. I thought you had to get back?' he added with a trace of suspicion.

Piers smiled whimsically. 'That was before I met your charming sister-in-law. Must admit I'm rather smitten with her and thought I would ride over and take her out. Poor thing can't have seen much fun for the past two years and a little jaunt here and there will do her good.'

Alexander stared at him, his face darkening. 'Do you think it wise? After all, she's not one of your good-time girls from London.' And as he said it, thoughts of the woman he had just married, Clementine's own sister, came to his mind.

Piers frowned. 'Your brotherly concern does you credit, but have no fear — I won't let you down. And for the record, old chap, I do realise she's different,' he said somewhat curtly.

Alexander watched as Piers cut a slice of Stilton and recalled something he had jokingly said the day before. *'I shall have an even better selection of women once you're safely married.'* Now those words mocked him, serving to make him aware of feelings to which he had no right. He began to wonder what Clementine must think of him. No doubt, that he was the worst kind of cad, and somehow, he knew he was going to have to speak to her. If only, when he had greeted Mrs Ellacombe at the church, he had acted more like a gentleman and gone to Clementine's aid. However, at the time he had been too preoccupied with feeling sorry for himself to think about a giddy young girl who was feeling faint because she had been too excited to eat breakfast. But what if he had gone, what then! What in truth could he have done?

'Your grandmother will die of hunger if you don't hurry with her meal,' said Piers, helping himself to another glass of champagne and making for the door. 'I left Miss Ellacombe describing her nursing adventures, so must tootle back.' However, Alexander passed him a minute or so later in the hall where he had been delayed by Claudia, who wished him to meet a relation who was in the Royal Flying Corps.

Clementine began to tremble when she saw Alexander approach, and she struggled, not only to finish what she was saying, but to make it coherent. Leaping up, she found a small table on which to place Lady Moundsmere's tray, and then in desperation cast her eyes about, searching for an excuse to slip away.

'Miss Ellacombe has been entertaining me with an account of her life near the Front Line, Alexander. It's most enlightening,' said Lady Moundsmere, who despite her age was still on the committee of the local Red Cross. 'I'm most indebted to her for sparing me the time, when I'm sure she'd rather have been dancing.' And when Clementine started to protest. 'Of course you would, all young girls love to dance, I certainly was no exception. I was the best dancer in the county, though I daresay you wouldn't believe it to look at me now.' And she glanced from Clementine to Alexander. 'You should get to know her, dear. She's a devoted young woman.'

Privately she wondered how two sisters could be so different. Try as she might, she couldn't take to Claudia. She'd known females like her before; each had taken from life what they could without thought or conscience of giving something in return — and that, as she had borne witness, was a recipe for disaster.

Shaking out the stiff white napkin, she tucked it beneath her chin and said, 'Well, Alexander, it's up to you to put matters right. Take Miss Ellacombe onto the dance floor and get better acquainted with her, and leave me to enjoy this delicious repast in peace. You know I can't abide an audience when I eat.'

It wasn't the ideal place; there were two other couples gliding gracefully across the floor, but Alexander seized what he saw might be the only opportunity to get Clementine alone. 'That sounds a splendid idea, Grandmama. Shall we?'

In silence they walked through into the drawing room, past the alcove where Mr Brecon and his sisters sat at their instruments with strained expressions executing a waltz.

Their hands made contact and they moved in unison, his very closeness disturbing Clementine, who knew with heart-sinking certainty that the magnetism, which had first drawn her to Alexander, was still as strong. In her head a pulse ticked like a clock. One of them had to break the silence and she feared it would be her. The way she was feeling, she wasn't sure whether she could trust herself.

Alexander found the moment every bit as uncomfortable. Holding her in his arms — close enough to smell the fresh scent of her newly washed hair — he knew it had been madness to dance with her.

'I suspect you did have breakfast, after all,' he said with a half-smile. It broke the tension between them and Clementine smiled too.

'It must have been quite a shock.'

'I think one of the more memorable ones.' He cleared his throat. 'I don't know what to say except that what happened between us was totally out of character. I acted like an absolute bounder, yet at the same time it seemed the most natural thing in the world.'

'Please forget it, I certainly have.'

'Have you?'

She blushed and glanced away, inadvertently revealing the truth.

'It's something I can't forget either,' he said softly. 'It has certainly given me something to think about over the last two days.'

A silence fell between them and Clementine became alarmed by the mix of emotions that were racing through her. His very presence caused her heart to pound, and his words led her to suspect that he felt the same. It was madness and the cold reality of the situation pulled her up sharply.

'Your hand seems better,' she said in as dispassionate a voice as she could summon.

'Almost as good as new.' He was about to say how lucky he was that he had been on the train, but thought better of it. Their eyes met and a long look passed between them; he felt sure she could read his thoughts. He was impatient for the dance to end. The unspoken attraction between them was telling on him, and he knew the safest thing to do was escape before he lost his reason. It was an impossible situation. Here he was, just married, and feeling like a lovesick schoolboy over his wife's sister.

Abruptly the music changed and several delighted youngsters, Timmy included, burst into song. They had persuaded the musicians to play a few popular war songs and their voices were raised in chorus.

'Tramp, tramp, tramp the boys are marching' Amongst them was Clementine's Cousin Philip who, according to his mother was counting the days to his eighteenth birthday, when he could enlist. In front of the small group stood his younger brother Rupert, who together with Timmy stamped their feet noisily to the march-like beat. 'Tramp, tramp, tramp ... Cheer up comrades they will come ...'

Tears of patriotic pride pricked their innocent eyes. Clementine felt sick, and for a moment forgot that Alexander was still there. Those young lads had no idea, no idea. She felt his hand on her arm and glanced up to see her own feelings mirrored in his gaze.

With a face like thunder, Claudia swept into the room at that moment. 'I said no war tunes,' she cried raising her voice above the din. Mr Brecon was apologetic, his sisters embarrassed, the singers frustrated. 'Anyway, you can take a break, everyone will be moving into the other room for a while. Oh!' She smiled broadly when she saw Clementine and Alexander, but it was forced and Clementine detected a note of nervousness in her tone. Clearly she was still anxious. However, she quickly relaxed when she decided that Clementine was only making an effort to be sociable, and grabbing Alexander's hand, dragged him away saying it was time to cut the cake.

Others followed and as guests filed into the dining room for the climax of the celebration, more glasses were filled with Brigadier Ellacombe's vintage champagne, and there was a hushed silence as Piers began the proceedings.

Clementine sank onto her knees in front of the library fire, and as the merriment spilled over from across the hall, so too did her tears. She couldn't hold them back any longer. She was in love with her sister's husband, and she was so miserable she wanted to die. Creeping out from beneath a chair where he had been hiding Jack snuggled up beside her, touching her hand with insistence, demanding a stroke. Clementine complied, glad of his company. 'You really do pong,' she chuckled as she wiped her eyes. 'You'd be wise to keep out of Claudia's way.'

She got up and looked out of the window. It was almost dark and looked very uninviting. Oh, to be back in France; the best place to put one's pain into perspective. There she would find no time to indulge her feelings. 'Where's your stiff upper lip?' she said, taking a deep breath and telling herself that tomorrow, the worst would be over. But it was hard to be brave, and no matter how often or convincingly she thought it, she didn't believe it.

Thinking she was alone, she started when a hand touched her shoulder. She turned to find Alexander. He stared at her, missing nothing; the red smudges beneath her eyes, her consternation at being caught unawares, her humiliation when she could see he was aware of her plight. He said nothing but took her hand and gently squeezed it. Their eyes held for what seemed an age and the silence between them was full.

'Come,' he said eventually. 'Come and have some champagne and join the others.'

*

Piers made a good job of doctoring Alexander's car. With Clementine's assistance he acquired a kipper from the kitchen which he placed on the exhaust manifold, and tied an impressive array of old tin cans to the rear bumper with lengths of string carefully hidden underneath. He was too boyishly happy to notice Clementine's lack of enthusiasm, but even she had to smile as she realised that the kipper was going to smell revolting after a few miles, and could well imagine her sister's vexation!

'I'm not at all sure that Claudia will ever forgive you, Squadron Commander Douglas, and besides, she's always hated kippers.'

'All the better!' he grinned, slamming the bonnet shut.

Suddenly the front doors of the house were thrown open and the wedding guests began crowding onto the steps, anticipating the couple's imminent departure. Then to a crescendo of cheers they appeared, Claudia looking elegant in a powder-blue coat and hat trimmed with fur, and Alexander casually dressed in country attire. As they boarded the car, Claudia turned and threw her bouquet to Clementine. 'Your turn next!'

Because of the gesture Clementine found herself the centre of unwelcome attention. She fought the urge to dash the already wilting flowers to the ground, but was conscious of the many eyes on her.

The engine burst into life and, amid cheers and applause, the newlyweds sped off down the drive, with Piers's tin cans, much to everyone's amusement, jangling behind.

As family and friends made their way indoors, Piers asked Clementine if he could see her again. She acknowledged how much his bright cheery company had helped her to survive the day, more than he would ever know.

'I had planned to go to Dorchester tomorrow to do some shopping. Perhaps we could meet up at lunchtime,' she suggested.

'I can't possibly wait that long. Meet me in Bright's tea shop at ten thirty sharp!'

Clementine could only laugh at his uncompromising tone. 'I shall look forward to it'

# 8

Brigadier Ellacombe dropped Clementine on High West Street by the Methodist Church. As she climbed from the car Timmy threw open the back door and jumped onto the pavement. He was en route back to school and besides saying goodbye to his sister, wanted to sit in the front. Clementine gave him a long hug, unsure when she would see him again.

'I'll try and get back later in the year,' she said.

'Make sure it's in the hols when I'm home.'

'I'll see what I can do, but don't forget to write.'

'And don't you forget to remind Squadron Commander Douglas that he promised to take me up in an aeroplane one day.'

'Over my dead body!' said their father, who was impatient to be on his way, concerned that the fifty miles he had to drive to Sherborne and back would make him late for luncheon.

Clementine waved as they drove off and laughed as Timmy pressed his nose against the window along with Jack, whose tail was wagging madly. She was going to miss her little brother; he was a dear boy and she was ever- thankful for the ten years that separated them; the war just had to be over before he reached eighteen.

She walked down South Street thinking that Dorchester was much the same as she remembered, though perhaps a little shabbier. Several shop fronts needed a coat of paint and a couple had been boarded up because the owners had enlisted and there was no one to keep them going.

Going into the leather shop to buy a pair of gloves, she encountered a new face across the counter. The man informed her that he had bought the business from Mr Thresher, who had decided to sell after the sudden deaths of his sons, both killed within two weeks of each other. Clementine was shaken; the boys had been of a similar age to herself and had helped out in the shop for years, always with a ready smile, and knowing every customer by name.

She remembered her first visit. Claudia and she had not long been back from India, and Great-Aunt Jane had taken them in to buy various things that they needed for school. The smell of hide had been quite pungent and she recalled asking whether the leather came from fallen cattle, cattle that had died naturally. Mr Thresher, not accustomed to eight year olds with ethics, had given her an odd look until Aunt Jane had explained that she was from India where cows were considered sacred. Mr Thresher had smiled knowingly and indulged Clementine with a tale of secret pastures where cattle roamed free and happy, until eventually at the end of their long lives, they died in their sleep. 'Of course they're not really dead, just moved on to another pasture which we can't see, and because they have new bodies, it's their wish that we make use of their old ones.'

Nothing much had changed inside the shop but for Clementine it would never feel the same without wise old Mr Thresher, Bob or Vic passing the time of day. But things moved on, as she was discovering.

The new owner beckoned to his female assistant to bring out a tray of gloves and Clementine sorted through them, settling for a pair similar to the ones she was wearing, but in brown and with a cashmere lining for extra warmth. Declining to try them on she took a ten-shilling note from her purse. Her hands had improved slightly since lavishing them with her mother's cream, but even so, one could be forgiven for thinking she had something contagious.

Outside, a soldier with a rifle watched as four German prisoners, armed with brushes, cleared the street of horse dung. It was clear from one soldier's expression that he considered the work demeaning. She was conscious of their eyes following her as she crossed the road to the confectioner's. One of them, a flaxen-haired lad, looked barely older than Timmy and she wondered if, like some Allied soldiers, he had lied about his age in order to enlist. How his family must worry about him, a prisoner of war, miles from home. I'm sure, if it was left to us ordinary folk instead of politicians, there would be no war, she thought.

The bell tinkled as she opened the door, which had a large panel of etched glass. The proprietor, a woman in her fifties with thin lips and greying hair, had been standing by the window.

'They were watching you; I saw them. They watch all us ladies. I don't trust them an inch. I've read of the disgusting things they did to those poor Belgian women. If the authorities insist on letting them out amongst us decent folk, they should be chained at the ankles. Just you think what might happen if one of them took off. '

'I've learned not to believe all I read,' said Clementine watching the woman weigh four ounces of sherbert lemons, followed by mint humbugs. 'Journalists just add to the gloom with lies and exaggerations and it wouldn't surprise me if, given the choice, those Germans would opt to stay in captivity; the likelihood being, if they did succeed in getting home, that they'd be sent straight back to the trenches. However, I'm certain other people share your opinion, and quite sure that German women are saying the exact same thing about our own prisoners of war.'

'You think the Germans are stupid enough to let the enemy

out with the general public?' the woman said, her face reddening as she twisted the tops of the paper bags. 'No! Our boys will be locked up, not fed buttermilk like we fools do.'

As Clementine handed over a sixpence the woman saw her glance at an open bible on the counter. 'I'm reading the lesson at church on Sunday,' she smiled. Picking up her purchases, Clementine walked to the door, turning back before escaping into the street. 'I seem to remember that Jesus told us to love one another as we would ourselves.'

Piers was already waiting for Clementine when she arrived at the tea room and was brimming with excitement because Lady Moundsmere had lent him her Rolls-Royce.

'It's all thanks to you,' he confided.' 'When I told her who I was meeting she insisted I take it. I don't think old Burrows, the butler-come-chauffeur was any too pleased. He gave me a list of do's and don'ts. I had to assure him I would be most careful and wouldn't drive more than twenty miles an hour.'

'I hope you adhered to that'

'But of course!' he grinned.

'So we're going for a drive, how exciting!'

'You bet! You're not in any hurry? You haven't arranged to meet your father?'

'No, I said I would catch the train back.'

'No public transport for m'lady. She shall be driven home in style. Now be a good girl and drink your tea. It should have cooled by now.

Clementine laughed. 'You remind me of Jack when he wants a walk.'

'I know just the spot, a perfect little cove with a good watering hole, and if you're feeling energetic there's a cracking good walk over the cliffs.'

'Sounds like Lulworth. I haven't been there since my fifteenth birthday.'

'When was that?'

'Never you mind.'

The driver's seat was quite unprotected from the elements, but rather than sit alone in the back, Clementine chose to brave it beside Piers. Fortunately the weather had improved since the previous day, and nearing midday the sun even made a welcome appearance for about half an hour.

They drove through small villages and along winding lanes where naked trees dotted the patchwork landscape. Eventually they reached an old thatched coaching inn just inside Lulworth village. Thawing out in front of the fire, they ordered boiled mutton, and Piers told Clementine he would no longer answer to 'Squadron Commander Douglas'.

'We're not strangers any more. We've been acquainted for almost twenty-four hours.'

'So long?' grinned Clementine noticing through the window a small crowd gathered round the car. 'Lady Moundsmere's Rolls-Royce has certainly caused a small sensation.'

'They've probably never seen one before. It was good of the old girl to offer it, especially with petrol scarce. She had the notion that I was going to take you for a ride on Alexander's motorcycle. She was horrified, but of course it served me to let her think that.'

'I'd say you were crafty. Please give her these mint humbugs as a thank you,' Clementine said handing him a cone-shaped paper bag. 'It would have been chocolate, but alas they didn't have any.'

'Just as well because I don't know whether I could have trusted myself. Now that we're on first name terms what about telling me more about yourself?'

'What is it you want to know?'

'Firstly, whether there's a man in your life?'

Clementine stared at him taken aback by the speed and bluntness of his question, but she wasn't entirely sure whether he was as earnest as he looked. She liked him enormously, and could tell he was attracted to her, but the last thing she wanted to do at this moment was give any encouragement.

'Yes, there is,' she lied.

'Oh! Who's the lucky man?'

'A doctor at the hospital where I work.'

'I thought it was forbidden for staff to fraternise.'

'It is, and the patients too, but it happens.'

He eyed her carefully. 'Is it serious?'

She felt herself blush and avoided his eyes.

'I thought it too good to be true,' he said, pulling a face. 'There was bound to be a snag.' It was said charmingly and with a smile, and once again Clementine couldn't decide if he really was as disappointed as he made out. However, she was certain that she could not cope with getting involved with anyone right now, and just in case he wasn't fooling, she thought it best to nip it in the bud.

'Now it's my turn to ask questions,' she said anxious to change the subject. 'You promised to tell me about your accident.'

'Did I? I'd much rather hear about you.'

'You promised.'

He gave a long sigh. 'It was on a reconnaissance flight. The Hun had brought in some heavy artillery and were inflicting untold damage to our Front Lines, so just before dawn one morning my co-pilot and I set off armed with cameras. We actually managed to get some good pictures, but then we were spotted and all hell was let loose. We turned tail for home, and got within a few miles of our own lines when we were seen by a dawn patrol of three Eindekkas — vastly superior to our plane. Needless to say, we didn't stand a chance. Alas, my co-pilot was killed, and I got wounded in the foot. Somehow, to this day I don't know how, I managed to keep airborne until we crossed no man's land where I promptly crashed and broke more bones than I care to remember. But I was alive — and believe it or not they managed to salvage the camera.'

'The pictures were all right?'

'Amazingly, they came out a treat.'

Two steaming plates of boiled mutton arrived which they washed down with a bottle of claret. As they ate, Clementine asked, 'What will you do after the war, Piers?'

'There's rumour of the Royal Flying Corps and the Royal Naval Air Service amalgamating. If so, perhaps I'll stay on and make a career in it. The war has really speeded up progress, shown the capabilities and potential of the aircraft. Until 1914 nobody took flying seriously. It was purely a sport for the rich and eccentric.'

Clementine felt happy and relaxed; the meal had been delicious and the portions surprisingly generous, but she struggled to finish the bread and butter pudding with clotted cream.

'I don't know about you, but I definitely need a walk, else I fear the plane might not get off the ground tomorrow,' chuckled Piers, finishing Clementine's portion.

They left the car outside the inn under the watchful eye of the landlord's son to whom Piers gave a sixpence, and followed the path down towards the cove, sniffing the briny air as they walked. Pretty cottages bordered each side. One with arched Gothic windows had several hens and a rooster scratching amongst the shrubs and snowdrops.

'The first snowdrops I've seen this winter,' said Clementine.

'The sea air makes it milder, though you would never guess.'

The cove, a bustling resort in the warmer months, looked bleak and devoid of life as if it had gone into hibernation. A few rowing boats lay upturned on the pebbles, and selecting a handful of smaller ones, Piers sent them one by one skimming across the water. Clementine tried, but only succeeded in slipping on the seaweed after catching her heel between the stones.

'Come on, we'll walk up the cliff,' said Piers grabbing her hand. 'Haven't been up there for years.' The wind whipped and whirled at them from every direction as they battled their way up the path leading over the hill to neighbouring Durdle Door. Clementine carried her hat and her hair blew freely. She had visited Lulworth several times but had never walked to the top of the hill before. Discovering the great arch the sea had carved out of the limestone rocks, she was thrilled and stared at the view in silence.

'It makes me feel quite insignificant,' she said eventually. 'Just imagine the amount of time it must have taken for that arch to evolve, and all the people who have stood on this very spot. Our lives are no more than a flash, like those waves down there crashing on the rocks.'

For a while they stood each lost in their own thoughts.

'It won't be long before I journey back across the sea,' she said, breaking the silence.

'Back to your doctor?' Clementine glanced sideways but Pier's gaze was firmly fixed on the violent ebb and flow of the ocean. Playfully she hit him with her hat.

'Come on, I'll race you back down,' she cried, turning on her heels and racing away. Piers stared in disbelief as she ran, hat in hand, her hair and coat flying behind.

'Crissakes, Clemmie! Stop! Stop, you'll break your neck! It's dangerous — you won't be able to stop.' His warnings were swept away with the wind, and she kept running and running, her feet barely touching the ground as the gradient forced her on.

Miraculously she did not fall, and when she finally reached the bottom, she sank to the ground laughing and panting from exhilaration. Piers followed closely behind.

'You're crazy! How you didn't come a cropper I'll never know,' he laughed, collapsing beside her. He put his arm around her shoulders and pulled her close; it was the protective arm of a brother, and still laughing, Clementine rested her head against him enjoying the warmth. They sat in silence listening to the sea crashing against the rocks and the piercing gulls circling above.

'Have you ever been in love, Piers?' Clementine found herself asking.

Her question seemed to amuse him. 'At least once every leave,' he replied.

'No, seriously, have you ever considered settling down and getting married?'

'You mean like Alexander?'

'I suppose I do. You're both in your late twenties or early thirties, and I thought some girl would have managed to tie you down before now.'

He laughed. 'Well, I think it boils down to the fact that I enjoy life too much to get involved in a lasting relationship. Besides, I feel it would hardly be fair to my wife and family, not only being in the war, but in the comparatively dangerous job of flying.'

'You're very considerate.'

'It's pure selfishness, I assure you. But don't worry, I have every intention of settling down one day, and believe it or not I should really like to have children. But in my own time.'

Her eyes lingered on him. 'Do you believe in love at first sight?'

He paused as he considered her question. 'To be perfectly

honest, Clementine, I don't think that I have ever really been in love. I thought I had a few times when I was very young, but it turned out to be mere infatuation.' She looked slightly puzzled and he explained. 'Well, a couple of times I've met girls and been instantly attracted, and thought of nothing else, day in, day out, but somehow when I got to know them better, the feeling has vanished. So you could say from my experience that I don't believe in love at first sight, because I think you have to know someone well to love them.'

Clementine was thoughtful, wondering if infatuation was indeed the source of her feelings for her sister's husband, in which case she prayed that it would quickly pass. It gave her hope and she felt more content.

'Actually, I was angry with Alexander the other day,' he said breaking into her thoughts. 'He told me he had fallen for a girl he had met briefly.' Clementine started and Piers went red in the face as he became aware of his blunder. 'Oh dear, talk about putting one's foot in it. But really it is nothing, believe me, nothing. Claudia has nothing to worry about.' He touched her hand reassuringly. 'It was just someone he met on the train… he doesn't even know her name, so he can't see her again.'

He was conscious of how clumsy it sounded and cursed himself for not having thought before he spoke. Glancing sideways he saw the tension in her face, and getting to his feet pulled her up. 'Do forget what I said, Clementine, it really is nothing to worry about. Alexander is the faithful sort, trust me.'

On the drive to Coppins Clementine told him a bit about her childhood in India.

'Claudia and I were sent back to England to go to school when I was eight. Having never been out of India it was very strange at first. Claudia being a year younger was particularly homesick.

101

However, we soon settled in, thanks mainly to the school. It was lovely, an old hunting lodge that overlooked Poole Harbour and had two headmistresses who were absolutely devoted to us all. We had a wonderful time there.'

'When did you next see your parents?'

'Not for some while. I think I was nearly eleven. Our great-aunt, with whom we used to stay at Coppins during the holidays, died. It was after that Papa retired from the Army and went into politics.'

'It must have been strange, seeing them again after so long.'

'It was, but meeting our new baby brother was even more so.'

'You and Claudia must be very close'

There was a noticeable silence before she answered. 'Perhaps not as close as we once were, but I suppose that's inevitable as you grow up.'

'Well, you're certainly different from each other, I'll grant you that. I can see the physical resemblance, but there the similarity ends. Never in a million years could I imagine Claudia doing your job.'

Talking about Claudia aroused a mixture of emotions that she wasn't ready to investigate and Clementine was relieved when they drew up outside Coppins. She thanked Piers for a lovely day, and invited him in for tea.

'I'd love to accept,' he said regretfully as he thought of Mrs Best's scones. 'However, I have to decline. It's getting late and Lady Moundsmere will be expecting me and I can imagine Burrows fretting that I've pranged the car.

'When are you returning to Calshot?'

'Early tomorrow. I was hoping for another day, but alas it's not to be.'

'Then it's goodbye.'

'Why, Clementine! Do I detect a note of sadness?'

'I've really enjoyed your company. In fact, I can't remember when I last had such fun.'

'Oh!' said Piers. 'He's the serious type, your doctor?' Clementine smiled uneasily.

'May I write to you?' Piers went on. He was as surprised as Clementine by his request.

'I would like that, though I must warn you that I shan't have much with which to captivate you unless you're fascinated by such things as Trenchfoot and Gaseous Gangrene. I anticipate I will find your letters far more entertaining.'

'The gorier the better,' he grinned. 'Really, I'd like to hear from you, doesn't matter what, and perhaps next time you're home we can arrange to meet. They have some good shows up in London. When are you leaving?'

'I've decided to leave on Sunday morning,'she said. 'I want to spend a couple of days in London.'

Piers looked surprised. 'What, you're not going to wait and welcome the happy honeymooners?'

'I'm sure they won't miss me,' she said, glancing away in order to avoid his eyes. She didn't want him questioning the reason for her hasty departure. But Piers wasn't thinking about Alexander and Claudia; his thoughts were heading in another direction, and he stared at her, arrested by a sudden idea.

'You'll be heading back by train, no doubt. Why not stop off on route. Beaulieu is only a few miles from me and the train pulls in there. I could meet you and take you out for lunch, and perhaps, if there is time, show you around the aerodrome. I might be tied up for a bit, but I'm sure I could get some young rooky to look after you — what do you say?'

Clementine's eyes brightened. 'What a lovely idea.'

# 9

As Clementine's train was drawing into the small New Forest station on Sunday morning, Claudia was stepping from Alexander's car onto the gravel sweep outside Coppins. Spotting her father approach from the side of the house puffing on his pipe, she assumed he had come to greet them and rushed into his arms in a manner she hadn't done for a long time. Father and daughter had never really been close, especially after the arrival of Timmy, 'the golden one' as Claudia liked to call him, but Brigadier Ellacombe was touched to see tears in her eyes.

'Missed your old pater?' he said.

'Oh, Papa,' she said, blinking hard. 'You shouldn't be outside in this temperature,' and she released herself from his embrace, embarrassed by her display of emotion.

'You're early! We hadn't expected you until later. We thought you were having luncheon with Lady Moundsmere.'

'No — well, not any more, it's all changed. Alexander has to get back to London.'

'Oh dear, well, we can't let him leave without something to eat. Better have a word with Mrs Best.'

'I believe he wants to get straight on, but you can try and persuade him,' she said as she watched Alexander lift her luggage from the car. 'Where's Mother?'

'I suspect she's in the library. I've only just arrived back myself from dropping Clementine at the station. It's good you're early, it will take your mother's mind off her departure.'

Claudia stared at him, anger warming her pallor. 'Clementine has left? She was not meant to leave until Tuesday!'

'Oh, well, like you her plans changed. She decided to attend some course which she felt would be beneficial.'

Claudia was so upset she wanted to hit something. Instinctively she glanced back to her husband, who was handing the cases to Best. 'That's awful. How could she be so cruel. Poor Mummy must be heartbroken.'

He smiled and patted her on the shoulder. 'Go and find her, she could do with cheering up.'

She started up the steps, pausing to watch Alexander and her father greet each other. She waited a moment in case he might join her, but soon realised he was in no hurry.

Knowing she would have to lie about the wonderful time she'd had and needing time to compose herself before meeting her mother, Claudia dashed upstairs to her bedroom, still livid that Clementine had left. But of course she wasn't fooled, it was her high-minded sister's way of showing her disapproval. Well, she'd had enough of her sort; hard-hearted individuals who thought they were whiter than white. She had just spent the four worst days of her life with another such individual.

She slammed the bedroom door shut and threw her hat onto the bed. 'Damn you Clementine!' she said aloud. Never had she felt so out of control as she did now, and she didn't like it. 'At least you might have waited to see how things had turned out.' Who else was there in whom she could confide but Clementine? She tidied herself, brushing her hair, then smoothing a little powder beneath her eyes to hide the tell-tale shadows. Desperate for a cigarette, she made for the window seat, where her packet of *Black Cat* were hidden inside a cushion. Her father heartily disapproved of women smokers, thinking them fast and loose, and she was careful to conceal her habit, though she had an inkling that her mother suspected. However, she could always count on her not to say anything.

Claudia wasn't a heavy smoker, but she had smoked more in the past few days than she normally did in a month. Having exhausted her supply over twenty-four hours before, she savoured the long-awaited draw, feeling an instant calm embrace her. Then, conscious of the incriminating smell, she moved to open the window but drew back behind the curtain when she spotted Alexander and her father below.

Keeping hidden, she watched them, anxious as to what they might be discussing. For once she hoped it was the war. Hearing Alexander laugh, she felt relief but it was only fleeting as all the fury and resentment she had been feeling, again coursed through both mind and body as she recalled his cruelty towards her. Helpless to stop herself, she went over the events of what should have been the happiest days of her life.

She had thought she had feigned the miscarriage well, and at first he had been all concern. He had wanted to call a doctor but she had stopped him, fearing her ability to fool a physician as easily as she had him. He had insisted she rest and had used the bed in the dressing room, not wishing to disturb her. Exhausted from the day's activities and satisfied with the way things had gone, she quickly fell into a deep sleep. However, sometime in the early hours she was rudely awakened when the blinding light above her head suddenly came on. Awoken from her slumbers, unable to focus properly, she could not, at first, think where she was. All she knew was that a dark menacing presence loomed above her. Scarcely able to breathe, an animal-like cry escaped from her, frightening her even more. Only as her eyes became accustomed to the light and she recognised Alexander, did her fear subside.

'What's the matter? You scared me half to death! What time is it?'

'Time to tell the truth.'

She looked at him in bewilderment, and growing alarm. 'What do you mean?'

There was a sinister look in his narrowed eyes and she felt a rush of fear such as she had never before experienced. Hardly a muscle flickered, yet the towering rage in his powerful physique was clear to her and caused her to cower in conviction that he was going to hit her. Instead he threw at her the box of Hartmann's towelettes that she had hidden in her case.

'I just needed to see your face, and it's as I suspected; you weren't pregnant at all. You tricked me into marrying you, and I was fool enough to believe you!'

'How dare you! How dare you insult me with your accusations!' she cried, finding her voice at last. But though she protested, and protested more, it was futile. With hindsight she wished he *had* struck her, for it might have cleared the air, but instead he remained silent and she discovered what a powerful weapon silence can be; far more cruel than a slapped face or a barrage of insults, and in that ugly stillness he left her frustrated, empty and scared. For the first time in her life she didn't know what to say or do.

Where he went she had no idea. She put on her dressing gown and waited for him to come back, but it was daylight before he returned and what hopes she had of him finding her grief-stricken on a damp pillow were thwarted when she fell asleep.

She awoke hearing him place a breakfast tray of tea and thinly sliced bread and butter on the chest of drawers opposite the bed. She sighed with relief. It was going to be all right. She would work her charm on him. 'Alexander …,' However, he cut her off in a voice as firm and hostile as a judge's hammer.

'Spare me, please! No more lies. The fact is, I don't believe you. I've no faith in anything you have to say. The only reason I'm here is to tell you that I am leaving. I'm going back to London.'

She stared at him, aghast.

'I need time to decide how I am going to deal with the situation.'

'You can't! You can't leave me here alone!'

'I shall return early Sunday morning in order to drive you to your parents' house, so make sure that you are ready to leave. By then I shall be clearer as to the future.'

Hope had flashed across her eyes but he had seen it and been brutal.

'But whatever the outcome, the future will not include you!'

The pain and humiliation of those days that she had spent alone would never leave her, not even if she lived to be a hundred. He had told the housekeeper that he'd been called back to London, but she was convinced that every servant in the place knew that he had left her. So all alone in that large freezing house, she had brooded away the hours, closeted in her room, until Alexander's return this morning.

She had been ready when he had turned up shortly after eight o'clock. Little had been said between them until they crossed from Devonshire into Dorset. Passing through Lyme Regis, past the shop where Mary Anning, the famous nineteenth-century fossil hunter, used to sell her finds, he told her that he had gone immediately to London after leaving her on Thursday morning, and seen his lawyer the following day about annulling the marriage.

'Annulment! You've no grounds!' She was shaken. How could she face people. What would they say?

'Really? That's not how I see it. What about marriage under false pretences, or non-consummation? Take your pick.'

'Well that's your word against mine, and I'm perfectly willing to be examined. So who do you think they will believe when they find I'm not a virgin!'

'I wasn't the first.'

'Prove it. Besides, should it come to it I have no doubt I will be able to convince any judge and jury that you and I have been intimate. How else do you suppose I know about those scars you hide.'

She knew immediately she shouldn't have said it; she should have been more clever.

Giving her a twisted smile he informed her that she exceeded all his expectations and promptly dropped the bombshell that in fact his intention was to divorce her. Hearing this, she had uttered some more unpleasant things. She hadn't been able to stop herself and only calmed down when she learned that his solicitor had advised him to wait until after the war before taking action.

'It most certainly is not my wish. I would far rather get the matter over and done with, but as he so tactfully pointed out, my chances of survival are not wonderfully encouraging, and that by waiting we at least might save our families a great deal of embarrassment.'

Hearing this, Claudia had felt a certain relief. At least time was on her side, if nothing else, but she wasn't pleased to hear that if, or when, he returned to England on leave, he would continue to use his old address and not move in with her. However, that was in the future and she would deal with it as and when. Besides, it was most unlikely he would get leave for another six months at least, and she was optimistic enough to believe circumstances could change by August. A part of her refused to believe that his animosity towards her could last. Perhaps when holed up in an icy trench with a few rats for company, he might think of her more fondly. Yet although she was confident of getting him back, she wasn't entirely sure how to go about it.

*

Clementine glanced again at the station clock above the deserted platform and began to wonder if Piers had forgotten she was coming. She was about to leave her things and enquire the time of the next train to London when she found herself being addressed by a panting youth in the dark uniform of the Royal Naval Air Service.

'I'm most dreadfully sorry to have kept you waiting, Miss Ellacombe, but I got a frightful puncture on the way here.' He had a slight lisp, which made Clementine want to smile.

'And you are?' she enquired.

He was even more embarrassed and, having apologised again, introduced himself as Flight Sub-lieutenant Tom White and explained that Squadron Commander Douglas had been called out on an emergency, and that he had been instructed to meet her and give her a tour of the aerodrome.

Although initially disappointed, Clementine found the tour so interesting she overcame these feelings, and surprised her guide with some pertinent questions. All who encountered her on her tour were curious as to her relationship with Squadron Commander Douglas. The majority assumed she was a relation, for he had never been known to bring a female onto the base before.

Leaving one of the large curved hangars, where she had watched resin being used to repair a damaged bi-plane, they paused a moment, deciding in which direction to go.

'Why are all those officers gathered in that field?' Clementine wanted to know.

'They're having a lesson observing.'

'Observing what?', she asked tying her scarf tighter as a gust from the Solent tore into them.

'Listen.'

Though still unable to see anything, she soon became aware of the distant yet distinctive sound of a rotary aircraft engine. It was somewhere in the low-lying clouds, and like everyone else she waited in anticipation. Within seconds the small aircraft burst through the grey clouds, and she watched as it gingerly, yet swiftly descended — not towards the grass as she had expected, but the water. As she put her hand over her mouth and gasped, she felt someone else's hand land on her shoulder. It was Piers.

'It's crashed!' she cried. 'It's crashed!'

Piers could hardly contain his amusement. 'No it's landed. It's a Sopwith Tabloid — a flying boat. It's designed to land on water.'

Clementine found it interesting to observe Piers at work. She had suspected he might be quite different when on duty, but was surprised at the extent. Over lunch in the local hotel, the conversation got around to discipline. Piers was a stickler for it, and admitted to being strict to a fault with his subordinates. Clementine learned that his father, a retired Rear Admiral, had instilled in him from an early age the essential qualities needed to become a good officer. He added that he had seen too many young pilots killed, simply because they had disobeyed orders, or tried to do things their own way.

'Our Matron is a rigid disciplinarian too,' Clementine said with a coy smile. 'So I have to confess I do somewhat sympathise with your men.'

Piers was keen to hear about Clementine's Matron, and was prepared to defend the woman to the hilt, until he learned how unreasonable she was. He was simply astounded to learn that a young nurse had been refused permission to take tea with her father, whom she hadn't seen for two years, because he was in uniform.

'Rules are that, father or not, nurses are forbidden to be seen out in the company of soldiers,' Clementine explained.

'I hope you're not suggesting that I'm in her category,' he said. 'It's lives I'm trying to protect, not virtues.'

Clementine gave Piers a wry smile. 'Well, I'm not sure if Matron even manages to do that. All she has succeeded in doing is to make everyone more careful. Girls continue to meet officers in Le Touquet on their days off — it's just a matter of knowing where.'

'She's a foolish woman if she thinks she can keep the sexes apart. She should invite the chaps in, have a coffee evening or a tea dance. At least she would have some control over proceedings, whereas outside in the dark, she has none.'

Clementine laughed at the very idea, telling him, 'Never in a million years would she even consider that.'

Time sped by, and after a pleasant walk in the New Forest with Piers and his black retriever Bonny, Clementine found herself back on the train, this time bound for London. Piers had been a tonic but as the miles lengthened, once again her mood began to darken as thoughts of Claudia and Alexander permeated her mind.. She knew that they should have returned to Coppins by now. There was no way she could have endured listening to tales of their honeymoon. If they'd been happy she'd have been eaten up with jealousy, if not she'd have been filled with compassion for the man she couldn't help loving. It had been right to leave even though she was suffused with guilt over the upset her premature departure had caused her mother.

Her parents rented a small house in the city, which Brigadier

Ellacombe used when he was at the House of Commons. Fortunately he planned to remain in Dorset until the end of the month, so she would have the place to herself, able to come and go as she pleased. Mrs Ellacombe had tried to insist that Clementine allow her to arrange for the part-time maid they employed to come in and attend to her needs, but Clementine would have none of it. She wanted to be alone and refused any help, saying adamantly, 'I'm more than capable of looking after myself.'

In the event, her mother conceded defeat and had to be content with having the woman stock the larder and air the place ready for her daughter's arrival. Clementine was aware that it would be a lonely way to end her leave, but it was infinitely better than staying at home.

# 10

A feeling of anxiety swept over Alexander as he descended the steps of the War Office in Whitehall. At last he had formally been told where he was being sent, putting an end to weeks of uncertainty and speculation.

Walking home in the twilight, he slowed his pace, making an effort not to think of what lay ahead and instead focused his attention on the blackened facades of the buildings. He imagined the difference if the acres of Portland stone were cleaned; the great city emerging from decades of grime, like winter's end; a massive scrubbing campaign filling the gutters with the filth that streamed down the walls. But immediately in his mind's eye he saw a German Zeppelin, silver and shaped like a Havana cigar, making him see that the camouflage of dirt probably served a purpose.

Immediately Alexander's thoughts raced to the following evening when he would be at Dover waiting to board ship, and the ensuing journey travelling inland was over. He was to take part in a major offensive from Ypres towards the Belgian coast; the final objective being the U-boat harbours.

Remembering the wholesale slaughter he had witnessed last summer on the Somme, and the discussion with George Ellacombe about the blunders of the War Cabinet and the Generals, he couldn't help wondering whether it could happen again. But it was something he didn't want to think of right now; the thousands more who might be sacrificed for each foot of ground gained. He only prayed the powers-that-be knew what they were doing this time.

The prospect of what lay in wait made him yearn to jump on a train and travel back down to Dorset instead. His heart had always belonged to the country, and to walk in the woods at Grangefield, amongst its ancient trees, was therapeutic, as if they transmitted vibrations from the Earth's core. Standing here, in a land where birds still had trees from which to deliver the dawn's chorus, it was impossible to imagine the carnage of the battlefields unless you had seen it first-hand, then it was something your mind would not let you forget. It was months after being wounded, but he still dreamed he was in hell's graveyard, still part of it; tangible dreams that disturbed his sleep, and forced him to relive those scenes again and again. And the cruel irony of it was, he knew that after tomorrow he'd be disturbed by dreams of the very same green fields and hedgerows teeming with wildlife that he longed for now.

The streets were in darkness by the time he reached home. Weary, he cast aside his gabardine and sank into the armchair in his study. A heavy shower beat against the window and he closed his eyes, but still his mind refused to rest, determined not to give him any respite. Already he was in France, knee-deep in a waterlogged trench watching bloated vermin feast on bits of decomposed bodies built into the parapets.

The door to the study opened, breaking the unwelcome reverie, and he glanced up to see his elderly manservant.

'Sorry to disturb you, sir, but Squadron Commander Douglas telephoned in your absence. He is most anxious to speak with you.'

Alexander sat up. He ran his hands through his silky black hair and watched the old retainer throw a log onto the fire.

'Did he say what it was about, Jarvis?' he asked as he rose to his feet and went to pour himself a measure of whisky from the side table.

'No, sir, he did not, only that it was urgent. Would you like me to connect you?'

'I'll do it myself, thank you, Jarvis.'

It took several minutes for the operator to put the call through, and a few more before Piers was on the line.

'Thank God, Alexander! I've been on tenterhooks waiting for you. I've been trying to locate you for hours. What are you doing tonight?' The line crackled and he had to shout.

'Nothing. Why, are you coming up to give me a send-off?'

'Only wish I could! I need your help, Alexander. I'm desperate, quite desperate. I've arranged to meet Clementine at seven o'clock at the Ritz, but I've had to perform some deck landings in the Solent, and I've been unable to contact her. Would you be an absolute sport and take my place? I'd hate to let her down, especially as it's her last night too.'

Alexander paused in bewilderment. The thought of seeing Clementine again disturbed him.

'I ... don't think so. Ferrers said he might look in. We — '

'Please, Alexander, this is important. I can't leave her standing there. If it's impossible for you to spend the evening with her, at least turn up and make my apologies.'

Alexander was silent in answer.

'Alex, are you still there?'

'All right, Piers, I'll go,' he said eventually.

'Bless you! Look, I'm sorry but I've got to dash, they're calling me. Don't forget, seven o'clock at the Ritz — give her my best and tell her I'll be in touch.'

*

Clementine was aware of being observed as she made her way along the cobbled street tightly packed with oppressive dwellings. No welcoming glow shone from any of the soulless windows that looked out onto the road. Only a splinter of light from the paint-smudged streetlamps lifted the dingy obscurity of brick and pavement.

It was her first visit to the East End and nothing had prepared her for the poverty she had witnessed in the short distance since alighting from the bus. She had thought that, before meeting Piers, she would pay a visit to Ruby Jacks, Danny Triggs's sister who used to be a housemaid at Coppins. Already she realised her mistake in coming this evening but it was too late to turn back now.

Two women, in thin shawls and worn faces, stood on their doorsteps following the progress of the elegant young woman in the long opera cloak and feathered hat, assuming she was just another of the fancy folk from the West End who had come to see the bomb damage.

'Excuse me, I'm looking for Ruby Jacks. I understand she lives in this street.'

'Over there with the brown door.'

There was no knocker and Clementine rapped with her knuckles. From inside she heard a child's voice. 'Mam — the door.' Slowly it opened and a small child of about five stood in a narrow hall with bare floors and damp walls. Her fine brown hair was tied in plaits and she had what Great-Aunt Jane would have called 'the eyes of an old soul'. She stared at Clementine.

'I've come to see your mother,' she smiled warmly.

'Who is it?' called a voice from within. Another door opened

117

and in the shadows appeared a tiny woman carrying a baby. Tugging at her skirts was a toddler and a child no more than three.

'Miss Clementine!'

'Hello Ruby. Can I come in?'

The commissionaire acknowledged Clementine as she entered the Ritz, and looking around she was surprised to find little had altered since a visit she had made before the war. If anything the place seemed even more lavish, but perhaps it was merely the contrast with similar establishments that had toned down their ambience to suit these austere times, or perhaps it was because of where she had just been.

She was shown to the lounge where she had arranged to meet Piers. How glad she was to be seeing him again; she desperately needed cheering up. Seeing Ruby had depressed her and she needed him to make her laugh and assuage the guilt she felt at being in such a frivolous place, her guilt at thoughtlessly spending money on a new dress, money that would have fed Ruby and her family for a month.

She scanned the room, an elegant backdrop to the beautifully groomed women and uniformed officers collected there. In his dark suit Piers would be easy to spot, amongst so much khaki. However, failing to see him she thought she would feel less conspicuous waiting in the lobby. Without thinking she spun round and collided with yet another of the soldiers. Firm hands on her shoulders righted her balance.

'I'm so sorry — Alexander!' Caught unawares, emotions flashed across her face like a child who has not yet learned to mask their feelings. Her eyes struggled to hold back the tears that had been fighting for release ever since her visit to Ruby. Now they threatened to overwhelm her until somewhere in the depths of this maelstrom she became aware of Piers's name. It was like a slap on the face, helping her to regain her composure. 'Has something happened to him?'

Alexander was quick to reassure her. 'No, he's fine, but he had to do some deck landings and asked me to come along and meet you.'

Her relief was short lived. 'It was kind of you to come,' she said hesitantly as her mind began to explore what this might mean. Did he intend to stand in for Piers? She glanced about as if an escape route would suddenly present itself.

Alexander recognised the delicate scent of Parma violets. He thought she looked utterly lovely and his resolve to make an excuse and leave deserted him. It would be like Cinderella arriving to find the ball cancelled, and before he could stop himself he had invited her to join him for dinner. Clementine tried to refuse but the words failed, and minutes later she was sitting opposite him in the restaurant trying to convince herself that this act of fate might be a blessing. Piers had spoken about the difference between love and infatuation. Perhaps in an hour or so she might realise what a fool she had been.

She watched the ancient-looking somelier pour champagne into their glasses, and fixed her eyes on the eruption of tiny bubbles, aware that Alexander was gazing at her. 'What exactly are deck landings?' she asked, seeking a neutral topic; one that didn't include her sister.

'I understand they've converted a cargo ship to enable planes to take off and land on it, and I believe Piers was one of the first to try.'

She was aghast. 'You mean he lands on a little ship bobbing about in the water! It sounds suicidal!' Alexander chuckled at her description. 'I admit it does sound rather tricky, but I'm sure he knows what he's doing. He's far too skilled a pilot to come to any harm, believe me.'

'Even so, it seems wrong that he should risk his life like that.'

'But flying *is* his life, and the more risk is involved, the better he seems to like it.' He paused and eyed her thoughtfully. 'I get the impression that you and Piers have grown rather fond of each other?' He hoped the envy he had no right to, did not show in his voice. 'Your mother mentioned that you have spent quite a lot of time together.'

Clementine answered briskly. 'Yes, it's true I've become quite fond of Piers. He's been very kind to me over the past few days.' He had actually made them bearable, but she didn't say that.

Alexander could only guess at the extent of her affection for his friend, but noted that she had not mentioned Claudia; not even an enquiry after her health!

'What have you been doing with yourself in London?' he asked.

'Some shopping and sewing.'

'You embroider?'

She smiled. 'Like a five year old. No, I need new aprons for work and Mother gave me some old sheets to cut up. I have made a start but I'm afraid sewing is not my forte. However, earlier this evening, I visited a former housemaid from home and she's agreed to finish them.'

'She lives near?'

'Poplar in the East End. She left to get married six years ago. Her husband was a visitor's chauffeur from London. I hadn't seen Ruby for ages. Her husband, Frank, is in the Army and the poor soul is having to cope alone with four children.'

'Was she not pleased to see you?'

His perception unsettled her and she shook her head. 'I confess I don't know. I felt like one of those ladies of high patronage arriving with toys for the children when it soon became clear that bread and potatoes would have been more welcome.' She stared at the chandelier overhead, ablaze with electricity, and thought of Ruby barely able to afford coal for the range.

'As I said, I hadn't seen her for years and had no idea what to expect.' There was a catch in her voice as she went on: 'The place was awful, sparse furnishings, so cold and damp … and this with a new baby. The pale creature who came to the door was barely recognisable as the bonny girl I once knew — her healthy complexion, sallow with poverty.' She bit her lip. 'I felt such guilt for having so much … I never fully realised just how hard life can be for the working classes. It made me see how spoiled I am.'

'I don't think you're spoiled. In fact, you're one of the least spoiled people I know,' he said gently. 'You mustn't blame yourself. The problem lies in the fact that the poorer classes don't have the resources to dip into when prices rocket as they have done. Somehow they have to make do.'

'Well, it's clear from what I saw that Ruby doesn't. She gets a separation allowance from the Army but it's barely enough to cover even basic living expenses. Until the latest baby arrived she worked in a canning factory in Limehouse, plucking chickens for a pittance, and left the children in a nursery. But then she got ill and lost both job and nursery place.'

'What about her family, are they not able to help?'

She shook her head. 'They live near us at home, simple country folk. I know Ruby wouldn't want to worry them. All I can do is write to Papa and pray he is able to do something.'

Alexander was silent as he pondered. He glanced at the other diners. He'd wager they were not discussing social welfare. He turned back to Clementine, wondering how it was that she and Claudia were so different. He could never imagine Claudia worrying about anyone other than herself.

'Might I make a suggestion?' he said. 'For I believe I may have a solution.'

Clementine studied his face. Was it possible he could do something or was he just being kind? He was going away tomorrow, and Ruby required help now. 'It's very kind of you, but she won't accept charity,' she said, deciding he must mean a donation. 'I had a little money which I offered, but all I succeeded in doing was offending her. In fact the only way I could get her to accept anything was to ask her to make my aprons. I'm going to take the material round tomorrow before I leave.'

He nodded. 'Sometimes pride is all one has and I've seen the poorest cling to it like a life-raft. However, I wasn't thinking of charity, and it would mean Ruby leaving London.' He went on to explain. 'My grandmother has a small cottage on her estate in Dorset. Her butler lived there with his wife but when she died he decided to move into the big house. More recently it has been occupied by Belgian refugees, but they moved north to be near relatives. I know if I asked, my grandmother would gladly help.' He watched Clementine's lips part in surprise as she absorbed what he was saying. It seemed too good to be true.

'I don't know what to say. Why should Lady Moundsmere agree to help a stranger?'

'The same reason as you would.' She looked at him questioningly. 'Because you care.'

She was lost for words yet had a strong feeling he was doing it for her, which gave her a moment's unquiet. However, whatever her misgivings Clementine knew she must accept. 'If you're absolutely sure …?'

'Absolutely!'

'Then I don't know how to thank you.'

'Your smile is more than sufficient.'

'Naturally Ruby will expect to work in return — that is, if she agrees to go.'

'That shouldn't pose a problem. Believe me, if she can cook, clean, sew or weed she will be welcomed with open arms. As you can appreciate, like most estates in these times, Grangefield has too few staff.'

'I only pray Lady Moundsmere will agree.'

'I wouldn't have mentioned it if I'd had the slightest doubt. It will just take a telephone call. All Ruby will have to do is get herself and the children down to Dorchester on the train. The rest will be taken care of.'

Clementine was jubilant and could hardly wait until tomorrow to tell her, and now with reason to celebrate, she felt more able to relax and rationalise being in such an extortionately expensive place.

The champagne played its part, smoothing the raw edges, and with a cheeky grin she even allowed Alexander to order both crème caramel and apple pie when she couldn't make up her mind which to have.

'I'm beginning to see the magic of this place,' she said. 'It's easy to forget the war exists. One can take a break from the outside, and live in the present moment.'

'Do I detect Piers's influence?' said Alexander. 'Well be warned, he once persuaded me to live in the present. As a result I regret the past and dread the future.'

She studied his expression. Was it possible he was referring to Claudia? 'Perhaps all the more reason to live in the present.'

He smiled. 'You have a point.' Then changing the subject he asked her to tell him about the village where she lived and worked in France.

She described the sprawling city of tents and huts near the coast in and around Camiers. 'Étaples, the nearest town,' she said, 'is almost medieval, with housewives depositing their slops and rubbish in the narrow streets. Twice a week there is a market with stalls laden with fruit and vegetables, rabbits and pigeons slaughtered in front of you. And nearby is the railway track that transports not only the sick and injured, but supplies, guns and equipment.'

As she spoke he studied her face and was surprised to discover that her eyes and mouth were the same shape as Claudia's. How strange that he hadn't noticed before. Yet even though he was now conscious of it, it didn't bother him. He recognised that two pianists were capable of interpreting the same piece of music quite differently and, in the same way he recognised that Clementine's smile was as shy and varied as sunlight, whilst Claudia's was poised, beaming and self-assured.

'It sounds like an active place,' he said hearing about the training of soldiers on the hills. 'What do you do with your free time?' He had a vision of admirers battling to take her out and hated himself for being pleased when she said that she got very little time off.

'This time of year there's nowhere to go. The ground is usually sodden and you can be guaranteed to have your ankles buried in mud. However, the recent cold spell has brought some compensation. There are two very large ponds hidden away from sight, which are popular places in the summer, and they've frozen over. Now you can usually find someone skating on them.'

Alexander looked thoughtful as he imagined the fun and revelry that went on there, but a brief glance at her hands stopped him from delving further. 'I hope you find time to enjoy yourself,' he said quietly, and he meant it.

He spoke to Clementine of some of the things he had

experienced during the war and she learned how frustrated he was with the present situation, and his disappointment at being sent back to France, instead of the Middle East. 'It's about the only place a rider and horse are needed these days. I think I've mentioned before that this war has rendered the Cavalry practically redundant. Piers and his flying machines have taken its place.'

As he talked Clementine became acutely conscious that time was ticking away and found herself wondering what his spotless uniform would look like in a month's time. She determined to turn the conversation to happier things, and encouraged him to tell her about his childhood and schooldays with Piers. He was happy to comply, and his humorous anecdotes, which revealed another side to his personality, caused Clementine to laugh repeatedly. She knew that tomorrow she would suffer, for no longer could she deny her feelings for him. But tomorrow was another day, and the next and the next; any of which might claim his life. At the moment she was content to believe that they were just two ordinary people enjoying each other's company at dinner. Neither had mentioned Claudia but she was omnipresent, and finally, Clementine plucked up the courage to ask the important question. 'Did you enjoy your time in Devon?'

He gave her a long and penetrating look. 'You knew!' he said simply. There was no accusation in his tone, but all the same her face flushed with guilt.

'I spent four days in London trying to find out how I could end the sham,' he went on.

It pained Clementine to meet his eyes and see the anger there.

'For what it's worth I pleaded with her to tell you,' she said, 'but it was just hours before the wedding and she insisted it wouldn't have made any difference to you anyway.'

He sighed and her heart ached for him.

'Are you able to forgive her?'

'Are *you*?' he returned, his words an acknowledgement of their mutual unspoken feelings.

He described how he had come to realise that he had been duped into marriage. 'She told me she'd miscarried and initially I was prepared to believe her, but then the more I thought about it, the more suspicious I became. My sister-in-law had a miscarriage shortly after my brother died and I witnessed first-hand her pain and distress. Claudia's behaviour didn't add up. Not only did she not appear upset, but she wouldn't let me call a doctor. Then about two in the morning this voice, intuition I suppose, told me to look in her luggage …'

He described his feelings when discovering the box of menstruation pads which Clementine remembered watching Claudia pack as she had pleaded with her to tell Alexander. The items new and expensive, a luxury, and it struck Clementine as ironic that it should be her sister's pursuit of comfort that had trapped her.

'I don't know what I had expected to find,' he continued, 'but when I found the box and read what they were, I just knew. Finally I saw her for the liar she was and nothing she said could convince me otherwise.'

Clementine sighed, pausing a moment for reflection. 'Where is she now?'

'I left her at Coppins with your parents.'

'Do they know?'

'No. My solicitor made me see that it is pointless to do anything until after the war. "Waiting might save everyone grief," is what he said.'

There was a long heavy silence as Clementine took in the

significance of his words. A picture of Claudia on her wedding day unemotionally stating that she could shortly be a widow came back to her; that was the moment Clementine had known for sure that her sister was not marrying for love.

'I'm sorry,' she said at last.

'It's not your fault.'

'Perhaps not, but she's still my sister and I'm ashamed of what she has done.'

He touched her hand wistfully. 'How can two sisters be so different? The irony is that I'm certain Claudia doesn't feel the slightest guilt, just anger that she's been caught.'

'You must have loved her once. Could you not again?'

He looked long and hard at her before answering, 'I loved her sexually, and that is quite different.'

Clementine blushed.

'I apologise. I knew it would shock you, but there is no other way to explain.'

'There is no need.'

'But there is.' He said quietly 'Claudia was there at a time when I needed to feel alive. I make no excuses for myself. I lived irresponsibly for two weeks. She was fun, extrovert, beautiful and more than willing to be seduced. Callous though it sounds, the ideal companion for my mood. Physically she was like a balm on my jangled nerves, but I was never in love with her, and eventually came to my senses. I realised I was using her and wasn't proud of it. I stopped seeing her and then a few weeks later she informed me she was pregnant. Needless to say I was horrified but never doubted that she spoke the truth. I did what I thought was the only decent thing, and asked her to marry me. The rest you know.'

He rested a moment, watching as Clementine kept her eyes fixed on the table napkin gripped in her hands. 'I certainly had never considered Claudia as a possible wife, and my one consolation was remembering my grandmother telling me that she had fallen in love with my grandfather *after* the wedding.'

He waited for some reaction from Clementine, but she seemed distant as if considering what he had said. Her face was pale and tense.

'I believe we both need something a little stronger,' he said, summoning the waiter and ordering some brandy.

The spirit coursed a warm path down Clementine's throat and revived her a little. She was more shaken by the turmoil of her own emotions than anything he had said. Anger, jealousy, revulsion combined to overpower her rational mind; feelings that were alien to her.

'It's not a pretty story,' he continued, 'but I felt you should know.' He watched her carefully, taking her silence to be a sign of disapproval. 'Are you very shocked?'

'You forget I've nursed soldiers for two years. I couldn't have done so without understanding something of their strengths and weaknesses. I'm only sorry you didn't see through Claudia.'

'With hindsight I see she was just waiting for someone such as myself to trap; if it hadn't been me it would have been some other fool.'

Clementine could only agree. Alexander was relieved yet troubled by her almost sullen mood. She became aware of his worried glances and, bolstered by the brandy, gave him a smile, but its brightness was as fragile as glass and shattered as tears filled her eyes. Alexander watched in consternation as they rolled down her cheeks and she brushed them aside.

'Clemmie?'

She turned away, murmuring, 'I'm sorry.'

'Come, I'll take you home.'

They spoke little on the short journey. She sat beside him in the car and every now and then he would glance sideways, checking to see how she was. Once he took her hand and squeezed it tightly.

He parked outside the house, and helping her from the car, walked with her up the steps to the front door. Taking the key from her hand he fixed it in the lock and pushed the door ajar, leading her into the narrow dark hall. Finding a gas lamp, he lit the mantle and turned to where she stood, framed in the soft light. Their eyes met and held. He had no need to ask her what was wrong: he knew. He reached for her.

'No, Alexander! You must go.' She tried to draw her hand away, but his clasp tightened and she found herself in his arms.

'Don't send me away, Clementine. You know I'm in love with you, and I dare to hope that you feel the same.'

'I can't help myself, and it's tearing me apart,' she said, feeling her strength drain away.

He removed her hat and she sighed as she felt his tender kisses on her hair and forehead. 'Alexander it's wrong…' She never finished. Their lips touched and the words vanished as passion flooded her senses. His kisses intoxicated her, destroying what little resistance she had.

# 11

Morning light filtered through the gap in the curtains bathing the sleeping couple in its rays and giving a surreal beauty to the scene. Alexander was the first to wake and, gazing at Clementine he reflected on the past hours. He could not remember ever feeling so alive. Only his awareness that they soon had to part and go their separate ways marred his happiness.

Clementine stirred and opened her eyes. Alexander kissed her tenderly, watching for any sign of regret.

'Don't look so worried,' she smiled, spotting his anxiety. 'No guilt — shows how wicked I must be.'

He relaxed. 'I should never have let you go, the night we met on the train. If only I had listened to my intuition we wouldn't be in this mess.'

'You did what you thought was right and I love you for it.'

He smoothed her tousled hair and kissed her again. The grandfather clock in the hallway chimed the hour. 'Eight o'clock. We have five hours,' he said quietly. He had no idea how he was going to be able to let her go. 'Monumental mess that it be, I'll sort it out, I promise.'

She nodded. 'Let's not think about it just now.' Time was so precious she wanted only to dwell in the here and now, where the future did not exist. She placed her hand on his unshaven face and ran her thumb across his lips. 'I can't believe it is possible to feel such joy.'

It was the same for Alexander, yet during the minutes before she had awoken he had pondered over their future. He too had no regrets, but it worried him what might happen should their relationship be discovered. The gossip columnists, who welcomed any scandal to brighten up their war-weary pages, would have a field day, bringing acute shame to both their families. But even worse would be the effect it would have on Clementine; it would be quite ghastly, and being away he would be impotent to protect her. Both agreed it was right to wait until the conflict in Europe was over before attempting to sort things out, and he only hoped that until then they could keep their love affair quiet.

They stayed in bed as long as they dared, then whilst Alexander shaved, using one of the Brigadier's razors, Clementine made omelettes and toast. Over their meal they discussed the possible dangers and practicalities of communicating with one another.

Instead of returning to his old regiment Alexander was to take command of some recruits. 'Everyone will be new and I shan't have a clue whom I can trust. Should anything happen to me, all my personal belongings will be returned to my next of kin.'

She understood what this would mean. Claudia would receive a bundle of love letters written by her sister. 'Couldn't you destroy them?'

'It would only take one, and that one could be in transit …'

'I need not put anything incriminating in them. I promised to write to Piers. Would it be so very different?'

Alexander stared at her. It was so tempting. He would be desperate to hear from her. But if anything did happen … He shook his head. 'No, darling, I don't want to put you in a position where you would have to lie or make Claudia suspicious. As far as all are aware, we've only met once.'

Then Clementine thought of Ruby and realised how moving to Grangefield might complicate matters. 'Naturally she will tell her parents she is back in Dorset, and it's bound to get back to Coppins one way or another.' She knew it would be easier for them if they forgot about Ruby, but she only had to remember the hungry look in those children's eyes to know she couldn't.

'In a few hours my life has become very complicated,' she said ruefully.

Alexander frowned. 'If they should find out, stick as closely as possible to the truth, and if needs be tell your parents that I stood in for Piers — though I wouldn't offer the information unless asked. But with regard to writing, I insist I first take someone into my confidence who will be under instructions to destroy all mail should anything happen.'

'Nothing's going to happen to you!' She gripped his hand. 'This hateful, hateful war!'

He raised her fingers to his lips and smiled. 'Anyway it's me who's going to suffer the most. There's nothing to stop me writing to you, but until I hear from you I shall be wondering whether you've changed your mind.'

'Don't even think it!' she said in a low, passionate voice. 'I shall never stop loving you. Oh Alexander, please be careful and don't do anything heroic. Just come back to me.'

'The time will pass quickly, you'll see. And when I do return I want to find a great improvement to these,' he said examining her work roughened hands. He knew only too well that many soldiers' wounds were pouring with sepsis; it would be so easy for Clementine to pick up an infection, even blood poisoning which so often was fatal. 'When I survive I want you there waiting for me!'

They left for the station at the very last minute, Alexander having promised to visit Ruby later. Both agreed it was best not to risk her guessing the true nature of their relationship. It was complex and, after all, it was barely a week since Alexander had married her sister ...

Hastily she wrote a letter introducing Alexander and telling Ruby of the cottage and the difference it would make for the children; the better quality of life that awaited them. She urged her to take the position and put a few pound notes into the envelope as payment for the aprons and for their train fares. Alexander promised to deliver it with the material after seeing Clementine off at Victoria.

Throughout the journey to the station there was an underlying tension in their conversation and as they drew nearer to their destination they became increasingly silent.

Victoria was bustling with activity. Soldiers were everywhere, from the seasoned who wore their old tunics with pride, to new recruits, some amongst them whose faces had never seen a razor. Many seemed in high spirits, but Alexander's experienced eye saw through their bravado. He could smell the sweet scent of alcohol wafting in the air; a potent sedative for quaking stomachs. A few women stood in small groups with a look in their eyes so raw it could disturb the hardest of soldiers. They were unable to hide the fear their men tried to mask.

Clementine and Alexander moved along the crowded platform until they met two nurses with whom Clementine had travelled on the outward journey. They greeted her cheerily, and noted with interest the handsome officer who carried her luggage.

A sudden stir amongst the crowd indicated the train's imminent departure. Clementine and Alexander stared at one another in quiet desperation. Suddenly he threw caution to the wind and took her in his arms and kissed her, oblivious to onlookers. The whistle reverberated throughout the platform and Clementine climbed into the carriage and leaned out of the window.

Alexander drew her head down and kissed her again; his hands tightly clasped about her face. There was a frenzy in their kisses which acknowledged that time had finally run out, and Clementine's tears spilled onto his face. The train began to move and they were torn apart as it chugged out of the station.

*

The low hills near Camiers were etched against the night sky, and Clementine knew that beneath them stood the start of the vast stretch of hospital marquees.

'Soon be there,' said the young female driver of the open-fronted ambulance. Her small head poked out of the top of a huge fur coat that had graced many fashionable residences in pre-war London.

Clementine sighed, exhausted and aching from the rigours of the journey. The delay at Dover had seemed interminable as every precaution had been taken to ensure the crossing was as safe as possible; but with the ever-increasing activities of German U-boats, a certain amount of luck was always involved. On this particular evening the sea had swelled to a storm, causing many passengers to suffer from nausea as the boat tossed about in the turbulence. It was a relief when her feet had finally touched terra firma.

The ambulance hit a pothole, causing Clementine to lurch sideways, knocking into the wounded soldier on her left. From the back of the vehicle, where the more seriously injured lay, a heart-stopping cry rang out.

'Blessed road,' snarled the driver. 'Just hope it's not that haemorrhage case. Already had a couple of enterics tonight. Can just imagine the horrors that will confront me tomorrow when I have to wash it down.'

'Shouldn't we stop?' asked Clementine, conscious of the groaning.

'Only five minutes now, best press on,' the girl replied, drawing nervously on her cigarette.

Clementine glanced sideways at the Tommy, who despite her efforts wouldn't speak. He continued to stare ahead, his expression only changing when a spasm of coughing gripped him.

The ambulance had met Clementine at Boulogne but the driver had been in such a rush that she'd scarcely had time to wave goodbye to the two nurses with whom she had travelled. They had raced off to catch a hospital train leaving Clementine to help with the stretchers that were carried from the train and slotted into the ambulances. The stench of those wretched men brought straight from the trenches had forcibly dragged her back to her duties.

Hospital orderlies rushed forward immediately the ambulance pulled up outside one of the marquees. Close up, the canvas lost its brilliance and it was possible in the moonlight to see where repairs had been made.

'Couldn't do without us, eh?' shouted one of the orderlies to Clementine as he went to lift a stretcher from the back. She smiled, barely able to hear him above the flapping of the canvas door, and then went to thank the girl for the lift. However, hearing her blaspheme at the mess she had discovered in the back, she picked up her bags and fled along the duckboards to the thin wooden hut she shared with five other nurses.

Only three were there, the others were either on night duty or in the Nurses Convalescent Home near Le Touquet that was run by a wealthy widow. Clementine couldn't remember the last time they had all been together. Used to the comings and goings of their colleagues at all hours they were not easily disturbed, and only Elizabeth Scott, a Canadian who had the bed next to Clementine's, heard her return.

As Clementine groped about in the dark and freezing room, Elizabeth, who preferred to be called Lisa, pressed her for information.

'Tell me all about the wedding' she whispered. 'What did your sister wear? Is the bridegroom handsome?'

Clementine was thankful for the blanket of darkness as Lisa persisted with her questions. Their work was often so gruesome that stories from home were like water to a thirsty man, and momentarily bringing a semblance of normality.

'Lucky old you,' Lisa said on hearing some details. 'When my cousin married last year it was such an anticlimax. It was more like a tea party with about half a dozen guests.'

Clementine started to undress, blinking away a treacherous tear. Yes, she *was* lucky! She was in love with a wonderful man who loved her back. Circumstances might not be as she would choose, but one day …

Stretching her coat and whatever she could find over the bed for added warmth, she climbed between the damp-feeling sheets. She ached all over, her body for sleep, her mind for peace. Alexander was in her every thought and she longed for him. Over and over she recalled the hours they had spent together, wondering how she would survive the coming months without him. Already desperate to see him, she knew her love for him was out of control. Only imagining her parents' distress, should they ever discover the truth, sobered her.

At the moment it still seemed unreal, as if it were a dream, but she knew it wasn't; she hurt too much. Two weeks ago she would never have believed it possible to be in such a position. She had never been a rebel, quite the opposite. Yet, all the time an uncontrolled passion had lain in the shadows waiting. Where had this raw craving, so alien, so intimate, been hiding before surging up and challenging all she had ever believed in? She had condemned Claudia for what she had done, but was she any better herself?

Regardless of the circumstances, there was no hiding from the fact that Alexander was a married man — married to her own sister — and she well knew how people would frown on their relationship. It was but a few years since Parliament had changed the law which prevented marriage between a deceased wife's sister and her brother-in-law. At the time it had aroused deep emotions, caused by the general belief that such a marriage was almost incestuous. Clementine remembered wondering what all the fuss was about as Parliament debated whether to abolish the Act. But though she might have considered it ridiculous there had been plenty of others who didn't.

Staring into the dark she felt afraid; the path ahead was daunting, with only her passion to guide her. But even so, she was realistic enough to acknowledge that even if she could change course there would be no escape from heartache.

*

The weather was particularly unpleasant. Clementine thought it was the coldest she had ever known, and sometimes wondered if she would ever feel warm again. Every morning she would don three pairs of stockings and as many layers as would fit comfortably beneath her blue frock. She was reminded of 1915 when the coal miners had gone on strike; there was so little fuel to heat the vast tents and poorly constructed huts. The battlefields were deep in snow, and although there was little fighting, the wards were filled with soldiers suffering from trench foot and frostbite. As Clementine changed their dressings, many told her how they had sunk up to their knees in icy slush whenever the sun had managed to make an appearance. Bronchitis and pneumonia were rife, and warmth was essential for recovery. However, in the draughty marquees that flapped like the sails of a ship turning into the wind, it was sometimes little warmer than an open deck.

About a week after her return Clementine went, as was usual at the end of her shift, to the mess for the inevitable stew and chlorinated tea, which unpleasant as it was, was nevertheless warming. As she sipped from a tin mug, feeling heat trickle into her body, Captain Hamilton the Medical Officer arrived with some post and handed her a grey envelope with a Dover postmark. Recognising the seal, she was unable to contain her relief, and it was a moment or two before she realised the doctor was still there.

Intuition warned her he was going to ask her to work overtime. Several of the nurses had measles and she guessed he would be seeking reward for arranging her impromptu visit home.

'Nurse Ellacombe, I once remember you saying that you assisted with your father's correspondence before the war.'

She stared at him, a trifle bewildered.

'I expect you've heard that Miss Maidment, the hospital secretary has contracted typhoid. The fact is, I have been endeavouring to keep the records myself in her absence, but unfortunately, they've got into a bit of a state and it occurred to me that you might be able to help sort things out. I'm sure once the backlog has been dealt with, just half an hour a day will suffice.'

Clementine nodded, surprised and a little flattered that this rather austere man should single her out for such a task. 'When would you like me to start?'

'The sooner the better — how about straight away? I have a little spare time and I can show you what needs to be done.'

She hesitated, her fingers clutching the letter, now in her apron pocket, trembling with anticipation. Captain Hamilton was a busy man, but how to concentrate with Alexander's letter unread? As he waited for her reply another doctor drew him aside. After a couple of minutes he returned. 'I have to see a patient. Can you meet me in half an hour and I'll run through things with you. Within seconds of his leaving, one of the regular nurses poked her head round the door and called to a VAD, huddled by the boiler in her gabardine, smoking a cigarette and engrossed in '*Red Cross Nancy — The Brave Hearted Nurse at the Front*'.

'Miss Frazer you are wanted by Matron, now.'

Millicent, looked anxiously at Clementine. 'Christ, Clemmie, you don't think I was spotted having coffee in Étaples with my fellow, do you? It'll be curtains if I was,' she said worriedly, before hurrying off.

Finding herself alone, Clementine sank into a shabby armchair and pulled the envelope from her starched apron pocket. Carefully she broke the seal.

*Dover*

*My darling,*

*I hope you're missing me as much as I you. In reality it's only a few hours since we parted, but already I wonder how I am going to survive the coming months without you.*

*I'm fog-bound in Dover. It seems your boat was the last to leave. How narrowly we missed being together for a little longer. It came down very suddenly, a real pea-souper, and they don't know when it* will lift. Everywhere is bursting at the seams but luckily I managed to get a room in a small hotel.

Here with only my thoughts for company, I fear you may be suffering, regretting what happened between us. I pray this is not so and that you remain strong. I urge you not to dwell on what might or might not happen in the future. Just focus on the feelings we have for each other, and should you ever feel anxious tell yourself that we are meant to be — a thousand times if necessary, to calm the treacherous inner voice.

I will never let go the vision of the day this ghastly war ends and we are together once more. For rest assured my love, I will return, and nothing will ever come between us again.

I feel such happiness that even my anger towards Claudia has diminished. Can you believe I feel gratitude? I know it sounds crazy and can imagine you smiling, but it was after all she who brought us together. Don't they say everything happens for a reason? Though with regard to the war, the longer it goes on the less I understand why, and the more I realise we have a duty to ourselves. Standing alone without country or family, I believe there would be no conflict. Responsibility of the individual is not easy because we have been taught to obey from fear. How infinitely braver are those Conscientious Objectors who go to prison and face untold disgrace for their beliefs, than we herds who don't fully understand the real reason we kill.

Finding it hard to live in the present after last night. If those memories were armour, then rest assured, I am indestructible.

I love you, Clementine, last night, now, forever!

Au revoir, my darling,

Alexander.


P.S. I went to see Ruby and by the time you get this letter she and the children should be safely settled at Grangefield.

*

A moment before opening the letter, 'the treacherous inner voice', had tried to convince her that Alexander was writing to tell her it had all been a ghastly mistake. But as joy surged through her it disappeared into oblivion. She hadn't dreamed it. He loved her! He loved her!

She read the letter again, absorbing each word until she almost knew it by heart. And then, as suddenly as a bird takes flight, tears filled her eyes and she leaned back and sobbed with misery. She wanted to sing from high of her feelings instead of all this furtiveness, to be open about her love for Alexander, instead of suffering this wall of shame that isolated them from the rest of the world.

She had barely dried her tears when Lisa appeared in gumboots and gabardine, needing a shoulder to cry on. 'What a horrible day I've had,' she sighed, looking close to tears herself, as she threw a piece of wood into the stove and cast her sou'wester aside.

Pulling herself together, Clementine asked what was wrong and watched with concern as Lisa buried her face in her hands and moaned with frustration. 'Oh, I've only myself to blame. I had to attend an operation and was so nervous I dropped one of the instruments as I was passing it to Captain Hamilton. He was livid and tore me off a strip.'

Clementine felt for her, knowing how long Lisa had waited for such an opportunity. 'There will be other times, Lisa I'm sure.'

'No, he'll just look at me as some clumsy fool. How could I have been so stupid?'

Lisa had taken to nursing as naturally as a child takes its first steps — it was instinct, and already she had decided to train professionally after the war. VAD nurses were largely girls from privileged backgrounds, who before 1914 would never have thought to seek gainful employment. They had been recruited to take some of the workload from the trained nurses, leaving them free to deal with the more serious aspects of their work. When the 'la-di-dah' VADs had first arrived, the professional nurses had tended to scorn them. However, before long they had been forced to admit, albeit grudgingly, that the 'gels' were capable of pulling their weight. In fact, they had proved to be an invaluable part of hospital life, and as pressure increased the VADs were no longer used solely for menial tasks.

Clementine understood that Lisa had a calling and how important it was to make a good impression. She rose from the chair and touched her friend's shoulder.

'Don't take it to heart, Lisa. There will be other opportunities, I'm sure. Everyone knows what a good nurse you are. But alas, talking of Captain Hamilton reminds me that I must fly. He's asked me to do some secretarial work.'

'Lucky you!' was the sarcastic reply. 'Make sure you dot the i's!'

*

The hospital secretary was slow to recover and Clementine struggled with what free time she had to keep the records in order. Captain Hamilton had not exaggerated when he said they were in a muddle, but eventually she managed to sort out the confusion. Despite his extremely full schedule, the doctor always found time to answer her queries, and she discovered he was not as unapproachable as she had assumed. Although the extra work was tiring on top of her normal duties, she was grateful that it gave her less time to fret about Alexander. The distant guns and the daily sights that she encountered would never let her forget the dangers that he encountered every hour.

After one particularly harrowing day on the wards, she felt so drained she fell asleep on her desk. It was late and Captain Hamilton was just going off duty when he noticed the light still burning in the small hut that was used for an office. Glancing in, he discovered Clementine with her head resting on books and papers. She was in such a deep sleep that she only stirred when he shook her gently by the shoulders.

Her initial surprise turned to embarrassment after realising what had happened.

'I'm so sorry' she mumbled. 'I couldn't keep my eyes open any longer.'

There was concern in his face as he gave her a scrutinising look.

'It's my fault, I've expected too much of you.' There was also a touch of annoyance in his voice, which, now she was better acquainted with him, she knew was directed at himself.

'No, really sir, I'm usually fine, but I have felt rather weary today. I didn't sleep well last night. I think it all just caught up with me.'

'Have you eaten today?' He noticed a little colour return to her pallid face as he awaited her answer.

'I had something earlier,' she replied, but didn't tell him it was just a bowl of soup and a piece of bread. The smell of today's mutton stew had almost made her wretch. Since falling in love with Alexander she had lost her appetite, and with it, weight she could ill afford to lose. He looked thoughtfully at her. In his opinion she looked tired and undernourished, and he wondered what had happened to bring about such a change in her appearance. He disappeared for a couple of minutes to return with a jug of milk.

'I'm going to make you a hot drink,' he said, placing a saucepan on the small burner in the corner. 'It should help you to sleep tonight.'

Clementine was touched and thought how different he was from her first impression. She had originally thought him aloof, but over the past weeks had caught glimpses of his compassionate side.

'There, drink it up. Doctor's orders,' he said, noting the slight grimace on her lips. She didn't like to tell him that she wasn't particularly fond of warm milk. They sat close to the burner and he asked about her family and home, and in return spoke a little about himself. Until the outbreak of war he had been a consultant surgeon in London. He spoke of a sister married to an MP and said he had once met Brigadier Ellacombe at their house some years before. Another coincidence was that he had attended the same school as Timmy, which led to them talking of Sherborne. He remembered the wonderful services at the Abbey, especially at Christmas.

'I think it has to be one of the most beautiful towns in England. I bet you didn't know the Saxons made it the capital of Wessex — Scirburne — *the place of the clear stream.*'

Time passed swiftly and when the clock struck midnight, they both glanced up in surprise.

'Goodness, have we been talking for three quarters of an hour? And with you so desperately in need of sleep. I do apologise.' He turned the lamp out and they stepped out into the dark; he walked with her towards the nurses' quarters. The night was still, and inside the marquees, all seemed calm and restful. The distant booming of guns, however, made Clementine very much aware of the ongoing hostilities. Looking at the moon, she wondered if Alexander could see it too. It was over two weeks since she had last heard from him, and she was becoming anxious. She knew he was back in the trenches. *Oh Alexander, my love, where are you?*

Charles Hamilton saw the distant look in her eyes as she stared at the sky. 'Will it ever stop?' she murmured.

'Have you got someone out there?' he asked eyeing her thoughtfully. She could only trust herself to nod and suddenly he understood the reason she hadn't been eating and sleeping. He felt for her; only able to guess what it must be like to have someone you love fighting in this war. He touched her arm. 'Go inside and get to sleep. Standing out here listening to that racket won't help.'

# 12

It was late March, and one afternoon Charles Hamilton felt the need to get away from the hospital and clear his head of all its sickness and associated smells. The cold weather had eased up of late, and he enjoyed a brisk walk on the hills. For him winter was generally a quieter period, as surgical operations were usually less serious. But as soon as the spring offensives got underway it all changed and then it was not an uncommon occurrence for the operating theatre to be in use twenty-four hours a day.

Captain Hamilton had recently returned from a spell of duty at a Field Dressing Station at the Front where he had tended to soldiers from the trenches. Having considered himself a hardened veteran, he had none-the-less been shocked by some of the sights he had seen, making him wonder just how many of the politicians back home had any idea of the real conditions these poor souls were encountering. He had also been disturbed and incensed when told, on authority, that the Generals never visited the Front; they were always too busy planning the next move. Perhaps if they did, these great and powerful men might think twice before sending their brave troops on suicidal attacks.

However, it wasn't only the ugliness that had affected him; he had been deeply touched by the sight of soldiers, out of the firing line, laying in fields of primroses and cowslips, enjoying the simple pleasures of life. It had given them a smack of home as they had relaxed, reading letters and playing football, and he had sensed their heightened awareness of the natural beauty that surrounded them. He'd heard a colleague call it 'a gift of war'. Charles himself called it fear.

He descended the hills where snow still lay in the hollows and came to the ponds. The buds on the branches, swelling with life, reminded him of all those faceless young men who would die before autumn. The ice — which had made the ponds a haven for skaters — had melted and, as he looked, he spotted a black swan amongst the reeds, its red bill dipping beneath the water. He'd seen plenty in Australia where he had lived for a few years as a boy, but this was the first since, and he wondered whether it was planning on nesting nearby. It swam out into the centre and disappeared somewhere on the opposite side where a small rowing boat, belonging to the chateau where the officers were billeted, was moored to a small jetty. As he watched, a nurse appeared from the path that meandered through some wild-growing shrubs. He saw her approach the boat and place a bag inside. Taking hold of the tethering rope she seemed to struggle to untie the knot.

'I'll come over and help,' he shouted across. Startled she glanced up, and it was only then he recognised her.

'Miss Ellacombe, I didn't expect to find you stealing boats?' he said as he came up beside her. Up close there was something in her pale expression that disturbed him. She looked caught out and guilty — but instinct told him it was more than that.

'I thought I'd like to explore as it's such a lovely afternoon,' she explained rather hurriedly. 'I didn't think anyone would mind … it's hardly ever used.'

He noticed a bag lying beneath a bush and knew it was the same one that he had seen her place in the boat minutes earlier.

'Are you meeting someone?' he asked guessing it contained food for a picnic. 'Don't look so worried. You can trust me. I shan't tell Matron.'

She blushed and stammered. 'I, …er … j-just wanted to be alone.'

He studied her, not sure whether to believe her. He remembered the night they had stood listening to the guns and decided it was probably one of the officers from the chateau she was expecting. Best be on his way and leave them to their fun, he thought, but seeing the deeply etched shadows beneath her eyes he felt a little concerned, for he knew that she had been ill with a feverish cold in his absence, and had spent a few nights in the hospital. To Charles she looked far from well, but it seemed she was back at work, for he remembered seeing her rolling bandages the previous evening when he had been doing his rounds.

'You are feeling all right? Nothing is bothering you, I trust, Miss Ellacombe?'

'Why should you think that?' she asked, her bottom lip trembling slightly.

His eyes brooded on her for a moment longer, and she grew awkward under his stare. 'I don't suppose you've noticed, but there aren't any oars.'

A slight smile lit her colourless face. 'How stupid of me. Clearly I was not meant to go boating this afternoon.'

'It would seem not.' Their eyes held for a second and then she started to move. 'In that case I shall return and write some letters. Good afternoon, Captain Hamilton,' and she hurried away before he could say anything else.

It was only after she had gone that he looked and saw that the canvas bag that she had deposited beneath the bush was still there. He called after her, but she didn't hear, so he picked it up intending to follow her to return it. The weight surprised him, and filled with a rush of foreboding he bent down and opened it.

In shock Charles Hamilton stared from the heavy stones to the boat, in sudden comprehension.

She was walking across the bridge when he caught up with her. He waved the empty bag in her face and grabbing her arm, pulled her towards the small church. 'We need to speak — now!' he said tersely.

She followed him like a lost child into the dark empty building and sat where he motioned her, in one of the pews. If she had looked at him she would have seen there was a tenderness in his eyes which belied his stormy face. But she couldn't, and trembling, buried her head in her hands.

'Do you think you would have carried it through if I hadn't disturbed you?'

Slowly she looked up, but he knew as soon as their eyes met that there was no point pressing her. He spoke gently to her. 'Miss Ellacombe, what can possibly have driven you to even contemplate such a thing? Nothing could ever warrant such an act.' He placed a hand on her shoulder and with the other turned her chin towards him. There was no escape, and bleakly she looked at him.

'I'm going to have a baby.'

*

Initially, Clementine had thought she was coming down with something. Her monthly courses had been irregular since working in France. When she had mentioned this to old Dr Gordon, after missing the wedding, he'd told her it was because she was so thin. 'I don't know whether you're thinking of getting married yourself, but believe me, that unless you put some weight on, you will never have children.' This thought had been foremost in her mind the night she had spent with Alexander and when they had parted she had persuaded him there was nothing to worry about.

However, eventually her changing body would no longer allow her to deny the truth, and she had been forced to face reality — that she was carrying her brother-in-law's child.

Night after night she had lain awake agonising over her dilemma, with no one in whom she could confide her dark secret. Her preoccupation made her careless with her health, and one evening she got soaked in a shower and allowed the damp clothes to dry on her whilst performing duties in one of the draughty marquees. She was lucky she only developed a severe cold, but she didn't think so. She wished she had died and could think of nothing but the shame she was going to bring on her parents and the cruel irony that Alexander was going to become a father, after all.

Lisa had noticed the change in Clementine too, not only in her appearance but also in her behaviour. They had been close, or so she had thought, able to talk about most things but, since her leave, she had been distant. On more than one occasion she had heard Clementine's muffled sobs in the night, and felt hurt because she wouldn't tell her what was wrong. She came close to guessing the truth the day she visited Clementine in the Nurses' Hospital. She had three letters for her, two from England, and another in a green military envelope. There was the usual signed declaration on the latter stating that all contents referred to only family and private matters. Lisa recognised the name to be that of her friend's brother-in-law, and was curious as to why Clementine only ever read out passages from her brother Timmy's and Piers Douglas's letters. The other she had slipped under her pillow unopened.

Clementine had been tempted to confide in Lisa that day, but knew no matter how hard she tried to tell her story, and make Lisa see how deeply she loved Alexander, the other girl would never fully understand, and might judge her. And later, when she had made up her mind what she must do, she was glad she had kept quiet, for it was important her parents be spared the truth. Also, it would have been difficult for Lisa, if pressed, to have kept such a burdensome secret.

That letter from Alexander had been the last Clementine received before meeting Captain Hamilton. A photograph fell out, the long awaited photograph he had promised, having asked Vandyk's in Buckingham Palace Road to send a copy of a Service picture. His eyes were dark and accusing — as if they saw into her soul and knew what she was planning to do. She began to cry and glanced away, unable to bear it.

Trembling, she read his letter. Nothing much had changed. He had still not found a safe way for her to correspond. He seemed to be frequently on the move, never staying in one place for long. Though he mentioned nothing about the dangers, nothing about being under fire, she knew the perils he faced and his reasons for not telling her. He spoke of them spending time together in Paris, but to Clementine it was just a dream. No longer could she bring herself to believe that there would ever be a Paris, or a future. That night in London was surely their quota!

She burned the letter and the others with the photograph in the Mess boiler. After doing it, something inside her collapsed and it was easy to give in and let her subconscious take control. She made her way to the largest of the ponds, aware that now the ice had melted, and the surrounding grass was little more than muddy furrows, she was unlikely to meet anyone. On the way she collected several heavy stones, which she put in the canvas bag she'd brought along. At first she had hurried, as if afraid that her nerve would run out, but the weight of the bag slowed her down and her pounding head forced her to face what she was doing. She knew it was wrong, but she could see no alternative. She couldn't have this baby, it was impossible. The scandal would be terrible; it would break her mother's heart, cause damage to her father's career, not to mention poor Timmy. What would it be like for him to have his schoolfriends snigger about the beloved sister he'd been so proud of? Even Claudia would suffer and for all Clementine felt about her sister, she still didn't wish it on her.

Such was the state of her mind that she told herself it wouldn't be much of a wait before she saw Alexander again; she believed that the war would claim him, as it claimed all beauty, and that wherever heaven was, she and their child would wait there for him.

The boat was in its usual place. There were no oars but it did not really matter. Once she had cast off she would drift into the middle. She placed the stones in the bottom of the boat, and catching hold of the rough wet rope, tried to undo the knot. She cursed her stiff, clumsy fingers and winced as a sore reopened. Tears of frustration filled her eyes as blood trickled onto the rust-stained rope. A voice pierced her darkness and looking up, she momentarily thought the tall officer across the pond was Alexander. Suffering from myopia she strained to see better, her initial excitement switching to alarm. Even he couldn't help her. Then she froze and looked again. Perhaps he had gone ahead, was already waiting for her. She always knew death was near when the patients began talking of deceased relations, saying they could see them. But no, the voice belonged to someone else.

Her breathing eased and her vision cleared, enough to realise it was Captain Hamilton. She pushed back her hair, trying to regain her senses. Her eyes fell on the canvas bag and she just managed to pull it out and place it under a bush before he appeared at her side.

*

There was an icy chill in the church and little sun permeated the stained-glass windows. The only warmth in the place was in Captain Hamilton's eyes. 'Do you want to tell me about it?' he asked gently.

'It's such a mess — I don't think I can.' Her voice mirrored the depths of her misery.

'What about the father? Have you told him? Surely he must be able to do something?'

*Oh, Alexander my love — what could you do for me?* The words raced around in her brain as tears welled in her eyes; the pain of it all becoming too much.

'You have told him? Does he know?' he persisted.

She shook her head.

'Why not?' She didn't answer and he eyed her perceptively. 'Is he married?'

She looked at him and nodded miserably. His face was expressionless and she lowered her eyes.

'Miss Ellacombe, I promise that what I have witnessed and whatever you tell me will be in complete confidence. I give you my word.' He squeezed her hand reassuringly and it soothed her as if she was a small child having suffered a nightmare.

'My brother-in-law is the father,' she heard herself say. 'Yes, the one who recently married my sister.' She looked at him, expecting to see disgust, but either he was hardened to such behaviour or he hid his feelings well; he didn't even seem shocked.

Having revealed the worst it was easier to continue and she told him everything, from the meeting on the train until the time they parted at Victoria. She found it strangely cathartic talking to him, but the confession took its toll, and by the time she had finished she was trembling.

Several seconds passed before Captain Hamilton spoke, but although his face was grave, his voice was kindly. 'Thank you for trusting me. I'm not here to judge, Clementine.' It was the first time he had used her Christian name and she felt comforted by it. 'I shall do all I can to help.'

'No one can help me. Why do you think I was at the pond?'

'I'm sure FitzPatrick will, if you give him the chance. Would you like me to find out where he is?'

'No!' she cried vehemently. 'He mustn't know!' Of course Alexander would come to her aid; never for a moment had she doubted this. But to be together now … she couldn't be so cruel or selfish as to hurt her family so blatantly.

'It's my parents,' she said hoarsely. 'If they found out … it would destroy them.'

'Don't you think what you were planning to do this afternoon would have destroyed them more?'

'I don't know … I don't know. I'd hoped they would think it was an accident. They could have coped with that but not a baby, not that shame.' Her eyes appealed for understanding. Captain Hamilton rose to his feet, his forehead lined with concern.

'My dear, I believe you are too emotional to think rationally. It is my belief you are making a grave mistake in not telling FitzPatrick or your parents. What you are effectively saying is that we must never make our parents sad even if this means giving up everything that makes *us* happy.'

She said nothing but his words hit home. She was a coward.

He looked down at her. 'And what now? I stopped you once but what about next time — will you try again?'

Still she said nothing.

'Clementine, I need an answer.'

'You ask too much. I don't know.'

He stared at her. 'It's my job to save lives. I can't leave here knowing that you may walk out after I'm gone and try again. I want your promise that you'll not do anything until we've had a chance to speak again. Will you at least do that for me?'

There was a pause. 'Yes.'

He sighed with relief and, taking her hands, pulled her to her feet. He was tempted to sign her off sick but decided that it would be better if her mind was kept occupied.

'I shall be waiting here early tomorrow morning when you go off night duty. Come as soon as you can.'

*

He was right to make her work. She had a busy night changing sheets, making poultices and massaging the swollen joints of those who could not sleep. Any spare time she got, Sister sent her off to make sure everyone was tucked in, regardless of discomfort, as tightly as possible. Such unnecessary acts always angered her. What did it matter whether the sheets were crumpled as long as the men were comfortable, but the trained nurses rigidly stuck to the rules.

However, that night, she got into trouble when she missed out a soldier whom she knew to be in pain from a recent amputation. Sister made sure she was suitably punished by making the poor soul cry out in agony, vindictively straightening the sheets herself. Clementine's anger remained with her throughout the night and when she went to meet Captain Hamilton she realised she'd had little time to think about her own problems.

He was waiting for her and experienced a tremor of trepidation when he saw her small wan face appear around the carved oak door. Over the previous hours, thoughts of her had haunted him, robbing him of precious sleep.

'It's freezing in here. I'm sure it's warmer outside,' he said, taking her icy fingers in his.

'I believe it is but someone might see us together, and after all I must protect my reputation,' Clementine told him. She, herself, wondered how she could joke at such a time, but all the same she was pleased that he smiled.

They sat at the back of the church and watched in silence as a peasant woman dressed in black entered and lit a candle before kneeling in prayer. Charles thought of the cemetery outside and then glanced at Clementine. Would she have been buried there, had he not discovered her in time? There was an air of resignation about her which disturbed him.

'Have you not considered adoption?' he asked, knowing they didn't have much time. He saw her lip tremble.

'I know that when the time came for me to give the baby up I wouldn't be able to. Oh Captain Hamilton, do you not think I haven't considered everything! I've even thought of staying in France and bringing him up in secret, but I know I'd be found out sooner or later.'

She looked despairingly at him. 'There is no solution. I can't have this child without destroying my parents. It was going to be bad enough without a baby, but with a baby — no, I can't do it to them. I cannot!' She looked wretched and a solitary tear rolled down her cheek.

Captain Hamilton was at a loss to know what to do, apart from comfort her. He drew her close but the warmth of his embrace served to overwhelm Clementine and she broke down.

'Why, oh why did you have to find me,' she wept. It would all have been over by now instead of this continual agony.'

He gently patted her head, still wearing the obligatory white headdress, listening to her sobs and understanding the enormity of the responsibility he now bore, and all the while his heart pounding with a mixture of fear and adrenalin. 'There is a solution,' he heard himself say. 'You could marry me.'

# 13

Clementine's voice was barely more than a whisper. 'Marry you!' She stared at him incredulously. 'You can't possibly mean it — you don't know what you are saying — you hardly know me.'

His steel-like eyes flashed with determination. 'I've never been more serious, Clementine. You see, despite being the son of a vicar, I don't believe in life after death, which is probably just as well for some of the pathetic souls I see on the operating table. I wonder if I would be so scrupulous each time I met a young soldier facing an existence of pain and dependence if I believed a happier life awaited him. No, I have no faith in another world. Life is here now — not tomorrow, not yesterday. *Now*! And the thought of you rotting in a grave when I have the means to save you is abhorrent to me.'

Clementine gaped in bewilderment. 'This is madness. I'm expecting another man's child, a man you know I love. What can you hope to gain from such a marriage?'

'It won't be easy, I don't deny that, but there is no way, knowing what you intend, that I shall ever be able to rest until you accept my proposal.'

His expression was earnest; she did not doubt his sincerity and was astounded by his goodness. But how could she contemplate such a union? What had she to offer this man but herself, and even that she had pledged to someone else. She had nothing and such merit deserved something. But he offered a future for herself and her child, and importantly her parents need never know the truth. Instead they would play a part in their grandchild's life, getting to know and love him, something she had never dreamed possible.

Was this God's answer to her cries for help? If so, it would seem He meant for her child to live. She looked at Captain Hamilton. What right had she to refuse?

As Clementine feverishly contemplated Captain Hamilton's proposal her head felt as if it was being tied into knots, so desperately was she trying to make sense of it all. She wondered why he had never married guessing that he was fast approaching forty. It was fairly certain he had had mistresses in the past. He was an attractive man, despite his sometimes haughty manner.

It served to show her how little she knew about him when he told her that he had, in fact, been married but that his wife, herself a doctor, had been killed in the bombings in the East End during 1915, whilst she had been working there.

'We had no children,' he said as if anticipating her next question. 'And apart from my sister who lives in London and a brother, I have no family. Our parents died some years ago.'

Charles had always admired Clementine, not just her beauty, but her intelligence and naturalness. In many ways she reminded him of a girl he'd had a crush on who lived in the village where he had grown up. Not long at medical school, he had known it would be years before he was in a position to support a wife and though he was prepared to wait, the girl wasn't. He still remembered how bruised he felt when coming home from college to learn that she was to marry his father's curate. The fact that Clementine reminded him of her made him wonder whether it was an omen. Was he mad? Would she end up hurting him too? From his own personal view he felt it would be easy to love her. He'd always thought her a good, gentle, generous girl, and had he been younger and Matron not so eagle-eyed, he would almost certainly have invited her out for tea. However, life never failed to surprise him and here he was, instead, inviting her to be his wife.

They stared at each other in silence for what seemed an age until he eventually spoke. 'I think you know that marrying me is your only real choice.'

Clementine continued to stare at him — she was utterly unable to speak.

*

The sudden marriage of Clementine to Captain Hamilton took everyone by surprise. No one had had any idea that the couple were so close. The haste with which it was arranged caused much talk and speculation and, although no one asked her outright, Clementine knew by the occasional veiled remark that pregnancy had not been ruled out. She weathered it, but at the same time felt guilty that Charles should be targeted too; overnight his respectability seemed in question.

Opportunely Matron was away on three weeks' leave and Charles connived in her absence to wield what influence he had and made arrangements for the wedding service. In view of Clementine's condition he also pressed for a transfer, and succeeded in obtaining one to a Casualty Clearing Station. It was nearer the Front Line, but he was familiar with the area and knew it would be possible for him to rent a cottage nearby where Clementine would be able to stay for the time being.

The wedding was a simple affair performed by the Army Chaplain, the morning before Matron returned, and attended by a handful of colleagues. Clementine was composed as she stood beside Charles before the small altar; the dark days were over and she knew she was fortunate to be exchanging vows with a man for whom she had the greatest respect. He had given her a future and she was determined to put her total commitment into this new relationship, even though she knew her heart would always belong to another.

After the ceremony they returned to the Officer's Mess and drank champagne; one of the guests took a couple of photos with his folding camera.

'Oh, Clemmie darling, I wish you all the luck in the world,' said Lisa giving her a hug. 'Promise me you'll be happy. Though I do wish you had trusted me — I would have understood.' The gentle reproach made Clementine's eyes water. She stared at Lisa … was it possible she knew?

'I'm sure it wasn't easy,' the other girl continued, 'but I think you've done the right thing. 'He's a good man.' Seeing Clementine's bewilderment she added, 'Let's just say I guessed you were in love, but was as surprised as everyone else to learn you were marrying Captain Hamilton.'

Clementine swallowed hard and hugged her. 'Oh Lisa, I'm going to miss you.'

Another nurse approached and playfully scolded her for taking the only single good-looking doctor away. 'Spare a thought for us poor Sisters of Mercy lying in our frozen coffin-like cots when you climb into your sumptuous marriage bed tonight.'

Clementine felt the colour rush to her face; it was something she tried not to think about, but she had committed herself to Charles and was quite certain he wouldn't be satisfied with a platonic relationship. For a moment she stared in silence as memories of her night with Alexander surfaced. Suddenly she was filled with trepidation. What had she done! Those hours with Alexander would live with her forever. She had given herself without reservation, and though she hadn't worn his wedding ring, she knew their love was pure, even without the blessing of the Church, and something she would never find with anyone else.

She glanced across the room to where her husband stood chatting to another doctor. He looked remarkably relaxed considering the heavy responsibilities he had just assumed, but she felt her body involuntarily stiffen at the thought of what lay ahead. Her anxiety showed and the nurse noted it with surprise. Perhaps the gossip was wrong!

With her eyes still fixed on Charles, Clementine acknowledged that she must put all thought of Alexander from her mind. She owed everything to Charles — her reputation, her family's happiness — she must never forget it. Alexander was the past. This new relationship was her and her unborn child's future.

*

They had two whole days before Charles was expected at his new post, a few miles from Amiens, and he made arrangements for them to spend them in a little fishing town on the coast before moving inland. There had been scant opportunity for their relationship to develop beyond the circumstances that had brought them together, and they both hoped that away from the pressure of hospital life they might unwind and come to know each other better.

By late afternoon they had arrived at their small hotel, and sensing Clementine's sudden awkwardness when shown to their room, Charles suggested they go for a walk. They strolled down towards the docks where gulls squawked above some of the returning fishing boats. It was breezy and there was a little crowd watching the fish and lobster pots being unloaded. Clementine took some deep breaths, hoping the briny air would calm her; it wasn't as quiet a place as she had hoped, and the number of officers milling about taking a rest from the Front unsettled her.

Charles noticed her disquiet when a tall cavalry officer walked towards them. Her grip on his arm tightened involuntarily and he didn't need to use his powers of perception to guess why. As they sat on the sea wall watching the local women in shawls and clogs inspect and haggle over the catch, he broached the subject, feeling it best to say something. 'Clementine, what happened between you and FitzPatrick is history for me, and I hope for you too. From now on it is you and I, and if one day you should meet him it will be as my wife, and I shall be there to support you.'

There was both shame and tenderness in her sideways glance. 'I'm sorry, Charles,' she sighed. 'How ungrateful I must seem. I'll get stronger, I promise.'

'You have nothing to fear.'

'I know. I just wonder how I am ever going to repay you. Who would have done what you've done?'

He looked mildly embarrassed. 'Don't put me on a pedestal. I don't know if I would have done it for anyone else.' Their eyes held for a moment, and she felt his arm draw her towards him. His kiss was gentle and though she couldn't respond she didn't recoil as she had feared she might.

They reached the end of the quay and decided to explore the maze of narrow cobbled streets. Voices and the smell of cooking wafted from inside tall terraced houses as preparation of the evening meal got underway. Two wizened fishermen sat on stools, smoking their pipes and mending nets. Beside them a gathering of children studied the movement of their gnarled hands. One of the old men nodded as the couple walked by.

Eventually they found themselves back near the quay, and passing a restaurant Charles suggested they stop and get something to eat. 'I'm sure you must be hungry. I certainly am. If the aroma is anything to go by, it should be good.'

'How the French love their food, even at times like this…' she said as they peered above the lace curtains and watched a sailor and his family tuck into a huge tureen of soup; the children breaking bread and dunking it into their bowls.

Seated in a quiet corner Clementine asked Charles about his parents. He had not spoken of them but she remembered him mentioning that his father was a vicar. There was so much to learn. 'My mother died ten years ago and my father had a stroke a few years later. But my sister, who I've yet to write to, will be delighted, I'm sure. She has always been a bit of a matchmaker, and after Mary my wife died, I knew she was worried that I might turn into a crusty old recluse.'

'You said you have a brother.'

'He's in the Flying Corps, but we haven't seen each other since 1915.'

'Does it upset you to talk about your wife? After all, two years is not a long time.'

'The pace we live these days, it seems much longer. Mary and I had a good life together and I count my blessings for the time that we shared. However, life goes on and I don't believe in grieving for something that can never return.'

'What was she like?'

'Strong, a fighter of women's rights, though she wasn't as radical as the Pankhursts. She set up a clinic in the East End for women and children. She tried to educate the women about health and contraception; make them understand it wasn't good for them to give birth every year, that there were ways of preventing pregnancy. You see she suspected many of the children she saw — the sickly ones that didn't thrive — were the results of bodged abortions, potions that didn't work, and not necessarily because there wasn't enough money to feed them all. She fought to educate women, make them stand up for themselves.'

'She must have made you very proud. What a loss it must have been for you. Apart from Great-Aunt Jane, who was old and unwell, I haven't had anyone close to me die.' But then she thought of Alexander and wondered if her grief would be any greater had he actually died. It brought to mind a conversation she had overheard years ago, between her mother and a friend whose husband had run off with another woman.

'Death would have been easier,' had sobbed the distraught friend. Only now could Clementine begin to comprehend.

'And what about your parents, have you told them yet?' he asked.

'I will as soon as we're settled,' she said realising she couldn't put it off for ever.

'How do you think they will take the news?'

'I don't know. They're bound to be shocked, and also hurt.'

'And, I imagine, concerned about the sort of man their daughter has married. Any decent fellow would, at the very least, have asked their permission first.'

Clementine sighed inwardly as she thought of her father. The brigadier had an unpredictable temperament, and knowing how outspoken he could be caused her some anxiety.

'We'll just have to wait. Though I feel it would be wiser to tell them we married in February.'

'But will they believe you, especially when in seven months from now you present them with a grandchild? I think I might suspect.

She couldn't deny it, nor the fact that her father had the means to check up if he so cared. 'But somehow, I feel he would rather not know the truth,' she said. 'He's always been proud of me, and I don't think he'd care to shatter the illusion. And also,' she avoided his eyes, but she had to say it, 'I feel it would be preferable for Alexander to believe we married then.'

Charles looked at her long and hard. 'You mean there is less chance of him suspecting the child is his,' he said levelly. 'Well, your father is going to think me a cad in any case, so why not a liar too.'

Suffused with guilt that such an upright and good man had been put in this position because of her, she vowed she would never make him regret marrying her.

It was dark when they arrived back at the hotel, and Clementine found the subtle combination of good food and wine had blunted the edge of her nerves. She felt relaxed and more confident. It was going to be all right. However, when Charles climbed into bed beside her, the cold reality of the situation hit her, and she burst into tears.

'I'm sorry,' she sobbed, but he seemed to understand and took her into his arms and held her gently.

'It doesn't matter, everything is going to be fine. There is no hurry. We have all the time in the world.' His empathy only made her cry more.

*

Charles took command of a new Casualty Clearing Station at Dernancourt, not far from Arras which was in the throes of a major battle. Though close to the Front Line, they were a safe distance from danger of enemy shells. However, at times the noise-levels from the incessant bombardment were so loud it felt as if they were in the thick of the action.

They rented a cottage on the neglected estate of an elderly landowner. It was close to the Clearing Station but so dirty that it took Clementine several days to make it habitable. Within minutes of their arrival Charles was whisked away to perform an emergency operation. The tiny hospital was packed to capacity and Clementine was soon to realise more than ever how tirelessly he worked, and she marvelled how he survived on so little sleep.

As soon as the cottage was straight, Clementine did something she knew she could no longer put off; she wrote to Alexander. She had in her possession three unopened letters from him and unopened they would remain for she knew she could not afford the anguish of reading his declarations of love. She had to tell him to forget her, tell him she had returned to France and married another man. As a nurse she had done things the faint-hearted could never have accomplished, but writing to Alexander was harder.

Although she kept the letter short, she agonised over it for hours, and was still very subdued when Charles returned home. He was quick to notice her puffy eyes, and the two letters on the mantelpiece waiting to be posted.

'What did you say to your parents?' he asked as he glanced at them.

'I told them we married quietly because it was so soon after Claudia's wedding and I wanted to spare them, both expense and upheaval. Now we can but wait and see how they accept it.'

He nodded and said nothing about the second letter. However, he was relieved that she had written to FitzPatrick. Maybe now she could come to terms with her past. But as he watched her ladle soup into bowls, he was aware that she was struggling to hide her distress. It disquieted him, for it told him she was mourning Alexander — and the reality of this truth stung him to the quick.

167

# 14

Alexander could not remember when he had last been in England in June, and guessed it must have been before the war. The sight of so many bees in the midday heat, buzzing round the wild flowers in the hedgerows, brought to mind halcyon summers of long ago. He drove leisurely, the roof down, on his Vauxhall Prince Henry, feeling that the vastness of the New Forest called to be explored on horseback. He liked motoring, but to him it bore no comparison to riding. He was a countryman through and through, and loved nothing better than being out in the open air, at one with nature.

Driving along the coast road with its contrasting landscape: grass meadows, lush from recent rain, and endless miles of sea, he thought of his boyhood summers which had always been split between Grangefield and Lyme Regis, where his grandparents had a house over-looking the bay. He and Patrick had eagerly looked forward to those weeks, so packed with adventures, that they had spent there each year, racing dinghies, scouring the cliffs and shores for fossils. What freedom they'd had.

Passing an inn advertising fresh lobster, Alexander was reminded of the time the pair of them had gone into the kitchen and witnessed the demise of two large lobsters. Used to the comings and goings of the animals at Home Farm, they were usually philosophical about animals and death, but the sight and sound of those poor creatures thrown into a vat of boiling water had horrified them. Agreeing that it had to be the most awful death ever, the youngsters decided to take action.

Over the coming weeks the local fishermen grew increasingly baffled and anxious about the depleting numbers of their lobster catches. Some thought cod were getting them, others that a giant eel was getting into the pots. Poaching was suggested but as the local restaurants were crying out for the creatures, few suspected this could be the reason, unless of course they were being transported further along the coast.

Every day Patrick and Alexander would do a round of the lobster pots, taking it in turn to dive in and liberate the prisoners, or if empty, remove the bait. Most of the locals knew the boys to be the grandchildren of Lord Moundsmere, and were used to seeing them playing, either on the water or the shore.

However, the mystery was finally solved as a result of Alex finding a dead lobster and thinking it would be a clever rouse to place it in a pot and *helpfully* tell the owner he had a catch. 'Just in case anyone suspects us — it should stifle any suspicion, don't you think, Patch?' They tried it twice — with the same dead lobster, but the second man, a younger fellow was not so appreciative. He told them off for ' 'avin a laugh.'

'What rude manners!' said Patrick. 'How's he to know whether we can tell a live lobster from a dead one.' However, it did made them think, that perhaps it wasn't such a good idea, after all.

But, too late — their luck had all ready run out. The hero-in-waiting was in the 'Fishermen's Haunt' later when he heard the boys first victim mention the dead lobster and the two brothers. He said nothing, just supped his ale and pondered; they looked all innocent, but there was something about them lads … Trusting his intuition he planted the now rather smelly same dead crustacion back in his pot, and waited.

Alexander recalled the shock of being caught red-handed, and arms as strong as a Boa Constrictor, hauling himself and Patrick, who pulled a face, up the hill to the house. Both brothers knew the reception they faced but Alexander, was more concerned about the fate of the lobsters.

There had been many angry words exchanged that night and the next morning long-suffering Lord Moundsmere had promptly received a visit from the local constabulary and had had little choice but to make good the losses of the season, costing him a small fortune.

Six weeks in Lyme was usually the maximum that their grandfather could stand, always anxious to get back to check on the running of the estate, but that particular year their stay had been cut short. However, much as the boys loved the sea, it was never any hardship for them to leave, for not so many miles away were Rough and Ready, their ponies, and a thousand acres which lay in wait for more adventures.

Alexander smiled sadly as he thought of his brother. 'We had some fun, didn't we, Patch,' he murmured, and thanked God for the memories, for he never forgot one of the last things his grandfather had said shortly before his death in spring 1914. 'The most important thing you can take with you is memories. Have plenty of happy ones.'

In the distance Alexander spied Calshot Castle, jutting out into Southampton Water. Since his last visit, new hangars had sprung up, obscuring part of the old fort from view. Overhead, two patrolling seaplanes sailed in and out of the clouds, lacing them together with ribbons of smoke. The gutsy noise from the rotary engines almost drowned his thoughts as the planes dipped and dived. He imagined the rush of adrenalin and the freedom these pilots must experience as they soared through the heavens. For a moment he envied them.

It was four months since the wedding, and apart from the odd letter, Alexander and Piers had not had any contact. He knew his reason for today's visit would come as a shock to Piers but felt he had little choice after his last two letters to Clementine had been returned unopened with a note from the Matron to say that Miss Ellacombe no longer worked there. She concluded by suggesting he write to her home address, informing him: *It is not our policy to forward mail or to supply a change of address without authorisation.* It was a situation neither he nor Clementine had foreseen. And until he found out where she had been transferred he had no means of contacting her. However, though irked, he knew he couldn't complain about these strictures, for the consequences had his letters been forwarded to Coppins didn't bear thinking about.

'Alex — speak of the devil! I've just been talking to Hunter. He was asking after you — said he saw Claudia recently in Town!' exclaimed Piers, getting up from his desk which was strewn with papers and maps. 'What are you doing here? I had no idea you were back in the country.'

'I got back yesterday,' Alexander' said as they greeted one another with a warm handshake and a pat on the shoulder.

'I hear congratulations are in order,' Alexander smiled, his teeth white against his tanned face. 'I learned on the way in that a couple of your chaps have just hit a U32.'

Piers grinned. 'Yes, a couple of crew dropped a hundred pounder from a White seaplane. We're delighted.'

'No doubt you'll all be celebrating.'

Piers gave him a knowing look. 'So what about you? Didn't expect you back so soon. No new injuries?'

'No, all in one piece. Good news for once, I'm joining the Desert Campaign.'

'I say, that's topping! I'm really happy for you. Think that calls for a double celebration,' Piers said. 'When did you hear?'

'Last night, and I leave tomorrow. In fact, I really shouldn't be here.'

'Tomorrow? Too right you shouldn't. Why aren't you with the beautiful Claudia?'

Alexander was silent and ignored his friend's searching glance.

'Look, I haven't much time,' he said evasively. 'I'm on my way to see my grandmother and want to be back in London tonight. Are you able to get away for an hour, I need to talk to you.' There were too many people floating in and out to risk it here.

Informing his crew that he'd be away for an hour, Piers jumped into the car and directed Alexander to an old coaching inn, well known for its ale.

'Try that,' he said, handing him a pint glass. 'Better than anything you've been used to, I'd wager.'

'That won't be difficult. You get swindled left right and centre in France; you're lucky to get beer that's not been watered down. There are always fights breaking out when some irate Tommy accuses the bar-owner of cheating.'

'That's the French for you, bloody ungrateful lot,' said Piers as he beckoned Alexander to follow him into the garden. They sat on an old wooden bench beneath the shade of an oak tree, and a middle-aged woman brought them a large plate of sandwiches. It was delivery day from the brewery and a heavily laden dray pulled by two horses halted at the side of the building. A short stocky man and a well-built youth jumped down, and aided by the ruddy-faced and overweight landlord, they began to off-load the barrels and carry them down to the cellar.

'I'm glad to see the essential supplies are getting through,' quipped Piers to the drayman as the man paused to catch his breath against the cart. 'My friend was just telling me about the damned awful beer in France. Pity you can't get out there to supply the troops.'

'That it is, sir, but someone's gorra stay here and look after you gentlemen,' he said, touching his cap.

Piers settled back down and took a mouthful of the good ale. Sighing appreciatively he turned to his friend. ' It's really good to see you, Alex.' And so it was; he hated scanning the casualty lists in *The Times*; it was a gruesome business searching those endless columns for names of people you'd once known, and he was relieved that Alexander had survived another stint.

'Well, what is it you want to talk to me about, must be important to be keeping you from Claudia,' he asked with a searching glance. 'Things *are* all right between you?' He hadn't seen Claudia since February but had heard that she had moved to London, into the new place. 'How is she?' It couldn't be long before the baby was due.

Alexander eyed him in silence for a moment. 'Piers this isn't easy. I'm here for a reason. I could have phoned but I thought it best I see you in person. The fact is, I need your help. Someone I've been corresponding with has moved and I don't have a forwarding address.'

Piers looked askance. Something in Alexander's expression made him uncomfortable. 'You've driven all the way here for an address?'

Alexander took a deep breath, knowing he had no choice but to confide in Piers. 'You mentioned Claudia but the fact is that the marriage was a mistake, and as soon as the war is over, if not before, I shall divorce her.'

Piers was astounded. 'For heaven's sake old man! What on earth has happened?'

'As I said, it was a mistake.'

'What do you mean a mistake? You've hardly been together five minutes. That's not exactly giving it a chance, is it? And what about the child? Have you forgotten he was the reason you married?'

'Well, some call it the oldest trick in the book. Unfortunately, I happened to fall for it.'

Piers's face softened. 'You mean … Oh, Alexander, I'm truly sorry, I really am, especially considering it was me who introduced you to her. But still, divorce … Have you thought it through? It's rather drastic, don't you think? Is there no way you could forgive her?'

Alexander shook his head. 'It was a mistake and one I mean to rectify.' Piers had rarely seen him so determined. 'The truth is, I've fallen in love with someone else and want to marry her.'

'My God, you certainly don't let the grass grow under your feet,' said Piers, his brows knitting together as the fog started to clear from his mind. 'Tell me who this person is you've been writing to. She's obviously someone I know too?'

'I understand you've been corresponding with her.'

The naturally high colour of Piers's face intensified. 'The only girl I write to apart from my sister is Clementine,' he said, his voice as heavy as iron. He banged his fist on the bench. 'Tell me I'm wrong, Alexander. Tell me!' The silence though short was overpowering, and gave him his answer.

'Clementine!' he shouted, leaping to his feet. 'You're not bloody well suggesting you're going to marry Clementine!'

Alexander was shaken by the extent of his anger. For a few seconds they glared at each other like angry bulls until Alexander eventually broke the silence.

'I'm sorry, Piers, I know how much you liked her, but we're deeply in love and I intend to marry her as soon as possible.'

'You rotten bastard!' His voice was like the crack of a whip. 'What's wrong with you that you keep falling in and out of love with every female you meet?'

'What are you talking about?'

'What about that girl you met on the train — remember? Or have you conveniently forgotten about her?'

'That *was* Clementine!'

Piers stared at him.

'It's true. I had no idea who she was until the wedding. You can imagine how we felt.'

Piers stormed off and silently paced around the garden; he was completely stunned. Alexander watched, not knowing what to say. He had not anticipated this violent reaction and, feeling rather bewildered, waited for his friend to calm down. ,

'I'm surprised at you, FitzPatrick,' Piers said. 'I always thought you were the sensible one. But now let me tell you some news that you're not going to like, and don't you bloody well deserve it too!' A vicious smile spread across his lips.

Alexander looked fiercely at him, the words filling him with foreboding. 'What the devil are you talking about?'

'Well, here you are, read it for yourself,' Piers said dragging a letter from his pocket. 'It's for you, and it's from Clementine, probably informing you of her marriage to her doctor love. So neither of us is going to get her, after all.'

At this Alexander lost control and threw himself at Piers. 'Liar!' They both hit the ground together. Rolling in the dust, their fists flew and tempers flared, and the uproar caused the landlord and the two draymen to come over and separate the two officers, much to the resentment of the small crowd that had gathered to watch.

'Come now, gents. You should be saving this for the Hun,' said the landlord, mopping his brow. Shamefaced, Piers apologised for their unfitting behaviour and dusted off his clothes, whilst Alexander retrieved the letter and stormed off to his car to read it alone. His hands shook as he tore open the envelope and took the single sheet of notepaper between his fingers.

*

*Dearest Alexander,*

*By the time you receive this letter, the chances are you will already have heard about my marriage. I regret you had to find out this way, but I had no choice. I loved you, Alexander, I always will, but know in my heart that we could never have found lasting happiness together. Too many lives other than our own were affected to allow us such luxury. I suppose I did not have your faith because I could not see a way forward.*

*I have married a surgeon from the hospital. He is a fine person, and I know in different circumstances you would like him.*

*I am sorry to have involved Piers, but did not know how else to contact you. Conscious that he was bound to wonder why I'm writing to you via him, I lied and told him it was to do with a surprise we were planning for Claudia. I pray you don't have to wait too long before it reaches you.*

*Forgive me Alexander but it was the only way.*

*Clementine.*

Numbly he stared at the letter in his hands, until gradually an agony so great filled his entire being. He was barely conscious of the strangled cry that escaped his lips. WHY? Had he imagined it, that night, so alive in his memory? Had it not really happened the way he remembered; their love and passion equal? Had separation fanned her feelings, diminishing them with the same force that had made his grow? Into his thoughts flashed a picture of a shrub which grew by the steps in the sunken garden at

Grangefield, its beautiful white flowers, as fragile as tissue. 'Twenty-four-hour blooms', his grandmother called them; intensive and lovely for their short duration, and every morning a gardener would be found bent over, gathering up the petals that had fallen in the night.

Tears filled his eyes, and burying his face in his hands, he wept.

Piers approached cautiously. The car door was open and seeing Alexander's suffering, his anger vanished. Perhaps he had been a little hard on him, and also guilty of allowing his own feelings to become involved. He knew Alexander was no fool and that he would never intentionally risk a marriage for a wild fling. His thoughts returned to the time he had walked with Clementine over the cliffs at Durdle Door and she had asked him about love at first sight. Of course now he realised that Alexander had been at the back of that question. If only he had known! Compassion getting the better of him, he placed a hand on his friend's shoulder.

'Come on, old fellow, do you want to tell me about it?'

There was an emptiness in Alexander's eyes that alarmed him. 'For the love of God, why?'

Piers saw the letter lying crumpled on his lap. 'May I read it?' Alexander shrugged. A little later Piers looked at him. 'How far did your relationship go? Did you sleep with her?' Their eyes met. 'Please don't tell me it was that night I asked you to meet her. Oh hell it was, wasn't it! Why the devil couldn't you have shown some restraint?'

'Because there's a bloody war on and neither of us knew when we would meet again. Look, whatever you're thinking, I didn't seduce her. I can't explain what happened. I only know it was what we both wanted.'

Piers frowned. 'Well, I don't doubt that you love her. I've never seen you in such a state, and from Clementine's letter it's clear that she felt the same. If it's any consolation I'm inclined to believe she married this fellow because she was scared of the consequences of your relationship. The situation must have played havoc with her conscience. How do you think Brigadier Ellacombe would have taken it? 'Oh, don't worry, son-in-law, we all make mistakes. Of course you can marry Clementine. I'll get Best to fetch the champagne.'

Alexander ran his hand through his hair. 'She knew it wasn't going to be easy, we spoke of the difficulties, but she assured me she was prepared to face anything.'

'Yes, while still warm with love, but when she got back to France things would have looked decidedly less attractive. You probably will not want to hear this, Alexander, but I think you should. Clementine told me that she was seeing a doctor.'

Alexander turned to Piers, pain flashing through his eyes like fork lightning. 'She told you that?'

'The second time we met — and that's why I wasn't entirely surprised when she married.'

Again Alexander shook his head, confused. 'I don't understand. I just assumed there was no one else. She never mentioned anyone.'

'Look, Alex, it's probably not a good time to say this, but in view of what's happened can't you put the past behind you and try to patch things up with Claudia? I'm sure it's what she wants, and possibly what Clementine intended.'

'Is this an attempt to make me laugh, because you're mad if you think there's any chance of that. Can you honestly imagine an occasion when we are compelled to meet, she with her husband, me with Claudia? Never! In fact, at this precise moment I never want to see either of them again!'

# 15

Spots of rain fell from the darkening sky and trickled down Alexander's forehead. In moments small puddles formed in the grooves of the leather upholstery. Pulling the motor off the road he hurriedly fixed the roof in place, just succeeding before the heavens opened. Back inside, the rain hammered and the windows misted around him. He sat awhile churning over and over what Clementine had done. To have returned to France and married another, after what they had shared was as incredible as learning that Britain had surrendered to Germany. The future that had sustained him over the past months was suddenly a black hole and he saw himself groping in the darkness, searching for answers he would never understand.

He cursed his caution, convinced it might never have happened, had he allowed her to write. He would have calmed her fears and misgivings. But instead, it would seem that she had turned to someone else; someone to whom Piers said she was close. But even now, with the facts before him, he couldn't really believe there had been anyone else in her life. He was convinced that he would have sensed it. But, whichever way he looked at it, it was obvious that by the time he had found a safe way to correspond, it was too late and she had already decided her fate.

The rain began to ease and glancing at his pocket watch he realised that he would have to postpone his visit to his grandmother. Having no idea when the opportunity would present itself again, he felt remorse for he was conscious of her age and what his visits meant to her. However, he knew that even if he went, he wouldn't be the best of company, and the inevitable questions about Claudia would prove difficult to cope with in his present mood.

Reaching for the starting handle he climbed out of the car and swung the engine into life. In a couple of hours or so he would be back in London. He hoped the ride might calm him.

As he turned the car round, he was struck by a sudden thought. Surely as Clementine's sister, Claudia would be able to give him some answers. Visiting her had been the last thing he had intended, but he was desperate and there would be no peace for him until he knew more. If that meant facing her ...

\*

'Major FitzPatrick to see you, madam,' said the young maid, interrupting her mistress, who was absentmindedly flicking through a magazine in the drawing room.

'Show him in,' she said in a cool voice which belied her confusion. Alexander had made it quite clear when they had parted that he'd no intention of seeing her again. Mr Edwards, his solicitor, handled everything from household bills to her allowance. What could he want? She hurriedly straightened her blue silk dress and slipped her shoes on.

'Alexander! This is a surprise,' she said guardedly.

'Don't get up,' he said taking her proffered hand but avoiding her cheek.

For one wild moment she thought her prayers had been answered. Now she eyed him with caution. 'I was not aware that you were on leave.'

'I'm not. I got back last night and set sail for the Middle East tomorrow.'

'The Middle East! That's practically on the other side of the world. Will you be away long?'

'That will depend on the success of the campaign.'

'Are you here for a particular reason, or are you just passing through?'

'I had a few things to tie up and felt it only courteous to let you know my whereabouts.' She smiled inwardly at his feeble excuse. 'How thoughtful. Well now you're here, won't you have a farewell drink?' She motioned to the side table where there was a decanter. 'I have a bottle of very good vintage brandy which I stole from Papa's cellar last time I was home.'

'How are your parents?' he asked as he filled two glasses.

'Very well, thank you, though Papa has gout again — no great surprise.'

Sitting opposite, Alexander became aware of her appraising eyes.

'How did you gash your lip, not fisti-cuffs, surely?' she teased. Colour rushed to his face at the accuracy of her guess. 'So what have you been up to?' he enquired, to distract her. 'Do you still help out at the canteen?'

'Four afternoons a week, and I also do hospital visiting, beastly depressing it is too. But you know how it is. One has to do one's duty. Imagine the fun, having to tell a fellow with no legs to stop sulking and count himself lucky.'

'Imagine how it must be for your sister as a full-time nurse,' he said seizing his chance.

'Clementine?'

'I wasn't aware you had another. I presume she's still in France?'

'Oh, very much so. She's married a doctor from the hospital where she worked. Though how she managed it baffles me, if what she used to tell us about discipline was true.'

'You didn't know about it?' he said, struggling to keep his voice flat and unemotional.

'Came like a bolt out of the blue.' She was still sore at Clementine for abandoning her when Alexander had dumped her at Coppins, and had taken sadistic pleasure in the furore her sudden marriage had caused at home.

'The first we heard about it was when it was already a fait accompli. An elopement! Can you believe it. Miss Goody Two Shoes! Poor Mother was quite beside herself until Papa discovered he was acquainted with the groom's relations. It seems he's rather older, a widower.'

Claudia studied Alexander as he put the glass to his lips, noticing the slight tremble in his hands and the pallor beneath his suntan. From her hospital visiting she had become familiar with nervous conditions, and what she saw convinced her that the war was getting to him. It was like a crack in a pane of glass, still in place, but irrevocably flawed, just awaiting a frost, and it gave her a surge of satisfaction and hope. Whereas before he had been the strong one, dictating, controlling, she could now see a time when he would come to need her. These past months fending for herself had not been wasted. She had learned patience and restraint, two qualities she would require if she was to succeed in winning back his confidence. She knew she must tread cautiously.

'So,' continued Alexander, 'She married in France — recently?'

'Not long after she went back,' she said, getting up to refill his glass.

Alexander drank it quickly — too quickly, he realised, judging from Claudia's expression, but he needed something to deaden the pain.

'Have you eaten?' she enquired in a tone her mother might have used. 'Why don't I get Cook to rustle something up, or better still we could go to the Ritz. Shall I phone for a table?'

He shot to his feet in horror, struck by memories of the last meal he had eaten there. ' No that's not possible. I have to get back.'

'Oh, come now, we won't be late, and you can do whatever you must on return. It will do you good. You owe it to yourself to have some fun and forget. Lord knows, you've little enough to look forward to.'

'I think not.' But she thought his voice less than convincing.

In fact, at that moment Alexander would have given anything to forget, but before she had time to press him further, a pinhead of light behind his eyes augmented like a firework. How could he forget that it was her actions that were responsible for his misery? Suddenly he had to get out of the place before he did something he would regret.

'Goodbye, Claudia.'

She hid her disappointment and smiled understandingly, knowing the importance of keeping her temper. She moved towards him. 'Well, perhaps next time, when you're not so hurried.' She smiled, and knowing it might be a long time before she got another opportunity, struggled not to overstep the mark. 'Do take care, Alexander, I'll be thinking of you,' and she reached up and pressed a kiss on his cheek.

He stared into those beguiling blue eyes, so like Clementine's. Their lips touched. 'Remember me to your sister,' he said, before wheeling round and marching out.

*

The thunder of heavy artillery was incessant throughout the summer of 1917, the constant boom a veritable heartbeat of war.

However, the constant rainfall, proved to be the worst enemy, for it caused a hideous quagmire. Whilst tanks and rifles were immobilised in the mud, many soldiers drowned in the plentiful shell-holes.

The casualties were horrendous, and initially Charles let Clementine use her nursing skills to help ease the burden of the overworked Sisters. It was commonplace to see a line of stretchers outside the marquee carrying men desperate for attention and she would tend to them as best she could. Charles showed her how to stitch wounds together and remove shrapnel from the lesser victims. He was very proud of the way she conducted herself and the Sisters grew to respect her. By June it was clearly obvious that she was pregnant, but she carried on regardless, working long hours, never complaining.

However, by the time August arrived she began to flag and Charles, conscious of some of the staff's anxiety, stepped in and stopped her from doing anything over-strenuous. From then on, she stuck to rolling bandages and writing letters for those soldiers who were too ill to do so, or who were illiterate. However, it wasn't easy and ever conscious that some casualties died because their injuries hadn't been tended in time, she defied him on numerous occasions. But then came the day when, after eight hours in surgery, he caught her, despite her heavily swollen stomach, bending over a young boy who was bleeding profusely on the churned-up earth. He ordered her home in a tone she found humiliating.

It was early the next morning before she saw him, and though still angry with him, the sight of his drawn face and bloodshot eyes smothered it. She could see he was overwrought with all the work.

'I see how foolhardy I've been allowing you to remain here, instead of sending you back to England,' he said exasperatedly.

'Why do you persist in making things difficult for me, Clementine? You know perfectly well you shouldn't be here. Think what would happen should you suddenly become sick, which you assuredly will if you continue to disobey me. Who will look after you?'

She acknowledged his point but said, 'It's not easy to turn away when you know you can make a difference.'

'Well, that's the price you must pay if you wish to remain. Can you not imagine my predicament if, through your very stubbornness, you become ill and need nursing. I would literally have to choose between you and possibly the lives of several good men!'

Clementine had no wish to return to England. It was her intention to have her child in France, as far away from her family as possible, and so from then on she was careful not to cause Charles further vexation.

In September Charles finally confined her to the house, and feeling large and weary she made little protest. The baby was very active, and apart from rolling bandages she spent the remainder of her time sewing and knitting for the layette. As the baby kicked and prodded with a fierceness that sometimes left her breathless, her thoughts would often turn to Alexander. What would he say if he knew? But this was a thought that brought only pain, not to mention pangs of disloyalty to Charles. Already she felt a strong bond with the baby, which like her stomach, was growing rapidly and she wondered whether in time she would be able to look at the life they had created and not be reminded of Alexander.

Because of the pressure of work she spent little time with Charles and was often lonely. She made enquiries in the local village about finding someone to help her after the birth. As a result she was introduced to the baker's twenty-year-old daughter who had previously worked as a nursery nurse. She took an instant liking to the dark-haired girl with melancholy eyes. Her name was Danielle Borde and when Clementine suggested that she might like to start immediately by helping with the cooking and cleaning, she readily agreed.

The French girl's quiet unobtrusive manner was perfect for the Hamilton household where Charles might return at any time to catch a few hours of sleep. Interestingly he now made an extra effort to be present at meal-times, which spoke volumes about Clementine's efforts at cuisine.

As she got to know Danielle better, she learned that she was still grieving for her fiancé who had been killed at Verdun, and of her conviction that her younger brother, holed up somewhere on the Front Line, would not survive. A while back Clementine would have tried to help her against such negative thoughts, but she understood better now. Only time could do that. Slowly but assuredly, time would once again sow seeds of hope. Meantime, there was nothing to do but wait. Grief could not be rushed.

They conversed in French, Danielle's English being poor, but hopeful of the opportunity of going to England, when her employers one day returned home, she was eager to learn and with Clementine's help was soon able to make herself understood.

By Charles's reckoning the baby was not due until late November, so when Clementine went into labour six weeks early he assumed it was a false alarm. By good fortune he was back at the cottage for something to eat when she got her first pain. He told her to lie down and rest, but by the time he had eaten his stewed pears, Clementine was screaming in agony and the baby rushing to be born. There was no time to be lost. Suddenly the place was a hive of industry, with Charles shouting instructions to Danielle.

The pains were fast and furious, and barely an hour later, Charles placed a lusty-voiced baby boy in her arms. As Clementine held him, mesmerised by his tiny, squashed features and fighting fists, and overwhelmed with love, she instinctively thought of Alexander. But as tears flooded her eyes she reminded herself how differently things could have turned out, had Charles not found her at the pond.

However, there was no time for maudlin thoughts, for barely had she drawn breath, before she was gasping once more with pain. Anxiously Charles took the baby from Clementine and handed him to Danielle whilst he examined her.

'What's wrong?' she cried as he felt her stomach, misinterpreting his expression of embarrassment for concern.

'It seems the little fellow wasn't alone!' Charles told her.

Fifteen minutes later she was delivered of a smaller, but equally noisy, daughter. Charles was as stunned as Clementine by the unexpected addition, and a little ashamed that he hadn't suspected. Nevertheless, he embraced her warmly and assured her that he was delighted.

All the emotions Clementine had felt for her son were duplicated when she held her daughter. Her heart was bursting and she radiated love. Charles thought he had never seen her look so beautiful. With both infants in her arms she looked at Charles and wondered whether he was as truly delighted as he said. 'I feel I've rather cheated you,' she smiled nervously.

'Put such thoughts away. I consider myself a fortunate man. Not only have I you, but now two little mites. What more could I wish for?'

She searched his face, not entirely convinced. He smiled and kissed her tenderly. 'Dearest one, I'd have married you had I known you were having triplets.'

*

Danielle became indispensable as her mistress struggled to cope with two hungry babies. Until the births the girl had continued to live with her parents, but now she moved into the spare room in order to help with the night feeds.

As a humble token of her gratitude Clementine named the children after Charles's parents, Charlotte and Peter, and nervously wrote to her own, breaking the news that they were grandparents. She well imagined their shock for she hadn't even told them that she was pregnant. She waited anxiously for their reply which came without delay, and sighed with relief when she read that her father had opened a bottle of his best champagne to wet the babies' heads. There was no reproach, only concern over Clementine's and the twins' safety. Both of her parents considered the edge of a battlefield no place to rear children, and urged her to return home as soon as she was fit to travel.

It was November before the battles ended, bringing the spring and summer slaughter to a finish, and, as always, due to exposure, the sick began to out-number the wounded, easing Charles's workload. It seemed to be the cycle of things, and it was easy to get depressed and wonder how many more years this terrible conflict would last. The United States had finally declared war on Germany in April, and at the time everyone had thought their entry would resolve matters quickly. But, as yet, few American troops had set foot on French soil. Then in early December something happened that caused grave concern amongst the Allies. Russia, in the throes of a revolution, signed an armistice with Germany, effectively eliminating the Eastern Front. General opinion was that the enemy would now bring their surplus troops over to the Western Front and launch a major offensive.

Anxiety ran high and opinions differed as to when the attack would happen. In the light of this news Charles grew increasingly concerned about the safety of Clementine and the children. They were too close to the Front to be complacent, and he knew the time was fast drawing near when he would have to send them home. Frequently he raised the matter, but Clementine was always ready to change the subject. She did not want to return. If the Germans broke through she would take the children back to one of the coastal ports.

It seemed she did not appreciate the severity of the situation. Charles had to remind her of the atrocities the Germans had allegedly inflicted on the Belgian people in 1915. The issue finally came to a head when a parcel of baby clothes arrived from Mrs Ellacombe. In the enclosed letter she expressed her deep anxiety.

*Papa has spoken to several people in high places, and is utterly convinced the Germans are planning a full-scale attack. If he's right, then you and the children will be in the thick of all the fighting. I implore you to come home, darling. I cannot emphasise too strongly the importance of your speedy return.*

The following day, Charles told Clementine that he had obtained a pass and was taking her back to England. She was miserable and pleaded with him to let her remain for the winter.

'You know the Germans won't attack before spring. Please, Charles.'

However, this time he was unrelenting. 'From the tone of your mother's letter, she obviously thinks you have married a brute who puts his own comfort before the safety of his family, and can you blame her? It would be foolhardy of me to allow you to stay a moment longer.'

From his manner Clementine knew it was futile arguing. Charles would not change his mind. 'I don't want to leave you,' she said heavily.

He kissed her fondly. 'That's nice to know, but remember that our family has just doubled in size, and as responsible parents we must give our children first consideration.'

Their eyes met and he continued in a more serious tone, 'I don't want you to go either, for all the obvious reasons. I'm aware how you feel about meeting FitzPatrick again, but at least we know that he's out in North Africa, which means we don't have to worry about that at the moment.'

Clementine lowered her eyes and glanced away. How astute he was. But he was right — she wasn't ready to meet Alexander yet. She wasn't strong enough to look him in the eyes and deny her love for him. At night, she lay beside Charles thinking of Alexander. She looked at the twins and thought of him. No, she was not strong enough yet.

She had grown to love Charles, but it was a different sort of love. If she hadn't experienced such glorious affinity with Alexander, her happiness with Charles would have been undeniable, but she had, and she believed only time would dull the memories. She felt safe with Charles; he protected her, but he could never replace Alexander, whose memory lingered and pervaded the very depths of her being.

# 16

Travelling back to England with two infants would have been difficult in any circumstances, but with a war going on and Christmas only days away, the journey was a nightmare. Every platform and port was congested with those soldiers fortunate to be granted leave, all hurrying in the same direction, home!

Danielle, having succeeded in making herself indispensable, and with her parents' blessing, happily agreed to accompany the family. Clementine would be eternally grateful, for Charles, like most fathers of his generation, had proved to possess limited skills regarding the management of babies. It was bad enough even with Danielle's assistance; without it Clementine dreaded to think how she would have coped. Needless to say, there was relief all round when the train drew into Victoria.

It was arranged that they break the journey by stopping a couple of nights with Charles's sister and brother-in-law, Grace and Alfred Riddett whom he was anxious for Clementine to meet. A car was sent to meet them and take them the short distance to the couple's home near Westminster. What with delays, et cetera, the entire journey had taken over twenty hours and the travellers were quite exhausted by the time they arrived. However, Grace, a sensible woman in her late thirties, had expected this and had her children's nurse whisk Danielle and the twins up to the nursery, leaving Charles and Clementine to unwind downstairs.

The following morning everyone awoke refreshed; the babies having slept the whole night for the first time. After their feed they were warmly wrapped and placed outside in a large black pram that had been given a thorough spring-clean after being pulled from the shed.

'The wind in the trees will soon lull them off to sleep,' said Grace to Clementine.

'They must wonder what has happened, they've never had it so quiet. '

'Mmmm — I don't know what Charles was thinking. He should have sent you back long ago. I can only suppose that having waited so long to have children he wasn't going to give them up so easily.'

'I'm afraid it was me who didn't want to come back,' said Clementine.

'Oh well, I suppose I can understand. You haven't been married very long. Not like we oldtimers — fifteen years next anniversary. Though I must confess, I quite look forward to when there's a late-night sitting at the Commons. I like nothing better than to take a relaxing bath and to climb into bed with a good book.'

The two women walked back towards the kitchen door. 'I was so happy when Charles wrote and told us about your marriage,' Grace confided, 'and now that I've met you, I'm even more so, for I can see you complement each other perfectly. Of course, I'm not saying he wasn't happy with Mary, but I don't think being in the same profession and talking shop all the time is necessarily good for keeping a relationship alive. I can see that your marriage will be quite different. Well, for a start there are the children … '

The family had lost most of their staff and Grace did the majority of the cooking herself. Clementine helped her prepare lunch.

'You did well to bring Danielle back. I don't know about down in deepest Dorset but up here, you'd have had trouble finding help.'

Clementine thought of Ruby and wondered how she was getting on working for Lady Moundsmere. She had lost touch since marrying, not wanting Alexander to discover her whereabouts. With a sigh she knew it would only be a matter of time before he learned she had returned home.

Meals were eaten in the kitchen, saving having to carry everything up stairs to the dining room. 'I should have thought we might have made the effort at least once, during your brother's stay, to eat in style,' said Alfred as the four of them gathered round the kitchen table for dinner that evening.

'It's cosier down here,' Grace told him, ' plus a darn sight warmer.'

Brother and sister caught up on news regarding family members and Alfred spoke to Clementine about a new law they were hoping to push through Parliament whereby children would not be allowed to leave school under fourteen. Before she had time to comment, the sudden distant boom of gunfire brought all conversation to a close.

'Oh dear, sounds like a raid,' said Grace, getting up from the table as another boom was heard, this one closer than the last. Clementine was on her feet immediately.

'The children!' But no sooner had she uttered the words than footsteps on the stairs heralded the arrival of Grace and Alfred's three children, followed by their nurse and Danielle, both carrying a warmly wrapped baby. 'Down to the cellar, quickly,' directed Grace, lighting a candle she kept at the ready.

As they all crowded in the dark damp space surrounded by wine and coal, they listened as the guns got closer until it seemed they were overhead. Everyone held their breath, no one making a sound.

'The Zeps fly too high for our planes, some twenty thousand feet, said Alfred, 'and it's not always easy to detect them.' There was another explosion but this time it sounded more distant. They waited patiently, filling the time with playing charades, until they were sure it was safe to return back upstairs.

'Excitement over, back to bed,' said Grace, clapping her hands and ushering her unsleepy brood back upstairs along with the twins, who were still slumbering peacefully.

'They never stirred.' said Alfred in surprise. 'You'd have thought the noise would have woken them.'

Charles laughed and explained that it was the quiet they seemed to find more disturbing, being accustomed to the din from the battlefields.

'If you ask me, it's a good thing they're going down to the country,' said Grace. 'I don't care what you say, babies need to be safe and quiet, otherwise you never know what nervous complaints they'll develop in later life. Fortunately Dorset seems to be well out of the danger zone.'

*

Mrs Ellacombe, wrapped in a festive shawl, was standing on the front steps holding an umbrella, as the car crunched to a halt on the gravel sweep. Throwing the door open, Clementine, climbed down and ran to embrace her mother. There was no hint of reproach, just her usual warmth, but she noted the moment of scrutiny before her mother took Charles's hand and welcomed him to Coppins.

'Well, where are they?' she then cried, raising her hands and making for the car. 'My grandchildren!'

Minutes later she was proudly presenting the babies to their grandfather, who due to gout, spent most of his days in the library, his foot resting on a stool.

'He's deuced strong! Look at him lift his head! And what lungs!' George Ellacombe exclaimed as Peter bawled.

'You are going to have to learn to lower your volume, George. You're frightening him,' his wife said, soothing the infant.

'Don't be ridiculous, woman. Well, Charles, how was the journey? I still remember going out to India when Clementine was a small baby. Not one of my favourite memories, I can tell you.'

'Nonsense! You hardly cast eyes on the poor child the whole trip,' countered his wife.

Charles smiled. 'I must admit it wasn't the most enjoyable of experiences.'

'Well, at least you'll have a more peaceful journey on the way back,' said Mrs Ellacombe, delighted that Clementine and the children would be living at Coppins for the foreseeable future.

The hubbub brought Claudia down from her room. She had returned the previous day and glided in just as her mother was happily mentioning that she had been invited to spend the New Year as a house-guest of Alexander's sister-in-law, Dulcie, the younger Countess of Moundsmere.

Clementine rose and the sisters embraced, and smiling with joy their mother said how wonderful it was that they were all together for Christmas.

'But where's Timmy?' asked Clementine. 'The twins have been looking forward to meeting their uncle.'

Charles noticed Claudia throw her eyes up.

'Aunt Meg picked him up from school with Rupert and took him back to town for a few days. They're due in an hour or so,' said Mrs Ellacombe.

Later, when Charles and Clementine were dressing for dinner, he confessed his relief at being so readily accepted into the family.

Clementine's smile masked her own misgivings, for she was conscious of the effort her mother had made. Also of the faint undertones of disapproval in her father's ostensibly congenial conversation. It seemed ironic to her that it was really the twins who had broken the ice; their grandparents' delight in them had given the delusion of intimacy. For Charles's sake she really wanted her parents to like him. If they only knew how much they owed him!

'What did you think of Claudia?' she said.

'I can understand how she managed to sweep FitzPatrick off his feet when he first met her. She's certainly very beautiful, but though I've hardly exchanged two words with her I don't think the two of us will find much in common.'

They were eight for dinner with Mrs Ellacombe's sister and Timmy and Rupert, who arrived shortly before they sat down. The conversation was lively and there was lots of laughter as the youngsters related some of the pranks they had got up to during the Michaelmas term. Clementine had not seen her aunt since Claudia's wedding and was sorry to learn that Cousin Philip, Rupert's older brother, had kept his promise and enlisted in the Army the day after his eighteenth birthday.

'He's so young,' she said.

'Well, ever since that dreadful woman stuck a white feather on him, when he was barely seventeen, he's been determined. He's in the Artillery and should be going out after Christmas,' said Aunt Meg. Her tone was such that she might have been describing a new school. Clementine wondered how she really felt.

' … and my poor devil of a husband,' she continued, 'is, at this very moment, cruising somewhere in the Mediterranean, bound for Egypt, no doubt bored to tears with all those pretty nurses I know to be on board.' She threw Charles a meaningful glance and he smiled.

'Well, Matrons do have a rather chastening influence, so I expect the Christmas festivities are well under control.'

'That's a comfort to know.'

Claudia turned to Clementine. 'Your Matron was a bit slipshod, wasn't she?'

Clementine blushed and there was an awkward moment which was saved by Timmy enquiring where Jack, his terrier, was. They'd been ushered into dinner so quickly after arriving he'd only just noticed his absence. Everyone looked blank except for Claudia.

'He's in the kitchen, drying out by the range. I asked Best to give him a bath.'

'How many times have I told you not to interfere,' said Timmy crossly, jumping up. 'He's getting old and it's too cold for him to have a bath.' He excused himself and sped out of the room.

'I understand Alexander is out in the Middle East?' said Aunt Meg to Claudia.

'Yes, he's with General Allenby.'

'He would have been one of those who rode into Jerusalem,' said Brigadier Ellacombe.

'How exciting. When did you last see him, Claudia?'

'Not since June. He came back from France and went straight off to North Africa. We only had one night.'

'Sounds familiar. Uncle Harry was sent to Africa the week after we married. I can sympathise.'

'Yes, it's been hard on poor Claudia,' said Mrs Ellacombe. 'I know she misses Alexander terribly.'

'I've been reading all about the campaign — they're calling it *the swan song of the British horse-soldier*,' said the brigadier. 'It's all been achieved under the most appalling conditions — sweltering heat, and little or no water. But at least Alexander realised his dream of charging with sword in hand.'

Charles was pleased to hear that FitzPatrick and Claudia had seemingly consummated their marriage, and he glanced at Clementine wondering whether her expression might betray her thoughts, but her face remained impassive.

'Do you hear much from him?' Charles couldn't resist asking.

'If he's anything like Harry, very little,' smiled Aunt Meg.

Claudia twisted her wedding ring. 'What do you suppose, when most of the Service mail ends up on the seabed.'

'Let's not upset ourselves by thinking of the Germans,' said Mrs Ellacombe. 'You're very quiet, darling,' she said, turning to Clementine. 'I'm sure you must be pooped after such a journey with the babies.'

Again Clementine felt Charles's eyes on her and she gave him a fleeting smile before answering. 'Well, our stay in London did much to revive us, but I think we're both feeling a little jaded, Charles especially. He's not used to the twins in large doses.'

'Well, now that you're home you can rest all you like. It's only two months since you gave birth. It takes time for your body to recover. I'm sure Charles will agree. Anyway, you're not to worry about Charlotte and Peter. I can help Danielle. I mean to enjoy my grandchildren. I know only too well how short childhood is.'

'I'll second that,' said Aunt Meg.

'Has Papa shown you the article the local paper did on the children, darling? It was blazoned across the front page — *Twins born on Western Front!* '

'Give me a chance, woman, they've barely been back five minutes,' bellowed the brigadier, who had wanted to show Clementine himself.

Timmy returned with Jack in his arms. He placed him in front of the log fire and told him to stay. 'Yes, I pinned a copy of it on the war board at school,' he said.

Clementine smiled, but for some reason she didn't have time to fathom out, she was not pleased.

'Actually the reporter telephoned yesterday,' said her father. 'He's keen to do a follow-up feature, take a photograph of you all.'

'Really! I don't think so, Papa.'

'Why on earth not? It's good for morale. People are interested. I'm always being asked how my grandchildren are. Someone in the House even enquired after them the other day.'

'Lady Moundsmere wrote such a charming letter after reading it,' said Mrs Ellacombe. 'I hadn't realised that Alexander and his brother were twins. She said they run in the family. Her husband was one too.'

'So there's a possibility we might have another set when you and Alexander get cracking,' said the brigadier to Claudia.

Clementine was barely conscious of her racing heart and erratic breathing; the room was closing in, spinning like a top, gathering momentum. As she tried to regain her composure she felt something brush against her hand.

'Oh dear, Clementine's spilled her wine. Ring for Best, Timmy.'

Her mother's voice, with its note of panic, penetrated her consciousness and she found herself staring at the red stain on the damask cloth. Clumsily she started to mop it up, and found Charles at her side helping her to her feet.

'If you'll excuse us, I'm going to take Clementine upstairs. She's utterly exhausted.'

'Never could take her drink,' said Claudia in an aside to her aunt.

Mrs Ellacombe became agitated. 'Oh dear, let me help. I thought she looked pale.'

Charles directed his mother-in-law to remain seated in the

same authoritative tone he used at work, but instead of taking offence she was impressed by his concern for her daughter's wellbeing.

When Clementine was safely tucked up in bed and propped against the pillows, Charles disappeared and returned with a glass of brandy.

'Drink this, it will make you feel better.'

She sipped it and felt it course its way down her throat. Charles sat on the bed and watched her.

'Are you really as calm as you seem, Charles?'

He took her hand. 'You must understand, Clementine, that there is no way FitzPatrick can prove those children are his.'

She started to protest but he cut her off. 'I don't deny he may suspect, we've always known that — but this business about twins proves nothing. For all he knows, I may have generations of them in my family too. Therefore if and when he should ever ask, which I somehow doubt, you will of course deny he has any connection to them.' He held her gaze and said pointedly. 'That is clear, isn't it?'

She nodded. The brandy made her feel stronger. She knew Charles was right. 'Forgive me, it was such a shock. I always assumed that Patrick was Alexander's older brother.'

Charles put his arm around her shoulders. 'There is no reason for you to be frightened. Now who is this Douglas fellow they were talking about downstairs when I fetched your drink? Would it be the aviator you told me about?'

'Piers?'

'That's the one. It appears that Claudia has invited him for Boxing Day.'

# 17

Thinking it could prove beneficial, keeping on good terms with Alexander's best friend, Claudia had pressed Piers to join them on Boxing Day. He was about to decline, having received a rather more appealing invitation, when she mentioned that Clementine and her husband would be there. His curiosity got the better of him, for he had often wondered what sort of man Clementine had married and more importantly, whether she was happy.

From what Piers had learned from Claudia, coupled with Alexander's confession, he was expecting to find some middle-aged academic, whom she had married to escape from an unsavoury relationship. So when he was finally introduced to Captain Hamilton and found him not only neither old nor stuffy, but striking in both looks and manner, he was convinced that it had to be the medic Clementine had mentioned; the one Alexander hadn't believed existed. He thanked God that she had come to her senses and gone back and married him.

After luncheon the younger members went for a walk, leaving the brigadier to have a nap and Mrs Ellacombe and her sister to catch up on family gossip.

It was a cold day but the brightness of the sky with the sun shining gave an illusion of high summer. The crisp wind did much to revive them from the dulling effects of the heavy meal and wine. They started out together, but parted when Piers and Claudia paused to light cigarettes. Timmy and Rupert threw a stick for Jack, who was excited at being out in the clement air, and before long the threesome disappeared into the woods, leaving the stragglers to wend their way back across the fields.

'I'm so glad you were able to come. I fear I should have died of boredom otherwise,' Claudia said to Piers as she leaned against a tree, sheltering her cigarette from the wind.

'Thank you for inviting me. It's good to be here.'

'So what do you make of Charles?'

'He seems a decent sort of chap, and they certainly seem happy.'

Claudia looked ahead to where Charles was helping Clementine over a stile and watched as they strolled off hand-in-hand, talking incessantly.

'Yes, don't they. They arrive home with two screaming brats, disrupting the entire household, and everyone welcomes them with open arms; and he's so in love with her it makes me sick!'

Piers turned to her with a look divided between disdain and amusement.

'My, you do sound bitter! Could it be that you've just been usurped as Papa's little girl?'

'Don't be ridiculous! I was usurped, as you put it, years ago when Timmy came along. No, I resent the time Clementine and Charles have had together. No wonder they're so close. Alexander and I have had little or no time together as husband and wife.'

'And that was a disaster, from what I heard,' said Piers pointedly.

She wheeled round. 'He told you! The bastard!'

Piers said nothing. He'd known Claudia for some time and he was aware that her reasons for inviting him today were self-serving; that he might put a good word in for her. He smiled to himself, wondering what she would say if she knew he was only here because of Clementine.

Claudia stared at him, tears welling in her eyes. 'Well, he was wrong ... he just wouldn't listen to me. It was almost as if he wanted an excuse.'

Piers didn't know whether he believed her or not, but in view of Alexander's infatuation for Clementine, it was probable that he hadn't given her a fair hearing. Whatever, Claudia looked so pitiable that he gave her his handkerchief and a bracing squeeze on the shoulder.

'Come now, I'm sure everything will work out. People say things in the heat of the moment that they later regret. Just give it time. Alexander isn't inhuman — I'm sure he'll come round.'

'If only I could believe you. It's terrible having to lie to everyone, pretend everything is fine when the truth is we have no contact, except through solicitors — though he did come to see me in June when he didn't really need to.'

She dried her eyes and returned Piers's handkerchief. 'He looked haggard and depressed, and for a moment I felt he wanted me — but that was six months ago. Six months is a long time. I suppose that's what makes me angry with Charles and Clementine. Of course they're happy, they've been together! Just give me six weeks, six days even. I could have made Alexander happy, I know I could. It's so unfair.'

Piers smiled. 'You know what they say, all's fair in love and war.'

'And what is that supposed to mean?'

'God knows' It had just rolled off his tongue, and now he wished he had given more thought to the glib words.

It was not the only discourse he was to have that afternoon. After the walk he took the opportunity of having a few minutes alone with Clementine. 'May I come and see the babies?' he asked springing up the stairs behind her. He followed her along the corridor, thinking the little extra weight she had put on not only suited her but was another indication she was relaxed and happy.

The twins were enjoying a rare sleep when they entered the yellow-painted nursery. Piers tiptoed across the wooden floor to where they lay side by side in their cots. He stood spellbound as he looked upon their tiny faces, each topped with a shock of black hair.

'Gosh, they look so tiny and fragile.'

'It's easy to be deceived, but they are tough little mites and rather strong-willed. As a rule they tend to spend more time awake than asleep.'

'So Claudia was saying.'

She grinned. 'I think my sister's idea of a baby is some angelic creature who coos and gurgles on demand, and never cries.'

Piers chuckled, his eyes fixed on Peter who was sucking his thumb. 'My sister's child was bald for the first year, looked like a little old man.'

'Oh dear, it won't be long before they're in full cry,' said Clementine, watching Charlotte's tiny fist find its way to her mouth. 'Nearly time for their feed.'

'They are perfectly lovely — you've a fine family,' he said, holding her eyes for a moment.

'Alexander told you, didn't he?' she heard herself say. There was a moment's silence before he nodded slowly, and she glanced away, feeling choked and unable to speak. She had suspected as much.

She felt Piers touch her arm. He smiled warmly. 'I wanted to talk to you, if only to tell you how glad I am to find you so happy.'

Her eyes looked sad. 'Thank you. I'm sorry I had to involve you, but I didn't know how else to contact him, and I knew I could trust you.'

He made a small gesture with his hand. 'That's what friends are for.'

She kissed him on the cheek. 'Thank you.' She knew it would be better to leave it there but she had to know. 'How did he take it?'

Piers threw his head back in a dramatic gesture. 'One could say he was rather shocked. Truth to tell, we actually came to blows over it! Had to be dragged apart.'

Her knuckles whitened as she gripped Charlotte's cot. 'What happened? Tell me.'

Piers thought he had said more than he should, but on the other hand he felt felt that she should be warned. 'It happened last June. He said he needed to talk to me so we went out for a bite to eat. I had your letter with me, meaning to give it to him, but before I got a chance, he announced that you and he were in love. Frankly, I was staggered, Clementine. I suppose I said some pretty harsh things. I don't often lose my temper. Anyway, when I gave him your letter he flipped, lost all reason. I'd never seen him like it before.'

The colour drained from Clementine's face.

'Clemmie darling, don't look so distressed. It's all in the past and let's face it, it's Alexander's own stupid fault if he's gone and got himself hurt. He was in no position to fall in love with you in the first place, understandable though it might be.'

She placed her hands over her eyes, wanting to say, 'I loved him, Piers, I still do,' but the words were spoken in the silence of her turbulent mind.

'I didn't mean to hurt him, Piers; there was no other way.'

He took her hand. 'I believe you.'

There was much he wanted to add, but they were interrupted by a sudden cry. Peter had kicked his way free of his blankets, his

205

features screwed in anger. In the adjacent cot Charlotte began to wriggle and it was clear that in no time at all, the twins would be screaming in chorus. Danielle appeared in the doorway with an armful of freshly laundered nappies, and she smiled shyly as Piers moved aside for her to pass.

'I'd better go down,' he said, making for the doorway where he paused with a thoughtful expression, watching Clementine comfort her son.

Tea was already in progress when Clementine reappeared. Piers was discussing aerial combat, much to the delight of the two youngsters, and Mrs Ellacombe glanced up from pouring tea to enquire why she hadn't brought the babies down.

'They're restless and I thought it would be more peaceful without them.' Her mother was always keen to pick them up and she knew it wouldn't be long before they recognised their grandmother's voice.

'I imagine life will be rather quiet when you return to France, Charles,' said Claudia.

He laughed. 'Meaning that yours won't. Well, I did tell Clementine to warn you all before we arrived.'

'I don't know what you're talking about,' said Piers. 'I've just seen the darlings and thought they looked perfect angels.'

Claudia snorted. 'I don't think I've ever seen them without their mouths open.'

'God help any poor children you might have, Claudia,' put in the brigadier as he helped himself to another slice of Christmas cake.

'Danielle seems a capable girl,' said Aunt Meg. 'You were lucky to find her, Clemmie. My house is undermanned. It's such a trial trying to find staff these days.'

Throughout the meal Clementine said little, unable to

concentrate on anything other than her conversation with Piers. She was now even more afraid of the time her path would surely cross with Alexander's. She was desperate to talk to Piers again and the opportunity presented itself when he announced that he was going to check the levels on his car, and went outside to the stable-block where he had left the vehicle. He was just returning the dipstick to the oil sump when she appeared.

'It's not frightfully reliable,' he said, wiping his hands as she admired the car. 'It's been using a lot of oil of late. However, it appears to be behaving itself today.' He turned to her. 'I was rather hoping you'd come out, for I just wanted to have a quiet word. I'm concerned that I may have upset you by what I said earlier about Alexander.'

She knew this was her chance to put things to rights. She just needed to keep her emotions in check. 'Well, there's nothing to worry about Piers. I've got over him, and I won't let anything jeopardise the happiness of Charles or the children. However, I have to confess I am rather worried about encountering him again, when he returns. I had hoped that he would leave me in peace, but from what you said in the nursery, I'm not so confident.'

Piers looked thoughtfully at her, wishing he could see her face more clearly. She sounded convincing, but was the truth concealed in the gathering darkness?

'You may put your mind at rest Clemmie, for the chances are that I will see Alexander before you, and you can count on me to tell him in no uncertain terms to leave you alone. But I really think you're worrying about nothing. Why should he pursue the matter now that you're married with a family?' He snapped the bonnet shut. 'I spoke to Claudia earlier and have every confidence that she will put matters right with Alexander.'

This time, he caught the fleeting shadow that flitted across her face. Let's hope for all your sakes that she is successful, he thought.

*

1917 had not been a good year for the Allies, so when General Allenby's Army marched triumphantly into Jerusalem on 9 December it was indeed a time for celebration.

Alexander was proud to be part of the success. The operation had taken months of preparation, then hard fighting, so when he and his fellow officers sat down to Christmas dinner, it didn't take long for them all to get into the festive spirit.

The Officers' Mess was part of a hotel the Army had requisitioned in the wealthy quarter of Jerusalem. Everyone was in dress uniform and seated at the long table in the marbled room. When the colonel toasted 'the beginning of the end' their cheers could be heard way down the street.

'Now for something I know you've all eagerly been awaiting,' he continued, beckoning to an orderly at the back of the room. 'The mail bag!' And to even greater cheers Father Christmas appeared from behind two enormous columns and began delving into his sack. 'Patience, everyone, there's something for you all,' he boomed above the rumpus.

One of their number was coerced into bashing out a few tunes on the piano and soon several officers, who were well on their way to being drunk, soothed away the months of tension by joining in the lyrics with gusto.

It was the first mail Alexander had received in months and he sifted through the envelopes with the same feeling of anticipation that would always result in the lowering of his spirits. Ridiculous though it was, a part of him still awaited a letter from Clementine telling him that it had all been a plot to separate them; that she wasn't really married. But though it still hurt, it was nothing like those early days when he had tried to drink away the pain on the outward voyage. Fortunately no one questioned his uncommunicativeness, assuming that like so many, he was suffering from mal de mer.

Since arriving in Africa there had been little time to focus on anything but the Campaign, and conscious that just one slip could result in the loss of countless lives, he managed to pull himself together. Though the past six months had been restorative, he was nonetheless aware of a rawness that lingered in his chest and had yet to heal.

Piers had been right when he told Clementine that Alexander would leave her alone, though wrong to raise Claudia's hopes for a reconciliation. Alexander wanted no association whatsoever with any member of the Ellacombe family. He intended to avoid them all, wanting no reminder of *her*. On his next visit to England, he had decided to start divorce proceedings; there was no longer any reason to delay the issue. He knew the sooner his connection with the Ellacombes was severed, the sooner he would be able to put it all behind him and get on with his life.

He opened the first envelope and sighed. It was from his brother's widow, Dulcie, wishing him a Merry Christmas and informing him that she intended inviting Claudia for New Year celebrations. However, his frustration lasted but seconds for he refused to let thought of either sister ruin what had so far been a splendid day.

There was a card from Piers and a note saying he had shot down a German aircraft in the Solent, and another from his grandmother, in her arthritic scrawl, sending her love and felicitations. She expected to be spending Christmas, as she had every year since war began, with Dulcie and members of her family. He smiled fondly, positive that she would soon be writing to tell him what a taxing time it had been, and that next year she'd be staying home.

' … *but it is always a delight to see young William. Patrick would have been so proud of him. Such a serious little chap for someone so young, but I am sure that it is because of the times we live in. Anyway, my dear, it goes without saying that I shall be thinking of you on Christmas Day and will make sure to drink your health, though assuredly it will be tea cups, not glasses we raise! Well, my dear grandson, let us hope that next year we will all be celebrating at Grangefield like we used to.*
    *Take care of yourself,*
    *Your ever-loving grandmama.*

Below, she had struggled to squeeze in a postscript by condensing her letters.

*I have just learned that Claudia's sister has recently given birth to twins. I shall drop her a line welcoming her to the club!*

Alexander stared blindly at the card, barely conscious of anything but the words he had just read. He felt as if he had been shot. Staggering to his feet, he rushed outside where, after taking several deep gulps of the cold air, he disappeared into the night.

# 18

A few days into the New Year, Clementine knew she was pregnant again. The shock was tempered by the knowledge that she would be giving Charles a child of his own, something she sensed was of importance to him. Ideally she would have preferred to wait until her body had fully recovered from the twins' birth, but as Charles would shortly be returning to France, she suspected the news would make him feel more secure; believe that she was committed to their marriage. Moreover, when she thought of what she owed him, it seemed but a small price to pay.

However, not all were delighted, namely Mrs Ellacombe. 'It's far too soon,' she said to her husband. 'The brute! Three children in less than a year — and he a doctor! You'd have thought he would have known better. The poor girl's barely over having the twins, and she's not strong. And what if he gets himself killed? What sort of a life will she have, a widow with three small children?'

The brigadier was careful to conceal his own misgivings. He had become rather fond of Charles; he admired his quick brain and found him to be a good conversationalist and extremely knowledgeable.

'Well, my dear, these things happen in the best of families. I've lost count of how many children Queen Victoria had but am certain, had it not been for Albert dying, the old girl would have had plenty more.'

'George! Don't be vulgar! Perhaps it *was* once normal to

multiply like rabbits, but have you forgotten how many poor women die in childbirth? I certainly don't want my daughter to become a wreck before she's thirty!'

Charles was not oblivious to his mother-in-law's wrath, but as her husband was largely responsible for the convivial atmosphere of the house, he ignored it. He was delighted about the new child and believed that as long as Clementine took adequate rest, there should be nothing to worry about. After all, she was young and healthy.

Claudia returned from her visit to Mannerling, Alexander's childhood home where she had seen in the New Year, looking rather subdued. The house-party had hardly been the dazzling gathering she had imagined, just old Lady Moundsmere and Dulcie's elderly parents, not forgetting the precious little heir whose idea of fun was to shut himself up in the library with a book — that is, when he wasn't showing everyone how clever he was by memorising the flags and capitals of the world. Though she would never admit it, she had been quite relieved when the visit came to an end and she was able to return to her parents' less grand but infinitely warmer abode.

Back home she embellished her stay, making it sound a great success. However, Charles was not deceived. 'I suspect she was bored to tears,' he said to Clementine as he sat in bed watching her brush her hair. Clementine glanced at his reflection in the dressing-table mirror.

'I doubt they had a lot in common. I've heard that Dulcie is quite an intellectual; she does Greek translations and reviews literary works.'

Charles smiled knowingly. Though he thought Claudia beautiful she did not strike him as having made the most of her education. She lived on the capital of her looks, and he imagined she must have felt out of place in a house where physical attributes meant little. 'Has she ever mentioned FitzPatrick to you? It's hard to know, without actually asking her outright, whether there is a rift or not. Clearly your parents have no idea there is anything amiss, if indeed there is.'

'She has said nothing to me,' said Clementine in a small voice, quite sure that if they were back together Claudia would have been bubbling with enthusiasm and planning all manner of ways to spend Alexander's money. Instead she assumed her sister was having to cope with the allowance he had afforded her, enough to cover general living expenses but not a lot else.

'It still bothers you to hear his name, doesn't it?' Charles probed gently.

'On the contrary, I'm getting used to it.'

Charles wished he could see her face, but her head was lowered as she searched in a drawer for something. He watched as she stood and removed her dressing-gown, and consciously made an effort to suppress thoughts that throbbed uncomfortably near the surface.

'Though I still wish you'd take us with you when you return,' she said, sitting beside him. 'I could rent a house on the coast. I'm sure it would be quite safe, and you could visit whenever you are free.'

'You know that's impossible, and can you not imagine what your mother would think of me?' His voice did not betray his faltering confidence. Would she ever love him like he loved her, like she had loved FitzPatrick? Was it only his protection she needed? But then he remembered she was pregnant and relaxed. 'You never know, with the arrival of the Americans the war could be over by summer, and perhaps I might be able to get back for the confinement.'

'I hope so. You'd have thought their arrival would have given everyone a sense of hope. There's such an air of desperation about since they raised the age of conscription to fifty. I suppose it was the final straw.' She gave a weary sigh as she began to wonder how it would all end; this unsettled world she had brought her children into.

*

With Charles's leave almost up, Claudia decided to cut short her stay and travel with him as far as London. She'd had enough of the countryside and planned to remain in Town for the foreseeable future. 'There's so little to do here and all my friends are there,' she announced when the family were gathered one evening in the library.

Mrs Ellacombe lifted her head from a magazine in which she had been catching up on the latest baby carriages.

'I've a better suggestion. Why not leave a couple of days early and take Clementine with you. You could do a show or something. I'm sure she would benefit from having a break.'

'I couldn't possibly go whilst I'm nursing the twins.' Clementine protested.

'I think your mother is right,' said Charles. 'A few days away would do you good, and bearing in mind your condition, I believe it would be best if the children are hand fed from now on. It will be better all round. Not only will it ensure they wont go hungry it will also mean we can be independent of them.'

'I have to agree,' put in Mrs Ellacombe gently, seeing her daughter's look of dismay. You now have your unborn child to consider, as well as Charlotte and Peter.

'I don't know how can you suggest it. You must know bottle fed babies don't thrive as well.'

'That was due to lack of hygiene, dear. It's a thing of the past; people are better informed nowadays. I was in the chemist in Wareham, recently, and they had a display of modern feeding equipment, which attracted my attention. I had a word with the assistant. She said there is nothing to compare with the Allenbury, which, unlike the old feeders is easy to clean and completely safe. Charles is right to be worried, you're too thin as it is, you'll be nothing but skin and bones if you continue to nurse the babies yourself. Even I know the early months of a pregnancy are vital to the wellbeing of an infant. You need ample rest and nourishment. How is that possible if you persist.'

Clementine glanced from her mother to Charles. For once they were in total accord and, angry though she felt, she knew she was in a untenable position. Charles would assuredly decide that she put Alexander's childrens' welfare before his own, if she refused.

'I'm more than capable of helping Danielle. I don't suppose you remember, being only five months' old at the time but your nanny, suffered so badly with sea sickness, on the trip out to India, I had to take sole charge of you. And believe me, that was no mean feat on the high seas.'

'She was a complete disaster if I remember,' said George. 'For once she got there she couldn't acclimatise — had to send her home.'

'It's true. The poor girl wept at the prospect of another voyage but she was useless in the heat. Anyway the point I'm making is, that any fears you may have about leaving the twins, are unfounded.' She looked at Charles who nodded and then back to Clementine. 'So, it's decided then,' she continued. 'You go to London with Charles and Claudia, and Danielle and I will look after the twins.'

Charles was grateful for his mother-in-law's support, and

delighted he and Clementine would have a few days to themselves before he left. He looked through *The Times* to see what entertainment was on offer. Claudia was surprisingly enthusiastic too, knowing it would give her the opportunity to show off her home.

'We can go shopping,' she said to her sister, already planning to persuade her to buy some new clothes. She once, a few years ago, had covered Clementine's eyes with her hands and asked her to describe what she was wearing. Guessing she had thrown on the first things she could find, she wasn't surprised when she got it wrong. It seemed to Claudia there was still something of that child in Clementine and she felt it high time her sister take her wardrobe in hand. Despite the war, fashions were changing all the time, and some of her clothes were positively ancient. Besides, the thought of meeting any of her friends with a country bumpkin in tow was not appealing. She could well imagine their sniggers.

'You need to brighten yourself up,' she said. 'Or you never know, Charles might fall for some pretty nurse.'

'Really, is that so?' said Charles, who had overheard. ' Actually, I rather put more importance on what's inside than out.'

'How perfectly droll! No wonder you became a surgeon. So you're more attracted by good intestines than a perfect complexion.' Though she laughed, Claudia wondered if his remark held undertones for over the Christmas period she had tried flirting with him, purely for amusement and to relieve the boredom. However, he had been infuriatingly indifferent to her charms and she had dismissed him as a bore whose idea of excitement was spending an afternoon poring over Homer. In fact now she came to think of it, he would have fitted in beautifully at Mannerling.

Clementine was surprised that Charles seemed keen to stay

with Claudia instead of Grace and Alfred. He said it would be quieter, having no children about, but she did wonder if it was some kind of test, and was careful not to object. She was quite sure, despite what her sister would have everyone believe, that Alexander had never spent the night there and that she would find nothing belonging to him that might upset her. And thankfully she was right, for apart from a framed wedding photograph, exactly like the one on the piano at Coppins, there was nothing in the place that indicated Alexander had ever been there. This, and the fact that he moved in different circles, eased some of her misgivings. Perhaps Charles was right when he said the chances of their paths crossing were slim.

Since she was a late riser, they saw little of Claudia during the day, for Charles was always eager to be up and about. Having lived in London before the war there was lots he wanted to do. Intent on writing some articles in the quiet period ahead, he spent several hours researching in various libraries, leaving Clementine free to meet up with Grace. Unlike Claudia who felt she should buy couture, she showed Clementine where to purchase fabric of high quality that didn't cost a fortune.

'I can see you're going to be busy during the winter months,' said Charles, glancing at her purchases one afternoon. They had arranged a rendezvous at Buszards, a fashionable place for tea. Claudia had arrived shortly before Clementine and snatching up the patterns, she gave each a cursory glance as she flicked through them.

'You can't be serious!' she sniffed. ' You surely don't intend to make your own clothes.'

Clementine smiled. She had discovered an ex-seamstress who had been forced to set up a business at home in the village, in order to help support her family in the absence of her husband.

However, she had no intention of telling her sister, who would probably be just as scathing. She turned to Charles, changing the subject. 'Grace sends her love but had to get back to prepare the evening meal.'

'I'd sooner starve than have to learn to cook,' said Claudia.

'You've obviously never gone hungry,' said Charles, watching her toy with a scone on her plate.

'I don't intend to.'

'As well you married a wealthy man!' There followed a moment of uncomfortable silence before he lightened the mood by regaling them with a description of a smart, fur-coated woman, laden with jewels, that he had encountered in the library that morning.

'She took command of a rather ingratiating assistant asking in a fatigued voice for 'something droll to read'. Claudia laughed, though she failed to see what was funny.

'I've done some shopping too,' he continued. 'I came across an antiquarian bookshop and found this.' He produced a history of Sherborne from his pocket. 'Someone said it's Timmy's birthday next week. I thought he might like it.'

'Perfect! He'll love it,' said Claudia, catching Clementine's eye with a knowing smile. It was the last thing their young brother would want to read.

'I'm sure he will be very touched that you thought of him,' said Clementine.

'Next time I'm back I'd like to pay a visit. Perhaps we could take him out for lunch? It would be good to see the old place again. I can scarcely believe a couple of my old masters are still there. They must be positively ancient.'

'So I suppose it goes without saying that Peter will go there,' said Claudia for want of something to say.

'Naturally. What about you? Where will you send your sons,

assuming, that is, that you have any. Eton?'

She hesitated a moment. 'I don't really know. Patrick, Alexander's twin, went to Eton, but Alexander went to Rugby. For some reason their parents decided to split them up. Maybe they thought it would make them more independent. Obviously it's not a decision you'll have to make.'

Clementine fidgeted uncomfortably, praying for a time when she would be able to think about Alexander and the children without her stomach twisting in knots. But maybe that was her penance. She began to gather her shopping bags.

'I think we should make a move. The restaurant is booked for seven and we have to get ready.'

Mrs Ellacombe had sent them back with a large hamper of freshly shot game and various other foods of the sort that were becoming more difficult to find in London. However, much to the dismay of Claudia's cook, who was delighted to have something decent to get her creative hands on, Charles took them out to dinner each evening and then onto the theatre or a show. On his last night, before returning to the flat, Claudia finally succeeded in persuading him to escort them to a popular nightclub where Ragtime was all the rage. She knew several people, but neither they, the smoke, nor the noise were congenial to Charles. After suffering for half an hour he began to get restless, and Clementine sighed. Claudia looked happier than she had for ages amongst these strange people, who seemed intent on making merry.

'Clementine is tired and not feeling well, Claudia. We're ready to leave.'

'But we *can't* go yet. Brackstone has just ordered champagne for everyone. You'll be most offended, won't you, darling?' she said to the effeminate-looking man beside her.

'Certainly will. Simply won't do, old girl. The night has not yet begun.'

Charles felt inclined to leave her, but his sense of responsibility would not allow this, and with a sigh of resignation he accepted that he would have to endure this place a little longer.

Clementine smiled with quiet amusement and braced herself. It just so happened she really was feeling unwell, but as yet hadn't mentioned it to Charles, hoping it would pass. It had started about an hour before when she got a mild stitch. At first it hadn't bothered her but in recent minutes it had become more like cramp. Knowing how much Claudia would resent an early departure had made her decide to keep it to herself. However, no sooner had the cork shot across the room than she was forced to speak up.

There was little conversation on the journey home, and upon arrival Claudia told Charles to ring for the maid if they required anything. Bidding them goodnight she promptly retired to bed. Clementine looked at Charles, her face tense and anxious. She had never felt like this with Charlotte and Peter. Hearing a small cry escape her lips, he swiftly carried her upstairs.

Charles informed Claudia the next morning that Clementine had miscarried in the night. To her credit, she looked remorseful. 'I'll go and see her,' she muttered.

'No. She's sleeping, she needs to rest. I've managed to delay my departure until the weekend, so I shall be able to look after her.'

'What do you think caused it?'

'These things happen in the early weeks.' His face was taut and grey.

'If you want my honest opinion, Charles, I think it's probably a blessing. I know Mummy was worried about her having another baby so soon — and besides, it's not as if it's your first-born!'

Charles stared at her, too stunned by the extent of his pain to reply.

Physically Clementine recovered quickly, but mentally it was harder, more from guilt than grief. She secretly wondered if the baby had known his mother hadn't really wanted him — not yet.

Last year when she had been alone and pregnant she had prayed for a miscarriage but the twins had gripped tenaciously to life. It seemed ironic that it should be the child whose welcome and future would have been assured, that was lost. She was able to see through Charles's outer shell and knew he was more upset than he would admit, and she was suddenly glad he was returning to France, and not to Coppins and Peter and Charlotte. He needed time to heal and so did she.

By Saturday, Clementine was recovered enough to see Charles off at Charing Cross station. An old hansom cab took them the short journey, rattling and jingling and reminding them of days past. The driver, unable to get through the crowds near the front entrance, dropped them a few hundred feet away. Charles had barely paid the cabbie when a large convoy of Red Cross ambulances, driven by young females, came blaring from the station laden with new casualties. The sudden hush was followed by loud cheering, and the old flower women, sitting by the entrance with their colourful baskets, threw some blooms into the backs of the lorries where soldiers lay, strapped onto bunk-style stretchers.

'God bless you, loves!'

'It must lift their spirits to get a welcome like that,' said Clementine as the last ambulance disappeared around the corner and the crowds began to disperse.

'How long before they are forgotten heroes?' said Charles, grabbing her hand and helping her through the crowd towards the station buildings.

They found the right platform. There were other officers; some standing in groups, others saying goodbye privately to their wives and sweethearts. Christmas was over, and they were returning to their world, a place far removed from cosy drawing rooms and Yule logs. Clementine glanced down the platform where a crowd had congregated outside the gates. They had no platform tickets and were making their farewells as best they could in the bottleneck. Tommies in newly laundered khaki stood with young children tucked under one arm, wives in the other, giving them a last hug and kiss.

Clementine watched wistfully, involuntarily recalling her parting with Alexander almost a year before. How oblivious they had been to everyone. No one else had mattered. And that last kiss. Even now, the memory of it made her tremble and her eyes prick with tears. It *had* been their last. Her face was flushed with guilt when she turned back to Charles, fearful that he could read her thoughts. Suddenly the final order to board was announced and in wild chaos, the Tommies rushed through the barrier, their heavy boots clattering on the platforms as they chased each other for a seat. Swiftly Charles lowered his head and kissed Clementine. She held him tightly, saying, 'I wish you weren't going.'

'So do I, but I hope it won't be for too long.' He squeezed her hands. 'Goodbye, darling, and take good care of yourself.'

With a sinking feeling, Clementine watched him climb aboard. There was bang after bang as all the doors slammed shut, and hundreds of heads tried to squeeze through the windows for a last look and a wave. A loud hiss of steam heralded the train's departure, and amidst a chorus of yells and cheers, it pulled out of the station leaving a crowd stripped of brave smiles, wiping tears away. Clementine walked out into the bleak winter afternoon feeling more alone than she ever had before.

# 19

Best was giving a last shine to the letterbox, and looking forward to a cup of tea with his wife, when a car pulled in from the road and swept up the drive. No one was expected and he guessed it was someone asking for directions. There were few road signs about and people often got lost. He strolled towards the old carriage lamp beneath which the vehicle had stopped.

'Good evening Best,' said the driver as he threw the door open and climbed out.

Best stared at the tall lean figure, his bristly moustache twitching in surprise. 'Goodness gracious, it's Major FitzPatrick!. Come in, come in. I thought you were out in the desert, sir.'

Alexander followed him into the hall and as he placed his swagger-stick on the rosewood side table, he explained how he came to be back in the country. 'They've sent sixty thousand of us back,' he said handing Best his Barbour.

'I suppose it's because of the German Offensive they're all talking about, sir.'

'The threat of it. Anyway, I think, what with more and more Americans arriving, each and every one of us is resolved to win this war once and for all. It's gone on far too long.'

'What was it like, sir — you know, out there in Africa? I should imagine it was quite different to what you've been used to.'

Alexander smiled. 'I confess, it was certainly more enjoyable, if that's the right word. For once it was real tactical warfare, nothing like the hell-hole of the Western Front.'

The large grandfather clock at the base of the stairs chimed six.

'My parents-in-law, Best — are they not at home?'

Best frowned. 'No, sir. They went to London yesterday and won't return till next week at the earliest. The brigadier's very busy at the moment with his work at Westminster, and I believe Mrs Ellacombe is going to spend a few days with her sister.'

'What a shame,' Alexander said, feigning surprise. 'I've been over to Bovington on military matters the past couple of days. I suppose I'm a bit out of touch. But not to worry, no doubt I shall see them in London. Actually, I was rather hoping for a bed for a night or two, but if it's a problem I can always put up at the local hotel.'

Best was predictably outraged at the suggestion. 'Sir, you'll do no such thing. We've a house full of empty beds, and your wife's room is always kept aired.'

Alexander smiled appreciatively, and cast another fleeting glance about. Where was she? Why hadn't she appeared? He felt a sinking feeling. *A house of empty beds.*

'So no one is at home then?' he said, conscious of the thread of tension in his voice.

'That is, apart from Miss Clementine, sir — or rather Mrs Hamilton as she is now, and of course the children. You won't have seen them, being on your travels like, but I warrant you'll soon be hearing them,' the man chuckled.

'And where is Miss Clementine?' He could not bring himself to use her married name. 'Is she in?' Perhaps she had seen him arrive and was hiding.

'She's at a Red Cross meeting, sir. Said she wouldn't be back till later.'

Alexander nodded. Perhaps it was for the best; it would give him time to prepare himself.

'You say the babies are here though?'

'Up in the nursery, sir. Mrs Hamilton brought a French girl back with her, very competent she is too, though her English isn't too hot.'

He saw Alexander glance towards the stairs. 'Let me take you up, sir, I expect you want to get to your room. I'll fetch your bags in a minute and move the car into the stable.' As they climbed the stairs he said that he would get Mrs Best to rustle him up something to eat.

'That's very kind, Best, but please tell her not to go to any trouble. I'm really not hungry. Perhaps just a bowl of soup.'

Best smiled knowingly. 'We'll see.' Reaching the landing he turned to Alexander. 'Perhaps you'd care to visit the nursery, sir? They're a bonny pair, the twins. I should imagine Danielle will soon be putting them down for the night.'

There was a moment's silence before Alexander nodded slowly. 'Yes, I would. I would like that very much!'

\*

The Red Cross meeting dragged on as one discussion followed another, and Clementine grew increasingly agitated about leaving Danielle alone to put the twins to bed. She had not anticipated it lasting quite so long, nor that when it finally ended, it would turn into a social gathering with refreshments. Dependent on a neighbour, Mrs Frobisher-Brown, for a lift, there was little she could do but smile politely. But it didn't stop her worrying, for she knew it wasn't easy trying to feed two hungry babies with one pair of hands.

It was well after seven before they got on the road and past eight when they reached Coppins. Mrs Frobisher-Brown, a nervous driver, rarely exceeded fifteen miles an hour. Her chauffeur had enlisted early in the war and, because she was so heavily involved in various charities, she had decided she had little choice but to get her own driving licence and learn to drive, which at seventy was no small achievement. She was an interesting woman and Clementine was very fond of her. However, after enduring her eternal chatter for the return trip it was a relief when she declined to break the journey. 'Thank you, but I must press on, my dear. I've an early start tomorrow.'

Without stopping to remove her coat, Clementine ran straight up to the nursery. The night candle and the glowing embers from the hearth provided enough light to reveal the twins lying still and content in their cribs; such a contrast to when in full cry demanding their feed. She crept softly across the room and gazed upon them, breathing in their delicious scent. Her heart swelled with love. They had brought monumental changes to her life, but she could never resent them and knew even at their worst she would walk on hot coals for them. Touching her fingers with her lips she brushed the kiss across their silky heads.

Hearing footsteps she turned with a ready smile to thank Danielle, but the shadowy figure, too tall, too male caused her heart to pound, her head to whirl. It couldn't be — but she knew it was.

Unable to speak or move she stared, trembling as he walked towards her, each step taking her back to where she had buried her pain. She knew what was coming, she had always known. He was so close, she could smell the faint scent of his skin; if she had reached out she could have touched him. Utterly helpless, she floated like a feather.

His eyes shining like ebony in the shadows were angry, bewildered. 'These are my children, aren't they, Clementine.' His voice was weary, as if he had travelled on a long journey.

Finally confronted by the nightmare she had lived with for months, she was unable to look at him. Alexander watched. For him her silence was proof enough and for a moment he was speechless. He really was a father. These children were his offspring; they had his blood coursing through their veins. He drew deep breaths trying to stay calm, but it wasn't enough, and gripped by the magnitude of what she had done something inside, fuelled by months of pain and frustration, snapped, and he took her by the shoulders and shook her. 'How could you,' he hissed. How could you. You know I'd have moved heaven and earth if you'd told me. You didn't give me a chance.' He pushed her away, frightened by the extent of his anger.

With shame Clementine lifted her eyes to his. Even in the shadows she could see his wretchedness.

'Why, Clementine? Tell me why!' He was silenced by a sudden cry from Peter's crib and watched in frustration as she settled the child down.

Realising they had to find another place else to talk, she directed him onto the landing where she paused, frantically wondering where she could take him without risk of being overheard. However, Alexander, impatient took command and pushed her into a nearby room. It was her bedroom and she pulled back.

'Have no fear, I only want to talk,' he said, the words cutting into her like an insult. The abrupt brightness of the electric light unveiled their faces and for a few seconds they stared at each other. Compelled by the force of his feelings, he turned away and strode over to the window, staring blindly into the darkness. It seemed a long while before he turned around, but when he did his voice was calmer.

'Surely you must have known that I would suspect. Why didn't you tell me, or is it because this man you've married thinks they are his?'

'How could you even think such a thing!'

'What do you expect me to think? All I know is that I obviously made you pregnant and rather than tell me, you chose to marry some other man. Why? Please, at least explain! You know damn well I'd never have turned my back on you.'

'Of course I knew. But surely you have not forgotten that you weren't mine to have? You already had a wife! Imagine the scandal and grief we would have brought to both our families. How, out of all that suffering, were we to have found happiness together? Tell me, Alexander! Tell me how that was possible.' The small strength left in her legs drained away and she sank onto the dressing-table stool.

He shook his head. 'It's not good enough, Clementine. Somehow we'd have found a way, but you chose to cut me out, and I don't know whether I can forgive you for that.' His words stung and there was a long silence.

'Piers mentioned that you were involved with this doctor before we met, is it true?' he said eventually.

She covered her face, her hands trembling. 'No, there was never anyone else.' She stared at the gold band on her finger, wondering what Charles would say about the situation. 'Deny it if FitzPatrick ever confronts you,' he had instructed. But it had been easy for him to say. For months she had lived in fear of Alexander's return, yet only now was she able to acknowledge that the person she had most been scared of was herself; deep down she had always known she could never deny Alexander the truth.

'Why should he say you were?'

'I didn't want any misunderstanding between us and made it up just in case he had romantic notions.'

'If that's the truth it certainly seems this Hamilton fellow turned up at a most opportune time.' The sarcasm was rich.

'He did, actually!' And though she didn't want to tell him, because she was ashamed, she felt he should know. Perhaps then he might understand how desperation had driven her.

'If it hadn't been for Charles we wouldn't be standing here now, neither would the children be sleeping safely next door.' Her quiet, desperate words left him in no doubt of what she meant. He stared at her, clearly shaken.

'Charles was the MO where I worked,' she went on. 'Our relationship was purely professional until the day he found me … ' Her voice died away.

Alexander lowered himself onto the window seat. 'Go on, I want to know.' He listened in silence to her confession. Its effect was instant and finally he began to understand the depths of her wretchedness and a changed picture began to emerge from the one he had painted. Charles Hamilton had actually been the Good Samaritan. Hard though it was to admit, he was clearly in the man's debt. Realising what her state of mind must have been, to drive her to such action was enormously painful for him, especially knowing that it had been through his own carelessness.

He looked at her afresh. She was very pale, as if she had been ill, and he could see how difficult it had been for her to tell him. He wanted to comfort her, but there was just one thing he needed to know, and which she had omitted to say. 'You said he married you because he felt sorry for you, but people don't do that unless they are fools. Is he a fool?'

'Of course not!' she retorted, colour returning to her cheeks.

A trace of a smile appeared on his lips. 'I didn't think so. Clearly he was in love with you. And you — are you in love with him?'

Clementine forced herself to meet his steady gaze, knowing

that this was the moment to put the past behind her. She had to remember what Charles had done, the vows she had made to him. She had to be strong for all their sakes. 'Yes, I am,' she said unfalteringly.

There was a terrible silence. 'I see,' he said eventually, his voice devoid of expression. Then turning abruptly, he strode from the room.

*

The little sleep Clementine had that night was fitful and troubled, but eventually at about five o'clock she fell into a deep slumber and didn't wake until after eight. Grabbing her dressing-gown, she ran straight to the nursery only to discover Alexander, standing beside a pile of nappies airing on the fireguard, watching Peter kick and splash in his bath, held by Danielle. Seeing Clementine, his expression sobered. 'Good morning.'

She gave him a curt nod, her stomach churning miserably.

'I trust you slept well?' he continued, his glance travelling from her tousled hair to her open dressing-gown.

'Did you?' she said knotting the tie round her waist.

'Like a log.' Her eyes lingered on him for a moment, before she turned away and busied herself with tucking in Charlotte, who had already fallen asleep. As she placed a discarded feeding bottle on the dresser, Alexander looked at his daughter. 'I rather think she resembles you, but Peter, Danielle tells me, is the image of his father.'

Clementine paled even more.

'Of course, not having had the pleasure of meeting your husband, I'm unable to offer an opinion.' His eyes burnt into her, and she fought to take a grip of herself.

'Danielle, you're wet,' she said. 'Let me see to Peter whilst you change. Then go and have some breakfast. I'll carry on here.' No sooner had the door closed than she turned to Alexander. 'I really don't think you should be here. Your presence serves no purpose.'

He watched her wrap their son in a large white towel. 'I'm becoming acquainted with my children, is that not purpose enough?'

'Surely you realise they must never know — no one must know?'

'Truth is a funny thing, Clementine. What was it Shakespeare said? 'Truth will come to light.'

Clementine's hands shook as she rubbed the infant dry, and began to dress his unyielding little body.

'Please, Alexander, please go and leave us in peace,' she said over Peter's cries.

He watched them thoughtfully for a moment, but his expression relaxed into a smile seeing Peter grab a handful of his mother's honey coloured hair and start to tug it.

'Now, you young scamp,' he grinned as the baby succeeded in tangling more hair in his tiny fingers. His powerful hands, browned by the desert sun, clasped the little fists that felt like gossamer, and gently released the hair from the iron-tight grips.

'How long it has grown?' he murmured, a finger brushing her cheek. 'But I think I preferred it shorter.'

'I should have tied it back,' she said, ignoring his remark.

'Let me take him whilst you do something with it. Don't worry, I shan't drop him.'

Clementine looked anxiously at him, feeling as helpless as a piece of flotsam in strong rapids. For the thousandth time she wondered what she was going to tell Charles.

Taking a ribbon from a drawer she watched as Alexander, with their son cradled in the crook of his arm, went to the window and pointed to the newly born lambs in the field. At five months the child was more interested in pulling Alexander's nose, and Clementine, torn between laughter and tears, turned away engulfed in misery. She still loved Alexander; she had known it the moment she had seen him in the nursery.

Tears filled her eyes and she busied herself with tidying up in order that he did not see. But his eyes were trained to miss little. However, he said nothing for beneath the veneer of his smiles, he was as miserable as she. He didn't know why he was still here. If he had any sense he would be long gone instead of remaining here torturing himself with something he could never have; letting these children find a place in his heart. He knew he was acting insanely but he could not let go.

With reluctance he handed Peter back and watched as Clementine laid him down for his sleep. After a few grunts the infant stuck his thumb in his mouth and settled. Alexander gazed at both children, his eyes heavy with sadness. Clementine began to walk away but he followed her and took her arm. 'We need to talk.'

'Yes, I know. I'll dress and then we can talk over breakfast,' she said, conscious of the pressure of his grip. She moved to leave but he called after her.

'Clementine, I'm leaving for France the day after tomorrow and I must visit my grandmother today. I'd like you and the children to come too.'

'You've told her!' She wheeled round, her face ashen.

'She knows nothing,' he assured her. 'The only reason I want you to come is so that I can spend some time with the twins.'

She looked uncertain as a host of reasons why she shouldn't, presented themselves. 'Would she not think it odd?'

'Not at all. I know she would like to see you, if only to say thank you for sending Ruby. From all accounts she has been a true asset. But I happen to know she's very fond of you and it goes without saying, being the mother of twins herself, she would welcome the opportunity to see the children. Her life is so monotonous these days it would give her great joy if you came.'

'You don't know what you ask,' she said, thinking of Charles. He would be livid if he ever found out.

'I ask only that for a few hours I might know what it feels like to be a father. Is that so very wrong?'

She turned away, her head and heart doing battle. How could she deny him, especially knowing he was going back to France. If anything happened to him she would never be able to forgive herself. Was he asking so much — a few hours with his children?

*

The twins still fitted into the wicker baskets in which they had travelled to England. About mid-morning, Alexander drew the car up outside the front of the house and placed them carefully on the back seat. They cried at first but before they had reached the highway the motion of the engine had rocked them to sleep. Clementine had wanted to bring Danielle, but there simply wasn't room. Pleased, Alexander knew her absence would afford him better opportunity to help with the twins.

From the moment the babies' eyes closed the journey became punctuated with long silences; the couple had been through too much to make polite conversation. It was a bright day with interludes of sunshine, the type that never failed to fill Clementine with optimism. Despite her reservations about the trip she couldn't help but enjoy all she saw and was appreciative when

Alexander slowed the car so she could take in more fully the beautiful view from the top of the Downs looking over Weymouth Bay.

He told her that he used to ride to hounds before the war, and knew practically every inch of the locality. However, it was only an interlude and for the most part there was only the wind beating on the canvas roof and the sound of the engine to accompany the silences.

She was glad when they finally arrived at Grangefield, but as they approached the house through an avenue of limes she suddenly became nervous. Something Alexander had said earlier made her turn to him anxiously.

'Are you certain your Grandmother doesn't know about us?' she asked. 'I did wonder that she appeared not to mention to Claudia that Ruby was working for her when they were together at New Year.' Clementine had been quite prepared for Claudia to come home and demand an explanation.

'I asked her not to.'

'Then you have told her!'

'Clementine, calm down. I assure you I have not. I gave the same reason I gave Ruby, that it would be better if it did not get back to Coppins. I let them believe your father might view it as poaching. Naturally, Grandmama wasn't going to jeopardise the opportunity of extra help, and neither was Ruby going to ruin the chance of a cottage.'

Clementine nodded but all the same she remained uneasy. 'I don't think I can do this, Alexander — I want to go home. Your grandmother's bound to know and if not, she will soon work it out.'

He placed his hand on top of hers. 'I think guilt is letting your imagination run wild. Besides, it's too late, she's standing at the door. Just believe me, there is nothing to worry about.'

234

Lady Moundsmere, clutching her stick and wearing a heavy shawl over her black frock, stood beneath the oriole window, looking very frail.

'Well, Alexander! How tanned you look,' she said, allowing her composure to drop a little as he kissed her. Every time he went away, she wondered if they would meet again in this life, and each night in her prayers she would ask for the war to end, always wanting to add, 'And for things to get back to normal.' But she never did for she had come to accept that some things were impossible.

'I wager that if you put on one of those native robes you'd pass for an Arab,' she chuckled, her old eyes glowing with a new radiance. He laughed, and she turned to Clementine who approached with Peter in her arms. 'How lovely to see you again, my dear, I'm delighted that you have come, and especially taken the trouble to bring the smalls.' She squeezed the baby's hand with her arthritic fingers. 'I've been wanting to see them ever since I first heard. I expect you know that we've a long line of twins in the family.'

The warmth of her welcome helped to relax Clementine a little. Maybe Alexander was right and she was getting paranoid.

'We should not linger out here, it's ghastly cold, not at all suitable for young babies. Let us go into the drawing room where the fire is roaring. Luncheon won't be for a little while so we can have a glass of sherry whilst we wait, and you can tell me all your news.'

The twins enjoyed the freedom of the rug stretched in front of the fire, and rolled back and forth gurgling gleefully as the adults watched.

'So where is Claudia?' the old lady asked. 'Why didn't she come too?'

Clementine met Alexander's eyes fleetingly. Why hadn't she stayed at home, instead of putting herself in a position where she was forced to lie.

'She has a heavy cold,' he said, leaning forward and stroking Charlotte's head. 'She didn't want to risk giving it to you.'

'That was thoughtful. I understand there is a lot of influenza about, and one can't be too careful. They say it's of a particularly virulent strain. Maxwell, my maid, had to attend the funeral of her nephew last week. He was home on leave when it struck. A great strapping boy, who was training to be a gamekeeper on the Holmes estate, before the war. You wouldn't have thought it would have made an impression on him, but I'm sure it's all this food rationing. Maxwell says his poor wife was reduced to giving him vegetable broth that had boiled and boiled, and the little meat afforded her. I daresay if the vegetables had been fresh it might have been a different story, but it seems her own crop had done badly and she was forced to rely on charity. Hardly fitting for someone fresh from the trenches in need of building up.'

Charlotte squealed with delight as Alexander tickled her tummy. 'You will spoil them, Alexander,' smiled Lady Moundsmere. 'And I am sure Clementine will not thank you.'

The warmth of the room, the sherry, the welcoming ambience combined to soothe Clementine's nerves and there were moments when she was lulled into imagining this mirage was real: a husband and wife, visiting with their family — but even so fleeting a folly caused her suffering, when reality awakened her and she acknowledged it could never be.

It would have shocked her to know that Alexander's frail old grandmother had also been beguiled into imagining the same. From the minute they had arrived she had been struck by how right they looked together, but it was more than that, it was like an inner knowledge that this sister would have been a far better match than the one he had married.

'Tell me about your husband, Clementine. I understand he's a doctor. Where are his family from?'

'Cumbria,' she replied, conscious of the way Alexander's lips tightened at the mention of Charles.

'Near the Lakes. Such a beautiful part. Doesn't Piers Douglas come from thereabouts, Alexander? Kendal, isn't it?'

He nodded, clearly more interested in playing with the babies than partaking in the conversation. Bemused, the old lady turned back to Clementine and they discussed Charles's family.

'I have always believed one has to have a calling to make a good doctor or a good vicar,' Lady Moundsmere said. 'I wonder which path young Peter will take?" She seemed unaware of any tension and Clementine was relieved when the next enquiry was about Piers.

'Have you seen him since getting back, Alexander?'

'I called in on the way down and we had lunch together,' he replied, and with sudden deliberation he lifted his eyes to Clementine's, saying, 'I understand he joined you at Christmas?'

'On Boxing Day,' she replied with sinking heart. 'Claudia invited him.'

'He seemed most taken with your husband — said you made a very happy couple.'

Clementine knew Piers had kept his promise.

'Ideal perhaps, but surely not happy,' said Lady Moundsmere breaking the silence. 'I defy any couple to be happy with this war blighting what little time they are afforded together.'

Clementine had to force her gaze away and trembling, she took another sip of sherry.

'My dear,' continued Lady Moundsmere in lowered tones, 'Did

not Claudia tell me, when we were at Mannerling at New Year, that you were enceinte again? I recall your mother writing to her.'

Unnerved at the old lady's indiscretion Clementine involuntarily turned to Alexander, who was busy piling old cotton reels on top of each other for the children to knock down. The most part of his face was hidden, but she was aware of a muscle twitching nervously at the side of his mouth.

'I miscarried,' she said softly.

Lady Moundsmere leaned across and touched her wrist. 'Oh my dear, I am sorry,' but before she could say more, Burrows the butler appeared and announced that luncheon was ready. Behind him a maid with enough frizzy red hair for two people smiled broadly, revealing a chipped front tooth.

'Ah Ruby!' said Lady Moundsmere. 'Ruby is going to take charge of the smalls,' she said to Clementine as Alexander helped her on to her arthritic feet. 'She will see to all their needs, so you're not to fret. With four children I rather think she knows what to do, don't you?'

It was a welcome interruption and Clementine rose to greet Ruby whose freckled face had filled out, obliterating the sallow look of poverty she'd had in London. She noticed the way Ruby handed Lady Moundsmere her walking stick and fussed with her shawl. There was clearly affection between the two women. Clementine was glad things had turned out so well and felt a surge of gratitude towards Alexander, who had made it all possible. At least some good has come out of that night, she thought. But as her eyes dropped on the twins she knew she could never wish they didn't exist.

There was only time for hurried exchanges between Clementine and Ruby but enough to learn how beneficial the move from London had proved. 'My older two go to school, Miss

Clementine. They's learning their letters, and when I'm working, the gard'ner's wife looks after t'others.'

Clementine introduced Ruby to the twins and pointed out a bag containing their necessities. 'Don't hesitate to fetch me should you need me,' she said, before hurrying off to catch up with the others.

She found them in the corridor near the dining room waiting by a large oil painting: a family group, mother, father and two boys of about seven, all mounted and in riding clothes. She didn't need to be told that it was Lady Moundsmere's son and his wife, Alexander's parents. It was a charming picture and the artist had captured well the closeness between them. She was surprised how unalike the two brothers were. Apart from the eyes there was little similarity, Alexander more like his French mother and Patrick his father. She would have liked to linger, to study it more but the others had already moved into the dining room, and she knew it was not advisable, for anyone's sake, that she show too keen an interest. The black ball of secrets she already carried was festering inside her like a cancer; the less she knew the better.

Seated opposite Alexander, without the children to hide behind, Clementine felt defenceless. It had been a while since their hostess had used the dining room, and viewing the portrait with her remaining grandson had affected her. She ate little and slowly, stopping frequently to put her knife and fork down as she remembered times gone by. She spoke much of Patrick, giving Clementine the feeling that out of all the deaths, his had been the most difficult to deal with, possibly because of his youth, possibly because age and tragedy had weakened her resilience. She told of the pet fox the brothers had secretly reared, the fateful summer their parents had deposited them at Grangefield, whilst they toured Europe, and the boys' growing excitement as the day of their return approached.

'They had been away several weeks and sent lots of postcards from all the wonderful places they had visited. The last one was from Florence, and in it they said they were going to drive along the coast road to France and would be home within the month. Well, as the days came and went with no sign of them, my husband and I became anxious.' She glanced at Alexander. 'Of course, we told the twins they had been delayed but every day they asked if we had heard any news. My son and daughter-in-law always came home laden with unusual gifts and their grandfather teased the boys, saying that was why they wanted them home. I remember Patrick in particular getting very angry and saying he and Alexander didn't want anything, just their parents.'

She paused. 'It was the rector who brought the news. Their car had been discovered at the bottom of a mountain road. It had caught fire and there had been some difficulty identifying the bodies …'

There was a heavy pause and Alexander looked at her with concern, but she moved her gnarled hand with its large ruby ring, dismissively. 'The boys were so traumatised they forgot to feed the fox. The animal was spotted approaching the house. I suppose he was hungry, had not yet learned to fend for himself, and of course with little or no fear of humans. Patrick saw him from an upstairs window at the exact moment the gamekeeper spotted him. Well, I don't need to tell you what happened.'

Clementine saw the fleeting glance Lady Moundsmere cast at her remaining grandson; such controlled desperation it made her eyes water and reminded her of something she had heard many times during the last four years. 'It's not natural to outlive your child.' Her heart reached out to her, certain her old soul would never find peace until the very last shell had been fired and she knew that Alexander was still alive.

Clementine watched as Alexander answered his grandmother's questions about what he would be doing in France. He reassured her that he would be in little danger, his role more on the planning side, but though Lady Moundsmere didn't question him, Clementine could see she wasn't fooled and found herself wondering what toll such family tragedy had taken on Alexander. He had lost both parents and his twin brother: his closest relations. She could only imagine the enormous effect it must have had on him, and whilst Alexander attempted to get his grandmother out of her maudlin mood by coaxing her to talk about Patrick's young son, she found herself thinking what he must be going through with Peter and Charlotte, knowing he could share no part in their lives.

Her sorrow intensified and, not for the first time, she acknowledged her mistake in coming with him today. She drifted in and out of the conversation, finding it difficult to keep from focusing on anything but the fact that this time together now was all there would ever be. Nothing more, just this present moment.

They stayed until late afternoon, when a darkening sky suggested an approaching storm; and Alexander, worried about a leak in the roof of the car, said they should leave.

Their return journey was punctuated with the same painful silences that had accompanied them before, but the closer they got to Coppins the more sure Clementine was that matters between them couldn't be left as they stood. Ignoring all thought of Charles and what she knew he would advise, she decided it was time to voice all the unspoken thoughts that enveloped them. Tomorrow would be too late; it must be now whilst they were alone.

Her eyes were heavy with unspent tears when he pulled onto the grass verge. She didn't know what she was going to say; only that she must speak.

'You have to understand that when I realised I was pregnant, all hope of you and I having a future together died. From that moment I knew it was impossible, could never be. Charles made me see I could still have a future. He gave me a choice and I chose to live. I wasn't in love with him, but I respected him. He was a good man and I felt that in time I could grow to love him. Having made that decision, I had no alternative but to pledge myself to him.'

She waited for a response but Alexander stared ahead, unable to focus on anything but this man in whose bed she must have slept night after night. Clementine knew instinctively what he was thinking, and realised she had only succeeded in making matters worse. What folly to have anaesthetised herself with wine and sherry.

'I am the one person in the world with whom it was totally unacceptable for you to father a child. Surely you see that,' she persisted.

It seemed an age before he turned, his dark eyes hiding nothing. 'I understand how frightened you were, alone and desperate, and for that I shall never forgive myself. But Clementine — there are far worse things happening in this world every day, and people accept and cope. Our only crime, if that is what it was, was to fall in love.' He paused a moment before going on. 'I don't care about others, only you, and our children. But that said, it has never been my wish to either hurt or make things difficult for you. Therefore I want you to know that when I leave tomorrow I won't try to see you again. You may not feel the same way as you did, but I shall always love you. Just promise me that should you ever need help, you will let me know.'

Clementine's eyes filled with tears and she glanced away, looking over her shoulder at the twins: their son and daughter. Eventually she turned back to face him, this man she loved above every living soul.

'I've never stopped loving you, I never will,' she said thickly, the words coming from a place over which she had no control. She could feel a vibration near her centre, an energy being drawn from her. The words had taken on a life of their own; it was too late to take them back. They were out there spinning round, deciding in which direction to go.

She sobered quickly, viewing her honesty as nothing but a gift of false hope, and wondered how she could have been so cruel. She was what her father would call 'a loose canon'. If Peter hadn't chosen that moment to wake up she would have jumped out of the car and let the wind and rain cleanse her. Hearing his cries, she looked at Alexander. 'We must hurry, for they will need feeding soon.'

# 20

Thankfully Peter's cries prevented further conversation and when they arrived at Coppins Danielle was waiting to help whisk the twins off to the nursery, leaving Alexander to bring in the wicker carry-cots.

'There was a call from the War Office sir,' said Best, relieving him of the babies' things.

'Ah, I rather expected there would be,' he replied with a note of resignation. 'Was there any message?'

'Only that you return the call, sir.'

He was deciding what to do when he noticed Clementine, still holding Peter, climbing the stairs. 'What time will dinner be, Best?' he asked.

'Half past seven, if that's convenient, sir?'

'It's fine with me, but what about you, Clementine? Will you be finished with the twins?'

Clementine stopped, their infant son wriggling in her arms as she glanced back at Alexander's handsome face. She was glad of the distance between them and that Best was still there. It made it easier.

'You'll have to excuse me, but I really couldn't eat another thing. It's been a long day and I have the most awful headache.'

Alexander's eyes narrowed. He wanted to ask what the devil she meant, but Best's presence made it impossible. 'Forgive me,' she murmured, before hurrying away.

'Shall I get the War Office for you, Major FitzPatrick?'

Alexander didn't appear to hear and Best repeated the question until finally the words penetrated. 'Yes, yes, thank you, Best. I would appreciate it,' he said heavily.

It took some minutes to put the call through, and then there was a long wait before someone in authority was able to speak to him and inform him of changes in his itinerary the following day. When at last he replaced the receiver, he went in immediate pursuit of Clementine. Expecting to find her in the nursery, he was surprised to discover Danielle coping alone with both infants. 'Where is your mistress?' he asked impatiently.

'She feel unwell, monsieur.'

A dangerous light flared in his eyes, and turning on his heels he marched from the room. If she thought, after telling him she still loved him, that he was going to let her off so lightly, she was mistaken. To him, her confession changed everything. He wouldn't go without a fight. He would do everything in his power to make her see they could have a life together.

'Clementine, open the door,' he called after trying the handle and finding it locked. 'I must speak to you.'

'There's nothing left to say. Please, please I beg you, leave me alone.'

'Look, I have to leave early in the morning and I'm not going without talking with you.'

'I told you there's …' Footsteps sounded on the stairs and reluctantly he moved away from the door. It was Mrs Best.

'I was just coming to check,' she puffed, 'if Miss Clementine was all right, Major FitzPatrick. Mr Best said she wasn't feeling very well.'

'I believe she's tired.'

She nodded. 'It's them little uns. They can be a right handful.'

Feeling conspicuous, and having no wish to arouse the woman's suspicions, he began to move away, then paused before descending the stairs. 'Mrs Best, I hope it's not too much of an inconvenience, but I shan't be in for dinner, after all. I have to go out.' Before she had time to respond he was gone, and seconds later the front door slammed.

It was a relief to hear Mrs Best's homely voice accompany the knock on the door and Clementine hurried to open it. 'You do look pasty, my dear,' the woman said, giving Clementine a scrutinising look as she followed her in. 'All done in.'

'I'm fine, Mrs Best. Really, it's just a headache. An early night will sort it out.'

'Are you sure I can't get you something, an omelette, perhaps? The chickens have started laying again.'

'No really, I've no appetite, but thank you all the same.' The sound of a motor made her go to the window.

'That'll be Major Fitzpatrick's car. He rushed out. I think it had something to do with his phone call. Now, Miss Clementine, you're not to worry about the babes. I'll go and lend Danielle a hand. You get some rest.'

After she had gone Clementine slumped down on the bed. How could she have been so stupid, so cruel. She loathed herself. She was weak and incapable of handling her emotions. She thought of Charles, wondering what he would say if he found out what she had done today. She knew she could never tell him. Oh, why had she not left things as they were, let Alexander believe Charles had stolen her affections. For she did love him, but it seemed a paltry emotion when compared to the feelings Alexander aroused in her. The love she felt for him consumed her mind and soul. Locking herself away was the only option and she prayed that by morning, both strength and common sense would be restored sufficiently to enable her to go downstairs and bid him goodbye without a show of emotion.

A shadow of light from the gas lamp on the bridge shone onto the water, lighting the path of two swans as they drifted by and out of sight into the thick reeds that ran alongside the River Frome. Alexander, from a quiet corner of the old coaching inn, blindly watched, a tumbler of whisky and an uneaten sandwich beside him. He felt at a loss to know what he should do. After months of believing the worst, Clementine had finally admitted that she still loved him, and wonderful though it was to hear, it was nevertheless painfully obvious she felt duty bound to honour her marriage of convenience. And as long as she refused to speak to him, he had no hope of persuading her otherwise; to make her see that life was too short and precious to sacrifice one's own happiness for the wants and desires of others. If nothing else, war had taught him that.

A young soldier and his girl sat in the opposite corner. Alexander watched them holding hands and whispering to each other, and experienced a stab of envy. Seemingly they had a normal uncomplicated relationship, something he and Clementine had never experienced. He thought of all the things he longed to tell her and knew if he didn't see her tonight, he might never get another opportunity. It had taken cunning to discover she was alone at Coppins, and the chances were that the next time he was back, either her parents or Charles Hamilton would be in residence. Somehow, he had to return and find a way.

It was just past ten o'clock when he arrived back. Best was there to take his coat and ask if he required anything. Alexander said he would attend to himself and told him not to wait up. He went to the library where the fire was still burning. There was a photograph on the side table of Clementine and Claudia sitting on an elephant when they had lived in India. Even at four or five years of age it was clear Claudia was going to be a beauty, but it was still the plainer sister that he couldn't take his eyes from.

Suspecting that Clementine had heard his return he had hoped that she might have second thoughts and come down so they could talk. However, the longer he waited the more he realised she had no intention of doing so. It was with resignation that he put the guard in front of the fire and went upstairs, his path lit by moonlight streaming through the window on the landing.

The nursery door was ajar and he couldn't resist going in to look at Peter and Charlotte. A nightlight flickered on the mantelpiece and he crept as softly as he could over to their cots, baring his teeth every time the floorboards creaked.

He lost count of how long he stood watching them sleeping peacefully, blissfully unaware of the torment surrounding them. It was going to be hard leaving them; they were part of him, part of Clementine. His blood, not Charles Hamilton's, flowed through their veins. Clementine's husband was father in proxy only and Alexander acknowledged that his feelings were a mixture of both loss and jealousy. He lowered himself into an old nursing chair, the seat of which was frayed by years of use. His mind was too agitated for sleep, and it soothed him to stay close to his offspring, to breathe the same sweet air.

Alexander began to wonder whether he should confide in his grandmother, seek her advice. He had a feeling she wouldn't be as shocked as one might suppose, but at her great age he decided it would be selfish to burden her so.

Peter suddenly coughed and began to cry, and when he didn't stop, Alexander picked him up and did his best to comfort him. Within seconds Clementine appeared. She frowned when she saw him and took the child from his arms.

'What are you doing here?' she hissed as she soothed the infant.

'I didn't wake him,' he protested, though he couldn't deny that the thought had crossed his mind. He watched as she gently settled their son in his cot and rocked him back to sleep.

'Come along out of here before they both awake.'

He followed her out into the corridor and as she stopped outside her door, she turned.

'Goodbye, Alexander.'

A disbelieving smile spread across his face. 'You really think I'm going to walk away? We can't part like this. We need to talk.'

'I'll be up early, I'll speak to you before you leave.'

'No! It will not do, Clementine. There will not be time.' And reaching out he quickly turned the door handle, pushed her inside and closed the door behind them. She turned on him in anger and tried to open the door.

'Please, Alexander. Please leave.'

Something inside him snapped and he grabbed her arms and forced her into the centre of the room. 'No, not until you listen to me!'

She struggled furiously but his grip was tight. He lowered his head, his mouth seeking her lips. Sharply she turned away. 'Please don't do this!' But he ignored her pleas and carried her over to the bed and pinioned her down. She had no escape, and he kissed her passionately. The effect was instant, her resistance draining like an ebbing tide.

As their lips parted, he whispered fiercely, 'Tell me you don't want me. Tell me!'

As tears welled in her eyes she tried to speak, but the words wouldn't form. The fury had died and for now there was only silence. Lightly, Alexander brushed his lips against hers and then pulled back watching, waiting. Eventually, with a sigh of resignation, she lifted her hand and touched his hair. It was soft and silky like the twins', just as she remembered. Their eyes met and held, and then sliding her hand round the back of his head, she drew it down.

*

Clementine awoke, alerted by the sound of a baby's cry, to discover herself cradled in Alexander's powerful arms. So it wasn't just a beautiful dream. The ecstasy of being together, for a moment, overrode her pangs of conscience; how could she feel guilt when she loved this man so desperately? How could anyone condemn them for expressing their love in the only natural way? She tensed as she heard Danielle scurrying along the corridor to the nursery and waited with baited breath until the crying stopped.

Dawn had broken and the pale early-morning sun splintered through the curtains so she could clearly see the man she adored lying beside her, deeply tanned from the African sun, still in a profound sleep. Downstairs, the hall clock struck six; it was like a death knell, and a ripple of fear rushed through her. Soon he would be gone, sucked once more into the madness of war. She stretched her arms about him and held him tight, tears falling onto his chest.

'Clemmie darling,' he said in a whisper as he awoke. He kissed her tenderly and becoming aware of her anguish, stroked her hair soothingly. 'There is always so little time.'

For a moment the shadows lifted. Buoyed up with his strength she felt safe, until her gaze fell on the fire in the grate, which Alexander had lit earlier.

'*Now in the falling of the gloom the red fire paints the empty room,*' she said heavily.

'*Armies in the Fire,*' he said, recognising the words. '*Armies march by tower and spire of cities blazing, in the fire.* It was a favourite when I was young.'

'A boy soldier,' she smiled sadly. 'I just pray Peter never knows what war is.'

'If what everyone is saying is right, this is the war to end all wars. I want so much to believe that, for it's the only thing that makes any sense out of it all.'

'I don't want you to go,' she said suddenly, panic-stricken.

'I suppose I could desert …' For a second she thought he was serious but seeing the playful smile on his lips she relaxed.

'Just hold the vision of us together, because one day I shall return and it will be for good, never again to be parted. We shall grow old together.' He saw the uncertainty in her eyes. 'Clemmie darling, you must have faith.'

'I shall pray for you.'

'Let me hear you say, we shall be together.'

'Oh Alex, how can it be? Nothing has changed.'

'Trust me, darling, it will. When I get back I'm going to put matters to rights. We'll find a way.'

She buried her face in her hands. 'Can we be so selfish as to think only of ourselves?'

'If we had done so in the first place, we wouldn't be in this mess.' He held her close, conscious of the fragility of her mood, and immensely aware of time ebbing away. In less than two hours he would be gone. He stroked her cheek then kissed her, wondering how he would find the strength to leave her.

Aware that it could be a long time before they met again they made love one last time. Their lovemaking contained an element of frenzied desperation; they were one body, one soul, bonded together. But without warning Clementine suddenly froze, filled with an overwhelming conviction that they weren't alone.

251

Alexander felt her stiffen and the pressure of her hands on his arms telling him to stop. Seeing the terror in her eyes, he glanced over his shoulder and saw Claudia standing pale and hostile at the foot of the bed.

'Heavens above, what have we here? My prudish sister and my poor deceived husband. No wonder you didn't want me to know you were home — you bastard!' As her voice rose it excited Timmy's Jack Russell that had followed her upstairs.

Alexander rolled from Clementine, who covered her face, but he, though stunned and embarrassed, managed to salvage some dignity. 'I don't know what you're doing here Claudia, but would you mind leaving now. If you go to your room, I will speak to you there.'

'Do not tell me what to do, bastard! No more! It's my turn to make the rules,' she shouted above Jack's barking. 'I want you in my bedroom now, not in a minute, *now!'* And she pointed her finger threateningly. 'As for you, you bitch, if you ever lay one finger on my husband again, I'll make you suffer!' And with that she spun on her heel and stormed out, slamming the door.

Clementine trembled violently, staring in shock as Alexander began throwing clothes on. Both understood that Claudia was capable of anything and that it was imperative to prevent her from doing something rash. However, before he went in pursuit, he took Clementine in his arms and prayed for a way to comfort her.

'Darling, it will be all right, you must believe me,' he said, trying to sound calmer than he felt. 'Let me sort it out.' He put a blanket around her shoulders and seeing Jack watching them with a quizzical expression, placed him on her lap. 'Look after her, old fellow.' Planting a kiss on her forehead he left to find Claudia.

Claudia stood by the window, her elbow cupped in her hand

as she drew on a cigarette in jagged breaths. Alexander paused inside the door, staring at her with loathing. 'What right have you to behave in so high and mighty a manner?' he demanded. 'You know perfectly well our marriage is nothing but a sham!'

'For you maybe, but not for me. You may have been sleeping around, but I've been as faithful as if you locked me in a chastity belt, so you can appreciate my being a teeny bit upset — more especially when it's my sister's bed in which I find you.'

'I told you more than a year ago I would divorce you when the war is over. I never deceived you, and what I do in my private life is my affair.'

'Not when it comes to bedding my sister.'

'You don't understand, do you? I happen to be in love with Clementine.'

She gave an hysterical laugh. 'Oh my God! When did you discover that — last night? Was she that good? You amaze me!'

'Your vulgarity does you little credit.'

Unable to bear the agony of not knowing what was happening, Clementine, looking pale and shaken, appeared in the doorway. Claudia could not bear to look at her. 'Get out of here, you slattern! Get out!' And she picked up a scent bottle and hurled it at her. It brushed past Clementine's ear and shattered on the floor. Alexander's temper snapped and he slapped Claudia across the face, causing her to fall backwards across the dressing table.

'You'll regret that!' she screamed, clutching her burning cheek. He had humiliated her and she hated him. She would make him pay.

'This has gone far enough, Claudia. I want a divorce and I don't intend to wait.'

His words brought an ugly smile to her lips. 'Is that so! Well you can get that idea right out of your head, because I've decided

I wish to remain your wife. Unless, that is, you don't mind me dragging both your good names through the courts.' Seeing the horror on Clementine's face made her smile. 'Now that would cause a merry little scandal. Can't you just imagine the headlines? Guaranteed to take everyone's mind off the war, don't you think? Such diversion for the readers. And I do think it's one's duty to do all one can to bring a little happiness into people's lives in these dire times, don't you?' Her lips pursed in mock sympathy. 'But poor Papa, do you think it would affect his career?'

Clementine felt sick. She knew Claudia would have no qualms about taking such action.

'You wouldn't dare!' said Alexander.

'Just try me!'

Alexander struggled to contain his anger. He knew if he didn't calm down the situation would escalate. It was already out of control and Coppins was clearly not the place to resolve the crisis. There was no way he could leave the two sisters under the same roof and it was imperative he sort something out with Claudia before returning to France.

'Get yourself ready, and I shall take you back to London. We can talk on the journey.' She started to protest but the challenge in his eyes silenced her. 'Meet me outside in half an hour,' and with that he took Clementine's arm and left.

Clementine stared at the bed where the rumpled linen lay exposed. 'We were never meant to be together,' she said, burying her face in his chest.

Alexander stroked her head, wishing he could take her pain away. Feeling utterly sick and drained, he struggled to find the right words. She was right, nothing had ever been straightforward for them; fate seemed to have been against them since the beginning. He had always known it was not going to be easy, but he had never envisaged this. How could he leave her to cope alone with the inevitable consequences: no family, no friends. The battlefields of France suddenly seemed paradise compared to what she faced, and once again it was his fault. He should never have stayed with her last night. Instead he should have waited until he was in a position to protect her.

'Darling, let me talk to her. When she's calmed down I might be able to reason with her.'

'You must know her better than that. We've played straight into her hands, and she'll take full advantage of it. There can be no future for us, we were just fooling ourselves.'

'Whatever she wants in order to keep quiet, she can have — anything. I shan't leave you at her mercy. Whatever it takes.' He clasped her to him, staring blindly ahead, his eyes heavy with unspent tears. 'Damn the bloody war! Damn everyone!'

Outside, Claudia began to get impatient and lit another cigarette. Alexander had said half an hour, but it was already forty minutes and she was getting cold standing about waiting. She wished she had put on a warmer coat, but she was not going back into the house. Sticking one hand inside the front of her coat, she started to walk up the drive in an effort to warm up. She felt the damp seep through the thin soles of her satin shoes and swore again. She was still wearing the same clothes she had gone out in the previous evening. However, for the first time in her life she didn't care about her appearance, she cared only for revenge. Clouds had gathered and rain looked inevitable; it would be a stormy ride back to London. She glanced over her shoulder, but still there was no sign of Alexander.

She frowned when she saw Freddie Durward's treasured Torpedo Tourer badly parked down the side of the house. He had been most reluctant to let her borrow it, indeed it had taken considerable persuasion. What was he going to say when she returned without it? She shrugged her shoulders; it was a minor problem, and besides she had never liked him anyway. Nevertheless, it had been a stroke of luck that he had driven her home from the party and still been there when her mother had called to ask whether she knew Alexander was at Coppins.

'Claudia, my dear, you didn't say Alexander was back. Papa spoke to Best earlier and he said Alexander had been down at Bovington and was staying for a day or two.'

Claudia had somehow managed to contain her surprise, not wishing to be pressed with awkward questions. 'Yes, he had to go down on military business. I've been tied up working at the canteen otherwise I'd have gone too. I felt I couldn't let them down, they do so depend on me.'

There had been a pause. 'But Best said he is going overseas tomorrow. You should have gone, Claudia. Lady Falkington would have understood.'

Claudia noted the chiding tone. 'Oh heavens, they must have cancelled his leave. The swines! I've been working and only just this minute got in. Mummy, I shall have to go. He's bound to call.'

Mrs Ellacombe had accepted her explanation for she too had been an Army wife and was well aware of the scant consideration given to family life by the leaders of the Forces.

'Try not to be upset, darling. Be strong. Don't let Alexander see you unhappy. Remember there is a war on. It's not as if it's his decision.'

Within minutes of replacing the receiver Claudia had decided to drive down to Coppins. She had been waiting for such an opportunity and it would be madness not to use it. She knew enough of soldiers on leave and their needs. There was no reason Alexander should be any different.

It had been a miserable journey and her flimsy evening dress had done little to protect her from the bitter chill of the night. She had kept her foot down hard on the accelerator, ever conscious that Alexander was to make an early start. It had taken forever, as again and again she had chosen the wrong turning and found herself on the wrong road. But the worst moment had been when she had run out of petrol near Ringwood, and had the unpleasant task of waking someone up and begging for fuel. It hadn't been easy, especially in view of petrol rationing, but her determination had been rewarded, and when she finally arrived and saw Alexander's car, she couldn't resist congratulating herself. She had made it, and now all she needed to do was put her womanly charms into action.

She went in by the kitchen door and found Mr and Mrs Best enjoying an early-morning cup of tea.

'Just what I need — I'm absolutely frozen,' she uttered through chattering teeth, as she warmed herself by the range and watched Jack climb from his basket and stretch.

'Miss Claudia, what on earth are you doing here so early?' said Mrs Best, as she fetched another cup.

Claudia rolled her eyes up. 'Why do you suppose? To see my husband, of course! I drove through the night to get here.'

'The madness of the young,' the housekeeper said, shaking her silvery head. 'Here, drink this quick or you'll catch your death.'

It was the best cup of tea she had ever had. 'Has Major FitzPatrick woken yet?' Claudia asked.

Shrugging her shoulders, Mrs Best glanced at her husband.

'The only sounds I've heard are them little uns, and they've not been awake long,' he replied.

'Then I shall go and surprise him. Would you prepare a pot of tea, Mrs Best, and I'll take it up.' Meantime she walked over to the mirror by the sink and checked on the damage of the night. After brushing her hair and adding a little rouge to her colourless cheeks, she felt satisfied. Picking up the tray, she made for the back stairs, pausing a moment to take a few deep breaths to settle the rush of nervous excitement that was gripping her stomach.

On the long drive down she'd had time to think and was now convinced that the only possible reason Alexander could be at Coppins was because he still cared for her. There simply could be no other reason. He could have stayed anywhere, but he had chosen Coppins. And remembering the last time she had seen him only seemed to endorse this; when he had visited her in London with the pretence of telling her he was going to Africa. There really had been no necessity for such a call, for his solicitor who handled her affairs would naturally have informed her. No, the more she mulled it over, the more certain she was that he wanted a reconciliation.

As she stepped onto the landing a baby's cry had broken the hushed silence. Noisy little beggar, she thought, and glanced down to see that Jack had followed her up the stairs. She shooed him away but he chose to ignore her. She quietly tiptoed in to her bedroom and, having imagined finding him asleep, she was bitterly disappointed to discover an empty room, with the bed already made. For a ghastly moment she thought he must have seen her arrive and slipped down the front stairs to avoid her, but then she spotted his luggage in the dressing room. She put the tray down and began to search for him. Finding the bathroom empty, she poked her head around the nursery door.

'Have you seen my husband, Major FitzPatrick this morning?' she asked the young French girl who was feeding Peter.

'*Non, madame*, I see no one,' she said, curious to see her mistress's sister in full evening attire at such an hour. Claudia turned away cross and confused, but hearing movement from Clementine's bedroom she grabbed the handle, opened the door, and walked in.

*

Claudia had almost reached the main gate when she heard Alexander's car start up. She had been walking round and round for almost three quarters of an hour and now, tired and cold, she was growing more and more incensed.

As he approached he couldn't help but think what a mess she looked; so unlike the polished socialite she usually was. He slowed down and she got in, neither speaking for a few minutes. Eventually she broke the silence. 'You've certainly got some explaining to do, Alexander,' she drawled.

He glanced sideways at her. 'I owe you no explanation!' he told her. 'You lost that right when you tricked me into marrying you.'

'Well, you're wrong about that!' she snapped. 'And ever since our wedding night you've denied me the opportunity of explaining my side of the story about my condition when we married.'

'You didn't have a condition, it was merely a plot to get me to the altar.'

'That's not true! When I told you I was pregnant I firmly believed I was. It was no pleasure for me, as the idea of having a baby so young was the last thing I wanted. However, I was deeply attracted to you, and I assumed that, as well as doing the decent thing, you actually cared for me too. When I discovered that it was a trick of nature, the wedding arrangements were so far advanced that it was almost impossible to stop. I know I should have told you, but I was frightened I would lose you. I admit I did wrong, but did I really deserve to be treated the way you treated me?'

There was a long silence and Alexander's face expressed little of what was going on in his mind. If what she said was true, then maybe he had been rather harsh, but she was a cunning little minx and quite capable of making any story sound convincing.

'However wrong I may have been,' she continued, 'it does not begin to compare with your contemptible behaviour last night. And as for my sister ...'

Alexander turned on her, his voice like a whiplash. 'I told you — that's none of your business.'

'It's very much my business, for whichever way you look at it, your actions are indefensible.' She smiled triumphantly. 'The tables have truly turned in my favour, don't you agree? Now I'm the one with the winning hand, so I suggest if you want me to keep your sordid little secret safe, you'd better start treating me like a wife.'

'Blackmail! But what else could one expect from someone of your sort?'

'Call it what you like,' she said smugly, 'but those are my conditions. In view of the circumstances, I think I'm being exceedingly generous. So tell me, Alexander, what's it to be: a convenient model marriage, or disgrace and ruin to you and *our* beloved Clementine?'

# 21

On 21st March, 1918, only days after Alexander landed in France, the Germans launched an attack on the Allies. Crack troops, rested from the campaign on the Russian Front and eager for victory, broke through the British and French defences between Arras and south of the River Somme. They swept through with terrifying speed, blasting the Allies from the trenches they had held for almost four years, and pushing them back towards the coast. Everywhere was in total chaos as the vast majority of the fighting Army and all its equipment fell back. Alexander was amongst the reinforcements who rushed forward in an attempt to stem further German advances.

Charles, stationed near the Front, grew increasingly anxious, for he knew that, unless help arrived soon, it would not be long before the Casualty Clearing Station would be over-run. Throughout the long day, streams of wounded with haunted faces and fear-filled eyes poured into the hospital, and as he and staff battled to alleviate their pain, he silently wondered if in the event of capture, compassion would be high on the advancing enemy's list of priorities.

Just when everything started to look ominous, a convoy of ambulances was sighted struggling towards them along the muddy track. A great cheer went up and within an hour, the place was cleared. All were evacuated to the relative safety of the large base hospitals near the coast. The next day Charles learned how close their escape had been. He described it all to Clementine in a letter.

*Before darkness the Germans had advanced more than a mile past the Clearing Station and I thanked God that you and the children were safe in England.*

By happy coincidence he found himself back at Camiers and related to her how dozens of tents had been hastily erected for use as temporary wards to house the horrendous number of new casualties. Again he was working into the night, and not at all hopeful that the situation was going to ease. *There is a depressing cloud above the camp. It's bad enough being wounded, but to be so in the face of retreat is utterly demoralising.*

It was a mood that spread rapidly, and as news of the retreat filtered back and the lengthy casualty lists were printed, the nation's morale reached its lowest ebb.

When Clementine wasn't in the nursery, she shut herself away in her room, and Mrs Best didn't fail to notice the change that had come over her in recent weeks. Several times she expressed her concern to her husband, but he only told her to stop worrying.

'It's the war, my dear, that's what's wrong with her,' he said one day in early April as he was about to set off with a bucketful of chicken feed.

She watched him place his cloth cap on his balding head and open the back door. 'I suppose you're right, luv. She's likely distraught over Captain Hamilton, bound to be with them devils bombing the hospitals — it's wicked, sheer wickedness!'

Best walked outside and glanced up at Clementine's window. The curtains were still drawn and he sighed, his mind drifting back to the morning Miss Claudia had arrived unexpectedly at some ridiculous hour. He had heard the ranting and raving and slammed doors. He knew what had happened and had taken pains to prevent his wife from knowing, even taking the trouble to open the Major's bed and make it appear that it had been slept in; something Alexander had overlooked in his haste to leave. Best did not consider himself a righteous man, and he'd certainly seen life in the Army. However, he would never have thought it of Miss Clementine — never! Moreover, her own sister's husband at that! But his lips were sealed; it wasn't his place to pass judgement, yet all the same it had shaken him deeply.

Clementine knew nothing of the pains Best had taken to protect her reputation; in fact, she was hardly aware of anything in those wretched days. She was only conscious that Alexander was gone, and that she would never see him again. The feeling of loss was excruciating and savaged any thought of the future. There was just blackness, and instead of time healing the pain, it seemed only to accentuate it. She was as flawed as her childhood doll, which Best had glued back together after it had been dropped. No matter how skilful the repair, she would never be the same, and this and guilt compelled her to write and confess to Charles what had happened.

Two weeks passed before she could bring herself to put pen to paper, two weeks during which she scoured the casualty lists over and over, two weeks during which she would cry herself to sleep only to wake up still weeping.

Best was in the hall repairing a pane of glass when she left to post a letter. He watched her don her mackintosh and slip an envelope into her pocket before venturing out beneath a darkening sky. There seemed something ominous about her decision to walk three and a half miles on such a day, instead of leaving her mail for the postman to collect when he next made a delivery. He insisted she took an umbrella and paused to watch her slight, hunched figure disappear down the drive.

Clementine's legs felt as heavy as her heart as she carelessly skirted puddles that were already forming in the lane. She was immune to the damp seeping through her shoes or the rain beating down in angry bursts. Even the sudden flash of lightning followed by a roar of thunder failed to arouse her; she was past caring.

Piers Douglas slowed down when he saw the bedraggled figure in his path, and wondered why she didn't make use of the umbrella, still rolled in her grip. Only when he pulled up alongside did he recognise her. 'Goodness gracious, it's you, Clementine! Get in at once!'

'What are you doing here?' she asked as droplets of rainwater ran off her coat onto the upholstery.

'It's lovely to see you too!'

She managed a smile. 'But what *are* you doing here?'

'Well, I had a few hours free and decided to drive down and see how you are.'

She studied his face whilst the rain punctuated the silence. 'You know, don't you? Alexander told you.'

'No, it was Claudia.'

'Claudia!' She was shaken. Who else had her sister told?

'She assumed I already knew,' he said. 'Don't worry, I think she realises that it's in her interest to hold her tongue.' He looked at her and shook his head. 'Oh, Clemmie, you fool. I thought you had more sense.'

'So did I once, but love seems to defy common sense.'

'It frankly baffles me, Clementine. I cannot believe you allowed it to happen.'

'I don't expect you to understand; all I know is that it is so powerful it leaves me helpless. Before the war I once went to a coming out party where some fool managed to spike my champagne. It tasted innocuous but within a short while I was physically helpless. I knew I was going to be ill, but could not move. I couldn't even speak. It was totally humiliating.' She grimaced at the recollection. 'When I'm with Alexander I'm as helpless and ashamed as I was then. I am drunk with love for him and though I know it's wrong, there's nothing I can do. Common sense takes a back seat until sobering up.'

Piers gazed at her with a quizzical expression. 'Well, you certainly look as if you've sobered up now, and got the devil of all hangovers. Oh Clemmie,' he said sadly, 'why couldn't you have fallen in love with me, it would have been so much simpler.'

She smiled, tears filling her eyes.

'Anyway count yourself lucky I haven't been able to get down until my temper cooled,' Piers went on. 'It has upset me a lot that two people I care about have got themselves into such a mess. I really thought after seeing you and Charles together at Christmas that all would turn out well; it was obvious he loves you, and from where I stood it looked mutual, so you can imagine my feelings when Claudia said she caught you *in flagrante delicto*.'

There was an awkward pause. Eventually Piers touched her arm, and when he spoke his voice held warmer tones. 'Look, Clemmie, I don't pretend to understand what you did, but I'm not here to judge you. You look as though you've suffered enough. I came because I felt you might need a shoulder to cry on. I don't suppose you've too many friends in whom you can confide.'

She gave a wry smile, and he grinned and shifted in his seat, saying, 'Look, old thing, I've two or three hours before heading back. What do you say I take you back to Coppins to change out of those wet things, and then we'll go in search of a roaring fire and something to eat — though perhaps you've other plans. I still haven't asked you what you're doing out in such beastly weather?'

'I was walking to the village to post a letter?'

'Must be pretty urgent,' he said as another flash of lightning zigzagged across the sky.

'It's for Charles.'

He looked hard at her. 'Does he know?'

'He will when he receives it.'

His eyes lingered on her a moment. 'Then it appears that I've arrived in the nick of time to prevent you from compounding your folly.'

Clementine stared at him. 'Are you suggesting I keep quiet in order to save my skin?'

'Most certainly not! You don't deserve such consideration. I am thinking of Charles and asking what he has done to deserve such treatment. He loves you, Clementine! Think what your confession will do to him. It will devastate him.'

'I should never have married him — it was wrong of me. It's been one wrong after another and it has to stop. I have to tell him. I don't think I could live with myself if I didn't.'

'Then let that be your penance. Too often, easing one's conscience is done at some poor innocent's expense — in this case a man who in my opinion deserves the highest consideration. There are not many who would knowingly take on some other chap's children.'

Clementine spun round.

'I guessed long ago,' he replied simply.

'And what about Claudia … did you discuss your suspicions with her?' She saw immediately that she had offended him and apologised. 'But how long will it be before she works it out?' she fretted.

'I don't think she will. As far as your sister is concerned, it was just a single night of lust. I doubt her vanity would accept anything else.'

'I pray you're right. I've had no contact with her since she left with Alexander. He phoned before leaving London and told me not to worry, that he'd sorted everything out and that she would keep silent.'

'What else did he say?'

'You want to know what we've planned if he gets back safely — whether we intend running off together?'

'Well do you?'

She said nothing and Piers looked troubled. 'Well, I'm sure you know the consequences if you do. It will not be so bad for Alex, the women always come off worse in these situations You will be a social outcast, forever known as the woman who stole her sister's husband — not an enviable position. As for your parents, how do you suppose they will survive it all? And whilst we're at it, let's not forget the twins. How will they cope with being taunted and teased all their lives. It's no fun to be illegitimate, but then I'm sure you know all this. At least with Charles they have respectability, grandparents, a background. Please don't throw it away, Clementine.'

He peered out through the windscreen and studied the sky. 'The weather seems to be lifting. I'll start the motor. What do you say we go to Corfe? There's an old coaching inn in the Square where they serve good food, and most importantly have a decent fire where you can burn that letter.' He shook his head firmly. 'No protests, my darling. You are just going to have to live with your guilt — alone!'

# 22

Charles glanced at the postcard showing the spectacular remains of the castle with the picturesque village at its foot, recalling from his school history lessons, that the Roundheads had destroyed it during the Civil War. As he turned it over to read the text it struck him what an awful war that must have been, with families and friends in conflict.

The large sloping hand of his wife's brought a smile to his face. *From the ruins of Corfe Castle to your own battlefield. Just a note to tell you all is well and that we miss you. Love, Clementine.*

He glanced at the postmark and saw that it had been posted nearly three weeks ago. It was the first time Charles had heard from her since the offensive began, and though he had not been too concerned, knowing that post did go missing in all the chaos, it was good to get word from her.

Nurse Elizabeth Scott, Clementine's old friend, was tending to a young sapper's leg when she noted Captain Hamilton's smile. For a fleeting moment he looked almost human, but his face soon resumed its impassive mask when an officer, who had been visiting some of his men, approached and enquired after their health. The sound of the wind on the billowing walls of the marquee concealed much of their conversation but she heard enough fragments to gather that Captain Hamilton was telling him, as he was apt to these days, that with influenza knocking the troops down like nine-pins, the only sure way back to Blighty was in spirit form. The tall officer, senior in rank, stared at him from eyes glazed with exhaustion, and said he had not long recovered from a bout himself. To Lisa it explained the pallor beneath his suntan and the uniform, which hung loosely from his shoulders.

She concentrated on her task, conscious of the patient's imploring eyes and set jaw as she removed the last of the dressing and began to clean the wound. 'Soon be over' she said soothingly to the lad, who began to relax and tell her that he had been a miner before the war. 'And now you tunnel under the German lines laying mines,' she said, with a quick glance towards Captain Hamilton whose voice rose in unveiled exasperation.

'It's about time those bureaucrats back home realise there is a war on and leave us to get on with the jobs we are here to do instead of trying to defeat us with blessed paperwork,' he said, slamming a folder on the table where Sister usually sat.

Lisa noticed the officer wince slightly and touch his brow. To her experienced eye she thought he should still be in bed, but doubtless the bed had been required for someone more needy.

As the MO resentfully sifted through the file, she saw the officer stoop to the floor. He staggered slightly and for a second she thought he was going to collapse. However, he quickly regained his balance, and seeing him pocket what looked like a photograph, realised that he had only dropped something. His gaunt frame had barely straightened when Captain Hamilton handed him a sheet of paper. He spent only seconds jotting down what he sought and then, still unsmiling, returned the document, apologised for taking up the Captain's time and bade him good day.

There was something about the good-looking officer that fascinated Lisa. She watched as he paused by the entrance and looked at the ward, as if trying to imprint it in his memory. Fleetingly, their eyes met, and she felt that she too was being stored, but acknowledged that it was likely the nurse and not the woman that he saw.

Major The Honourable Alexander Rufus Henry FitzPatrick had every right to be pleased as he rode away from the vast expanse of white hospital marquees; had it been a military exercise it would have been a resounding success. It had not been easy to locate Hamilton, and to contrive a meeting without arousing his suspicion made the manoeuvre even more successful. But Alexander was depressed as he led his horse towards the hills. Clementine had told him little of her husband, and what his imagination had conjured bore small resemblance to reality. He knew he had been wrong to come, but during his recent illness, he had thought much about her husband, until finally a mixture of curiosity and jealousy had driven him to seek Charles out.

There had been a moment back there when he had come close to introducing himself and informing Hamilton of his intentions regarding Clementine. Thankfully, he had stopped himself. Just in time he had acknowledged that it would be an act of gross selfishness to seek to destroy a marriage when his own future was so uncertain. He knew that he had to suffer the present situation until the war was over and he was in a position to make the changes he so desperately wanted. For as much as he hated the thought of her with someone else, he would not wish her to be alone.

He had been profoundly shocked when Clementine confessed that she had planned suicide upon discovering she was pregnant; and it had made him realise how vulnerable she was. Hamilton's timely rescue had forged a bond which Alexander knew would be hard for Clementine to sever. Indeed, he himself would be eternally grateful to this man. But, that said, he also knew that if, God willing, he survived, nothing would stop him from doing all in his power to put matters to rights. Nothing — neither her protestations nor thought of the furore to come — would stop him. In recent years he had learned the difference between living and merely existing, and knew that sometimes one had to fight for one's beliefs. However, reading the postcard Hamilton had so carelessly dropped, and which he had stolen, he had been stabbed by emotions. Those few words of affection with which Clementine had addressed Hamilton had cut deeply, and his reflex had been to throw it into the rhubarb patch that grew alongside the duckboard paths surrounding the camp.

Perhaps if Charles had been short, fat and ugly, he would have reacted differently, but his rival was of striking appearance with intelligent eyes that reminded him of his brother.

What must Patrick be thinking, Alexander wondered, as he looked down from heaven and saw the mess he had got himself into? As boys they'd got into plenty of scrapes together and it was usually Patrick's quick thinking that got them out of trouble. Alexander lifted his head to the skies, ablaze with the setting sun. 'If you're listening, Patch, help me,' he said.

*

Summer arrived and the Army, still short of soldiers, launched a fresh campaign for new conscripts up to the age of fifty-one. Military Police frequently turned up in public places such as football grounds and theatres, with orders to root out shirkers. The conscription of such mature men, old enough to be grandfathers, caused a public outcry. Such measures made them fear that the situation was more desperate than they were being told.

Brigadier Ellacombe had his work cut out with complaints

from many constituents. Suddenly people seemed more critical of the war than before. Too many soldiers had laid down their lives and victory seemed more distant than ever.

A feeling of hopelessness grew among the nation as newspapers raged at German savagery on nightly bombing raids, which resulted in the devastation of Allied hospitals. Photographs of the atrocities in the popular press caused anti- German feeling to intensify. The Hun were the cause of everyone's misery, from the loss of loved ones to food shortages, and the wave of hatred reached new heights.

Early in June 1918, Brigadier Ellacombe suffered a mild stroke. The doctors said it was a result of overwork and stress, and he was ordered to take things easy for the coming months. He retired to Coppins where Mrs Ellacombe and Clementine nursed him back to health. Not having suffered more than an occasional attack of gout, his illness shook him more than he cared to admit. He was not yet seventy and had hoped to be around to watch his son Timmy and grandchildren grow. Although he resented all the restrictions imposed on him, not least the ban of alcohol, he was not prepared to risk his life. Bored and disgruntled, he proved a demanding patient, and his devoted wife had a fulltime job trying to amuse him and hold the fort with Constituency matters until he made a full recovery.

Claudia drove down from London in Alexander's car in order to visit her father. Clementine was in the nursery when she saw the vehicle, with its distinctive pointed bonnet, approach the house. For a moment she thought it was Alexander, but as the car got closer she saw the distinctive silvery-blonde hair.

With a heavy heart she watched Claudia step from the car. As if knowing Clementine was watching, the other girl looked up with a smug smile. Sinking onto the window seat, her nerves jangling, Clementine imagined her sister informing their parents of her shocking discovery two months before and their disbelief as they demanded an explanation she could not give. She had to keep reminding herself that Alexander had made certain his wife would not expose them, but this being their first encounter, she was fearful that Claudia, incensed at the sight of her, might lose control.

Clementine didn't think her legs would carry her down the stairs, let alone walk into the drawing room and greet her sister as if nothing was wrong. A summer-sweet voice pierced her sorrow and she turned to see Charlotte standing in her cot, her plump arms outstretched. Peter had been pulling himself up for a few weeks now but this was the first time his little sister had managed it. Clementine's eyes filled with tears as she thought how proud Alexander would have been. She lifted the child into her arms and held her close. Pressing her lips against the soft curls, she felt stronger. Whatever the future held, she would always have her children. Nothing could prevent that.

As Piers had assured Clementine, Claudia said nothing. At long last she had something worth keeping and was determined that the life she had always yearned for would finally be hers when her husband returned.

Over dinner, Clementine learned the cost of Claudia's silence. She spoke about her home in London and the improvements she was making. Also, she made a point of letting Clementine know that it was Alexander's home too. It seemed she had wasted no time in disposing of his old accommodation by renting it out for the duration. She seemed in her element as she described the study she was decorating in the modern style for his use, and humoured her father by asking his advice on what books she should purchase to fill the shelves.

Thankfully both their parents were so preoccupied with their own affairs they failed to notice that the sisters spoke only when it was unavoidable, and that their paths only crossed at mealtimes. Claudia stayed for two nights, insisting duty summoned her back to the city; canteen work and hospital visiting occupying her days. However, Clementine's relief was short-lived, for within a few weeks, her sister returned, with plans to stay longer this time.

'The woman in the house next door has gone down with this Spanish Influenza,' she said at dinner. 'I felt it a tad close for comfort and decided it was time to get out. I don't think London's a safe place to be at the moment. Everyone's talking about it.'

She was right to be concerned, for the epidemic was of a particularly vicious strain, arriving without warning and, according to what one read and heard, which frequently killed its victims within the first twenty-four hours. It was like a plague, believed by many to have started in the trenches. Tragically, the disease seemed to favour young adults, and many soldiers who had thus far survived the war did so only to die of this sudden virus for which there was no cure.

'They've closed so many meeting places that London is like a morgue,' Claudia complained. 'And they're using gallons of chemicals to fumigate the buses, trains and trams to prevent it from spreading.' She shuddered affectedly. 'If there's one smell I can't abide it's disinfectant, and it's positively everywhere.'

'So much for their efforts,' said Brigadier Ellacombe, who had been following the spread of the disease. 'I read somewhere that a large party of American soldiers en route to France, camped out on Southampton Common and went down with it overnight, like flies. Apparently they had no room for them in the hospitals and the poor fellows were left in the open. It appears hundreds died.'

'How tragic! Their poor mothers,' grieved Mrs Ellacombe. 'To have travelled so far only to die of some foul disease.'

'Listen to this, Clemmie,' said her father later on, when they were gathered in the library and he was reading the evening news. 'This will make you laugh. They report that so far, the present epidemic of influenza has not affected the British troops in France. What poppycock!'

Had it not been for the seriousness of the subject she might well have laughed, for Charles had written much about the mortuary tents that were crammed with row upon row of corpses, and of the men arriving at the hospital tents semi-conscious and with raging temperatures.

'Why don't we ever get the truth?' she replied and instantly regretted it when she saw Claudia looking at her with a sly smile.

\*

The next day, Clementine welcomed the opportunity to drive her father to Sherborne to collect Timmy for the summer holidays. After the end-of-term service in the Abbey, during which the names of fallen alumni were read out, her brother introduced her to his House Master, a bespectacled man in his seventies, who had been brought out of retirement. He fondly remembered Charles as a good all-rounder. 'A bright boy with an enquiring mind. Captain of the First Eleven too.'

On the return journey Timmy jabbered nonstop, catching up on all the news, asking about Jack and the size of the twins. He was especially longing to see Peter, who was almost walking, planning to teach him to kick a ball before the end of the holidays.

Clementine laughed, glad to have her young brother home again, knowing his presence would inject a much-needed shot of gaiety into their lives.

Mrs Best made a special effort with dinner that evening and Brigadier Ellacombe insisted on opening a bottle of claret to go with the roast duck. As Timmy was helping himself to a second helping of raspberries and describing a pillow-fight that went wrong, Best appeared wearing a sombre expression and carrying a silver plate. Clementine was the first to spot the telegram.

'It's for Mrs FitzPatrick,' she heard him whisper to her father.

She could barely breathe, feeling as if someone had gripped her by the throat. Death, wounded or missing … One by one, the others stopped talking. Clementine pressed her fist to her mouth struggling to remain calm.

'Let me open it, my dear,' said Brigadier Ellacombe to Claudia.

'No, Papa, it's something *I* must do,' she said, taking the telegram from him. To Clementine's horror, it seemed as if her sister relished the occasion, almost as if she had rehearsed it.

'He's in a Base hospital in Boulogne. They advise I make an immediate visit.' Clementine saw relief register on her mother's face but all she could think of was the countless wives and mothers she had comforted, having arrived in France only to discover they were too late.

'You must leave immediately,' said her mother. 'Clementine will accompany you.'

Claudia protested vehemently. 'No! If I've got to go, I'd rather go alone.'

'Don't be ridiculous,' said her father. 'Someone must travel with you. Your mother is needed here so Clementine is the obvious choice. Let's hear no more about it,' and he rose from the table to telephone Lady Moundsmere.

*

The rattle of the machine guns was unrelenting, bullets zipping through a sky pockmarked by rifle-fire and exploding hand-grenades. The formation had broken and every man clawed his way forward, diving into shell craters, crawling over splintered trees, inching past dismembered bodies, some belonging to old friends. All around there were screams but still they pushed on.

'Anaesthetise him, the leg has to come off,' said the blood-splattered surgeon to the chaplain, as he hurriedly inspected the injuries of one of the six wounded soldiers who lay on the operating tables in the make-shift theatre. Reverend Thomas Ryan, though medically untrained, looked disconcertedly at the growing pile of newly amputated limbs that awaited removal and felt compelled to speak.

'Is it not possible to save the leg?'

Their distant voices gradually penetrated the soldier's nightmare.

'I'm not God!' the surgeon snapped. 'The sort of operation he needs requires time — time I don't have, time that might save a couple of other poor blighters from being added to your burial list tomorrow!'

Alexander's whole being rebelled, and he half-rose from the table. He tried to speak but no sound would come and he felt himself falling, falling, to a place of escape.

*

After arranging for Best to drive Claudia and Clementine to the station to catch the early-morning train, Mrs Ellacombe spent the remainder of the evening comforting her younger daughter and helping her pack her case. 'I know you would have preferred me to accompany you, darling, but Papa needs me — and besides

277

I'm sure you'll find Clementine with all her experience invaluable. She will be a great comfort to you.'

Before retiring for the night, Mrs Ellacombe came into Clementine's room for a quick word. She found her by an open window staring at the sky.

'It goes without saying that you will do your utmost to take care of Claudia, and I know she'll be grateful for your support. The poor child is in shock.' She removed the counterpane and turned back the sheet. 'Come and get into bed. You've a long day ahead of you tomorrow and I want you in a fit state to look after your sister. You know as well as I do that it's not going to be easy for her.'

After her mother left, Clementine climbed back out of the bed.

'May I have a word?' she said, slipping into Claudia's room where she found her sitting on the bed unscrewing a bottle of aspirins. Claudia looked at her with naked hostility. Clementine noticed how pale she was, more than usual, and the dark circles beneath her eyes.

I've been wrong, she thought. She does love him.

'Claudia, I know you don't want me there but I've just come to say that for Alexander's sake we must try and get on as best we can. We don't know how ill he is, but I suspect it must be very serious, and above all else we must remember that he will need all his strength if he is to recover. We must give him no cause for anguish.'

Claudia picked up a glass of water and swallowed the pills. 'I don't need *you* to tell me about my husband. I may not be able to stop you from coming, but I can and will prevent you from seeing him. Now get out of my room.'

Clementine slept little, and about four in the morning was on her way to the kitchen to get a drink when she became conscious of groaning; long intermittent groans, the kind she had heard every day of her nursing career. They led her to Claudia's room, and seeing the thin light which escaped from beneath the door, she ventured in. 'Are you all …' The stench of vomit from the floor was overpowering, and sprawled on the bed, Claudia lay as lifeless as a cloth doll, staring from unseeing eyes. Swiftly Clementine lit the bedside lamp, drawing in her breath when she saw the deep flush on her face. Instinct told her it was the killer influenza that Claudia had left London to escape.

*

The room was hot and oppressive and Clementine threw up the window and sat resting on the sill. The early-morning breeze revived her a little after the night she had just endured. Down below she saw Alexander's car still in the same haphazard position Claudia had parked it in the week before when she had returned after a trip into Wareham. Thinking of Alexander, her fingernails dug into the window surround. It was four days since the telegram had arrived and although her father was using his contacts, they were still waiting for news. *Oh Alex, Alex!*

The door opened and old Dr Gordon appeared, wearing a kindly smile. Wiping her eyes, Clementine went to greet him.

'How is she this morning, my dear?' he asked, concerned by how tired and anaemic Clementine appeared.

'She's been feverish most of the night,' she said as they walked over to the bed where Claudia lay in a restless sleep. 'And though I've forced fluid down her, she brings it up within minutes.' The tension in her voice was mirrored in her eyes; she felt so helpless, so worried. Each day she had hoped for some improvement, but still her sister's temperature remained dangerously high, still she was delirious most of the time, and since the early hours Clementine had noticed a change in her breathing.

Dr Gordon removed the stethoscope from the patient's chest and turned to Clementine, his face grave. 'The lungs are congested.'

The words caused a sinking sensation in her stomach. 'Pneumonia?' she said feebly.

'I'm afraid so, but take heart. You're doing a fine job, and with your expert care I'm sure she'll pull through. Now you have a bronchitis kettle, I presume? No — well, I'll mention it downstairs and tell them to get one immediately. It will release warm vapours and help your sister to breathe more easily.'

Clementine watched as he lit a rod of cotton dipped in alcohol and placed it in a small glass for a few seconds. 'Cupping can be even more effective,' he said, pressing the cup to the back of Claudia's thorax. It remained in place by suction, and satisfied, Dr Gordon closed his bag. 'It cannot be easy for you, coping alone, but I do feel that for the safety of the rest of the household, you are wise to contain the virus here. It could be disastrous if either of the twins or your father were to contract it, but I'm sure you know that.'

Clementine nodded and Dr Gordon patted her on the shoulder.

'Chin up, my dear. With your nursing experience she has a better chance than most. Keep the room at an even temperature and continue with the fluids, for if she gets dehydrated she won't have a hope.'

After he left Clementine stood staring at the little cup that clung leechlike to Claudia's throat. For all Dr Gordon's praise and encouragement, she felt utterly helpless. She was sure they were not doing enough, but when she had voiced her fears he had told her to write to her husband 'For with most of the country's bright young medical people on the Western Front, it seems the most likely place a cure will be found.'

Clementine had looked at the ageing man who should have been enjoying retirement, and said quietly: 'Surely, Dr Gordon, my sister will either be well on the road to recovery or dead by the time my letter would even be acknowledged.'

More days passed and Claudia continued to cling to life by a gossamer thread. Her body, wracked with fever, tossed and turned, and as Clementine battled to keep her alive, her ears echoed with her sister's disjointed ravings.

Mrs Ellacombe lived in constant dread. Every morning, after little sleep, she would leave a breakfast tray outside the quarantined room and wait anxiously for Clementine to acknowledge her presence. She was convinced it was only a matter of time before Clementine too fell victim to the disease. Through the oak door she would nervously enquire of any progress, and upon hearing Clementine's voice would say a silent prayer, and another, when she learned that her beloved Claudia was still holding on.

*

Clementine did not hear the door open. Lying on the chaise-longue at the foot of the bed, she had fallen into a deep slumber. Charles, careful not to wake her, crept in and gazed at her bedraggled figure. He recalled the time he had found her slumped over his desk. He would never forget it, for he believed that this was the moment he had fallen in love with her.

Clementine forced open her heavy eyes and lifted her head to check on Claudia. Sitting on a chair near the window she saw a figure, and wondered if she was still dreaming. The curtains were drawn and the room was shadowy, like looking through muslin, reminding her of the mosquito nets they had used in India. She registered the uniform, and the lean powerful body within, but she could not see his face. It was hidden beneath a fragment of light. Involuntarily, her whole being went rigid.

Swiftly Charles was at her side. 'Charles ...' She started to tremble. 'You scared me — I thought you were a ghost.' But she didn't say whose. She sat up. 'What are you doing here?' Her eyes filled with tears and she could not stop shaking.

'They sent me home, darling,' and then she noticed the plaster cast on his arm. 'I broke my wrist, slipped on a wet duckboard. All your fault too,' he teased, 'for I dropped the postcard you sent me from Corfe Castle amongst the rhubarb, and as I bent down to pick it up, my feet went out from under me. As you can imagine, I'm not too handy with a scalpel at the moment.' Smiling, he pulled her to her feet. 'Let me look at you, it's been so long.'

'I look a fright,' she said awkwardly, and hearing Claudia groan she hurried to her side. Charles joined her. After a week she was still very ill, and Clementine feared she was getting worse. Her temperature was rising even higher, and the only way Clementine had managed to keep it from raging further was to frequently sponge her down with the cold water she kept by the side of the bed in a tin bath.

'I wondered why your mother was so welcoming,' said Charles. 'I seem to have arrived at an opportune time.'

'She's been frantic with worry. She wanted to nurse Claudia herself, but thankfully Papa forbade her. Can you imagine if she got it. I'm sure she wouldn't stand a chance.'

'One would think so, but there is nothing normal about this

disease. It's unlike anything I've yet encountered. It attacks without discrimination but seems to kill mostly the young,' Charles said as she refilled the bronchitis kettle. 'I'd say Timmy's more at risk. Make sure he stays well away.'

'Papa sent him to stay with Aunt Meg until Claudia's recovered.'

'That's sensible. I examined Claudia whilst you were sleeping and the indications are that she's reaching crisis point. The next few hours will be crucial.'

Clementine nodded, having suspected the same. 'She's so weak.'

Charles placed his hand on her shoulder and steered her away from the bed. 'I'm here now, so let me do the worrying. Just for a minute let's forget Claudia. I've missed you, more than I ever thought possible, the twins too.' He grinned. 'How they have grown. I wouldn't have recognised them, but neither did they me. I thought Charlotte was going to cry.'

She sighed. 'I fear they're going to forget me too. I've only seen them from the window since Claudia's been ill. If the weather's nice Danielle puts a rug on the lawn and I sit and watch them play, but I so long to hold them.'

'And are you longing to hold me too?' He went to kiss her but she moved her head. He frowned playfully. 'You do still love me, don't you?'

'I've virtually lived in this room, in these same clothes, for the past week. I …'

'You look fine to me, a little pale perhaps and rather tired, but nothing that a good sleep won't put to rights.'

However, the tension wouldn't leave her, and his eyes lingered on her, making her more uncomfortable.

'Claudia will be all right. You must stop worrying about her.' Choking with misery she nodded, and he placed his hand on the side of her face, running his thumb over her lips. 'You *are* pleased to see me, aren't you?'

'What do you think!'

He lowered his head and kissed her, and swallowing hard she steeled herself to respond, horribly conscious of the comparison that was running amok in her mind. His touch, scent, the texture of his hair and skin, his lips: everything so different to Alexander.

'Poor little darling, you've worked so hard,' he breathed softly. 'But I can take over now and give you the rest you deserve.'

'Don't be silly, Charles. How can you manage with your arm in plaster?'

'Well enough.' He squeezed her tightly with his good arm and kissed her again. Clementine's embrace was feeble in comparison.

'Now off you go. Run yourself a bath and have a sleep. Leave me to look after Claudia. Mrs Best is going to bring me something to eat and I've taken a book from the library I've been wanting to read for a long time.'

She protested but in truth was desperate to escape, to be alone.

'No buts. You do as the doctor orders.'

Minutes later she was standing in her own bedroom, leaning heavily against the door, staring at the bed where she had lain with Alexander and remembering what Piers had said as they had watched her confession to Charles burn. 'It won't be easy for you, I'm sure, but believe me, there are times when honesty is *not* the best policy.'

# 23

Brigadier Ellacombe's maiden Aunt Matty had once told Clementine that great happiness and great sorrow were destroyers of sleep. She had been a quiet lady of small income, whose only excitement had been infrequent visits to relatives. Claudia had thought her a bit of a joke and nicknamed her Aunt Musty.

'Reminds me of Miss Haversham in *Great Expectations*,' she said to Clementine. 'Though I can't for the life of me ever imagine Aunt Musty having had a beau.'

As Clementine tried to sleep that night she thought of that rather prim lady, remembering the certainty with which she spoke, and wondered what had happened in her seemingly uneventful life to have caused her to utter the words with such conviction. Then she thought of the small portion of happiness that she and Alexander had shared, and how it had always been the precursor of sorrow. It would seem there was a price to pay for such extreme emotions, and she wondered if that was why Aunt Matty had settled for a humdrum existence.

Until falling in love with Alexander, Clementine had considered herself fairly happy and content, but after experiencing such intense joy she realised she had only been half-alive. Perhaps Aunt Matty had been able to return to her half-life — but could *she*?

As her misery kept her awake she turned restlessly, imagining how different her life would have been, had they not met. But despite all the suffering it had brought, she felt strongly that it had been no accident. She and Alexander had been destined to meet, and until a few days ago, she had thought they had been destined to remain apart.

Watching her sister's strength fade she saw for the first time the possibility of a future with Alexander. But it brought no happiness. She could not deny that she longed more than anything to be with him, but not at the cost of Claudia's life, and this awareness, coupled with the burden of bearing the responsibility of her recovery, only heightened her torment. For Claudia's sake she was glad Charles was home, for she believed that if anyone could save her, it would be him.

Burying her head in the pillow to smother her sobs, she recalled what Charles had said about arriving at an opportune time. Yesterday, Lady Moundsmere had telephoned to break the news that besides internal injuries, Alexander's leg had been amputated. The report had come from his uncle who had visited him and spoken to the doctors. It seemed the worst was over and as soon as he was fit enough to travel, he would be shipped back to England.

Before Charles's return, Clementine had tried not to think of the future, but now she could no longer hide from it. Against her instinct she had allowed Piers to influence her, convince her that her future lay with her husband. She had thought it a cowardly path but he had insisted that it was the right thing to do. Charles had not sinned. Why should he suffer for her adultery, and learn that she continued to betray him in thought, every waking hour. From near-drowning she had survived, learning to swim in those rivers of guilt and deceit. Alive she was, but she loathed what she had become, and Charles's return only added to this self-loathing, for she was no longer able to hide from the ugly reality. She now knew that if Claudia were to die, she would ask Charles to release her from their marriage so that she could be with Alexander.

*

It had been a long and exhausting day for Charles. He yawned wearily, but try as he would, he could not sleep. The chaise-longue was lumpy, besides being too small for his frame, and his wrist ached, yet it was something else that kept him awake. His thoughts were engrossed with Clementine, the change in her. She was as she had been when they had first married, shying at his touch. It had taken months of patience on his part to make the physical side of their marriage work, and now it would appear she had taken a step backwards, and he couldn't understand why.

Before he had gone up to see her, he had spent a little time with his in-laws catching up on recent events. He had learned the fate of FitzPatrick and about the thwarted visit that Clementine and Claudia had planned. He couldn't deny his relief that it had not come about.

He shifted position as the muscles in his leg contracted, and with a grimace he waited for the pain to subside. It was a marked contrast to the way he had envisaged spending his first night back. He noticed Claudia move, as if she too couldn't get comfortable. She had been restless for the past hour and her breathing more laboured. He stretched his leg, sighed and then closed his eyes again and made a determined effort to put Clementine from his mind. Claudia seemed quieter and gradually he drifted off into a deep sleep. But within what seemed like minutes he was rudely awakened when a cry penetrated his dream. Dazed, he pulled himself up and went over to the bedside.

The rivulets of sweat on Claudia's forehead glistened in the lamplight as short angry bursts of incoherent words escaped her lips and faded into oblivion. Hurriedly, he lit another lamp and in the process knocked over the tray with the remains of his dinner. Seeing her burning with fever he knew he had to lower her temperature quickly, and pulling the sheet from her, he placed it in the tub of water by the bed. Clumsily he wrung from it what water he could, before spreading it over her naked body. Vapour began to rise almost immediately, and pulling up a chair he remained by her side watching her battle with the disease, mopping her brow, and re-soaking the sheet as it dried. He knew she had reached crisis point and that her life was in the balance. He could do no more to ease her suffering; she alone would have to win this fight. A peculiarity of the illness was that it seemed to take the strong. Charles had seen many die from this deadly virus that no one could cure. Claudia was drawing on her inner reserves and to Charles it seemed a futile fight.

The stench hit Clementine immediately she opened the door. She had escaped it during the night and wondered how she would ever get used to it again. It was awful, like nothing she had experienced before. Dr Gordon said it was the poison in the virus. Sometimes it amazed her that she had avoided catching it herself, and could only think that her time as a nurse had made her immune. She longed to throw the windows up and rid the room of the evil stench, but there was a cold wind and she remembered what she had been told about keeping the room at an even temperature.

The sight of Charles sprawled on the chaise-longue, his head resting precariously near the edge, stirred her. Even in the early morning shadows she could see the mess he was in; his shirt stained and crumpled and his hair, damp with sweat, had formed soft curls. She glanced again at Claudia, suddenly conscious that she lay so still, so still she could see no sign of breathing. Gripped with fear, she shook Charles. 'Wake up, wake up!' Befuddled with sleep, he opened his eyes. 'Charles, she's not moving! Claudia's not moving!'

He shot off the sofa without a word and she watched him place his hand on her sister's jugular vein. Barely breathing herself, she saw his shoulders relax. It was all right. She was alive. Thanking God for His mercy, Clementine threw her arms around Charles and held him tight. Wearing a broad grin he said, 'I wonder how many poor souls you've shipped off to the mortuary tent when they were only sleeping.'

Watching as he briefly checked her sister, she collapsed onto the dressing- table stool, trembling with relief and drying her eyes. Eventually Charles placed his hand on her shoulder. 'She's going to get better, darling.'

While Charles took a bath, Clementine tried to put the room back in some sort of order. He allowed her to open the windows, but she was careful to leave the curtains drawn to prevent draughts. Repeatedly she would stop and glance at her sister, checking, just in case.

Gradually the air began to change, and through the curtains a breeze filtered, circulating and banishing the evil smell of disease.

Light-headed with relief, Clementine felt as if she was caught up in it, as if she was part of the change, and that the past was escaping; sucked out through the sash windows. She knew she could not hold on, that the time had come for it to go. She felt a little of the same mood she'd had the first New Year's Eve after leaving school; nostalgia for the past and uncertainty for what was to come; only then it had held a certain amount of excitement as she had wondered what jewels lay ahead. The difference now was that the future seemed to her as lifeless as a beach of pebbles; she'd had her jewels, and the future, such as it was, had to be faced.

Clementine knelt on the floor picking up the smashed dinner-plate Charles had dropped during the night, and hearing movement glanced up to see him standing inside the door with just a towel around his waist.

'Where's my luggage?' he asked.

'It's unpacked. I'll come and show you.'

Watching him awkwardly search through the wardrobe, her compassion was aroused at the sight of a large damp area in the centre of his back, and picking up another towel she rubbed it dry.

'I knew there had to be some benefit to having fractured my wrist,' he teased, pleased that she had touched him voluntarily. He turned and looked longingly into her eyes, as he traced a line down her cheek. 'I've missed you, Clemmie.'

The urge to run was strong; she wasn't ready for this. He stroked her hair and drew her closer, but she put her hands on his chest, keeping him at a distance, mumbling, 'I've got to get back to Claudia.'

'She'll be fine. I doubt she will wake for hours.' Pulling his wife towards him again, he buried his head in the nape of her neck, kissing her tenderly. 'I've missed you, darling,' and he squeezed her tightly, making her aware of how much he wanted her. 'I've waited nine months to be alone with you.' He fumbled with the buttons on her blouse, cursing his clumsiness.

Clementine began to panic. 'No, Charles, not now!'

'Are you menstruating?'

She shook her head.

'Then what's wrong?' Eyes that only seconds before had been brimming with desire now bore into her. Clementine stared back, her own pale eyes reflecting her torment. This was the key to turn the lock on the past and open the door to the future. She needed more time; she was not ready! But there wasn't any more time, not the sort she wanted, and somehow, she forced a smile.

'Nothing is wrong,' she murmured. 'Nothing.' And when he drew her close again there was no resistance.

Clementine lay on her side bearing the weight of Charles's arm as he dozed contentedly beside her. She lay wide awake, staring at the fireplace; the grate was empty but she saw flames. Great flashing spears of fire, painting the room.

'What are you thinking?' asked Charles, seeing her stare into the fireplace.

'I was just remembering a poem I learned when I was little — *Armies in the Fire*,' she said, glad that he couldn't see her tears.

Charles looked curiously at her; he knew the verse about the boy seeing armies in the flames, but all he could see was an empty grate.

*

There was rejoicing when it became known that Claudia was on the road to recovery. Confident that she was no longer infectious, Charles later permitted Mrs Ellacombe into the sickroom. Although delighted to see her daughter, she wept when she saw the emaciated, jaundiced figure asleep in bed, and needed repeated assurance that she would be her old self in a few weeks.

Mrs Ellacombe was present when Claudia awoke that afternoon. She had to tell her how ill she had been, for the girl had little recollection of the previous fortnight. Though dazed and weak, it did not please her to learn that she owed her life to Clementine.

'But it was Charles who was with you when your fever broke. He really couldn't have arrived at a better time.' And having saved her daughter, she was happy to forgive him anything. She brushed Claudia's lifeless hair, trying to sound cheerful while inwardly sighing.

Claudia nodded weakly; she felt utterly exhausted and did not want to think about it. 'Pass me the mirror, Mummy.'

Mrs Ellacombe pretended not to hear for she feared her daughter's looks might not recover. Claudia noted her reluctance. 'Oh Christ, do I look so bad?' she groaned.

'It's a clear sign you're on the road to recovery when you start worrying about your appearance,' said Charles, coming in to check on his patient. He briefly examined her and smiled. 'Well, everything seems to be in working order. Now all we have to do is build up your strength. Mrs Best is under strict instruction to feed you plenty of nourishing meals, lots of broth.'

Claudia sighed. 'I've no energy for anything, I only want to close my eyes and sleep. I'm so tired.'

Claudia waited until the next day when she was alone with Clementine before asking about Alexander. Their mother, believing the matter would distress her, felt it best to keep the news from her as long as possible. She watched as Clementine placed a cup of hot Bovril and milk on the bedside table, saying 'Mrs Best said you're not to leave any this time.'

Claudia pulled a face. 'She knows perfectly well I hate the stuff.'

'It must be doing you good, you're already looking much improved.'

They were not easy in each other's company and there was an awkward silence while Clementine straightened the counterpane.

'Why has no one mentioned Alexander?' Claudia asked suddenly. 'Is he dead?'

It was the lack of emotion in her voice that shook Clementine. She stared at her sister, sure that her features must betray her true feelings, but her face was set and revealed nothing. It was only later that she suspected Claudia had set a trap, watching her carefully, gauging her reaction to Alexander's name. If that had been her intention, then she had been easy prey.

'No,' Clementine said at last when she was able to control her voice. 'He's been very ill, but apparently he is now recovering. Lady Moundsmere keeps us posted of his progress and is confident he will soon be brought back to England.'

'Does that mean he can come home?'

Clementine paused. 'I should imagine he will be sent somewhere to convalesce,' and feeling the tears well in her eyes, as they so often did when she thought of him, she began to move away, missing the frown that etched a line on Claudia's brow.

'What sort of injuries has he suffered?' she asked as Clementine went to open the door.

'Some internal ones and ... his leg. He'll need nursing for a while.'

'What's wrong with his leg?' Claudia demanded, holding Clementine's gaze. 'I

trust he's still got it?'

In danger of breaking down, Clementine fled.

*

'I do wish you had been more careful, Clemmie,' scolded Mrs Ellacombe that evening when the family were at dinner. After Clementine's hasty exit Claudia had called for her mother and demanded to know the truth about Alexander. She had not taken the news well. 'You know how squeamish she is, and in her mental state it can only seem worse than it is.'

Charles defended his wife. 'She had to find out sooner or later. Besides, I've spoken to her. It seems she had visions of Alexander with a peg leg, but I was able to reassure her that things have moved on since the days of Long John Silver. Moreover, that he was lucky to retain his knee.'

'All the same, it's bound to make a huge difference to his life,' said Brigadier Ellacombe as he carved the chicken Best had killed earlier that day.

'Not so great as it might once have been. One good thing that has come out of the war is the enormous progress that has been made with artificial limbs. In time I don't see why he shouldn't be able to ride again.'

'Well, whatever way you look at it the war is over for Alexander and now the Allies have taken Amiens and the tide has turned, I predict it will all be over in a matter of weeks.'

Time enough in which more soldiers will die, and more will be maimed, thought Clementine who had heard that casualties on both sides had been horrendous. Even if it ended tomorrow it would still be too long.

Pleading a headache, she excused herself. On the way up to bed she looked in on the twins and found them sleeping. Peter had kicked his blankets off and she stared at his chubby legs. He was nearly eleven months old and already walking. She thought of Alexander. How long before *he* walked again.

Charles found her there. 'I thought you'd be here,' he whispered glancing at the children. 'I can't get over their size; they were so small when I left at Christmas.'

'They change constantly in their first year. The sun is turning Charlotte's hair blonde.'

'She's going to look like you.'

And every day Clementine thought Peter was growing more like his father. She could see it clearly. Charles placed his arm round her shoulders and led her back to their room. As soon as the door closed she turned to him, her face unsmiling. 'I have something to tell you that I've no doubt will upset you.' She knew she could not keep if from him; it was too risky, and she knew that eventually he would find out.

He stared at her with foreboding, impatient for her to continue.

'I should have told you before, but there hasn't been much opportunity.' She took a deep breath. 'Alexander knows that he is the father of the twins.'

Charles's features froze and the silence between them was leaden until he eventually spoke. 'I think you had better explain,' he said with the politeness of a man about to draw a sword.

Conscious of his eyes burning into her, she explained how Alexander had caught her unawares in the nursery after she had returned from the Red Cross meeting. 'Any doubts he might have had vanished when he saw my face. I'm sorry.'

Charles banged his fist down on the chest of drawers. 'How could you be so damned, stupid! You, who were so worried about FitzPatrick finding out. Surely you must have prepared yourself for such an occasion?' Clementine's gaze dropped to the floor and Charles watched her carefully. 'Well — are you going to tell me the rest?'

'The rest?'

'Yes! What else happened? Surely that's not it?'

'He was extremely angry and we argued. He said he would never forgive me.' Seeing Charles's face, she knew better than to tell him she had accompanied Alexander to Grangefield; he would never understand. She could only pray he didn't find out.

'And where was Claudia when all this was taking place?'

It took a tremendous effort to look him in the face. 'I don't know. I didn't see her until they left together the following day.' It was almost the truth, but even so the deceit made her wretched.

'I presume she knows then.'

Clementine shook her head. 'I don't think so. I'm sure she would have said something.'

Charles was silent in thought for a while. 'Well, as you can see I'm far from happy, but I suppose what is done is done. The fact is, FitzPatrick will never be able to acknowledge Peter and Charlotte as his own, even if he wanted to.' His eyes lingered on her a moment longer and his expression softened. When he next spoke, his voice was kinder and he caught her wrist and pulled her towards him. 'I knew there was something on your mind. You've been fretting about telling me, haven't you?' He stroked her cheek. 'I'm sorry I shouted, but I suppose, if nothing else, it proves I care.'

Engulfed by misery, tears blurring her vision, she choked, 'Oh Charles, you deserve so much better than me.'

Lifting her chin, he told her passionately: 'But I've got the best. I've never doubted it.'

\*

'You can relax again now, Major FitzPatrick,' smiled Sister as she tidied away her instruments and straightened the bedcovers. 'No more dressings today.'

Relief showed in Alexander's face. 'Is there any news of when I'll be shipped home?'

'Aren't we nurses pretty enough for you then?' she teased in her lilting Welsh voice. He smiled, for it seemed — not only to him, but also to his fellow wounded officers — that she had an aversion to having unattractive nurses on the ward. Opinion was divided; some thought it was because she liked her team to have the reputation of being beautiful, whilst others argued that she

296

believed looks and good nursing to go hand in hand. But whatever the reason it was practically certain a plain-looking nurse wouldn't last long, that Sister Jenkins would somehow find fault and get them moved.

'It's the MO's decision. You will just have to be patient until he sees fit,' she said aware of a stranger entering through the flap of the marquee entrance, a fair-haired man in a dark naval uniform.

'I do believe you have a visitor Major FitzPatrick,' seeing the stranger's boyish grin upon spotting Alexander.

'Piers! This is a surprise.'

'How are you, old friend?'

'He's doing nicely,' interjected Sister Jenkins, moving away. 'Don't tire him.'

Piers made a face behind her back, making Alexander chuckle. 'Well you don't look too bad,' he said cheerily. 'I was expecting worse, but how do you feel?'

'With my hands.' The old school boy joke made Piers laugh. He guessed Alexander was trying to put him at ease. 'We *are* on good form.' He sat on the chair beside the bed. Close up Alexander didn't look so good as his first impression; he could see the suntan was in fact a yellow pallor.

'How did you hear?' asked Alexander casting a brief glance where the remains of his leg was.

'Clementine.'

There was a pause. 'How is she?'

Piers nodded. 'Oh, I think she's well. I expect you know about Claudia. She's had this wretched flu. Apparently it was touch and go, but she's over it now, though apparently still quite weak.' He saw that Alexander wasn't interested, so went on: 'Charles, Clementine's husband, is back. He broke his arm, and I reckon the way things are going, now that the Americans are here, the war will be over before the plaster is removed. Pity they hadn't come in sooner. I suppose you've heard about the peace offer Germany has made to Belgium?'

'Peace offer!' scorned Alexander. 'No indemnity and no reparation. What nerve! There must be no conditions and they should be made to pay for all the suffering they have caused.' He started to cough and Piers watched anxiously wondering what his friend was really feeling.

'Are you here on active service?' Alexander asked, taking a sip of water.

Piers grinned. 'Here to help deliver the fatal blow.'

'I hear the RNAS. and the Flying Corps have amalgamated.'

'Yes. It's the Royal Air Force now. Squadron Leader Douglas. Impressive, don't you think?'

'Same uniform?'

'Not much point getting a new one if the war ends soon, is there?'

'You're thinking of leaving?'

Piers shrugged his shoulders. 'To be honest, I really don't know. The Air Ministry certainly get far more done for us. When I was last here, the RNAS were the poor relations and it was you chaps who were given priority. Now things are different. We've the planes, the pilots, and we're giving the Hun what for!'

He chatted on, throwing out scraps of conversation with the intent of imparting some surface gaiety until finally Alexander stopped him.

'I thought she might have written, but there's been nothing.' And sinking back against the pillow, he turned his head away.

Piers watched, not knowing what to say; feeling that whatever he said would be wrong.

Suddenly Alexander turned back, his face wrought with tension. 'That bastard cut my leg off!'

Piers frowned in bewilderment. 'What are you talking about?'

'It was him! I know it was. I recognized his voice. Hamilton did this.'

# 24

'Poppycock! You're imagining it, Alex!' scoffed Piers. 'How can you be so sure it was him when you say you only met the fellow once — and then fleetingly. How can you possibly insist it was him, especially when by your own admission you were barely conscious?'

'I tell you, I recognised his voice.'

Piers laughed. 'Oh, come now, Alex, that's no proof at all. Isn't there a record of the surgeon's name?'

'Apparently it was lost in the turmoil, but I rather doubt anything was recorded. It happened at some clearing station; it was hell, bodies everywhere, and when I came round days later I was here and no one seemed to know anything.'

Piers shook his head. 'Even if you're right, which I doubt, are you suggesting he did it as an act of revenge?'

Alexander shrugged. 'I don't know what I think.'

'For goodness sake, man, the chances of it being Charles Hamilton are minuscule! Moreover, I'm certain that if it *had* been him, he'd have done far more than cut your leg off.' He gave Alexander a meaningful look, and the wounded man was unable to resist a smile.

'Maybe you're right,' he conceded. 'Maybe I have let my imagination get the better of me.'

'Exactly. You've been lying here with little else to occupy you. Anyway, enough of that. What are your plans after the war?'

'You mean when I'm on my feet again?' he said wryly. 'Retire to the country and became a recluse. The lease on Waverly is only for the duration, so I suppose by the time I get my new leg, it will have been vacated.' He paused, looking into the distance. 'Then I intend to bury myself there among its beauty.'

'And what about your beautiful wife — does she come into your plans? When I last saw her she was busy doing up the place in London.'

Alexander's eyes narrowed. 'My feelings for Claudia are unaltered. I'm surprised you even ask. After discovering me with Clementine, she had me over a barrel — and believe me, her silence wasn't cheap. She'll never blackmail me into loving her, not that she'd want that now, for I rather imagine she's not overly thrilled at the thought of having a cripple for a husband. Anyway, I become more confident as each day passes, without any word from her enquiring after my health, that she won't be too adverse to accepting a settlement in return for a divorce. If I can achieve that, it will make losing my leg seem almost worthwhile.'

*

It was another week before Charles decided Claudia was well enough to go downstairs and then only for a couple of hours in the afternoon. Still weak and nauseous, she spent the time curled up in front of the sofa fire with magazines.

Her convalescence was slow and it was not until the end of September, when the country was celebrating breaking through the Hindenburg Line, that she began to look more like her old self. However, despite longing to get back to London she knew she wasn't ready, having neither the energy nor the inclination to exert herself more than necessary to carry out normal everyday tasks. It was a tiresome period, particularly as she had to suffer her parents repeatedly tell her how lucky she was to have such a wonderful sister.

'I'm certain had it not been for Clementine you wouldn't be here now,' said her father, who felt a little show of gratitude wouldn't go amiss.

Sometimes it took all her strength not to inform them exactly what her wonderful sister had done. But even if she did, they would probably think the virus had damaged her mind. In her opinion Clementine was a hypocrite of the worst kind. Never would she forget the things she had said on her wedding morn, calling her a scheming hussy and saying that she deserved all she got. Claudia considered her own transgression slight in comparison to Clementine's adulterous liaison with Alexander.

Witnessing Charles's devotion to his wife only augmented Claudia's bitterness, and when boredom got to her she would amuse herself by imagining telling Charles what she had caught his precious wife doing. And sometimes, as they all sat round the dining table, she would catch her sister's eye, and smile. Clementine never failed to flinch, but even so it seemed small retribution for what the slut had done.

Alexander had been right when he told Piers that his injury would cause Claudia serious misgivings. She had many quiet moments in which to think over her fate, and eventually faced up to the fact that even if he were willing to give their relationship another chance, he would never again hold the same attraction for her. Shellshock or gas poisoning she might have handled, but not a stump. She had once seen one when hospital-visiting, raw and grotesque. The memory of it still sickened her. It wasn't her fault she was squeamish; it was just the way she was made.

Watching Charles and Clementine depart for long walks, she would brood about the injustice of it all; he striding so confidently on his long legs. Her sister seemed to have everything, a good-looking, intelligent husband, affection and children, and very soon, a home of her own. The iniquity of it stung.

Certain that the war would soon be over, Charles knew it was unlikely he would return to France, and therefore made enquiries as to whether he would be able to return to his old position at Charing Cross Hospital in London. Confident that they would welcome him back on receipt of his discharge, he decided to spend a couple of days with his sister, and begin to look for somewhere for the family to live. Clementine couldn't wait to leave Coppins. She knew she should never have come back, that she should have listened to her intuition and not been swayed by Charles and his trust in her. Now all she wanted was to escape before anything else happened.

Lady Moundsmere paid an unexpected visit, whilst Charles was away. She came to enquire after Claudia and discuss plans concerning Alexander. Brigadier and Mrs Ellacombe were out, and Clementine was alone in the sitting room sewing when Best showed the old lady in.

'Ah my dear, how lovely to see you again,' she said, taking Clementine's hand. 'What trials since we last met, but at least the worst is over. Alexander is at Roehampton where he is to be fitted with an artificial leg.'

The few minutes they were alone were insufficient to answer Clementine's many questions. Lady Moundsmere had yet to see him, but according to reports she had received it would appear he was on the mend.

'No one tells me very much. I think they do not want me to worry, but between you and me I am planning to visit him. I need to see him with my own eyes.'

Claudia's arrival cut short further conversation. With a mere glance she made it patently clear that Clementine was not welcome.

Picking up the smocking she had been working on, Clementine excused herself. Lady Moundsmere looked disappointed and tried to persuade her to stay, but she explained it was time to take the children for a walk.

'Do bring them in before you go. I'm sure they've grown since you brought them to Grangefield.'

Not daring to look at Claudia, Clementine somehow managed a smile.

The twins were dressed in their outdoor clothes when she returned. Charlotte was wary of the old lady and stayed in her mother's arms but Peter was not the least frightened of the stranger in black who peered at him through her pince-nez. He studied her from a distance until his attention was attracted by the large ruby and diamond ring she wore.

'My husband gave it to me on my wedding day. It's a family heirloom,' she said watching the child's plump fingers explore its many facets. 'You're a sharp little fellow, aren't you? You like the sparkles. When Alexander is home you must come and visit, my dear. Claudia will arrange it.'

Out in the drive, Clementine was strapping the twins into the pram, and worrying what Claudia had thought upon hearing of her visit to Grangefield when she noticed Charles walking towards them. He hadn't been expected back until the following day, and she tried her best to look happy.

'I finished my business early,' he explained, 'and it being such a lovely afternoon, decided to walk from the station.' He put his case down and kissed her. 'Visitors?' he said, spotting the Rolls-Royce.

'It belongs to Lady Moundsmere. She's here to visit Claudia.'

'Isn't that FitzPatrick's grandmother?'

Clementine nodded. 'She's here to discuss what is to happen after his discharge. I gather she would like them to live at Grangefield, at least for a while. She thinks it would be better for Alexander.'

'And what does Claudia say to that?'

'I don't know because I left. She's quite private about her affairs.' With a sinking heart Clementine couldn't see how she could avoid Charles and Lady Moundsmere meeting. Having just walked three and a half miles from the station she guessed he was anxious for some refreshment.

However, dispensing with his hat and coat over a bench, he turned to Clementine. 'I'm not in the mood to make polite conversation.' It was inevitable, he said, that the conversation would turn to FitzPatrick and his medical expertise would be called upon. At this moment, he had more absorbing things on his mind. 'I'll come with you and tell you about my trip.'

In London the plaster had been removed from Charles's arm, but apparently it would be several weeks before he could perform surgery again, he was told, and he returned to Coppins evermore convinced that for him, the war was over. He felt some remorse, that after four years he would not be there at the end, but took solace in the fact that he was able to use the time in setting down roots with Clementine and the children.

Whilst there, he had agreed to buy a Victorian terraced house with a small garden in West Kensington, less than thirty minutes walking distance from the hospital. It had five bedrooms with further space in the attic. 'The garden is about the same size as my sister's,' he said, 'and has a rhododendron tree, which I know you will love.' The move was planned for early November and the preceding weeks were taken up visiting salerooms for furniture.

Brigadier Ellacombe kindly lent him his car whenever he did

not require it, but there were occasions when public transport had to suffice. Charles had lived in the city before the war and there had been no necessity for him to own a vehicle. However, with a growing family he began to see the advantages of having one, and succeeded in acquiring a motor from a local farmer, who was selling it on behalf of his widowed daughter-in-law.

Claudia watched with mixed emotions as Clementine began packing. On the one hand she was delighted to see them go, the noisy brats too, but on the other, she resented everything they had to look forward to. Knowing what her own future held in store might have helped, but it was full of uncertainty and she began to feel very much alone.

The depression left over from her illness seemed only to increase. Her parents had each other. Clementine had Charles and the twins, but who had she to grow old with? Who was going to love and cherish her when her beauty had faded? Just a glance in the mirror was like a glimpse into the future. Pinched hollow cheeks, lifeless hair and circles so deeply etched beneath her eyes, it didn't seem possible they would ever disappear and that she would look young again. She was a stranger to herself. A few months before, she thought she had everything — beauty, wealth and a fine home — but now she realised that without anyone to share her life with, she had very little.

Lady Moundsmere had professed a wish that Claudia should move to Grangefield when she felt sufficiently recovered, in order that together they might start planning for Alexander's return. She had seemed determined that he should spend his convalescence there, and Claudia had shown neither objection nor enthusiasm to her proposal.

'He will need all the support we can give at first, my dear,' the old lady had said. 'And it is up to us to supply it.'

Claudia had little choice but to agree. After all, she was his wife — and what were wives for, if not to be a source of strength at times such as these. However, where, she wished to know, was *she* to get the strength to see her through the ordeal, and who was going to be there to support *her* in her hour of need? There could be no opting out: she had to see it through, had to know if and what kind of future she had with Alexander.

Once it was assumed that she would move to Grangefield, she turned to Charles for reassurance regarding Alexander's injury. Strangely, for someone used to seeing human flesh at its worst, he was sympathetic and confessed to having almost passed out the first time he had attended an operation.

'I really thought I had chosen the wrong profession.'

She suspected he exaggerated, but little by little he boosted her confidence until once again she began to look more positively to the future, even to the point where she came to view the loss of Alexander's leg in a different light. Perhaps it could prove instrumental in bringing them together; a blessing in disguise.

A few days before Clementine and Charles were due to move, Claudia suddenly announced her decision to return to London where it would be easier to visit Alexander at Roehampton. She had received a letter from him expressing a wish to see her; it seemed Lady Moundsmere had been to see him and told him of her plans.

*We need to talk*, his letter had said and she took this as a positive sign that he was prepared to give their marriage another chance.

Clementine was setting off with the twins for their afternoon walk when Best began piling Claudia's luggage into Alexander's car, ready for an early start the next day. Mrs Ellacombe was baffled as to why her daughter was taking so much. 'You'll only have to bring it all back again,' she said as she watched her empty her wardrobe.

'I think I might be there a while, at least until Alexander is ready to leave the hospital. Charles says it's a lengthy process, learning to walk again.'

The back seat was full of suitcases and hatboxes, and searching for a safe place to put her jewellery, she emptied the glove box of some road maps, and a scrunched-up piece of paper at the back. Thinking it an old invoice or something equally uninteresting, she was about to toss it away when curiosity made her hesitate. Placing her jewellery box on the seat she smoothed out the creases.

*

Clementine smiled as Peter toddled ahead of the pram, stopping frequently to pick up whatever caught his interest. Charlotte, content to remain seated, leaned over the side jabbering with glee. They loved being outdoors, as did Clementine, who thought the countryside seemed particularly beautiful this autumn with the trees a riot of red, brown and gold. Soon the earth would be covered with a deep rust carpet, leaving boughs stripped naked. What fun the twins would have playing in the fallen leaves!

Her thoughts turned to the house in West Kensington, which she had seen for the first time last week. She would have preferred something more rural, but understood Charles's reasoning, being but a short journey to work. In a few days they would be discovering new walks, new places to go. She glanced back to the house expecting to see Charles starting the car. He had a solicitor's appointment to sign the final purchase documents, but there was no sign of him, only Claudia, who was perched on the running board of Alexander's car reading something.

A sharp smack on the temple interrupted her thoughts. Peter, having come across some fallen walnuts, was throwing them in all directions. She persuaded him to place them in the pram, but Charlotte, squealing with delight, threw them out as fast as they arrived. Clementine laughed with quiet amusement, but sadness tinged her mood as it sometimes did when alone with the twins, and she would think of Alexander. It saddened her to think he would never share these simple joys.

*

Cold reality enveloped Claudia as she stared at the letter Clementine had written to Alexander back in 1917 telling him of her marriage to Charles. Short though it was, it was abundantly clear to her that they had been lovers. She was stunned; it was almost like finding them together all over again, only now it seemed even worse, especially when she realised from puzzling over words and dates that the most likely time it had happened was after her own wedding, when Alexander had abandoned her on their honeymoon, or possibly in France. It hardly seemed credible, yet the more she thought about it, the more certain she was.

One of the things that had most shocked her when she had caught Alexander and Clementine together in spring had been the fact that it had seemed so completely out of character for either of them to indulge in casual sex. She had certainly not found Alexander easy to seduce, for he had been of the old school where it was simply not done to sleep with single women of a certain class. And as for Clementine, she had always regarded her as more prim than promiscuous.

But now awakened to the truth, her thoughts flew back to her wedding day when she had introduced them to each other. From what she could remember, she was fairly certain neither had met beforehand — though he had become distant and Clementine had absented herself from the wedding. But on the other hand Clementine had shown no sign of recognising Alexander's name, and he had proffered little interest in the fact that she had a sister. However, it just wasn't feasible they had been intimate then and she could not bring herself to believe so. Yet, if not — when had it happened?

Her brain jerked back and forth, like a motion picture out of control, as it presented her with a jumble of images, searching for something significant. But it found nothing until the distant screams of the twins cut through the ribbons of confusion and focused her attention on Lady Moundsmere's recent visit, when she had casually mentioned that Clementine and the twins had accompanied Alexander to Grangefield. Clearly she would not have mentioned the trip had there been anything untoward about it. Lady Moundsmere's attitude had been largely responsible for Claudia putting little importance on the incident, persuading her that what had started out as an act of kindness on Alexander's part had later led to adultery.

She struck a fist against her forehead as the truth became blindingly obvious! What a fool … what an utter fool she had been!

In a daze she staggered to her feet, and staring into the small clearing off the drive saw her sister's honey-coloured hair shining like a halo in the sunlight. Claudia's strides quickened until she was running.

'Clementine!'

Clementine straightened, dropping the small harvest of nuts gathered in her skirt. Peter stooped to pick them up, unperturbed by the sudden appearance of his aunt, who burst into the clearing, shouting and gesticulating at his bewildered mother.

'You bitch! You thought you had me fooled, didn't you? But

no longer! Now I know everything! These are Alexander's bastards, aren't they? Conceived a few days after my wedding!'

Clementine paled, her heart bolting like a frightened stallion. She was helpless to do anything but stare dismally as the tirade continue.

'My God! If anyone had told me you were capable of such an act, I'd never have believed him. I hate you! I could kill you! You've ruined my life and you don't give a damn. What do you care about taking my husband? Nothing! Because you soon found another man to pander to you and bring up your bastards!'

'Don't speak of Charles like that. You don't understand anything,' Clementine retorted, colour returning to her face. 'It's not as it seems.'

'Yes, so Alexander said,' Claudia sneered. 'But to me it's crystal clear. What do you suppose your devoted husband would say if he knew your guilty little secret? My husband left me because he thought I had tricked him. What do you suppose Charles would do if he discovered these are not even his own children? But perhaps you don't care. Perhaps you're just using him until Alexander gets back and you can run off together.'

'You're wrong, Claudia. Listen to me, please. It's all over between Alexander and me. I promise I'll never see him again.'

'Why? Does the thought of his stump make your flesh creep?'

'Don't be so hateful!'

'No, of course not! It wouldn't matter to Florence Nightingale, would it? I daresay she's used to more gruesome sights.' Claudia laughed hysterically and Clementine tried to keep calm.

'Please Claudia, you must believe me when I say I won't jeopardise my marriage.'

'Of course not! But you jeopardised mine, didn't you? You didn't worry about that!'

Clementine was desperate to calm her down. 'Yes, it was wrong, but we were in love and nothing else seemed to matter.'

'Really! And what now? How long before you end up in his bed again?'

'I've told you — It's over. You must believe me.'

Claudia stared at her, pausing for a moment as if thinking, and Clementine, filled with dread, saw the dangerous flicker behind her eyes.

'But I do,' she said eventually. 'I really do believe that you think it possible to settle down in your new house with Charles and your little bastards and forget that any of this ever happened.'

The turning of a car engine created a marked silence between them, and aware of Clementine's unease, Claudia gave an acid smile.

'Is that Charles I see setting off? Of course, it's completion day, I'd quite forgotten. Well, we'll see, shall we? Remember how you pleaded with me on the morning of my wedding to tell Alexander the truth? Well, you were right, I should have told him. Now it's your turn. Let's put Charles to the test, see if he is as loving and forgiving as Alexander.' And throwing Clementine a glance loaded with menace, she turned and sprinted through the trees and hedges, just managing to reach the drive as Charles turned the corner.

Clementine watched helplessly as her sister flagged him down, climbed in and drove away.

# 25

Snatching his eyes from the road, Charles watched as Claudia fought to catch her breath and wondered why, with FitzPatrick's car sitting in front of the house, she had to ride with him when he was in a hurry to get to his appointment.

'Have you the time?' he asked curtly..

'Nearly four,' she said, her breathing starting to settle.

He cursed loudly. It was even later than he had thought. 'Well, I hope you're not expecting me to drop you anywhere off my route. I'm already late.'

She shook her head. 'I'm not going anywhere, Charles. I just want to talk.'

He swore, inwardly this time, thinking she was going to raise the subject of FitzPatrick's injuries again. 'Well, I'm afraid it will have to wait until the journey home. Just let me concentrate on getting to Wareham and the business I have to attend to, and you'll have my undivided attention.'

The car slowed and he glanced from left to right as he pulled onto the main highway. Claudia fell back against the seat as he pressed his foot down on the accelerator.

'Charles, slow down!' she cried, gripping tight to the door-hold. 'What I have to say won't wait, and I'm quite certain that once you've heard what it is, you won't be requiring that house any more.'

He looked askance and saw the smug smile that was forming on his sister-in-law's face. 'What do *you* know?' he demanded.

313

'You've never set eyes on the place. There is nothing wrong with it. It has been thoroughly surveyed, so whatever you've heard will hold little interest for me.'

His rebuff only seemed to increase her smugness. 'Oh, it has nothing to do with the house. It's about your wife and my husband. I think you should prepare yourself for a shock, Charles. Clementine has deceived you. You are not the father of the twins! Alexander is!'

She wanted to savour the moment, her moment of revenge, but the spiteful light blazing behind her eyes dimmed when she saw Charles's twisted smile.

'She tricked you — as she tricked us all,' she continued, bewildered by his lack of interest.

'I hate to disappoint you, Claudia, but you've had a wasted journey. You see, I already know.'

There was a stunned silence.

'You mean to tell me that you married her knowing she was pregnant by Alexander?'

'Really Claudia, do you honestly think Clementine would have married me without telling me?' She was silenced and humiliated, and Charles felt justified in giving vent to his fury. 'Think yourself very lucky that I'm in such a hurry, for if I didn't have such a pressing engagement I would stop the car and give you a damn good shaking.'

Claudia stared ahead, oblivious to the blur of hedges and trees that sped by even faster. *He had known all the time and still married her.*

'What's wrong, Claudia? Does it upset you to see us so happy? Well, don't worry, it won't be for much longer. Just as soon as I've signed the completion papers, we'll be able to move.' He was too angry to notice the dangerous glint in her eyes.

314

'And what of Clementine and Alexander now, Charles? I must say it's very magnanimous of you to turn a blind eye to their continuing relationship.'

He turned violently. It was too much. Now she was going too far!

'There's nothing between them, as well you know, so stop trying to pretend there is.'

She smiled triumphantly. 'Then perhaps you'll be interested to hear how I caught them in bed together whilst you were toiling away in France. Didn't Clementine tell you about it?'

'You filthy little liar — you'll sink to the lowest depths, won't you!'

'It's the truth. I saw them with my own eyes.'

'Shut up, you vixen — just shut up!'

'Then go back and ask her, if you don't believe me. Go back!'

'No, because I don't believe you. You're a compulsive liar.'

'Stop the car immediately and take me home.'

'No, I damn well will not. Nothing you say will make me change my mind.'

'Stop the car now!' she screamed. But Charles simply drove faster. In frustration she glanced about, searching for the means to stop the vehicle. Her eyes fell on the handbrake. Without another thought, she pulled it up as hard as she could.

*

'Still no sign of them, I wonder where they've got to,' said Mrs Ellacombe, finding Clementine still sitting in the nursery window. 'Perhaps they've gone for a drive,' the woman fretted. 'It's ages since Claudia has been out of the house.'

Clementine nodded, knowing her mother was anxious but

315

wishing that she would go back downstairs and leave her to her vigil alone.

'It's not like Charles not to have mentioned the possibility of being late,' she said. 'He's usually very punctual, knowing how Papa dislikes being kept waiting for dinner.' She refrained from expressing her greatest fear — that, in her opinion, Charles's wrist had not sufficiently recovered for driving.

Although there was nothing but blackness, no stars or moon, it was an effort for Clementine to tear herself from the window. But Peter, standing in his cot, demanded attention and she dragged herself to her feet, horribly aware that Charles and Claudia should have returned over two hours ago.

Alarmed by Clementine's pallor, Mrs Ellacombe did her best to reassure her, saying, 'I expect the car has broken down. After all it's been laid up for over two years in the Neillands' barn. Probably a puncture. If they're not back shortly I'll get Best to go over the route. Try not to worry, darling, we're bound to hear soon. In the meantime, I suggest you dress for dinner. Papa's getting hungry and it's not fair on Mrs Best to hold the meal back much longer.'

As she turned to leave, Clementine had an overwhelming urge to call her mother back and confess all — rid her soul of its enormous burden — but it would be too cruel, and she managed to control herself.

She busied herself, tidying up and folding away baby clothes — jobs that Danielle usually did. Finally she turned down the lamps but, before going to her room she was drawn again to the window, where she lingered a while longer, staring into the night.

The thought of dinner made her nauseous. How could she sit with her parents and pretend nothing was wrong; talk excitedly of the new house and eat a meal whilst wondering where the others were and what Claudia had said. It seemed hours since her sister had climbed into Charles's car, and she was beginning to fear he would not return. How he must hate her.

Resigned to the fact that she had to get ready and join her parents, she went to draw the curtains, and as she did so she saw two beams of light in the distance. A mixture of relief and fear rushed through her. They were back! Numbly she turned away, wondering how she could face him.

She went to her room and waited for Charles to come. Minutes passed, more still. They were telling her parents! It was too ugly to imagine, but though crippled with fear she knew she must go down.

Then she became conscious of footsteps on the stairs, slow and weighted as if the climb was too steep. They became louder and her heart beat erratically. She wanted to hide, but all she could do was shut her eyes and wait. Standing motionless, she opened her eyes and fixed them on the door. Guilt pounding in her ears, the handle turned.

Her father, not Charles, stood before her, his normal high colouring having paled. He looked old and waxen, and with sudden conviction she knew his days were numbered. Dear God, what had she done!

They stared at each other for a long moment and then with a grotesque sigh he stretched his arms out. 'There has been an accident, Clemmie … you must be brave.' There was immense sadness in his eyes and she backed away as if in a trance.

'Charles is injured. He has head injuries and has been taken to Dorchester Hospital.'

'And Claudia …?'

'Claudia was not so lucky.'

It was as if someone had hurled a grenade at her; the explosion was enormous burying the thud of the floor as she fell.

*

Dr. Gordon had brought the news, having been visiting a patient when the two casualties were carried in. It had been Claudia's pale blonde hair that made him take a closer look.

'It is believed she died at the scene of the accident. The car hit a tree. It was most fortunate that an Army ambulance passed almost immediately. They found Captain Hamilton lying on the ground. He was unconscious but came round on the way to hospital. He was extremely lucky. He's badly cut and bruised, but he will make a full recovery. I managed to speak to him, and though he's groggy he's aware of what happened. He said a deer ran out and he skidded on some wet leaves and lost control.'

He looked at Clementine, who was sitting beside her mother. Blood had spilled onto her blouse from a gash on her lip when she had fallen, but otherwise he thought she was all right, just very shocked like everyone else.

Best busied himself pouring everyone brandy whilst his wife hovered anxiously, trying to be of help.

'Mrs Hamilton,' the doctor continued, taking Clementine aside, 'your husband asked me to assure you that his condition is not serious and that in the circumstances he feels your place this evening should be at your parents' side.'

Best drove Clementine to Dorchester the next morning, dropping her off at the hospital before continuing on to Sherborne to collect Timmy from school.

Charles was sitting up in bed, his face so black and swollen that Clementine failed to recognise him at first. She had packed some things he would need and handed the bag to a nurse. A lump came to her throat as they looked at each other and she braced herself, not wanting to break down. She waited for him to say something and was surprised when he took her hand and motioned her to sit on the bed.

'How are you?' she asked.

'A bit sore but otherwise fine. How are your parents?'

She told him that her mother had been awake most of the night and that Dr Gordon had administered a sedative so she could rest.

'I think it's hit her this morning. Last night it was all so surreal. Papa numbed the pain with brandy He looks dreadful. I left him at his desk writing letters and telephoning.'

All the while she was with Charles she lived in expectation of his accusations, but he said nothing. Finally she had to know.

'Tell me how it happened,' she asked, searching his bloodied eyes for wounds of a different nature. She held them for long seconds, yet all she could see was sorrow — no anger, and no hatred — only sorrow.

He repeated what he had told Dr Gordon, that all he could remember was a deer appearing from nowhere and then braking.

'The wet leaves on the road caused me to skid.'

Clementine remained until Timmy came to fetch her, his eyes red from crying. Clementine hugged him tightly.

Over the coming days, friends and neighbours would arrive at Coppins bearing flowers and to offer their condolences. Brigadier Ellacombe had telephoned Lady Moundsmere that first evening to break the news. Though deeply shocked by this latest tragedy to affect her family she somehow managed, during their conversation, to inject into him a shot of her indomitable spirit, which helped bolster him to face the difficult period ahead.

Charles remained in hospital for five days, discharging himself in order to attend Claudia's funeral. Clementine wondered if Alexander would come, aware that his presence would make the occasion even more difficult to handle. She was certain he was sensitive to this when his black-bordered envelope dropped through the letterbox. He wrote to her parents saying it wouldn't be possible to attend, owing to a recent operation. He chose his words carefully, expressing his sorrow at their loss but not dwelling on his own. He promised to visit as soon as he was released from hospital.

In the days preceding the funeral no one paid much attention to what was happening abroad, but when the day finally arrived and the family were seated at breakfast, Brigadier Ellacombe told them all of the call he had received a short time ago from a colleague.

'This is a momentous day for us in more ways than one,' he said, clearing his throat, 'Not only is this a very sad occasion, being the day our darling Claudia is laid to rest, it will be forever a time of celebration. For, this morning at five a.m., Germany surrendered. They have signed an armistice. And at eleven minutes past eleven, whilst we are in church, hostilities will cease.'

And so it was that as the mourners filed into the small graveyard and Claudia's coffin was lowered into the earth, distant guns from Bovington Camp could be heard firing a victory salute.

# 26

The following weeks brought great change as survivors from the four-and-a-half year-old conflict started to return home. The euphoria that the end of hostilities had brought was short-lived as people began to take stock of the loss of life. Three quarters of a million British men would never return; plus there were two million casualties, many of whom would be scarred for life, both mentally and physically.

Clementine read in the newspapers how the rest of the country had celebrated, whilst they had returned to Coppins with a feeling of emptiness that could not be filled. Many thousands had packed into London, on overladen buses, singing and shouting, as streetlights were unmasked and blackout curtains were torn from shop windows. Like a chrysalis the capital discarded its dark shell, bathing in a blaze of colour from the Allied flags, hastily erected on the rooftops. And to the delight of the masses, King George and Queen Mary ventured from the Palace, making an informal drive through Hyde Park. Peace at last!

Though people talked about getting back to normality, the majority accepted that the world had moved on since 1914 and that there would be no going back; it was a matter of getting used to the changes.

Following the cessation of hostilities a General Election was immediately called, and George Ellacombe, feeling the worse for wear, decided it was time to step down. He no longer had the energy or enthusiasm that he once had to make a difference. All he wanted was a quiet life with time to enjoy his family, and see his grandchildren grow.

Clementine postponed the move to London as long as she could, and Charles was very understanding, knowing how important it was to her to spend as much time as she could with her parents. He went up several times on the train to prepare the house for her arrival, wanting everything to be perfect.

His sister Grace was a great help, arranging the furniture, finding a housekeeper and gardener, and getting a painter to decorate the nursery. Before long it began to feel more like a home than a house. The only thing it lacked was his family.

Though he had recovered fairly swiftly from his injuries he had nevertheless managed to put off taking up his old position at Charing Cross until the New Year, making Clementine aware that she would be unable to delay her departure any further.

Christmas arrived, and thanks to the twins it was a happier occasion than anyone had anticipated. As Timmy and Clementine began to adorn the house with holly and mistletoe, Danielle suddenly expressed a longing to see her family. Clementine insisted she return to France, and after arranging her passage, drove her to the station herself. Saying goodbye, she wondered whether Danielle would return. She had been invaluable and the twins loved her, but she was a clever girl and, now fluent in English, must realise she had better prospects than before.

Her departure threw Clementine into a panic, wondering how she was going to cope with two exuberant infants needing constant attention, but in fact it proved to be a blessing in disguise. The attention their presence demanded, as the pair learned to spread their wings away from the nursery, kept everyone on their toes, their grandfather included, leaving little time to dwell on matters of a sad nature.

Even Mrs Ellacombe came to realise that life still had its funny moments and instead began to dread the New Year when Timmy would return to school, and Clementine and the twins would depart for their new life in Croydon. As an MP's wife, she had spent a lot of time in London, always finding plenty to keep her occupied. However, Brigadier Ellacombe had decided it was not economical to keep the house in the city, and though part of her worried how she was going to adapt to this life of retirement, she knew Clementine would always welcome her. Besides, as she kept telling herself, West Kensington was close to the centre and not too far from her sister in Wimbledon. Tragedy had shown her the importance of making the most of what she had, and she only hoped Charles did not tire of his mother-in-law's visits.

As usual, on Christmas Eve Best cut down a spruce and placed it in the hall. The decorations were then brought down from the attic and Timmy set about decorating it whilst Jack slumbered by the fire. Beneath it presents were placed, but this year only for the twins and Timmy, Brigadier Ellacombe having decided they should instead give a donation to the Red Cross memorial fund.

Most afternoons, weather permitting, Charles would leave his books to join Clementine and the twins for their walk. They would discuss matters to do with the new house, but no matter how hard she tried, he could tell she didn't share his enthusiasm — so different from the reaction of his late wife when they had purchased their first little house. Recently he had begun to think of Mary quite a lot. Until he had met Clementine, Charles hadn't thought it possible to fall in love again. He had always known what Mary was thinking and she likewise, even though their busy lives prevented them from spending the time together they would have wished.

Three days after Christmas the General Election was held, and for the first time in history women were allowed to vote. It was something Mary had fought for, but Charles knew she would have considered it only a step in the right direction as the vote was conditional on a woman being, not only over thirty, but also a home-owner.

Clementine noticed how Charles had recently started to slip Mary's name into the conversation, and wondered why. Did he suspect what a faithless wife he had replaced her with? Though he had always maintained he couldn't remember the lead-up to the crash, intuition told her otherwise.

On Wednesday 2nd January the couple took their final walk: the following day they would be leaving. Watching Peter and Charlotte chase after Jack as he fetched his stick, Clementine turned to Charles. 'Do you think if I was no longer here you might meet someone else and ...'

Her sentence trailed into silence. She waited, but he said nothing.

He looked at her, his expression grave, and they carried on walking in silence.

It was not until they undressed that evening, when Charles came over to the dressing-table, where Clementine sat brushing her hair, that she saw his reflection in the mirror and noticed how tired he looked. But it was not the sort of tiredness she was used to seeing, when he had worked round the clock in the hospital. This was a different sort of exhaustion, the exhaustion of his spirit. Sighing inwardly, Clementine rose to her feet and turned to face him. Charles took her hands and smiled sadly.

'I know you've tried to love me Clementine, and I know you do, but I know it's not me you dream about. It's not your fault. We don't choose who we fall in love with. Naïvely I thought you might grow to love me the way I love you, but I know it's not going to happen.' She wanted to protest, to tell him he was wrong, but she couldn't.

'I've watched you struggle with your feelings, your sense of right and wrong. I wanted to save you and take you away to a new life. However, knowing that your heart lies elsewhere, it could only be a hollow victory. Every time you look at Peter and Charlotte you are reminded of the man you really love, and I can't compete with that.

'Fear of losing you made me selfish, but how can you lose something you've never had? But perhaps worst of all, I realise what a hypocrite I am. I abhor caged birds, believe they should be free as God intended, but it's exactly what I am doing to you. So, dearest Clemmie, I'm setting you free. Tomorrow when I leave it will be alone.'

He paused, watching her tears fall, and in a low voice he told her. 'No matter what happens after tomorrow, I shall never regret marrying you.' And he pulled her close and held her. 'Your parents need only know you've decided to stay longer, but eventually they will accept I'm not coming back.'

Clementine swallowed hard. There was no blame in his eyes, only love and sadness. She owed him her life and the life of her children, and now he was releasing her. Never had she loved Charles more.

# Epilogue

*June, 1920*

It was a warm evening, and shadows were falling fast in the churchyard. Two lambs darted in and out of the gravestones, finding the cooler temperature more conducive to their antics than the sleepy heat of earlier. They paid scant attention to the man and woman who slowly weaved their way over the parched grass, dotted with clover and daisies, and continued to make the most of the fading light.

That morning, Clementine and Alexander had returned from their honeymoon in Italy. Everyone had been delighted when they had announced they were getting married. After the shock of her divorce from Charles, Clementine's parents had thought her future bleak. Marriage to Alexander was a dream nobody had dared to voice. The small civil ceremony took place in London attended by Piers, and Alexander's sister-in-law, Dulcie, who acted as witnesses.

Clementine thought of the twins, who were almost three. They could not remember Charles and would never know what they owed him. Alexander had been an almost daily part of their lives since he had called by a few months after the war ended. He and his grandmother had come to pay their respects, but really, he had wanted to see Clementine and the children as soon as he had learned they were still in residence.

Clementine and Alexander hadn't seen each other since that

dreadful day when Claudia had discovered them together. For Alexander, watching their children at play during his visits, their chubby little bodies bursting with energy, together with his love for their mother, had put back meaning into his life. He felt a solace that he thought he had lost forever.

Clementine spotted the Purbeck stone angel that watched over Claudia's grave, and took Alexander's hand. Nineteen months had passed since Claudia had died. Charles had always maintained a deer had run out, causing him to skid on wet leaves. Clementine had never spoken of the day that she had gone with her father to the accident spot and seen the skid marks, which heavy rain and early frosts had failed to obliterate. She'd never know for sure — and had had to accept that — but standing there beside the death path, despite everything Charles and the police had told her, she suspected there had been another cause for her sister's death.

Tomorrow the couple would collect the twins. Together with Charlotte and Peter, Clementine and Alexander would begin their life as a family. She was staring at the angel watching over her sister. Clementine wanted to put to one side her own feelings of guilt. She wanted a new start, not just for herself but, after the horrors they had witnessed over the last few years, for all mankind.

She lowered her eyes and prayed — *Oh Lord, forgive us our trespasses.*

Lightning Source UK Ltd.
Milton Keynes UK
UKOW01f2209201016

285733UK00003B/91/P